Praise For Rosamunde Pilcher

'Rosamunde Pilcher's warm spell is charming and utterly convincing' *Daily Mail*

'Pilcher's strength is knowing what she can do well and writing about what she knows. She has a way of tapping into the emotional life of her readers and making them care about characters not unlike themselves' *Daily Telegraph*

'Especially good on atmosphere . . . Pilcher's storytelling skills are serene and beguiling' *The Times*

'Much-needed balm to soothe the troubled mind' *Sunday Express*

'It is never too soon to discover Rosamunde Pilcher' *Good Housekeeping*

Also by Rosamunde Pilcher

Sleeping Tiger
The End of the Summer
The Empty House
Wild Mountain Thyme
The Shell Seekers
September
Coming Home
Winter Solstice

SHORT STORY COLLECTIONS

The Blue Bedroom
Flowers in the Rain

ROSAMUNDE PILCHER

Another View

and

The Day of
the Storm

HODDER

ROSAMUNDE PILCHER

Another View

HODDER

1

In Paris, in February, the sun was shining. At Le Bourget Airport, it gleamed coldly from an ice blue sky, and this was reflected, with much dazzle, from the runways, still wet after a night's rain. From inside, the day looked inviting, and they had been tempted out on to the terrace, only to discover that the bright sun held no real warmth and the gay breeze that blew the wind socks out at right angles had an edge to it like a knife. Defeated, they withdrew to the restaurant to wait for Emma's flight to be called, and sat now, at a small table, drinking black coffee and smoking Christopher's Gauloises cigarettes.

Unselfconscious, absorbed in each other, they nevertheless attracted a certain amount of attention. This was inevitable, for they made an arresting pair. Emma was tall and very dark. Her hair, worn back off her forehead and held in place by a tortoiseshell band, fell in a straight black tassel to below her shoulder-blades. Her face was not beautiful – it was too clearly boned and strongly built for beauty, with a straight nose, and a square and determined chin. But these features were redeemed and given much charm by large and unexpectedly grey-blue eyes, and a wide mouth, which, although it was quite capable of drooping disconsolately if she did not get her own way, could grin, from ear to ear, like a boy's, when she was happy. She was happy now. She wore, on this cold bright day, a bitter green trouser suit and a white polo-necked sweater that made her face look very brown, but her sophisticated appearance was off-set by the mass of luggage with which she was surrounded, and which appeared, to the casual passer-by, to have been salvaged from some disastrous act of God.

It was, in fact, the accumulation of six years of living abroad, but no one was to know this. Three suitcases, at enormous expense, had already been checked in. But there was still a canvas grip, a Prisunic paper carrier sprouting long French loaves, a basket bulging with books and records, a raincoat, a pair of ski-boots and an enormous straw hat.

Christopher surveyed it all, speculating, in a detached and unbothered fashion, as to how it was all going to be conveyed into the aeroplane.

"You could wear the hat and the ski-boots and the raincoat. That would make three less things to carry."

"I've already got a pair of shoes on, and the hat would blow off. And the raincoat's disgusting. I look like a displaced person in it. I can't think why I bothered to bring it at all."

"I'll tell you why. Because it will be raining in London."

"It may not be."

"It always is." He lit another Gauloise from the stub of the first. "Another good reason for staying in Paris with me."

"We've had this out a hundred times. And I'm going back to England."

He grinned without rancour. He had been teasing her. When he smiled, his yellow-flecked eyes slanted upwards at the corners, and this, combined with his lanky, idle body, gave him a curiously feline appearance. His clothes were colourful, casual, faintly Bohemian. Narrow cord trousers, battered chukka boots, a blue cotton shirt worn over a yellow sweater, and a suède jacket, very old and shiny about the elbows and the collar. He looked French, but in fact he was as English as Emma and even related to her in a tenuous way, for, years ago, when Emma was six and Christopher ten, her father, Ben Litton, had married Hester Ferris, Christopher's mother. The arrangement had lasted, with only the smallest degree of success, for eighteen months, before it finally fell apart, and now Emma remembered it as the only time in her life when she had ever known anything vaguely approaching an ordinary family life.

It was Hester who had insisted on buying the cottage at Porthkerris. Ben had owned a studio there for a number of years, since long before the war, but its conveniences were non-existent, and after one look at the squalor in which she was expected to live Hester went straight out and acquired two fisherman's cottages, which she proceeded, with taste and charm, to convert. Ben was disinterested in any such activity, so it became very much Hester's house, and it was she who insisted on a kitchen that would work, and a boiler that would heat water, and a big fireplace blazing with driftwood, a heart to their home, a focal point around which the children could gather.

Her intentions were splendid, her methods of carrying them out not so successful. She tried to make allowances for Ben. She had married a genius, and she knew his reputation and she was prepared to turn a blind eye to his love affairs, his disreputable companions and his attitude towards money. But in the end, as so often happens in quite ordinary marriages, she was defeated by the small things. By meals, forgotten and uneaten. By trivial bills left unpaid for months. By the fact that Ben preferred to drink in the local pub, rather than in a civilised fashion, at home, with her. She was defeated by his refusal to have a telephone, to own a car; by the stream of apparent derelicts whom he invited to sleep on her sofa; and finally by his total inability to show at any time any sort of affection.

She left him at last, taking Christopher with her, and sued almost immediately for a divorce. Ben was delighted to let her have it. He was delighted, too, to see the back of the small boy. The two of them had never got on. Ben was jealous of his male priority, he liked to be the only man of importance in his household, and Christopher, even at ten years old, was an individual who refused to be ignored. Despite all Hester's efforts, this antagonism endured. Even the boy's good looks, which Hester truly believed would charm Ben's painter's eye, had the very opposite effect, and when Hester tried to persuade Ben to do a portrait of him, he refused.

After their departure, life at Porthkerris slid easily back into its old seamy routine. Emma and Ben were cared for by a series of messy females, either models or student painters, who moved into and through and out of Ben Litton's life with the monotonous regularity of a well-ordered cinema queue. The only thing they had in common was an adulation of Ben, and a lofty disregard for housekeeping. They took as little notice of Emma as possible, but, in fact, she did not miss Hester as much as people thought she would. She had become weary – as Ben was – of being organised, and perpetually buttoned into clean clothes, but Christopher's going left a great void in her life which refused to be filled. For a little, she had mourned for him, tried to write him letters, but had not dared to ask Ben for his address. Once, in the desperation of loneliness, she ran away to find him. This entailed walking to the station and trying to buy a ticket to London, which seemed as good a place as any to look for him. But she had only one and ninepence in the world, and the stationmaster, who knew her, had taken her into his office which smelt of paraffin lamps and the black railway coal he burnt in his grate, and had given her a cup of tea out of an enamel pot, and walked her home. Ben was working, and had not noticed her absence. She never tried to look for Christopher again.

When Emma was thirteen, Ben was offered a teaching fellowship at the University of Texas for two years, which, without thought of Emma, he instantly accepted. There was a small hiatus while Emma's future was discussed. When taxed with the question of his daughter, he announced that he would simply take her to Texas with him, but someone – probably Marcus Bernstein – persuaded Ben that she would be better off away from him, and she was sent to a school in Switzerland. She stayed in Lausanne for three years – never returning to England, and then went to Florence to study Italian and Renaissance Art, for another year. At the end of this time, Ben was in Japan. When she suggested that she should join him, he replied by telegram. ONLY SPARE BED OCCUPIED BY CHARMING GEISHA GIRL WHY DONT YOU TRY LIVING IN PARIS.

Philosophically, for she was now seventeen and life was no longer surprising, Emma did as he suggested. She found herself a job with a family called Duprés who lived in a tall scholarly house in St Germain. The father was a professor of medicine, and the mother a teacher. Emma cared for their three well-behaved children, taught them English and Italian, and took them, in August, to the modest family villa at La Baule, and all the time waited patiently until Ben should return to live in England. He stayed in Japan for eighteen months, and when he did return it was by way of the United States, where he spent a month in New York. Marcus Bernstein flew out to meet him there, and it was typical that Emma learned the reason for this reunion, not from Ben himself, nor even from Leo, who was her usual source of information, but from a long and fully illustrated article in the French *Réalités*, which dealt with a newly built

Museum of Fine Arts in Queenstown, Virginia. This museum was a memorial created by his widow, to a rich Virginian called Kenneth Ryan, and the opening of the Art Section was to be a retrospective exhibition of the paintings of Ben Litton, ranging from his pre-war landscapes, right through to his latest abstractionisms.

Such an exhibition was an honour and a tribute, but inevitably suggested a painter to be revered, a Grand Old Man of the arts. Emma, studying one of the photographs of Ben, all angles and contrasts, dark-tanned skin and jutting chin and snowy hair, wondered how he felt about such veneration. He had been a rebel all his life against convention, and she could not imagine him tamely submitting to being a Grand Old anything.

"But what a man!" said Madame Duprés, when Emma showed her the photograph. "He is very attractive."

"Yes," said Emma, and sighed, because that had always been the trouble.

With Marcus, he returned to London in January, and went straight back to Porthkerris to paint. This was confirmed by a letter from Marcus. The day the letter arrived, Emma went to Madame Duprés and gave in her notice. They tried to coax, cajole, bribe her into changing her mind, but she was adamant. She had scarcely seen her father for six years. It was time they got to know each other again. She was going back to Porthkerris, to live with him.

In the end, because they had no option, they agreed to letting her go. Her flight was booked, and she started to pack, throwing out some of the accumulated possessions of six years, and cramming the rest into a variety of battered and much-travelled suitcases. But even these were sadly inadequate, and Emma was eventually driven to going out and buying herself a basket, a huge French marketing basket that would accommodate the number of awkwardly-shaped objects that refused to go into anything else.

It was a grey and cold afternoon, two days before she was due to fly home. Madame Duprés was at home, so Emma, explaining her errand, left the children with her, and went out alone. To her surprise, she found that it was raining, lightly, in a chill drizzle. The cobbled pavements of the narrow street shone with wet, and the tall bleached houses stood quiet and closed against the murk, like faces which give nothing away. From the river a tug hooted, and a solitary gull hung, high above, in the mist, screaming dismally. The illusion of Porthkerris was suddenly more real than the reality of Paris. The resolve to return, which had for so long been in the back of her mind, was crystallised now into the impression that she was already there.

This street would lead – not to the busy Rue St Germain, but out on to the harbour road, and it would be flood tide, the harbour full of grey sea and bobbing boats, and a heavy swell running out beyond the north pier, the Atlantic crested with white horses. And there would be familiar smells – fish from the market, and hot saffron buns from the baker's; and all the little summer shops would be shuttered and closed for the season. And back at the studio Ben would be working, hands mittened against the cold, the brilliance of his palette a scream of colour against the sweep of grey cloud that was framed by his towering north window.

She was going home. In two days, she would be there. The rain was wet on her face and all at once she felt that she could not wait, and this sense of happy urgency made her run, and she ran all the way to the little épicerie in the Rue St Germain, where she knew she would be able to buy the basket.

It was a tiny shop, fragrant with fresh bread and garlic-flavoured sausage meat, with onions strung like white beads from the ceiling, and jars of wine, which the local workmen

bought by the litre. The baskets hung at the door, strung together
and suspended by a single piece of rope. Emma did not dare untie
it and choose herself a basket in case the whole lot fell to the
pavement, so she went into the shop to find someone to do it for
her. There was only the fat woman with the mole on her face, and
she was busy with a customer, so Emma waited. The customer
was a young man, fair haired, his raincoat streaked with damp.
He was buying a long loaf and a pat of country butter. Emma
eyed him and decided that, from the back at least, he looked
attractive.

"*Combien?*" he said.

The fat woman did a sum with a stub of pencil. She told him.
He felt in his pocket and paid, turned, smiled at Emma and made
for the door.

And there he stopped. With his hand against the edge of the
door, he swung slowly around, to take a second look. She saw
the amber eyes, the slow, incredulous smile.

The face was the same, the familiar, boy's face on the
unfamiliar man's body. With the illusion of Porthkerris so near
and so strong, it seemed that he was simply an extension of that
illusion, a figment of her own highly-stimulated imagination.
This was not him. This could not be . . .

She heard herself say "Christo," and it was the most natural
thing in the world to call him by the name that only she had ever
used. He said, quietly, "I simply don't believe it," and then he
dropped his parcels and held out his arms and Emma fell into
them, pressed close against the shiny, wet front of his raincoat.

They had two days to spend together. Emma told Madame
Duprés, "My brother is in Paris," and Madame, who was kind-
hearted, and had, anyway, resigned herself to being without
Emma, set Emma free to spend them with Christopher. They
used up these two days in slowly walking the streets of the city;

8

hanging over the bridges to watch the barges slip away below them, bound for the south and the sun; sitting in the thin sunshine and drinking coffee at the small, round iron tables, and when it rained, taking refuge in Notre Dame or the Louvre, perched on the stairs beneath the Winged Victory and always talking. They had so much to ask and so much to tell. She learned that Christopher, after a number of false starts, had decided to become an actor. This was much against his mother's wishes – after eighteen months of Ben Litton she had had enough of artistic temperaments to last her for the rest of her life – but he had stuck to his guns and even managed to get a scholarship to RADA. He had worked for two years in a repertory theatre in Scotland, had moved, unsuccessfully, to London, done a little television work, and then had been diverted by an invitation from an acquaintance, whose mother owned a house in St Tropez.

''St Tropez in the winter?'' Emma could not help asking.

''It was then or never. We'd never have been offered it in the summer.''

''But wasn't it cold?''

''Freezing. Never stopping raining. And when the wind blew all the shutters rattled. It was like some ghastly film.''

In January he had returned to London to see his agent, and had been offered a twelve-month contract with a small repertory company in the south of England. It was not the sort of work he wanted, but it was better than nothing, and he was running out of money, and it was not too far from London. The job, however, did not start until the beginning of March, and so he had returned to France, finished up in Paris, and finally met Emma. Now, it irked him that she was returning so soon to England, and did everything he could to make her change her mind, postpone her flight, stay in Paris with him. But Emma was adamant.

''You don't understand. This is something that I have to do.''

"It's not even as though the old boy asked you to go. You're just going to get in his way, and interfere with all his amorous adventures."

"I never have before – interfered, I mean." She laughed at his stubborn expression. "Anyway, there's no point my staying, if you're coming back to England next month."

He made a face. "Wish I wasn't. That lousy little theatre at Brookford. I shall get lost in the jungle of fortnightly rep. Besides, I'm not due there for two weeks. Now if you would only stay in Paris . . ."

"No, Christo."

"We could rent a tiny attic. Think of all the fun we could have. Bread and cheese every night for supper and lots of rough red wine."

"No, Christo."

"Paris in the Spring . . . blue skies and blossom and all that rot?"

"It isn't spring yet. It's still winter."

"Were you always so unco-operative?"

But still she would not agree to staying, and in the end he admitted defeat. "Very well, if I can't persuade you to keep me company, I shall simply behave in a very well-bred and British way, and come and see you on to your plane."

"That would be perfect."

"It's very self-sacrificing of me. I hate saying goodbyes."

Emma agreed with this. Sometimes, it felt as if she had been saying goodbye to people all her life, and the sound of a train moving out of a station, gathering speed, was enough to reduce her to tears. "But this goodbye is different."

"How is it different?" he wanted to know.

"It isn't really goodbye. It's *au revoir*. A stepping stone between two hellos."

"My mother and your father are not going to approve."

"It doesn't matter if they approve or not," said Emma. "We've found each other again. For the moment, that's all that matters."

Above them, the loudspeakers gave a click, began to speak with a feminine voice.

"Ladies and gentlemen. Air France announce the departure of their flight Number 402 for London . . ."

"That's me," said Emma.

They stubbed out their cigarettes, stood up, began to gather in the baggage. Christopher took the canvas grip and the Prisunic paper carrier, and the great bulging basket. Emma slung the raincoat over her shoulder, carried her handbag, the ski-boots and the hat.

Christopher said, "I wish you'd wear the hat. It really would complete your ensemble."

"It would blow off. Not to say look funny."

They went downstairs, crossed the expanse of shining floor towards the barrier where a small queue of passengers was already forming.

"Emma, are you going down to Porthkerris today?"

"Yes, I'll get the first train I can."

"Have you got any money? Pounds, shillings and pence, I mean?"

She had not thought of this. "No. But it doesn't matter. I'll cash a cheque somewhere."

They joined the queue behind a British businessman who carried only his passport and a slim brief-case. Christopher leaned forward.

"Oh, sir, I wonder if you could help."

The man swung round, and found to his surprise Christopher's face only inches from his own. Christopher was wearing his sincere expression. "I am sorry, but we're in rather a predicament. My sister's returning to London, she's not been home for six years, and she has such a lot of hand luggage, and she's only just recovered from a serious operation . . ."

Emma remembered Ben saying that Christopher never told a small lie if he could get away with a bigger one. Looking at him as he came out with this outrageous fabrication, she decided that he had chosen his career wisely. He was a wonderful actor.

The businessman, thus approached, could make no excuse.

"Well, yes, I suppose . . ."

"It's more than kind of you . . ." The canvas grip and the carrier with the bread went under one arm, the basket in the other along with the slim brief-case. Emma felt sorry for him.

"It's just till we get on to the plane . . . it is so kind of you, and you see my brother isn't coming with me . . ."

The queue moved forward, they had reached the barrier.

"Goodbye, darling Emma," said Christopher.

"Goodbye, Christo." They kissed. A brown hand whipped away her passport, riffled the pages, stamped it.

"Goodbye."

They were divided by the barrier, by the formalities of the French government, by other travellers, surging forward.

"Goodbye."

She would have liked him to wait and see her safely on to the plane, but even as she waved, flapping the sun hat, he had turned, and was walking away from her, the light shining on his hair, and his hands buried deep in the pockets of his leather coat.

2

In London, in February, it was raining. It had started to rain at seven o'clock in the morning, and it had rained without ceasing ever since. By half past eleven only a handful of people had visited the exhibition, and those enthusiasts, one suspected, had simply come in order to get out of the rain. They shed wet raincoats and dripping umbrellas, and stood around, bemoaning the weather before they had even bought themselves a catalogue.

At eleven-thirty, the man came in to buy a picture. He was an American, staying at the Hilton, and he asked to see Mr Bernstein. Peggy, the receptionist, took the card which he proffered, asked him politely if he would mind waiting for a moment, and then came through to the office to speak to Robert.

"Mr Morrow, there's an American outside by the name of . . ." she glanced at the card. "Lowell Cheeke. He was here a week ago, and Mr Bernstein showed him the Ben Litton of the deer, and thought he was going to buy it, but he went off without making up his mind. Said he wanted to mull it over."

"Have you told him Mr Bernstein's in Edinburgh?"

"Yes, but he can't wait. He's going back to the States the day after tomorrow."

"I'd better see him," said Robert.

He stood up, and while Peggy went to open the door and

13

invite the American in, did a swift spring-clean of his desk, squaring some letters, emptying the ash-tray into the wastepaper basket and shoving the basket under the desk with the toe of his shoe.

"Mr Cheeke," said Peggy, announcing the visitor like a well-trained parlourmaid.

Robert came around the desk to shake hands.

"How do you do, Mr Cheeke? I'm Robert Morrow, Mr Bernstein's partner. I am sorry, I'm afraid he's in Edinburgh today, but perhaps I could help you . . . ?"

Lowell Cheeke was a short, powerful-looking individual in a dacron raincoat and a narrow-brimmed hat. Both of these were very wet, indicating that Mr Cheeke had not arrived in a taxi. He began divesting himself, with Robert's help, from these sodden garments, and revealed an uncrushable navy blue terylene suit and a pin-striped nylon shirt. He wore rimless spectacles and behind them his eyes were cool and grey, and it was impossible to assess any sort of potential either financial or artistic.

"Thank you very much . . ." said Mr Cheeke. "What a terrible morning . . ."

"It doesn't look as though it's going to let up either . . . A cigarette, Mr Cheeke?"

"No, thank you, I no longer smoke." He coughed self-consciously. "My wife made me give it up."

They grinned at this female idiosyncrasy. The grin did not reach Mr Cheeke's eyes. He reached for a chair and settled himself into it, hitching a polished black shoe across his knee. He already looked very much at home.

"I was in here a week ago, Mr Morrow, and Mr Bernstein showed me a painting by Ben Litton – your receptionist probably told you."

"Yes, she did, the deer painting."

"I'd like to see it again if I may. I'm returning to the States the day after tomorrow, and I have to make up my mind."

"But of course . . . !"

The picture waited for Mr Cheeke's decision, resting, where Marcus had left it, against the wall of the office. Robert drew the padded easel into the centre of the room, turned it towards the light, and gently lifted the Ben Litton into position. It was a large picture, an oil of three deer in a forest. Light filtered through the barely-suggested branches, and the artist had used a quantity of white which gave the work an ethereal quality. But its most interesting feature was the fact that it had been painted, not on stretched canvas, but on jute, and the coarser weave of this textile had blurred the artist's brush, like the outlines of an action photograph taken at high speed.

The American swung his chair into position, and turned the cold beam of his spectacles on to the painting. Discreetly, Robert removed himself to the back of the room so as not to obtrude in any way upon Mr Cheeke's own assessment, and his own view of the painting was obscured by the round crew-cut head of his potential customer. Personally, he liked the picture. He was not a fan of Ben Litton's. He thought his work affected and not always easy to understand – a reflection, perhaps, of the artist's own personality – but this swift sylvan impression was a thing to be looked at and lived with and never tired of.

Mr Cheeke got out of his chair, moved up to the painting, examined it minutely, backed away once more, and finished up leaning against the edge of Robert's desk.

"Why do you suppose, Mr Morrow," he said, without turning round, "that Litton was inspired to paint it on burlap?"

The word burlap made Robert want to laugh. He longed to say irreverently, *Probably had an old sack lying around* but Mr Cheeke did not look as though he would appreciate irreverence.

Mr Cheeke was here to spend money – always a serious business. Robert decided then that he was buying the Litton as an investment, and he hoped it would pay him off.

He said, "I'm afraid I have no idea, Mr Cheeke, but it does give a most unusual quality to the work."

Mr Cheeke turned his head to send Robert a cold smile over his shoulder.

"You are not as well informed on such aspects as Mr Bernstein."

"No," said Robert. "I'm afraid I'm not."

Mr Cheeke relapsed once more into contemplation. The silence settled and lasted. Robert's own concentration had begun to wander. Small sounds intruded. The ticking of his own wristwatch. A murmur of voices from the other side of the door. The thunderous rumble, like distant surf, that was Piccadilly traffic.

The American sighed gustily. He began to feel in his pockets, one by one, searching for something. A handkerchief, perhaps. Some change for his taxi ride back to the Hilton. His attention had strayed. Robert had not convinced him that the Litton was worth buying. He was going to make some excuse and go away.

But Mr Cheeke was simply searching for his pen. When he turned round, Robert saw that he already held his cheque book in the other hand.

Their business finally completed, Mr Cheeke relaxed. He became quite human and even took off his glasses and stowed them away in a tooled leather case. He accepted the offer of a drink, and he and Robert sat for a little, with two glasses of sherry, and talked about Marcus Bernstein and Ben Litton, and the two or three paintings which Mr Cheeke had purchased on his last visit to London, with which to form, with his latest acquisition, the nucleus of a small private collection. Robert told him about the retrospective Ben Litton exhibition which was being held in

16

Queenstown, Virginia, in April, and Mr Cheeke made a note of it in his diary, and then they both stood up, and Robert helped Mr Cheeke into his raincoat, and gave him his hat, and they shook hands.

"I've enjoyed meeting you, Mr Morrow, and doing business with you."

"I hope we'll see you next time you come to London."

"Most certainly I shall pay you a visit . . ."

Robert held the door open and they moved out into the Gallery. Bernstein's were showing, that fortnight, a collection of bird and animal paintings by an obscure South American with an unpronounceable name, a man of humble origins, who had somehow, sometime, incredibly, taught himself to paint. Marcus had met him last year in New York, had been instantly impressed by his work, and invited him then and there to stage a London exhibition. Now, his brilliant pictures lined the straw-green walls of the Bernstein Gallery and on this gloomy morning seemed to fill the room with the verdancy and sunshine of a more salubrious climate. The critics had loved him. Since the exhibition opened ten days ago, the Gallery had never once been empty, and within twenty-four hours there was not a picture that had not been sold.

At this moment, however, there were only three people in the Gallery. One of them was Peggy, neat and unobtrusive behind her kidney-shaped desk, busy with the proofs of a new catalogue. Another was a black-hatted man, stooped as a crow, doing a slow round of inspection. The last was a girl, who sat, facing the office door, on the circular buttoned sofa in the middle of the room. She wore a bright green trouser suit and was surrounded by luggage, and appeared to have wandered into Bernstein's under the mistaken impression that it was the waiting-room of a railway station.

Robert, with considerable self-possession, managed to behave as if she was not there. Together he and Mr Cheeke moved across the thick carpet towards the main door, Robert's head bent to catch the last of Mr Cheeke's small talk. The glass doors opened and swung shut behind them, and they were swallowed into the gloom of the dismal morning.

Emma Litton said, "Is that Mr Morrow?"

Peggy looked up. "That's right."

Emma was not used to being ignored. The single swift glance had made her feel uncomfortable. She wished that Marcus was not in Edinburgh. She crossed her legs and then uncrossed them again. From outside came the sound of the departing taxi. In a moment, the glass door opened, once more, and Robert Morrow came back into the Gallery. He did not make any comment, simply put his hands in his pockets, and calmly regarded Emma and her attendant chaos.

She decided that she had never, in her life, seen a man who looked less like an art dealer. His was the sort of face that, groggy and unshaven, is helped from a small sailboat at the end of a single-handed circumnavigation; or, darkly goggled, looks down from the peak of a previously unconquered mountain. But here, in the precious and rarefied atmosphere of the Bernstein galleries, he did not fit at all. He was very tall, wide-shouldered, long-legged; all this emphasised – and yet made incongruous – by his smoothly-tailored dark grey suit. In his youth his hair might have been red, but the years had tamed it to a tawny brown, and in contrast his grey eyes seemed pale as steel. He had high cheek-bones and a long, stubborn jaw, and she was diverted by the discovery that such a collection of features could be so attractive, and then remembered that Ben always averred that the character of a man lies, not in his eyes, where emotions are fleeting and can always be masked, but in the physical shape of his mouth, and this man's mouth was wide, with a jutting lower lip, and looked now as though it was trying, hard, not to laugh.

The silence became uncomfortable. Emma tried a smile. She said "Hello!"

For enlightenment, Robert Morrow turned to Peggy. Peggy was amused. "This young lady wants to see Mr Bernstein."

He said, "I am sorry, he's in Edinburgh."

"Yes, I know, so I've been told. The thing is, I only wanted him to cash me a cheque." He looked more puzzled than ever. Emma decided it was time to explain. "I'm Emma Litton. Ben Litton's my father."

His puzzlement cleared. "But why on earth didn't you say so? I am sorry, I had no idea." He came forward. "How do you do . . ."

Emma stood up. The straw hat, which had been on her knee, floated to the carpet and lay there, adding to the confusion which she had already wrought to the elegantly designed room.

They shook hands. "I . . . there wasn't any reason why you should know who I was. And I'm terribly sorry about all this stuff, but you see I haven't been home for six years, so there's bound to be quite a lot."

"Yes, I can see that."

Emma was embarrassed. "If you can just cash me a cheque, I'll take it all out of your way again. I only want enough to get back to Porthkerris. You see, I forgot to get any sterling when I was in Paris, and I've run out of traveller's cheques."

He frowned. "But how did you get this far? From the airport, I mean?"

"Oh." She had already forgotten. "Oh, there was a kind man on the plane, he helped me to carry my stuff on, and off again at London, and he lent me a pound. I'll have to send it back. I've got his address here . . . somewhere.'' She felt vaguely in pockets, but could not find the man's card. "Well, anyway, I've got it somewhere.'' She smiled again, hoping to disarm him.

"And when are you going down to Porthkerris?''

"There's a train at twelve-thirty, I think.''

He glanced at his wrist-watch. "You've missed that. When's the next?''

Emma looked blank. Peggy broke into the conversation in her usual polite and practical fashion. "I think there's one at two-thirty, Mr Morrow, but I can check.''

"Yes, do that, Peggy. Would the two-thirty be all right for you?''

"Yes, of course. It doesn't matter what time I arrive.''

"Is your father expecting you?''

"Well, I wrote him a letter and told him I was coming. But that doesn't mean he's *expecting* me . . .''

He smiled at this. "Yes. Well . . .'' He glanced at his watch again. It was twelve-fifteen. Peggy was already on the telephone, inquiring about train times. His eyes returned to the turmoil of suitcases. In a feeble effort to improve the situation, Emma stooped and picked up her sun hat.

He said, "I think the best thing would be to get all this out of the way . . . we'll pile it up in the office, and then . . . Have you had anything to eat?''

"I had some coffee at Le Bourget.''

"If you catch the two-thirty, there's time for me to give you lunch before you go.''

"Oh, you don't have to bother.''

"It's no bother. I have to eat anyway and you might as well eat with me. Come along now.''

He picked up two of the suitcases, and led the way into the office. Emma gathered up as much as she could carry, and followed him. The deer painting was still on the stand, and she saw it at once and was diverted.

"That's one of Ben's."

"Yes, I just sold it . . ."

"To the little man in the raincoat? It's good, isn't it?" She continued to admire it, while Robert toted the remainder of her luggage. "Why did he paint it on sacking?"

"You'd better ask him when you see him tonight."

She turned and grinned at him over her shoulder. "Influenced, do you think, by the Japanese school?"

"I wish," said Robert, "I'd thought of saying that to Mr Cheeke. Now, are you ready for lunch?"

He took an enormous black umbrella out of a stand, and stood aside for Emma to go out through the door ahead of him, and they left Peggy to hold the fort, sitting in a gallery restored once more to its usual ordered calm, and they went out into the rain and walked together, beneath the black umbrella, shouldering their way through the lunch-hour jostle of Kent Street, London, W1.

He took her to Marcello's where he normally lunched if he was not expected to entertain some important expense-account customer. Marcello was an Italian who ran a small upstairs restaurant, two streets from Bernstein's, and a table was perpetually reserved for either Marcus or Robert, or both of them, on the odd occasion when they were able to lunch together. It was a modest table, in a quiet corner, but today when Robert and Emma came up the stairs, Marcello took one look at her, with her long tassel of black hair, and her green trouser suit, and suggested that they might prefer to sit in the window.

Robert was amused. "Would you like to sit in the window?" he asked Emma.

21

"Where do you usually sit?" He indicated the small corner table. "Well, why don't we just sit there?"

Marcello was charmed by her. He led the way to the smaller table, held Emma's chair for her, gave them each an enormous menu written in dubious purple ink and went to fetch two glasses of Tio Pepe while they decided what they were going to eat.

Robert said, "My stock with Marcello will have gone up. I don't think I've ever brought a girl here for lunch."

"Who do you usually bring?"

"Just myself. Or Marcus."

"How is Marcus?" . . . her voice was warm.

"He's well. He'll be sorry to have missed you I know."

"It's my fault. I should have written and told him I was coming. But as you've probably realised, we Littons aren't very good at letting anybody know about anything."

"But you knew Ben had gone back to Porthkerris."

"Yes. Marcus wrote and told me that. And I know all about the retrospective exhibition, because I read an article on it in *Réalités*." She smiled wryly. "Being the daughter of a famous father does have some compensations. Even if he never does anything except send telegrams, you can usually read up what is happening to him in some paper or other."

"When did you last see him?"

"Oh," she shrugged. "Two years ago. I was in Florence, and he stopped off on his way to Japan."

"I didn't know you went through Florence when you went to Japan."

"You do if you happen to have a daughter living there." She put her elbows on the table, and rested her chin in her hand. "I don't suppose you even knew Ben had a daughter."

"Yes, of course I did."

"Well, I didn't know about you. I mean, I didn't know Marcus had a partner. He was still on his own when Ben went to Texas and I was bundled off to Switzerland.''

"It was about that time that I joined Bernstein's.''

"I . . . I never knew anyone who looked less like an art dealer. Than you, I mean.''

"Perhaps that's just because I'm not an art dealer.''

"But . . . you just sold that man Ben's painting.''

"No,'' he corrected her. "I simply accepted the cheque. Marcus had already sold it to him a week ago, but even Mr Cheeke didn't realise that.''

"But you must know something about painting.''

"Now, I do. One couldn't work with Marcus for all these years and not have some of his boundless knowledge rub off. But I'm basically a business man, and that's why Marcus asked me to join him.''

"But Marcus is the most successful business man I know.''

"Exactly, and so successful that the whole venture of the Gallery grew too big for him to handle on his own.''

Emma continued to regard him, a slight frown between her thickly-marked brows.

"Any more questions?''

She was not disconcerted. "Were you always a very close friend of Marcus?''

"What you really mean is, why did he take me into the firm? And the answer is that Marcus is not only my partner, but my brother-in-law as well. He married my older sister.''

"You mean Helen Bernstein is your sister?''

"You remember Helen?''

"But of course. And little David. How are they? You'll send them my love, won't you? You know I used to go and stay with them when Ben came up to London and there wasn't anyone to leave me with at Porthkerris. And when I went to Switzerland, it was Marcus and Helen who put me on to the plane, because Ben had already gone to Texas. Will you tell Helen I'm home, and that you gave me lunch?''

''Yes, of course I will.''

''Do they still have that little flat in the Brompton Road?''

''No, as a matter of fact, when my father died, they moved in with me. We all live in our old family house, in Kensington.''

''You mean you all live together?''

''Together and apart. Marcus and Helen and David live on the first two floors, and my father's old housekeeper lives in the basement, and I roost in the attics.''

''Aren't you married?''

Momentarily, he looked put out. ''Well, no, I'm not.''

''I was sure you'd be married. You have a very married look about you.''

''I don't quite know how to take that.''

''Oh, it wasn't meant in a derogatory fashion at all. It's really quite a compliment. I only wish Ben had that look about him. It would make life so much easier for all concerned. Especially me.''

''Don't you want to go back and live with him?''

''Yes, of course I do, more than anything. But I don't want it to be a failure. I was never very good at coping with Ben, and I don't suppose I'll be any better now.''

''Then why are you going?''

''Well . . .'' Under Robert Morrow's cool grey regard, it was difficult to be coherent. She picked up a fork and began to make patterns with it on the white damask cloth. ''I don't know. You only have one family. If people belong to each other, they should at least be able to live together. I want to have something to remember. When I'm old I want to be able to remember that once, even if it was only for a few weeks on end, my father and I were making some sort of a life together. Does that sound crazy?''

''No, it doesn't sound crazy, but it sounds as if you might be disappointed.''

''I learned all about being disappointed when I was a little girl. It's a luxury I can well do without. Besides, I only plan to stay until it becomes painfully obvious that we cannot stand each other's company for another hour.''

''Or,'' said Robert gently, ''until he prefers some other person's company.''

Emma's head came up, her eyes a sudden furious blaze of blue. She was, in that instant, her father at his most unscrupulous, when there was no retort too cruel or too cutting to be made. But her anger provoked no reaction, and after a cold pause, she looked down again, and continued to draw patterns on the tablecloth, and only said, ''All right. Until then.''

The small tension was broken by the return of Marcello bringing their sherry and ready to take the order. Emma chose a dozen oysters and fried chicken; Robert, more conservatively, a consommé and a steak. Then, taking advantage of the interruption, he tactfully changed the subject.

''Tell me about Paris. How was it looking?''

''Wet. Wet and cold and sunny all at once. Does that convey anything to you?''

''Everything.''

''You know Paris?''

''I go over on business. I was there last month.''

''On business?''

''No, on my way back from Austria. I had three weeks' splendid ski-ing.''

''Where did you go?''

''Obergurgl.''

"So that's why you're so brown. That's one of the reasons you don't look like an art dealer."

"Perhaps, when my tan fades, I shall look more authentic and be able to command higher prices. How long did you spend in Paris?"

"Two years. I shall miss it. It's so beautiful, and doubly so now all the buildings have been cleaned. And somehow, at this time of the year, there's that special feeling in Paris. That the winter's nearly over and the sun's just a day or so away and it's going to be spring again . . ."

And buds unfolding, and the scream of gulls, swooping over the chopped brown waters of the Seine. And barges, strung like necklaces, slipping away beneath the bridges, and the smell of the Metro, and garlic, and Gauloises. And being with Christopher.

All at once it became important to talk about him, to speak his name, to reassure herself of his existence. She said, casually, "You never met Hester, did you? My stepmother? At least for eighteen months she was my stepmother."

"I know about her."

"And about Christopher? Her son? Do you know about Christopher? Because, quite by chance, Christopher and I met up again in Paris. Just two days ago. And he came, this very morning, and saw me off at Le Bourget."

"You mean . . . you just bumped into each other . . . ?"

"Yes, we really did . . . in a grocer's shop. It could only happen in Paris."

"What was he doing there?"

"Oh, filling in time. He'd been to St Tropez, but he comes back to England in March to join some repertory theatre or other."

"He's an actor?"

26

"Yes. Didn't I tell you that? There is just one thing . . . I'm not going to say anything to Ben. You see, Ben never liked Christopher, and I don't think Christopher lost any love over him. To be truthful, I expect they were a little jealous of each other. But there were other things as well, and Ben and Hester didn't exactly part company on the best of terms. I don't want to start off by having a row with Ben about Christopher, so I'm not going to say anything. At least not right away."

"I see."

Emma sighed. "You've got a very stuffy expression on your face. You obviously think I'm being underhand."

"I don't think anything of the sort. And when you've finished making patterns on the tablecloth, your oysters have arrived."

By the time they had finished lunch and drunk their coffee, and Robert had paid the bill, it was half past one. They got up from the table, and said goodbye to Marcello, and collected the big black umbrella and went downstairs. They walked back to Bernstein's, asked the doorman to get Emma a taxi.

"I'd come with you and put you on to the train, but Peggy has to go out and get herself some lunch."

"I'll be all right."

He took her into the office and unlocked the safe.

"Will twenty pounds be enough?"

She had already forgotten her reason for coming to the Gallery in the first place. "What? Oh, yes, of course . . ." She began to feel for her cheque book, but Robert stopped her.

"Don't bother. Your father has a sort of petty cash account with us. He's always running out of small change when he's in London. We'll put your twenty pounds down to that."

"Well, if you're sure . . ."

"Sure I'm sure. And, Emma, there is one other thing. The man who lent you the pound. Somewhere you have his address.

If you find it and give it to me now, I'll see he gets the pound back again."

Emma was amused. Searching for the card, finding it at last, entangled with a French bus ticket and a book of matches, she began to laugh, and when Robert asked her what was so funny, she simply said, "How well you know my father!"

3

It stopped raining at tea-time. There was a subtle lifting of the atmosphere, a freshness in the air. An errant shaft of sunlight even found its way into the Gallery, and by five-thirty, when Robert locked up his office, and went out to join the rush hour torrent of home-going humanity, he found that a small breeze had got up and blown the clouds away, leaving the city to sparkle beneath a pale, pellucid blue sky.

It was somehow more than he could bear to plunge into the subterranean stuffiness of the tube, so he walked as far as Knightsbridge, and then got on a bus and rode the rest of the way home.

His house, in Milton Gardens, was separated from the busy artery of the Kensington High Street by a maze of small streets and squares, a pleasant neighbourhood of miniature, early-Victorian houses, cream-painted, and with bright front doors and small gardens that in summer bloomed with lilac and magnolia. The streets had wide pavements where nannies pushed prams and small, well-dressed children walked to their expensive schools and the local dogs were rigorously exercised. After this, Milton Gardens came as something of a let down. It was a terrace of large and shabby houses, and Number Twenty-three, which was Robert's – the centre house, and crowned with the main pediment of the terrace – quite often looked the shabbiest. It had a black front door, and two dried-up bay trees in tubs, and a brass letter-box that Helen always meant to polish, but quite often forgot. The household cars were parked at the pavement's edge – a big dark-green Alvis coupé which was Robert's, and a dusty red Mini which was Helen's. Marcus did not own a car because he had never found time to learn how to drive.

Robert went up the steps, feeling in his pocket for his latch-key, and let himself in. The hall was large and spacious, a surprisingly wide and shallow staircase curved up to the first floor. Beyond the staircase, the hall continued in a narrow passage, which led to a glassed door, and the garden. This beguiling vista of distant grass and sun-touched chestnut trees gave the immediate impression of being in the country, and was one of the most endearing aspects of the house.

The front door slammed shut behind him. From the kitchen, his sister Helen called his name.

''Robert.''

''Hello!''

He chucked his hat on to the hall table, and went in through the door at the right of the hall. In the old days this room, facing out over the street, had been the family dining-room, but when Robert's father had died, and Marcus and Helen and David had moved in, Helen had converted it into a kitchen dining-room, with a scrubbed country table, and a pine dresser, crammed with patterned china and a counter, like a bar, behind which she could work. There were also a great many plants in pots, straggling geraniums, and herbs, and bowls of bulbs. Bunches of onions and marketing baskets hung from hooks, and there were recipe books, and racks of wooden spoons, and the cheerfulness of bright rugs and cushions.

Helen was behind her counter now, in a blue and white butcher's apron, peeling mushrooms. The air was filled with fragrant smells – of baking and lemons, and warm butter and the lightest suggestion of garlic. She was an exceptional cook.

She said, "Marcus called from Edinburgh. He's coming home tonight. Did you know?"

"What time?"

"There's a plane at a quarter past five. He was going to try and get a seat on that. It gets in to the terminal at half past seven."

Robert pulled a high stool up to the counter, and perched on it, like a man sitting at a bar.

"Does he want to be met at the airport?"

"No, he'll get the bus in. I thought one of us would go and pick him up. Are you in or out for dinner tonight?"

"It smells so good, I think I'm in."

She smiled. Facing each other across the counter, the family resemblance between them was very marked. Helen was a big woman, tall and heavy-boned, but when she smiled her face and her eyes lit up like a girl's. Her hair, like Robert's, was reddish, but softened by streaks of grey, and she wore it drawn tightly back into a knot, to reveal a small and unexpectedly neat pair of ears. She was proud of her pretty ears, and always wore ear-rings. She had a whole boxful of them in her dressing-table drawer, and if you didn't know what to give her for a present, you simply bought a pair of ear-rings. This evening they were green, some sort of semi-precious stone, set in a narrow rope of woven gold, and their colour brought out the green lights in her indeterminate, speckled eyes.

She was forty-two, six years older than Robert, and she had been married to Marcus Bernstein for ten years. Before that she had worked for him, as secretary, receptionist, book-keeper, and – on occasions when finances were shaky – as office cleaner as well, and it was as much due to her efforts and faith in Marcus that the Gallery had not merely survived the initial lean patches, but had grown to achieve its present international reputation.

Robert said, "Did Marcus tell you anything . . . about how he got on . . . ?"

"Not much, there wasn't time. But the old Lord of the Glens, whoever he is, has three Raeburns, a Constable and a Turner. So that should give you all something to think about."

"Does he want to sell them?"

"Apparently. He says that at the current price of whisky, he can no longer afford to keep them hanging on the wall. Anyway, we'll hear all about it when Marcus gets back. How about you . . . what have you been doing today . . . ?"

"Nothing much. An American called Lowell Cheeke came in and wrote a cheque for a Ben Litton . . ."

"That's fine . . ."

"And . . ." he watched his sister's face ". . . Emma Litton's home."

Helen had started to slice the mushrooms. Now, swiftly, she looked up and her hands were still.

"Emma. You mean Ben's Emma?"

"Flew back from Paris today. Came into the Gallery to collect enough money to get her back to Porthkerris."

"Did Marcus know she was coming back?"

"No, I don't think so. I don't think she wrote to anyone except her father."

"And of course Ben wouldn't say a word." Helen made an exasperated face. "Sometimes I could just strangle that man."

Robert was amused. "What would you have done if you'd known she was coming?"

"Well, met her at the airport. Given her lunch. Anything."

"If it's any comfort to you, I gave her lunch."

"Well, good for you." She sliced another mushroom, considering this. "What does she look like now?"

"Attractive, in a rather unusual way."

"Unusual," Helen repeated dryly. "Tell me she's unusual and you tell me nothing I don't already know."

Robert picked up a slice of raw mushroom and ate it, experimentally. "Do you know about her mother?"

"Of course I do." Helen rescued her mushrooms, whisking them out of his reach, and taking them to her cooker, where a pan simmered with warm butter. With another deft movement, she spilled the mushrooms into the butter, and there were faint sizzling sounds and a delicious smell. She stood there, moving the mushrooms around with a wooden spatula, her strong features profiled.

"Who was she?"

"Oh, a little art student, half Ben's age. She was very pretty."

"Was he married to her?"

"Yes, he did marry her. I think, in his way, he was very fond of her. But she was simply a child."

"Did she leave him?"

"No, she died, having Emma."

"And then, later on, he married someone called Hester."

Helen turned to look at him, her eyes narrowed. "How do you know about that?"

"Emma told me today at lunch."

"Well, I never did! Yes, Hester Ferris. That was years ago."

"But there was a boy. A son. Called Christopher?"

"Don't say he's turned up again."

"Why do you sound so alarmed?"

"You'd sound alarmed, too, if you'd lived through those eighteen months when Ben Litton was married to Hester . . ."

"Tell me."

33

"Oh, they were murder. For Marcus, for Ben . . . I suppose for Hester, and certainly for me. If Marcus wasn't being roped in to referee some sordid domestic fracas, then he was being showered with ridiculous little bills which Hester said Ben refused to pay. And then, you know how Ben has this phobia about telephones, and Hester put one into her house and Ben tore it out by the roots. And then Ben ran into some sort of mental block and couldn't do any work, and spent all his time in the local pub, and Hester would get hold of Marcus and say that Marcus must come because he was the only person who could do anything with him, and so on, and so on. Marcus aged, visibly, before my eyes. Can you believe that?"

"Yes. But I don't see what it has to do with the boy."

"The boy was one of the bones of contention. Ben couldn't bear him."

"Emma said he was jealous."

"She said that? She was always a perceptive child. I suppose in a way Ben was jealous of Christopher, but Christopher was a devil. He looked like a saint, but his mother spoiled him rotten." She drew her pan of mushrooms away from the heat, and came back to lean her elbows on the counter. "What did Emma say about Christopher?"

"Just that they'd met in Paris."

"What was he doing there?"

"I don't know. I suppose having a holiday. He's an actor. Did you know that?"

"No, but I can well believe it. Was she looking very starry-eyed about him?"

"I should say so, yes. Unless it was the thought of going back to live with her father."

"That's the last thing in the world for her to be starry-eyed about."

34

"I know that. But when I started to say as much, I near as dammit got my head bitten off."

"Yes, you would. They're as loyal as thieves to each other." She patted his hand. "Don't get involved, Robert; I couldn't bear the strain."

"I'm not involved, simply intrigued."

"Well, for your own peace of mind, take my advice and keep it that way. And while we're on the subject of involvements, Jane Marshall called at lunch-time, and she wants you to ring her up."

"What about, do you know?"

"She didn't say. Just said she'd be in any time after six o'clock. You won't forget, will you?"

"No, I won't forget. But don't you forget, either, that Jane is not an involvement."

"What you're jibbing at, I cannot imagine," said Helen, who had never, with her brother at any rate, bothered to mince words. "She is charming, attractive and efficient."

Robert made no comment on this, and exasperated by his silence, she went on, justifying herself. "You have everything in common, interests, friends, a way of life. Besides, a man of your age should be married. There's nothing so pathetic as an elderly bachelor."

She stopped. There was a pause. Robert said politely, "Have you finished?"

Helen sighed deeply. It was hopeless. She knew, had always known, that no words would provoke Robert into any action that he did not choose to make. He had never been talked into anything in his life. Her outburst had been a waste of breath and she already regretted it.

"Yes, of course I've finished. And I apologise. It's none of my business and I have no right to interfere. It's just that I like

35

Jane, and I want you to be happy. I don't know, Robert. I can't work out what it is you're looking for."

"I don't know either," said Robert. He smiled at his sister, and ran a hand over his head and down the back of his neck, a familiar gesture made when he was either confused or tired. "But I think it has something to do with what exists between you and Marcus."

"Well, I just hope you find it before you drop dead of old age."

He left her to her cooking, collected his hat and the evening paper and a handful of letters, and went upstairs to his own flat. His sitting-room, which looked out over the big garden and the chestnut tree had once been the nursery. It was low-ceilinged, close-carpeted, lined with books, and furnished with as much of his father's stuff as he had been able to get up the staircase. He dropped his hat and the paper and the letters on a chair, and went to the antique bombé cupboard where he kept his drink, and poured himself a whisky and soda. Then he took a cigarette from the box on the coffee table, lit it, and, cradling his glass, went to sit at the desk, to lift the telephone receiver and dial Jane Marshall's number.

She took some time to answer. While he waited, he doodled on the blotting paper with a pencil, and glanced at his watch and decided that he would have a bath, and change before he went to pick Marcus up at the Cromwell Road terminal. And, as a peace offering to Helen, he would take a bottle of wine downstairs and they would have it with their dinner, the three of them, sitting round the scrubbed table in Helen's kitchen and, inevitably, talking shop. He discovered that he was very tired, and the prospect of such an evening was comforting.

The double burr stopped. A cold voice said, "Jane Marshall here."

She always answered the telephone in this manner, and Robert still found it chilling, although he knew the reason for it. At twenty-six, Jane, with a broken marriage and a divorce behind her, had been forced to start earning her own living, and had ended up with a modest interior decorating business which she ran from her own house. Thus, a single telephone number had to do double duty, and she had long since decided it was prudent to treat an incoming call as potential business until it proved to be otherwise. She had explained this to Robert when he complained about her frigid manner.

"You don't understand. It might be a client ringing up. What's he going to think if I sound all sexy and treacle-voiced?"

"You don't need to sound sexy. Just friendly and pleasant. Why don't you try it? You'd be ripping out walls and running up curtains and loose covers before you knew where you were."

"That's what you think. More likely to be fending him off with a curved upholstery needle."

Now he said, "Jane . . . ?"

"Oh, Robert." Her voice was at once its normal self, warm and obviously pleased to hear him. "I am sorry, did Helen give you my message?"

"She asked me to call you."

"It's just that I wondered . . . Look, I've been given two tickets for the ballet on Friday. It's La Fille Mal Gardée and I thought you might like to come. Unless you're going away or something."

He looked down at his own hand, drawing boxes, in perfect perspective, on the blotting pad. He heard Helen's voice. *You have everything in common. Interests, friends, a way of life.*

"Robert?"

"Yes. Sorry. No, I'm not going away. I'd love to come."

"Shall we eat here first?"

37

"No, we'll go out. I'll book a table."

"I'm glad you can make it." He could tell that she was smiling. "Is Marcus back yet?"

"No, I'm just going to meet him."

"Send him and Helen my love."

"I will."

"See you Friday, then. Goodbye."

"Goodbye, Jane."

After he had replaced the receiver, he did not get up from his desk, but sat there, his chin in his hand, putting the final touches to the last box. When it was finished, he laid down the pencil and reached for his drink, and sat, looking at what he had drawn, and wondered why it should make him think of a long line of suitcases.

Marcus Bernstein came through the glass doors of the terminal building looking, as he always looked, like a refugee or a street musician. His overcoat sagged, his old-fashioned black hat had somehow got turned up in the front, his long, lined face was sallow with tiredness. He carried his bulging brief-case, but his grip had travelled from the airport in the luggage compartment of the bus, and when Robert found him, he was standing, patiently, by the circular conveyor-belt, awaiting its arrival.

He managed to look both humble and dejected, and the casual passer-by would have found it hard to believe that this modest and unassuming man was, in fact, a powerful influence in the art world on both sides of the Atlantic. An Austrian, he had left his native Vienna in 1937, and after the horrors of an alien's war, had burst upon the post-war art world like a bright flame. His obvious knowledge and perception quickly drew attention, and his backing of young artists showed an example which other dealers were quick to follow. But his real impact upon the lay public was made in 1949, when he opened his own gallery in Kent Street with an exhibition of abstracts by Ben Litton. Ben, already famous for his pre-war landscapes and portraits, had been moving for some time towards this new medium, and the 1949 exhibition was the beginning of a working friendship which rode all personal storms and quarrels. It also marked the end of Marcus's initial struggles, and the start of a long, slow haul to success.

"Marcus!"

He gave a small start, and turned and saw Robert coming towards him, and looked surprised, as though he had not expected to be met.

"Hello, Robert. This is very kind of you."

After thirty years in England, his accent was still strongly marked, but Robert no longer noticed it.

"I would have come to the airport, but we weren't sure if you'd get on the plane. Did you have a good flight?"

"It was snowing in Edinburgh."

"It's been raining here all day. Look, there's your bag." He whipped it off the conveyor-belt. "Come on, now . . ."

In the car, waiting for the lights in the Cromwell Road to change, he told Marcus about Mr Lowell Cheeke returning to Bernstein's to buy the Litton of the deer. Marcus acknowledged this with a grunt, giving the impression that he had known all along that the sale was simply a matter of time. The lights went from red to yellow to green and the car moved forward and Robert said, "And Emma Litton is home from Paris. She flew in this morning. Didn't have any sterling, so she came to the gallery to get you to cash her a cheque. I gave her lunch and twenty pounds and sent her on her way."

"On her way to where?"

"Porthkerris, and Ben."

"I suppose he is there."

"She seemed to think he would be. For the time being, at any rate."

"Poor child," said Marcus.

Robert made no answer to this, and they drove home in silence, each busy with his own thoughts. Back at Milton Gardens, Marcus got out of the car, and went up the steps, feeling for his latchkey, but before he could run it to earth, the door was opened by Helen, and Marcus, in his sagging coat and comic's hat, was silhouetted against the hall light.

She said, "Well, how lovely!" and because he was so much smaller than she, stooped to embrace him, and Robert, extracting Marcus's grip from the boot of the Alvis, tried to work out why it was that they never looked ridiculous.

It seemed to have been dark for a long time. But when the London express came to the junction where she had to change for Porthkerris, and Emma got out of the train, she found that it was not really dark at all. The sky was bright with stars, and the night blown through with a buffeting wind that smelt of the sea. When she had unloaded all her luggage, she stood waiting on the platform for the express to pull out, and above her the tattered leaves of a palm tree rattled incongruously in this restless wind.

The train moved on, and she saw the single porter on the opposite platform, occupied, in a leisurely fashion, with a barrow-load of parcels. When at last he noticed her, he set down the handles of his barrow, and called, across the lines, "Want some help, do you?"

"Yes please."

He jumped down on to the tracks and walked across to her side, and somehow gathered all her belongings into his two arms, and then Emma followed him back across the tracks, and he gave her a hand up on to the other platform.

"Where are you going?"

"Porthkerris."

"Taking the train?"

"Yes."

The smaller train waited on the single line branch track that ran round the coast to Porthkerris. Emma appeared to be the only passenger. She thanked the porter and tipped him and collapsed into a seat. Exhaustion consumed her. Never had a day seemed so long. After a little she was joined by a country woman in a brown hat like a pot. Perhaps she had been shopping, for she carried a bulging, checked leather bag. Minutes passed, the only sound the wind thudding at the closed windows of the train. At last, the engine gave a single whistle and they were off.

It was impossible not to feel excited as familiar landmarks loomed up through the darkness, and were recognised, and then fled past. There were only two small halts before Porthkerris and then, at last, the steep cutting which in spring was quilted in primroses, and then the tunnel, and then the sea was below them, dark as ink, the tide out, the wet sands like satin. Porthkerris was a nest of lights, the curve of the harbour seemed strung with a necklace, and the riding lights of fishing boats were reflected in a maze of shimmering black and gold water.

They had begun to lose speed. The platform slid alongside. The name PORTHKERRIS passed and fell behind. They finally stopped alongside a shiny tin advertisement for boot polish which had been there ever since Emma could remember. Her companion, who had spoken not a word the entire journey, now stood up, opened the door, and stepped sedately out, disappearing into the night. Emma stood in the open door, looking for a porter, but the only visible official was up at the other end of the

train, unnecessarily shouting, "Porthkerris! Porthkerris!" She
saw him stop to chat to the driver, pushing his cap back off his
forehead, and standing with his hands on his hips.

There was an empty barrow by the boot polish advertisement,
so she loaded her luggage on to this, and then abandoned it,
carrying only a small overnight bag. She began to walk up
the platform. In the stationmaster's office, the lights were on,
they shone out in warm yellow patches, and a man sat on a
bench, reading a newspaper. Emma walked by him, her footsteps
ringing on the stone flags, but as she passed, he put down the
newspaper and said her name.

Emma stopped, and slowly turned. He folded the newspaper
and stood up, and the light seemed to turn his white hair
into a halo.

"I thought you were never going to arrive."

"Hello, Ben," said Emma.

"Is the train late, or did I get the times all wrong?"

"I don't think we're late. Perhaps we were late starting from
the junction. We seemed to wait there a long time. How did you
know what train I'd be on?"

"I had a telegram from Bernstein's." *Robert Morrow*,
thought Emma. *How kind.* Ben glanced at her bag. "You haven't
much luggage."

"I have a barrow-load at the other end of the platform."

He turned to vaguely peer in the direction that Emma indicated. "Never mind. We'll fetch it some other time. Come on,
let's get back."

"But someone might take it," Emma protested. "Or it might
rain. We'd better tell the porter."

The porter had by now finished his social chat with the
engine driver. Ben attracted his attention, told him about
Emma's luggage. "Put it somewhere, would you, we'll collect

it tomorrow.'' He gave him five shillings. The porter said, ''Yes, Mr Litton, don't worry, I'll do that,'' and went off down the platform whistling, tucking the money in the pocket of his waistcoat.

''Well,'' said Ben again, ''what are we waiting for? Come on, let's get moving.''

There was no suggestion of a car or a taxi, they were simply going to walk home. They did this by way of a series of narrow short-cuts, steep flights of stone steps, tiny sloping alleys, always leading downhill, until finally they emerged on to the brightly lighted harbour road.

Emma, trudging beside her father, still carrying the overnight bag which he had not thought to carry for her, took a long sideways look at Ben. It was the first time she had seen him for nearly two years, and she thought that no man changed as little as he. He was no fatter, no thinner. His hair, which had been snow-white as long as Emma could remember, was neither thinning nor receding. His face, weathered by years of working in the sun, in the outdoors, by the sea, was darkly tanned and netted with fine lines which could never be described as anything so prosaic as wrinkles. From him, Emma had inherited her strong cheek-bones, and her square chin, but her pale eyes must have come from her mother, for Ben's were deep-set beneath craggy brows, and of so dark a brown that in certain lights they looked black.

Even his clothes did not seem to have changed. The sagging corduroy jacket, the narrowly cut trousers, the suède shoes of immense elegance and age – they could have belonged to no one else. Tonight his shirt was a faded orange wool, a paisley cotton handkerchief did duty as a necktie. He had never owned a waistcoat.

They came to his pub, the Sliding Tackle, and Emma half expected him to suggest that they should go in for a drink.

She did not want a drink, but she was ravenously hungry. She wondered if there was any food in the cottage. She wondered, in fact, if they were actually going to the cottage. It was quite within the bounds of possibility that Ben had been living in his studio, and would expect Emma to shake down there with him.

She said, tentatively, "I don't even know where we're heading for."

"The cottage, of course. Where did you imagine?"

"I didn't know." They were safely past the pub. "I thought perhaps you might have been living at the studio."

"No, I've been staying at the Sliding Tackle. This is the first time I've been to the cottage."

"Oh," said Emma, glumly.

He caught the inflexion in her voice and reassured her. "It's all right. When they knew at the Sliding Tackle that you were turning up there was a positive deputation of eager ladies all wanting to get the place ready for you. In the end Daniel's wife saw to it for me." Daniel was the barman. "She seemed to think that after all these years everything would be covered in blue mould, like Gorgonzola cheese."

"And was it?"

"No, of course it wasn't. A bit cobwebby, perhaps, but perfectly habitable."

"That was kind of her . . . I must thank her."

"Yes, she'd like that."

The cobbled road climbed steeply away from the harbour. Emma's tired legs ached. Suddenly, and with no word of explanation, Ben removed her bag from her grasp.

"What the hell have you got in this?"

"A toothbrush."

"It weighs like pig-iron. When did you leave Paris, Emma?"

"This morning." It seemed a lifetime ago.

"And how did Bernstein's know about you?"

"I had to go there to get some money. Some sterling. I was given twenty pounds out of your petty cash account. I hope you don't mind."

"I don't give a damn."

They passed his studio, shuttered and dark. "Have you started painting yet?" asked Emma.

"Of course I have. That's what I came back for."

"And the work you did in Japan?"

"I left it in America for the exhibition."

Now, the air was full of the sound of surf, of breakers rolling up on to the beach. The big beach. Their beach. And then the uneven roof of their cottage came into view, illuminated by the street lamp which stood by the blue gate. As they approached it, Ben felt in his jacket pocket for the key, and he went ahead of Emma, through the gate and down the steps, unlocking the door, and letting himself in, switching on the lights as he went, so that in a moment every window was blazing.

Emma followed more slowly. She saw at once the bright flicker of firelight and the almost inhuman cleanliness and order which Daniel's wife had somehow created out of neglect. Everything shone, was scrubbed and whitewashed and polished to within an inch of its life. Cushions had been plumped and placed with geometrical precision. There were no flowers, but the house was pervaded with a strong smell of carbolic.

Ben sniffed and made a face. "Like a bloody hospital," he said. He had put down Emma's bag, and now disappeared in the direction of the kitchen. Emma crossed the room and stood at the fireplace, warming her hands at the blaze. Cautiously, she was beginning to feel more hopeful. She had been afraid that there would be no welcome. But Ben had met her train and there was a fire in the fireplace. No human being could ask for much more.

Over the mantelshelf was the room's only picture, the painting that Ben had done of Emma when she was six years old. It was the first time in her life – and, it transpired, the last – that she had been the centre of his attention, and, for this reason alone she had borne uncomplaining the long hours of sitting, the boredom, the cramps, and his unleashed fury if she moved. For the picture, she had worn a wreath of marguerite daisies, and each day had brought the recurring pleasure of watching Ben's clever hands make a fresh wreath, and then the pride of having him place it on her head, solemnly, as though he were crowning a queen.

He came back into the room. "She's a good woman, that wife of Daniel's. I shall tell him so. I told her to stock up with a few supplies." Emma turned, and saw that he had found himself a bottle of Haig and a tumbler. "Get me a jug of water, would you, Emma?" A thought occurred to him. "And I suppose another glass, if you want a drink."

"I don't want a drink. But I'm hungry."

"I don't know if she laid in *those* sort of supplies."

"I'll look."

The kitchen, too, had been scoured and scrubbed and swept. She opened the fridge and found eggs and bacon and a bottle of milk, and there was bread in the bin. She took a jug off a hook on the dresser and filled it with cold water, and carried it back into the sitting-room. Ben was wandering about, fiddling with the lamps, trying to find something wrong. He had always hated this house.

She said, "Do you want me to cook you some scrambled eggs?"

"What? Oh, no, I don't want anything. You know, it's odd being back here. I keep feeling Hester's going to appear and tell us to start doing something we don't want to."

Emma thought of Christopher. She said, "Oh, poor Hester."

"Poor nothing. Interfering bitch."

She went back to the kitchen, found a saucepan, a bowl, some butter. From the living-room, she could hear the continued sounds of Ben's restlessness. He opened and shut doors, drew a curtain, kicked a log back on to the fire. Presently, he appeared in the kitchen doorway, a cigarette in one hand, his glass cradled in the other. He watched Emma, stirring eggs. He said, "You've grown up, haven't you?"

"I'm nineteen. Whether I've grown up or not, I really wouldn't know."

"It's odd, your not being a little girl any longer."

"You'll get used to it."

"Yes, I suppose so. How long are you going to stay?"

"Let's say I've made no plans for going away again."

"You mean, you want to live here?"

"For the time being."

"With me?"

Emma glanced at him, over her shoulder. "Would that be so painful?"

"I don't know," said Ben. "I've never tried it."

"That's why I came back. I thought perhaps it was time you did."

"You couldn't, by any chance, be reproaching me?"

"Why should I reproach you?"

"Because I abandoned you, and went off to teach in Texas. Because I never came to see you in Switzerland. Because I wouldn't let you come to Japan."

"If I really minded about those things, I shouldn't have wanted to come back."

"And supposing I decide to go away again?"

"Are you going to go?"

"No." He looked down at his drink. "Not for the moment.

47

At the moment I'm tired. I've come back for a bit of peace." He looked up again. "But I shan't stay here for ever."

"I shan't stay here for ever, either," said Emma. She put the toast on a plate, the egg on the toast, opened a drawer to find a knife and fork.

Ben watched all this with some agitation. "You aren't going to be an efficient little housewife, are you? Another Hester? If so, I shall throw you out."

"I couldn't be efficient if I tried. If it's any comfort to you, I miss trains, burn food, lose money, drop things. I had a sun hat, this morning, in Paris, but by the time I'd got to Porthkerris, it had gone. How could anyone lose a sun hat in this country, in February?"

But he was still not convinced. "Won't you want to be driving around in a car all the time?"

"I don't know how to drive a car."

"And television and telephones and all that rubbish?"

"They've never figured largely in my life."

He laughed then, and Emma wondered if there was something wrong in thinking your own father so attractive.

He said, "You know, I wasn't sure how well this was going to work. But under such favourable circumstances, I can only say I'm glad you came back. Welcome home."

And he raised his glass to Emma and finished his drink, and then went back to the sitting-room to retrieve the bottle and pour himself the other half.

4

The bar of the Sliding Tackle was small and snug, blackly panelled, very old. It boasted only one tiny window, which looked out over the harbour, so that a visitor's first impression, as he came in from the glaring outside light, was one of utter darkness. Later, when his eyes became accustomed to the gloom, other peculiarities became evident, the most prominent being that there were not two parallel lines in the place, for over the centuries the little pub had settled into its foundations, like a deep sleeper in a comfortable bed, and various irregularities, like optical illusions, were apt to make potential customers feel intoxicated before they had even downed their first drink. The flagged floor sank in one direction, displaying a sinister gap between stone and wainscoting. The blackened beam, which formed the framework of the bar itself, sloped in another. And the whitewashed ceiling had such a lethal tilt to it that the landlord had been driven to put up notices saying "Watch That Beam" and "Mind Your Head".

Over the years the Sliding Tackle had remained, stubbornly, itself. Set in the old and unfashionable part of Porthkerris, slap on the harbour, with no space for chi-chi terraces or tea gardens, it had managed to resist the spate of summer tourism which engulfed the rest of the town. It had its regulars, who came to drink, and talk in comfortable, undemanding grunts, and play shove-ha'penny. It had a dart board and a small blackened grate where, winter and summer, a fire always burned. It had Daniel, the barman, and Fred, turnip-faced and squint-eyed, who was employed in the summer cleaning trash from the beaches and hiring out deckchairs, and spent the rest of the year blissfully drinking his takings.

And it had Ben Litton.

"It's a matter of priorities," said Marcus, as he and Robert set forth in the Alvis to run Ben Litton to earth. It was so fine that Robert had put the hood down, and so Marcus wore, with his habitual black overcoat, a tweed cap like a mushroom that looked as though it had been bought for some other person. "Priorities and timing. At mid-day on a Sunday, the first place to look is the Sliding Tackle. And if he isn't there, which I very much doubt, we'll go on to the studio, and then try the cottage."

"Or maybe, on such a wonderful morning, just out and about?"

"I don't think so. This is his drinking time, and as far as that is concerned, he has always been a creature of habit."

Still only March, it was indeed a freak day of unbelievable beauty. The sky was cloudless. The sea, driven obliquely into the curve of the bay by a buffeting north-west wind, lay streaked before them in every shade of blue, from deep indigo to palest turquoise. From the top of the hill, the view stretched to infinity, distant headlands merging into a haze that suggested the full heat of midsummer. And below, down the twisting road, the town dropped steeply, a jumble of narrow cobbled lanes, and whitewashed houses, and bleached, crooked roofs, clustered around the harbour.

Each year, during the three months of summer, Porthkerris

became a small hell on earth. Its inadequate streets were jammed with cars, its pavements overflowed with underdressed humanity, its shops spilled over with postcards, sun hats, sand-shoes, shrimping-nets, surfboards and inflatable plastic cushions. On the big beach the tents and the bathing huts went up, and the cafés opened, their terraces crammed with round iron tables, speared by umbrellas. Orange banners flapped in the wind, advertising Raspberry Sticks, and Frozen Chocolate-Coated Clusters and other horrors, and if these were not sustenance enough, there were Cornish splits for sale, and pasties, filled with soggy grey potato.

And around Whitsun, the amusement arcade opened up, with pin-ball machines and juke boxes blaring, and perhaps another cluster of ramshackle but picturesque houses would go down before the bulldozers, to clear the space for yet another car park, and the residents, and the people who loved the town, and the artists, would be horrified witnesses to this rape and say, *It's worse than ever. It is ruined. We can stay no longer.* But each autumn, once the last train had borne away the last peeling-nosed invader, Porthkerris settled back, miraculously, in its normal tempo. The shops put up their shutters. The tents came down, and the beaches were washed clean by the winter storms. The only flags which flew were lines of washing, flapping from house to house, like pastel-coloured bunting, or propped high over the greenswards where the fishermen spread their nets to dry.

And it was then that the old magic reasserted itself, and it became easy to understand why a man like Ben Litton should return time and time again, like a homing pigeon, for refreshment, and the security of familiar things, to be caught up once more in the painter's obsession with colour and light.

The Sliding Tackle was at the far end of the harbour road. Robert drew up outside its crooked porch and killed the engine.

It was very warm and quiet. The tide was out, the harbour full of clean sand and seaweed and screaming gulls. Some children, coaxed out by the sunshine, played with buckets and spades, watched over by a couple of knitting grannies in pinafores and hairnets, and a scrawny black cat sat on the cobbles and washed its ears.

Marcus got out of the car. "I'll go and see if he's inside. You wait here."

Robert took a cigarette from the packet on the dashboard and lit it, and watched the cat. Above his head the inn sign creaked in the wind, and a gull came and sat on it and eyed Robert with malevolence, screaming defiance. Two men came down the road, walking with the slow righteous gait of a restful Methodist Sunday. They wore navy blue guernseys and white cloth caps.

" 'Morning," they said as they passed.

"Lovely day," said Robert.

"Yes. Lovely."

After a little, Marcus appeared once more. "All right, I've found him."

"What about Emma?"

"He says she's back at the studio. Whitewashing."

"Want me to go and get her?"

"If you would. It's . . ." he glanced at his watch, "twelve-fifteen. Suppose you're back here at one. I said we'd lunch at one-thirty."

"Right. I'll walk. It's not worth taking the car."

"Can you remember the way?"

"Of course." He had been before, twice, to Porthkerris, chasing up Ben Litton for some reason or other when Marcus had not been available to do it for himself. Ben's phobia about telephones and cars and all forms of communication, presented, from time to time, the most hideous complications, and Marcus had long since accepted the fact that it was quicker to make the journey from London to Cornwall and beard the lion in his den than to wait for an answer to the most impassioned of reply-paid telegrams.

He got out of the car and slammed the door shut. "Do you want me to tell her what it's all about, or shall I leave that pleasant task to you?"

Marcus grinned. "You tell her."

Robert pulled off his narrow tweed cap and dropped it on to the driving seat. He said, amiably, "You bastard."

He had had a letter from Emma, a week or two after she passed through London.

Dear Robert,

If I call Marcus Marcus, I can't possibly call you Mr Morrow, can I? No, of course I can't, not possibly. I should have written at once to thank you so very much for the lunch and for letting me have the money, and for letting Ben know that I was on the train. He actually came to meet me at the station. Everything is going wonderfully well, so far we haven't had a row, and Ben is working like a fiend on four canvases at once.

I didn't lose any of my luggage except the sun hat, which I'm sure someone stole.

> *My love to Marcus. And you.*
> *Emma.*

Now, he made his way through the baffling maze of narrow streets and tightly-packed houses that led to the north shore of the town. Here, there was another beach, a bleak and unprotected bay only esteemed for the long surfing rollers which poured in, straight from the Atlantic. Ben Litton's studio faced out over this beach. Once, long ago, it had been a net store and its only access was a cobbled ramp which sloped down from the street to a double, black-tarred door. There was a printed sign with his name, and an immense iron knocker, and Robert took hold of this and banged it, and called "Emma."

There was no reply. He opened the door, and it was immediately almost torn from his hand by a gust of wind which poured, like a torrent of water, through the open window on the far side of the studio. Once the door had slammed shut again behind him, the draught subsided. The studio was empty and bitterly cold. There was no sign of Emma, but a step ladder and whitewash brush and bucket bore witness to her recent occupation. She had finished the whole of one wall, but when he went to touch it with his hand, he found that it was still cold and damp.

From the middle of this wall protruded an ugly old-fashioned stove, empty now and unlit, and beside it a gas ring, a battered kettle, and an upturned orange box containing blue and white striped mugs and a jar of sugar lumps. On the opposite side of the room stood Ben's work table, littered with drawings and papers, tubes of paint, and hundreds of pencils and brushes all contained on sheets of corrugated cardboard. The wall above this table was dark and dirty with age, and smeared with the scrapings of countless palette knives, that had built up, over the years, into a crustaceous shell of colour. At the top of the desk was a narrow level shelf, and on this ranged a selection of *objets trouvés* which at some time or another had caught Ben's eye. A stone from the shore, a fossilised starfish. A blue jug of dried grasses. A postcard reproduction of a Picasso; a piece of bleached driftwood, carved by sea and wind to abstract sculpture. There were photographs, a fan of curling snapshots, arranged in an old silver menu-holder; an invitation to a private view that had taken place six years ago, and, finally, a heavy, old-fashioned pair of binoculars.

At floor level, the walls were stacked with leaning canvases, and in the middle of the room the current work stood, easeled and shrouded with a faded pink cloth. Turned towards the empty stove was a sagging sofa, draped in what looked like the remains of an Arabic rug. There was also an old kitchen table, with its legs cut short, and on this a tin of cigarettes, and an overflowing ash-tray, a pile of *Studios*, and a green glass bowl, full of painted china eggs.

The north wall was all glass, squared off by narrow wooden partitions and designed so that its lower portions would slide aside. Along the foot of this was a long seat, piled with cushions, and from beneath this protruded further ill-assorted flotsam. The spars of a boat, a stack of surfboards, and a crate of empty bottles, and, in the middle, beneath the open window, two iron hooks had been screwed into the floor, and on to those were looped the spliced ends of a rope ladder. This disappeared out of the window, and Robert, going to investigate, saw that it dropped straight down to the sand, twenty feet below.

The beach appeared to be empty. The ebb tide had left it a sweep of hard clean sand, divided from the sky by a narrow line of frothing white breakers. Further inshore, there was a stratum of rock, crusted with shellfish and seaweed, and over this the seagulls hovered, occasionally pouncing to fight and scream over some prize. Robert sat on the window-seat, and lit himself a cigarette. When he looked up again, a figure had appeared on the horizon, right on the edge of the sea. It wore a long white gown, like an Arab's, and as it walked back towards the studio, appeared to be wrestling with some large and unidentifiable red package.

He remembered the binoculars on Ben's table and went to

fetch them. Focused, the figure sprang into relief, and revealed itself as Emma Litton, long hair blowing, dressed in a huge white towelling robe and lugging, with some difficulty, for the wind kept catching it broadside and jerking it out of her grasp, a scarlet surfboard.

"You surely haven't been swimming?"

Emma, struggling with the surfboard, had not seen him at the window. Now, with a hand on the rope ladder, she nearly jumped out of her skin at the sound of his voice. She looked up, trailing the surfboard in the sand, her wet black hair ripped to ribbons by the wind.

"Yes, I have, and what a fright you gave me. How long have you been there?"

"About ten minutes. How are you going to get the surfboard up the ladder?"

"I was wondering that, but now you've turned up all my problems are solved. There's a rope under the seat. If you chuck one end down, I'll tie it on, and you can pull it up for me."

This was duly accomplished. Robert hauled the board through the open window, and hard on its heels came Emma herself, her face and hands and feet crusted with dry sand, and her black lashes spiked like starfish.

She knelt on the window-seat, and laughed at him. "Now, wasn't that the luckiest thing! What would I have done? I could hardly get it over the beach, let alone up the ladder."

Beneath the sand, her face looked blue with cold. He said, "Come along in, and get the window shut . . . that wind's freezing. How could you bear to go and swim? You'll die of pneumonia."

"No I won't." She stepped down on to the floor, and watched him furl the ladder in and slide the window shut. It did not fit properly and there was still a draught like the edge of a knife. "Anyway, I'm used to it. We always used to swim in April when we were children."

"This isn't April. It's March. It's winter. What would your father say?"

"Oh, he wouldn't say anything. And it's such an utterly gorgeous day and I was sick of whitewashing . . . have you seen my lovely clean wall? The only thing is, it makes the rest of the studio look like a slum. Besides, I wasn't swimming, I was surfing, and the breakers kept me warm." And then, without any noticeable change of expression, "Have you come to see Ben? He's down at the Sliding Tackle."

"Yes, I know."

"How do you know?"

"Because I left Marcus there with him."

"Marcus." She raised her strongly-marked eyebrows, considering this. "Has Marcus come too? My goodness, it must be important business!"

She shivered slightly.

Robert said, "Do get some clothes on."

"Oh, I'm all right." She went to take a cigarette from the table, and lit it, and then collapsed on to the old sofa, flat on her back, with her feet propped on the arm.

"Did you get my letter?"

"Yes, I did." With Emma taking up all the sofa, there was nowhere to sit but on the table, so he eased the pile of magazines on to the floor, and sat there. "I was sorry about your sun hat."

Emma laughed. "But glad about Ben?"

"Of course."

"It's amazing how well it's working. Unbelievable. And he really likes having me around."

"I never imagined for a moment that he wouldn't."

"Oh, don't start being gallant. You know you did. At lunch that day, you were all quizzical eyebrows and scepticism. But you see, it really is the perfect arrangement. Ben doesn't have to pay me to keep house for him, or be bothered with tedious details like days off and insurance stamps, nor does he have to become emotionally involved. He never knew that life could be so simple."

"Have you heard from Christopher?"

Emma turned her head sideways to look at him. "How do you know about Christopher?"

"You told me yourself. At Marcello's. Remember?"

"So I did. No, I haven't heard. But he'll be at Brookford by now, in the thick of rehearsals. He won't have had time to write. Anyway, there's been such a lot to do here, getting the cottage organised and cooking and things. Don't believe people when they say that artists never eat. Ben's inner man is quite insatiable."

"Have you told him you met up with Christopher again?"

"Good heavens, no! And spoil the even tenor of our life? I haven't even mentioned his name. You know, you look much nicer in those tweedy sort of clothes than you do in the London kind. I thought when I first saw you that you weren't the type to spend his days buttoned up in a charcoal grey suit. When did you get down here?"

"We drove yesterday afternoon. We spent last night at The Castle."

Emma made a face. "In with all the potted palms and the cashmere cardigans. Ugh!"

"It's very comfortable."

"The central heating gives me hay fever. I can't even breathe."

She stubbed her half-smoked cigarette out in the overflowing ash-tray, and swung her feet off the sofa, and stood up and walked away from him, towards the window, untying the sash of the robe as she went. She took a pile of clothes from beneath a cushion, and with her back to him, started to dress. She said, "Why did you and Marcus come together?"

"Marcus doesn't drive."

"There are trains. And that wasn't what I meant."

"No, I know." He picked up one of the painted china eggs and began to play with it as an Arab handles a string of worry beads. "We've come to try and persuade Ben to go back to the United States."

There was a sudden great squall of wind. It broke over the glass window of the studio like a wave, poured, roaring over the roof above them, with the thunder of a passing train. A cluster of gulls rose screaming from the rocks, were flung across the sky. And then, as suddenly, it was over.

Emma said, "Why does he have to go back?"

"This retrospective exhibition."

She dropped the white towelling robe, and stood silhouetted, in jeans, pulling a navy blue sweater over her head.

"But I thought he and Marcus fixed all that when they were in New York in January."

"We thought so too. But you see, this exhibition is being sponsored by a private individual."

"I know," said Emma, turning, and flipping her dark hair free of the turtle-neck of the sweater. "I read all about it in *Réalités*. Mrs Kenneth Ryan. The widow of the wealthy man whose memorial is the Queenstown Museum of Fine Arts. You see how well informed I am. I hope you're impressed."

"And Mrs Kenneth Ryan wants a private view."

"Then why didn't she say so?"

"Because she wasn't in New York. She was sunning it in

59

Nassau or the Bahamas or Palm Beach or somewhere. They never met her. They only saw the curator of the museum.''

''And now Mrs Ryan wants Ben Litton to go back, so that she can throw a nice little champagne party and show him off, like a trophy, to all her influential friends. It makes me sick.''

''She's done more than decide, Emma. She's come to persuade him.''

''You mean come to England?''

''I mean come to England, come to Bernstein's, come to Porthkerris. She drove down with Marcus and me yesterday and at this very moment, is sitting in the bar of The Castle Hotel, drinking very cold Martinis and waiting for us all to go and have lunch with her.''

''Well, I for one am not going.''

''You have to. We're all expected.'' He glanced at his wrist-watch. ''And we're running late. Do hurry up.''

''Does Ben know about the private view?''

''He will by now. Marcus will have told him.''

She picked up a brown sailcloth smock off the floor and pulled it on over her sweater. As her head came through the neck, she said, ''Ben may not want to go.''

''You mean you don't want him to go?''

''I mean that he's settled down here again. He's not prowling, he's not restless, he's not even drinking very much. He's working like a young man, and what he's doing is fresh and new and better than ever. Ben is sixty, you know. Looking at him, it's hard to believe, but he's nearly sixty. Isn't it possible that all this hopping about all over the world may no longer stimulate him, but simply wear him out?'' She came back to the sofa to sit down, facing Robert, her earnest face on a level with his own. ''Please. If he doesn't want to go, don't try to persuade him.''

Robert still held the china egg. He looked at it intently as though its convolutions of blue and green would miraculously provide the answer to every problem. Then, with care, he laid it back in the glass dish, along with its fellows.

He said, ''You talk as though this were something important, as though he were returning to the States to teach again, as though he weren't going to come back for years. But it isn't. It's simply a party. He needn't be away for more than a few days.'' She opened her mouth with a fresh protest, but he talked her down. ''And you mustn't forget that this exhibition is a great tribute to Ben. A lot of money's been ploughed into it, and a great deal of organisation, and perhaps the least he can do . . .''

Furiously, Emma interrupted. ''The least he can do is go and parade up and down like a pet monkey for some fat old American. And what makes it so awful is that he likes that sort of thing. That's what I hate, that he likes it.''

''So he likes it. So, if he wants to, he'll go.''

She was silenced. She sat, eyes downcast, her mouth sulky as a child's. Robert finished his cigarette and stubbed it out, and stood up and said, more gently, ''Now, do come on or we're going to be late. Have you got a coat?''

''No.''

''Some shoes then, you must have some shoes.''

She felt under the sofa and produced a pair of thong sandals, and stood up, thrusting her bare feet into them. Her feet were still covered in sand, and the sailcloth smock spotted in whitewash.

She said, ''I can't go to The Castle, for lunch, looking like this.''

''Nonsense.'' He tried to sound bracing. ''You'll give the residents something to talk about. Brighten their dull lives no end.''

''Isn't there time to go back to the cottage? I haven't even got a comb.''

61

"There'll be a comb at the hotel."

"But . . ."

"There simply isn't time. We're late already. Now come along . . ."

They went together, out of the studio and up the ramp, and into the sunlit street, and began to walk back towards the harbour. After the chill of the studio the air felt warm, and the brightness of the sea was reflected from the whitewashed walls of houses, and assailed the eye like the glare of snow.

5

Emma did not want to go into the Sliding Tackle.

"I'll wait here. You go and prise them out."

"All right."

He went across the cobbles, and she noticed how he had to duck his tall head to get in under the porch. The door of the pub swung shut behind him. She wandered over to his car and inspected it with interest, because it belonged to him, and should therefore provide further clues to his character, as a shelf of book-titles will do, or the pictures that a man hangs on his walls. But, apart from the fact that it was dark-green, had fog lights and wire wheels and a couple of car-club badges, the Alvis gave little away. Inside on the driving-seat was a tweed cap; cigarettes in the dashboard cupboard, a book of maps. On the back seat, neatly folded, a thick, expensive-looking tartan rug. She decided that he was either trusting, or careless, but also lucky, for the rug had not been stolen.

A gust of wind blew in from the sea and Emma shivered. After the swim and the session in the draughty studio, she still was very cold. Her hands had gone numb, quite colourless, the fingernails tinged with blue. But the metal of the car was warm, and, for comfort, she leaned against it, spreadeagled across the bonnet, with her hands splayed like starfish.

The pub door opened and Robert Morrow emerged once more, ducking cautiously. He was alone.

"Aren't they there?"

"No. We're late, and they got fed up with waiting, so they got a lift back to the hotel." He opened the driving-seat door, picked up his cap and pulled it on, jerked down over his nose, to add yet another sharp angle to his formidable profile. "Come on . . ." And he leaned over and opened the other door, and Emma unpeeled herself from the bonnet, and slid in beside him.

They left the harbour behind and below them, roared up through the town, up the steep narrow streets, up between terraces of prim houses, and the signs which said Bed and Breakfast, and front gardens where sad palm trees tossed their heads in the alien wind. They came out on to the main road, still climbing, turned into the drive of The Castle Hotel; climbed on, between banks of hydrangeas, and landward-leaning elm trees, and at last came out at the very top of the hill, into an open space of tennis courts, and lawns, and a miniature golf course. The hotel had once been a country house, and prided itself on its authentic atmosphere. A white post and chain fence kept cars away from the gravel sweep in front of the hotel, and here, in deckchairs, sat a handful of hardy residents, scarved, gloved and swaddled in rugs, like the passengers of some trans-Atlantic liner. They read books or newspapers, but when the Alvis roared up the drive and drew up with a massive scrunch of gravel, these were lowered, and in some cases, spectacles were removed, and Robert and Emma's progress observed and noted as though they were visitors from another planet.

Robert said, "We're probably the first exciting thing to happen since the manager fell into the swimming-pool."

Once inside the revolving doors, the heat of the place struck like a newly-opened oven. Emma professed to despise such comfort, but today it was blissfully welcome.

She said, "I expect they'll be in the bar. You go, I'll be there in a moment. I must try and get rid of some of this sand."

In the Ladies', she washed her hands and her face, and rubbed the sand off her feet on to the back of her jeans, like a schoolboy trying to polish his shoes. There was a pretentious set of brushes and combs on a beruffled dressing-table, and she used the comb on the snarls of her hair, breaking half the teeth, but reducing the tangled mass into some sort of order. As she turned back for the door, she caught sight of herself in the long mirror. No make-up, faded jeans, whitewash stains. She pulled off the offending smock, and then was infuriated with herself for minding about anything so trivial as her own personal appearance, and pulled it on again. They would think she was a beatnik art student. A model. Ben Litton's mistress. Let them. As Robert Morrow had so rightly said, it would give them something to talk about.

But as she emerged from the Ladies' and went down the long, carpeted hall, she was grateful to see that Robert Morrow had not abandoned her and gone to join the others, as she had told him to, but was waiting for her by the porter's desk, reading a Sunday paper which had been left on a chair. When he saw her coming, he folded the paper and tossed it down again, and gave her a grin of encouragement.

"You've done splendidly," he said.

"I've ruined the hotel comb. Ever so nice it was, too, one of a matching set. You didn't need to wait. I've been before and I know the way . . ."

"Come along, then."

It was a quarter to two, and the busy Sunday lunch-time session was over. Only a few serious drinkers still sat at the bar, cradling their gin and tonics and beginning to look a bit red in the face. Ben Litton, Marcus Bernstein and Mrs Kenneth Ryan were over on the other side of the room, grouped in the bay formed by a huge picture window. Mrs Ryan was on the window-seat, against a backdrop like a travel agent's poster — a shout of blue sea, a sweep of sky, and the green undulations of the miniature golf course. The two men, Ben in his French workman's *bleus*, and Marcus in his dark suit, were talking, turned slightly towards her, so that it was Mrs Ryan who first saw Emma and Robert.

"Well, look who's here . . ." she said.

They turned. Ben remained sitting, but Marcus stood up and came to greet Emma, his arms outstretched, his pleasure at seeing her both genuine and demonstrative and very un-British. He could on occasion be almost embarrassingly Austrian.

"Emma, my darling child. Here you are at last." He put his hands to her shoulders and kissed her, formally, on both cheeks. "What a pleasure to see you again, after this very long time. How long is it? Five years? Six years? What a lot we have to talk about. Come along, and meet Mrs Ryan." He took her hand to lead her over. ". . . But your hand is like a block of ice. What have you been doing?"

"Nothing," said Emma, catching Robert's eyes, and daring him to say more.

"And your bare feet . . . how can you stand it? Mrs Ryan, this is Ben's daughter, Emma, but don't shake hands with her, or you will die of shock."

"I can think of worse ways to die," said Mrs Ryan, and held out her hand. "How do you do?"

They shook hands. "I must say, you are very cold."

On an insane impulse, Emma said, "I was swimming. That's why we're late. And why I'm so untidy. There wasn't time to go back to change."

"Oh, but you don't look untidy, you look charming. Sit down
. . . we have time for another drink, don't we? The dining-room
isn't going to shut down on us or anything like that. Robert,
would you be a darling, and order another round for us. What
would you like, Emma?"

"I . . . I don't really want anything." Ben gave a small cough.
"Well . . . a glass of sherry."

"And we're all drinking martinis, Robert. If you want one
too?" Emma lowered herself carefully on to the chair that
Marcus had vacated, aware of her father watching her from the
other side of the table.

"I simply don't believe," said Mrs Ryan, "that you really
have been swimming."

"Not really. I just went in and out again. There were huge
waves."

"But won't you get the most terrible chill? It can't be good
for you." She turned to Ben. "You don't approve, surely, of
swimming when it's as cold as this? Haven't you got any
influence on your daughter?"

Her voice was gay and teasing. Ben made some reply, and she
went on, telling him that he should be ashamed of himself . . .
that she could see he was an outrageous father . . .

Emma did not listen. She was far too busy looking. For Mrs
Ryan was not old and fat, but young and beautiful and very
attractive, and from the top of her smoothly-coiffed golden
blonde head to the tips of her shining crocodile pumps there
was no single detail that did not give active pleasure. Her eyes
were enormous and blue as violets, her mouth full and sweet-
tempered, and when she smiled, as she did now, revealed two
perfect rows of even, white, American teeth. She wore a most
becoming suit of rose-pink tweed, the collar and cuffs edged
with starched white pique. Diamonds sparkled from her ears,

67

her lapel, her neatly-manicured hands. There was nothing vulgar about her, nothing brash. Even her scent was flower-like.

". . . The fact that she has been away from you for six years is all the more reason for you to take care of her now."

"I don't take care of her . . . she takes care of me . . ."

"Now there is a real man talking . . ." Her soft, southern voice made the words sound like a caress.

Emma's eyes moved round to her father. His attitude was a characteristic one, legs crossed, right elbow resting on his knee, his chin supported by his thumb, a cigarette between his fingers, its smoke rising before his eyes. The eyes were dark as black coffee, deeply shadowed, and they watched Mrs Ryan as though she were a fascinating new specimen, caught between the glass plates of a laboratory slide.

"Emma, your drink."

It was Marcus. She dragged her eyes from Ben and Mrs Ryan and turned to him in relief.

"Oh, thank you . . ."

He sat beside her. "Robert has told you about the private view?"

"Yes, he told me."

"Are you angry with us?"

"No." And this was true. You could not be angry with such an honest man who came so instantly to the point.

"But you don't want him to go?"

"Did Robert say that?"

"No, he didn't say. But I know you very well. And I know how long you've waited to be with Ben. But it's only for a little while."

"Yes." She looked down at her drink. "He really is going, then?"

"Yes, he really is going. But not until the end of the month."

"I see."

Marcus said, gently, ". . . if you wanted to go with him . . ."

"No. No, I don't want to go to America."

"Do you mind being alone?"

"No. It doesn't bother me. And, as you say, it won't be for long."

"You could come to London, and stay with Helen and myself. You could have David's room."

"Where would David sleep?"

"It is so sad, he is away at boarding school. It broke my heart, but I am now an Englishman and my son was torn from me at eight years old. Come and stay, Emma. In London, there is a lot to see. The Tate Gallery has been re-hung, and it is a masterpiece . . ."

Despite herself Emma began to smile.

"What are you laughing about, you horrible child?"

"I'm laughing at your shamelessness. You take my father away with one hand, and offer me the Tate Gallery with the other. And," she added, dropping her voice, "nobody bothered to tell me that Mrs Kenneth Ryan was the Beauty Queen of Southern Virginia."

"We didn't know," said Marcus. "We had never seen her. She flew to England on an impulse, she walked into the Bernstein Galleries the day before yesterday and said she wanted to see Ben Litton, and that was the first time I had ever set eyes on her."

"Well, she's certainly worth setting eyes on."

"Yes," said Marcus. He looked across at Mrs Ryan with his sad, hound's eyes. He looked at Ben. He looked back into his Martini, and touched the sliver of lemon peel with his forefinger. "Yes," he said again.

Their arrival, late, in the dining-room caused something of a stir. The best table had been reserved for them, the round one in the window, and it was necessary to cross the length of the floor to get there. Mrs Ryan led the way, aware of adulation from every eye in the room, and apparently unconcerned. She was quite used to it. Behind her came Marcus, shabby, but oddly distinguished and obviously interesting. Then Robert and Emma, and finally Ben. Ben fell behind to stub out his cigarette and made what amounted to a star entrance, stopping for a moment in the doorway to speak to the head waiter, so that by the time he did move forward into the room, he was the sole centre of attraction.

Ben Litton . . . There's Ben Litton, the whispers went up, as he walked between the tables, magnificent in his blue French overalls, the red and white scarf knotted at his throat, his white hair thick as a young man's, a quiff like a comma falling across his forehead.

Ben Litton . . . you know, the painter.

It was exciting. Everybody knew that Ben Litton had a studio in Porthkerris, but if you were determined to actually see him, you had to make your way down to the town, and find a fisherman's pub called the Sliding Tackle, and there sit, in the stuffy gloom, making a glass of warm beer last as long as possible, and wait for him to come. It was rather like a strange form of bird-watching.

But today, Ben Litton had abandoned his usual haunts, and was here, at The Castle Hotel, about to eat Sunday lunch, like any other ordinary human being. The mountain had come to Mahomet. An elderly lady stared openly at him through her lorgnette, and a visiting Texan was heard mourning the fact that he had left his flash camera in the bedroom.

Emma caught Robert Morrow's eye, and just managed to suppress a snort of laughter.

Ben reached the table at last, settled himself in the place of honour at Mrs Ryan's right, picked up a menu, and suggested, simply by raising a finger, that the wine waiter should be fetched. Gradually, the excitement in the dining-room died down, but it was obvious that for the rest of the meal they would be the object of all attention.

Emma said to Robert, "I know I shouldn't approve – I should be ashamed of such blatant exhibitionism, but somehow, he gets away with it every time."

"Well, at least it's made you laugh, and you've stopped looking all pinched and nervous."

"You might have told me Mrs Ryan was young and beautiful."

"She's certainly beautiful. But I don't think she's as young as she appears. Well-preserved more like it."

"That's the sort of bitchy remark a woman would make."

"I'm sorry. It was meant with the best will in the world."

"You still should have told me."

"You never asked."

"No, but I made some remark about fat old Americans, and even then you didn't put me right."

"Perhaps I didn't realise that it was so important to you."

"A beautiful woman and Ben Litton, and you didn't realise it was important? It's more than that; it's lethal. One thing, you and Marcus won't have to do any persuading. Ben is going to America. One sweep of those lashes, and he was already mid-Atlantic."

"I don't think you're being entirely fair. The longest lashes in the world wouldn't sweep him into anything he didn't want to do."

"No, but he could never resist a challenge."

Her voice was cold.

71

Robert said, "Emma."

She turned to look at him. "What?"

"Your resentment is showing." He measured between his forefinger and thumb. "Just the very smallest amount."

"Yes . . . well . . ." She decided to change the subject. "When do you go back to London?"

"This very afternoon." He glanced at his watch. "We're running late, as it is. We'll need to leave, as soon as I can coax Little Miss Millions away."

But Mrs Ryan was not to be hurried. The luncheon wore on through four courses, through wine and brandy and coffee, served in the now-empty dining-room, because she did not want to move from their table. At last, taking advantage of a pause in the conversation, Robert cleared his throat, and said, "Marcus, I am sorry to interrupt, but I really think we should make a start, we've got a three hundred mile drive."

Mrs Ryan seemed astonished. "But whatever time is it?"

"Nearly four o'clock."

She laughed. "Already! It's like being in Spain. I once went to a lunch party in Spain, and we didn't get up from the table until half past seven in the evening. Why does time have to go so fast when you're really enjoying yourself?"

"Cause and effect," said Ben.

Across the table, she smiled at Robert. "You don't want to leave right away, do you?"

"Well . . . as soon as possible."

"But I wanted to see the studio. I can't come all the way across the Atlantic, and all the way down to Porthkerris and not see Ben's studio. Couldn't we drop in just for a moment, on the way back to London?"

This light-hearted suggestion was received in silence. Robert and Marcus both looked momentarily confused; Robert, because he did not want to put off any more time, and Marcus, because he knew that of all things, Ben hated to have his studio inspected. Emma also experienced a sinking of the heart. The studio was in chaos – not Ben's chaos which was of no account, but her own chaos. She thought of the step ladder, and the whitewash bucket, the wet towelling coat, and the bathing-suit which she had left abandoned on the floor, the brimming ash-trays, and the sagging sofa, and the sand everywhere. She looked at Ben, praying for him to refuse. They all looked at Ben, waiting like puppets, to see which way he would jerk the strings.

But for once he did not let them down.

"My dear Mrs Ryan, despite the pleasure it would give me to show you my studio, I think I should point out that it is not on the way to London."

They all looked at her, to see how she would take this. But she merely pouted, and they laughed in relief, and Mrs Ryan laughed too, with good grace.

"All right, I know when I'm beaten." She began to collect her bag and gloves. "But there is just one thing. You've all been so sweet to me, and I don't want to feel like a stranger any longer. My name's Melissa. Do you-all think you could manage to call me that?"

And later, when the men were loading the car, she got Emma to herself.

"You've been specially sweet," she said. "Marcus told me that you'd come back from Paris to be with your father, and here I am, taking him away from you again."

Emma, who knew that she had not been specially sweet, felt guilty. "The exhibition has to come first . . ."

"I'll take good care of him," Melissa Ryan promised.

Yes, thought Emma, *I'm sure you will*. And yet, despite herself, she liked the American woman. And there was something

73

about the set of her chin and the clarity of her violet-blue eyes that made Emma wonder if perhaps, this time, Ben would not enjoy his usual walkover. And if things did not go his way from the very beginning he was apt to become discouraged. She smiled at Mrs Ryan. She said, "I don't suppose it'll be long before he's home again." And she picked up the honey-coloured mink which lay across the back of a chair and helped Mrs Ryan into it. They went out of the hotel together. It was colder now. The warmth of the sun had left the sky and a chill, like frost, swept up from the sea. Robert had put up the hood of the Alvis, and Melissa, wrapped in the mink, went to say goodbye to Ben.

"But it isn't goodbye," he told her, holding her hand, and gazing darkly down at her. "It's au revoir."

"Of course. And if you let me know when your flight arrives at Kennedy Airport, I'll arrange to have you met."

Marcus said, "I will do that. Ben has never in living memory let anybody know anything, least of all his time of arrival. Goodbye, Emma, my darling child, and don't forget that I have invited you to stay with us for as long as you like when Ben is in America."

"Bless you, Marcus. You never know. I might come."

They kissed. He got into the back of the car, and Melissa Ryan into the front, her elegant legs wrapped in Robert's car rug. Ben shut the door, then stooped to continue his conversation with her through the open window.

"Emma." It was Robert.

She turned. "Oh, goodbye, Robert."

To her surprise he took off his cap and bent to kiss her. "You'll be all right?"

She was touched. "Yes, of course."

"If you want anything, give me a ring, at Bernstein's."

"What could I want?"

"I don't know. Just a thought. Goodbye, Emma."

They stood, she and Ben, watching until the car had disappeared down the tunnel of trees. After it had gone, neither of them spoke, and then Ben cleared his throat, and said, portentously, as though he were giving a lecture, "What an interesting head that young man has. The narrow skull and the strong facial bones. I should like to see him with a beard. He would make a good saint – or perhaps, a sinner. Do you like him, Emma?"

She shrugged. "I suppose so. I scarcely know him."

He turned to move off, and caught sight of the small gathering of hotel guests, who, setting off for walks, or coming in from golf, or aimlessly snatching at the smallest straw of entertainment, had stayed to witness Melissa's departure. As Ben fixed them with his dark eyes, they became discomfited, turned away and moved on as though they had been caught doing something shameful.

He shook his head in amazement. "I think," he said, "I have had enough of being stared at as though I were a two-headed chimpanzee. Come along, we'll go home."

6

Ben Litton left for America at the end of March, travelling from Porthkerris to London via British Railways and from London to New York on a BOAC Boeing. At the last moment Marcus Bernstein decided to go with him, and the evening papers carried photographs of their departure, Ben with his white hair a coxcomb in the breeze, and Marcus almost obliterated by his black hat. Both looked faintly self-conscious.

It was from Marcus that Emma received the airmail bundle of American newspapers, carrying in their columns the comments of every worthwhile art critic in the country. They were unanimous in their praise of the whole concept of the Queenstown Museum of Fine Arts, acclaiming it as a perfect example of architecture, lighting, and immaculate display. And the Ben Litton exhibition was on no account to be missed. Never again would the artist's work be available to the public in its entirety, and the two or three pre-war portraits, lent by private individuals, were alone worth a visit, if only to see how a single man could be painter, psychiatrist and absolving priest at one and the same time.

"Ben Litton uses his brush as a surgeon's scalpel, first laying bare the hidden sickness, then treating it with the utmost compassion."

77

The word compassion was used again for his war-time drawings, the shelter groups, the fire-fighters, and a handful of sketches salvaged from the time of the Allied advance in Italy. And of his post-war work they said, "Other painters abstract from nature. Litton abstracts from imagination, and an imagination so lively that it is difficult to believe that these vital paintings were not turned out by a man of half his age."

Emma read these and allowed herself to feel proud. The private view took place on the 3rd of April, and by the tenth there was still no word of Ben's return, but she filled in the days with time-consuming household chores, and eventually moved back to the studio to finish the whitewashing. This took little mental concentration, and her mind wandered aimlessly into the future, indulging in the sort of day dreams that, a month ago, she would never have allowed herself. But now, she truly felt that things had changed. When she had gone to the station to put Ben on to the London train, he had kissed her goodbye – absentmindedly to be sure, as though he had forgotten for the moment who she was, but still, he had kissed her and that surely marked a milestone. And when he did eventually tear himself away from the adulation of the American public and returned to Porthkerris, she saw herself meeting the train, cool and composed, the perfect social secretary. And, maybe the next time he took off for some far-flung, but obviously colourful, corner of the globe, he would take Emma with him, and she would book flights, and see that he caught connections, and keep Marcus informed as to his movements.

And then, a day or two later, there was a letter from Marcus, postmarked London. She opened it hopefully, thinking that it would tell her that Ben was coming back, but, in fact, it was simply to say that Marcus had returned to London alone, and Ben had stayed in Queenstown.

The Ryan Memorial Museum is fascinating, and if I had been able, I should have stayed as well. It embraces all forms of art, has a small theatre and concert hall and a collection of Russian jewellery which has to be seen to be believed. Queenstown itself is charming, full of red brick Georgian houses, set in green lawns and veiled in flowering dogwood ... they all look as though they have been there since the days of William and Mary, but in fact, I saw one in the process of being built, the mature lawn being laid in turves, and the dogwoods planted, fully grown. What it is to have a warm and temperate climate, to be sure.

Redlands (the Ryan homestead) is a great white house with a pillared "porch" where Ben sits in a long chair and gets brought mint juleps by a coloured butler called Henry. Henry comes to work each day in a lilac Chevrolet, and hopes, in the not-too-distant future, to become a lawyer. He is a bright young man and should achieve his ambition. There are also a couple of tennis courts – a paddock (corral) full of spirited horses, and the inevitable swimming-pool. Ben, as you can imagine, neither rides nor plays tennis, but spends long hours, when he isn't adding a little local colour to the retrospective exhibition, floating around the pool on a rubber mattress. I am sorry that he has stayed away from you for so long, but honestly believe that he needs this rest. He has been working hard for the last few years, and a little harmless relaxation will do him no harm. If you are lonely, our invitation still stands. Come and stay with us. We should so love to have you.
Always your loving Marcus.

The whitewashing was finished, the studio floor scrubbed. Ben's drawings had been stacked and stowed in numbered folios. His pens and brushes graded and various tubes of solidified oil paint, used once, and then abandoned, had been discreetly shovelled into the dustbin.

There was nothing left to do.

He had been gone two weeks when the postcard came from Christopher. Emma was in the kitchen of the cottage, making coffee and squeezing orange juice, still wrapped in her dressing-gown and with her hair tied back in a pony tail, when the postman, who was a cheeky young man in an open-necked shirt, put his head round the door and said, "Well, and how are you this morning, my handsome?"

"Splendid, thank you," said Emma, who had been putting up with this camaraderie ever since she returned from Paris.

He flapped a bundle of letters at her. "All for your old man. But . . . here . . . is a postcard for you." He inspected the picture before Emma snatched it from him. "So vulgar those things are; I don't know how decent folks can buy them."

"No, you wouldn't," said Emma rudely, scarcely glancing at the bulging lady in the bikini before turning the card over to see who it was from. The postmark was Brookford.

Emma darling, when are you coming to see me? I can't come and see you, because we're up to the ears in rehearsals for Dead on Time. *Phone number Brookford 678, best about ten in the morning before we start work. Producer nice chap, stage manager bloody, all girls have spots, and not as pretty as you. Love Love Love Christo.*

The nearest phone box was a mile away, so Emma went down the street to the ramshackle grocer's where she bought cigarettes and tins of food and soap flakes, and used the telephone there.

It was an old-fashioned one, in two separate bits, and with a hook that you jiggled to get the operator. She sat on a beer crate and waited while the call was put through and a grey and white cat, fat as a cushion, came and lay exhaustedly across her knee.

The phone was answered at last by a cross-sounding female.

"Brookfield Theatre."

"Can I speak to Christopher Ferris?"

"I don't know if he's in yet."

"Could you go and look?"

"Oh, I suppose so. Who shall I say it is?"

"Say Emma."

The cross female departed. Various voices could be heard, chattering. A man in the distance shouted, "*Here I said, you clot, not there.*" And then there were footsteps and a voice, and it was Christo.

"Emma."

"You are there. They didn't know if you were in."

"Yes, of course I'm in . . . we're rehearsing in five minutes . . . Did you get my postcard?"

"This morning."

"Did Ben read it?" (He obviously hoped that he had.)

"Ben isn't here. He's in America. I thought you'd know."

"How should I know?"

"It's been in all the papers."

"Actors don't read papers and if they do it's always the *Stage*. But if the old boy's in America, why didn't you let me know and come and stay with me?"

"For a hundred reasons."

"Name two."

"Well, he only meant to go for a week at the most; and I didn't know where you were."

"I told you. Brookford."

"I don't even know where Brookford is."

"Thirty-five minutes from London, trains run every half hour.

81

Look, do come. Come and stay. I've been moved into a sinister basement flat. It smells of dry rot and old cats, but it's ever so cosy."

"Christo, I can't. I must be here. Ben'll be home any day now, and . . ."

"Did you tell him about meeting me again?"

"No, I didn't."

"Why not?"

"The subject never came up."

"You mean you were scared?"

"I was nothing of the sort. It was simply – irrelevant . . ."

"Nobody's ever called me irrelevant and got away with it. Oh, do come, ducky. My little basement nest needs the touch of a woman's hand. You know, scrubbing and all that jazz."

"I can't come till Ben's home. Then I'll try."

"It'll be too late by then. I'll have got it clean. Please. I'll get you a free ticket for the show. Or two tickets and you can bring a friend. Or three tickets and you can bring them all."

His voice dissolved into amusement. He had always laughed at his own jokes.

"Oh, very funny," said Emma, but she was laughing too.

"You're just playing hard to get. You wouldn't stay with me in Paris, and you won't come and keep house in the wilds of Surrey. What have I got to do to win your heart?"

"You won it years ago and you've had it ever since. Truthfully, I'm longing to see you. But I can't come. I simply can't come till Ben gets back."

Christo said a rude word.

The telephone went pip-pip-pip.

"That's it, then," said Christo. "Let me know when you make up your mind. Goodbye."

"Goodbye, Christo." But he had already hung up. Smiling

foolishly, going back over every word he had said, she put the receiver back on to the hook. The cat on her knee purred momentously, and Emma realised it was about to produce a family at any moment. An old man came into the shop to buy two ounces of plug, and when he had gone Emma picked up the cat and placed her gently on the floor, and felt in her pocket for loose change to pay for the call.

"When are the kittens due?" she asked.

The old woman behind the counter was called Gertie, and wore, indoors and out, an enormous brown beret pulled down over her eyebrows.

"Only time can tell, my dear." She put Emma's money into her till, which was an old tin box, and gave her her change. "Only time can tell."

"Thank you for letting me use your phone."

"It's a pleasure," said Gertie, who always listened, shamelessly, and relayed every word she heard.

In March it had been like midsummer. Now, in May, it was cold as November, and pouring with rain. He had never imagined Porthkerris in the rain; had always pictured it painted in the bright blues of summer, gay with the white wings of gulls and yachts, everything dazzling in a glaring sunlight. But now squalls, borne in on a cutting east wind, were flung against the windows of the hotel, sounding like fistfuls of pebbles. The gusts rattled the casements and then whined away beneath doors, down chimneys, blowing curtains, chilly and inescapable.

It was a Saturday, and Robert, flat on his bed, had been asleep. He looked at his watch and saw that it was five to three, so he reached for a cigarette, and lit it, and lay, watching the leaden sky race across the window, and waiting for the telephone to ring.

It did, at precisely three o'clock. He lifted the receiver.

"Three o'clock, sir," said the hall porter.

"Thank you very much."

"Sure you're awake, sir?"

"Yes. I'm awake."

He finished the cigarette, and stubbed it out, and got up, pulling on his white towel robe and heading for the bathroom for a hot shower. He hated sleeping in the afternoon, hated waking with the feeling that his teeth were itching, and that he was on the verge of a splitting headache, but after driving all through the night from London it had been impossible to stay awake. He had had an early lunch, and left word with the porter to call him. But the wind, blown up while he slept, had wakened him first.

He dressed, put on a clean shirt, tied his tie, picked up the jacket of his suit, and then changed his mind, and pulled on a polo-necked sweater instead. He combed his hair, slid his belongings from the top of the dressing-table into his trouser pockets, took a raincoat from the back of the door and went downstairs.

The lounge was thick with the silence of mid-afternoon. Elderly residents snoozed, snoring lightly in dry heated air. Frustrated golfers watched the rain, rattling loose change in the pockets of their tweed knickerbockers, wondering if the weather was going to let up, if there would be time for nine holes before it got dark.

The hall porter took Robert's key and hung it up.

"Going out now, sir?"

"Yes, and perhaps you can help me. I want to get to the Society of Artists Gallery. I believe it's an old chapel, converted. Have you any idea where it is?"

"That's down the old part of the town. Know your way round, do you?"

"I know the Sliding Tackle," said Robert, and the hall porter grinned. He liked a man who used pubs as landmarks.

"Well . . . say you're going to the Sliding Tackle, but turn up the street before you get there. Up, away from the harbour. Narrow little road, very steep, and there's a square at the head of it. Gallery's on the other side of the square. You can't miss it. Got great posters up outside . . . not that any living soul can make head nor tail of them . . ."

"Well, we'll have to see. Thank you very much."

"You're welcome." The porter swung the revolving door, and Robert was ejected into the bitter cold. Rain hammered at his unprotected head, he hunched himself into his raincoat, and picked his way across the gravel, trying to avoid the worst of the puddles. Inside, his car smelt damp and musty, an alien smell over the usual one of leather and cigarettes. He switched on the engine and the heater began to hum. A leaf was stuck in the blade of the windscreen wiper, but when he turned it on, the leaf was dislodged and torn from the wet glass by the wind.

He drove down to the town, and it was all deserted, abandoned, the inhabitants in a state of siege from the weather. Only a drenched policeman stood at point duty at the foot of the hill, and an old lady fought with an umbrella. The narrow streets acted as chimneys for the wind, which funnelled up them, cold and ferocious as a torrent of water, and when he came out on to the harbour road, he saw that the tide was full, and the harbour itself grey and choppy, fleeced with white-capped waves.

He found the street the porter had described. It climbed away from the harbour between crowded cottages, the cobbles wet and shining like the scales of a newly-caught fish. It crested the hill, and opened out into a picturesque square, and he saw the old chapel, a solid, gloomy building, quite at odds with the poster at its door.

85

PORTHKERRIS SOCIETY OF ARTISTS
SPRING EXHIBITION
Admission 5/-

Beneath this was a strange motif in purple – the suggestion of
a staring eye, a six-fingered hand. Robert decided that he could
see the hall porter's point of view.

He parked the car, and went up the streaming steps, and
through the door, and was immediately assailed by the smell of a
paraffin stove. He saw that the old chapel had been whitewashed,
the walls soared to high private windows, and liberally hung with
every sort and size of painting.

Just inside the door, her knees covered with a rug, sat a lady in
a felt hat. On one side of her was a wooden table, with catalogues
and a bowl for money, on the other was the paraffin heater, at
which she was trying to warm a pair of purple-knuckled hands.

"Oh, close the door, close the door," she implored as Robert
blew in on a gust of wind. He leaned against the door, shutting
it, and feeling in his trouser pocket for two half-crowns. "What
a freezing day," she went on, "and this is meant to be summer.
You're my first visitor this afternoon. You are a visitor, aren't
you? I haven't seen your face around the place."

"No, I haven't been here before."

"We've got a most interesting collection, you'll have a catalogue, of course. Another half-crown, please. But I think you'll
agree, well worth it."

"Thank you," said Robert, feebly.

He took the catalogue, decorated with the same purple hand-
and-eye motif as the poster outside, and opened it casually,
running his eye down the list of artists for the name he wanted.
". . . er . . . any particular artist?" The woman at the desk

managed to sound diffident, but she had an inquisitive gleam in her eye.

"No . . . not really."

"Just generally interested, I expect. Are you staying in Porthkerris?"

"Yes . . ." he began to move away from her. "For the moment I am."

He took it slowly, pacing down the long room, feigning interest in every picture. He had found the name, Pat Farnaby. Number 24. The Journey, by Pat Farnaby. He stayed a long time at number 23, then moved on again.

The colour pounced at him. There was a sensation of great height, a dizzying sensation, like vertigo. And yet with it, a sense of elation, as though he were above the clouds, caught, suspended, between the blue and the white.

You must go, Marcus had said. *I want you to form an opinion of your own. You can't remain the man who keeps the books for the rest of your life. Besides, I'd like to see your reaction.*

And this was it. This pure, high note of simple colour.

After a little, he went back to the persistent lady. He was aware that all the time she had been watching him. Now, he thought, she was bright-eyed as a greedy robin, waiting for a bread crumb.

"Is that Pat Farnaby's only exhibit?"

"I'm afraid so. It was all we could persuade him to let us have."

"He lives around here, doesn't he?"

"Oh, yes. Out at Gollan."

"Gollan?"

"That's about six miles away, out on the moor road. It's a farm."

"You mean he's a farmer?"

"Oh, no." She laughed. *Merrily*, thought Robert, as though

87

she were following the directions in an old-fashioned play. "He lives in the loft over the barn. Here," she drew a scrap of paper towards her, wrote an address. "If you want to see him, I'm sure you'll find him here."

He took the paper. "Thank you very much." He started for the door.

"But don't you want to look at the rest of our exhibition?"

"Another time, perhaps."

"It's so *interesting*." She sounded as though her heart would break if he did not look at some more pictures.

"Yes, I'm sure. But another time." It was at this moment that he thought of Emma Litton. His hand on the doorknob, he turned back. "By the way, if I wanted to find Ben Litton's house . . . is it near here? The house, I mean, not the studio?"

"Well, of course, it's just round the corner. About a hundred yards down the road. It's got a blue gate. You can't miss it. But you do know that Mr Litton's not at home?"

"Yes, I know."

"He's in America."

"Yes, I know that, too."

It was still streaming with rain. He got back into the car, and started the engine, and nosed it forward down a street as narrow as a burrow. At the blue gate he left it, parked, completely filling the road, and went through the gate, and down a flight of steps which led to a flagged courtyard where tubs stood, filled with drowned-looking plants, and a painted wooden seat disintegrating slowly in the damp. The house itself was long and low, single-storied, but the uneven roofs and ill-matched chimney pots indicated that it had once been two small cottages, or even three. The front door was painted blue to match the gate, and had a copper dolphin as a knocker.

Robert knocked. From above a stream of water poured down upon him from a faulty gutter. He stepped back and looked up to see where it came from, and as he did so, the door was opened.

He said, "Good afternoon. Your gutter's leaking."

"Where on *earth* have you sprung from?"

"London. You should get it mended or it'll rust away."

"Have you come all the way from London to tell me that?"

"No, of course I haven't. Can I come in?"

"Of course . . ." She stood back, holding the door open for him. "But you are the most disconcerting man. You keep just turning up, with no notice at all."

"How can we give you notice if you aren't on the telephone? And there wasn't time to write a letter."

"Is it about Ben?"

Robert went into the house, ducking his head beneath the lintel of the door, unbuttoning his wet raincoat.

"No. Should it be?"

"I thought he might be home."

"As far as I know he's still basking in that balmy Virginia sunshine."

"Well, then?"

He turned to face her. It occurred to him then that in an odd way she was unpredictable as the weather itself. Each time he met up with her, she seemed a different person. Today she wore a dress in red and orange stripes, and long black stockings. Her hair had been caught back on the nape of her neck with a tortoise-shell slide, and her fringe had grown. It was too long, it would get into her eyes, give her a squint. As he watched her, she pushed it back, off her face, with the heel of her hand. It was a gesture both defensive and disarming and it made her seem very young.

He took the scrap of paper out of his pocket and handed it across to her. Emma read it aloud.

"Pat Farnaby, Gollan Home Farm." She looked up at him. "But where did you get this?"

"From the female at the Art Gallery."

"Pat Farnaby?"

"Marcus is interested."

"Why didn't he come himself?"

"He wanted a second opinion. Mine."

"Have you formed one?"

"It's difficult to say after seeing only a single painting. I thought I might be able to see some more."

Emma said warningly, "He's a very odd young man."

"I should expect him to be. Do you know where Gollan is?"

"Of course. It belongs to Mr and Mrs Stevens. We used to go out in summer for picnics on the cliffs. But I haven't been since I got back this time."

"Will you come with me now? Show me the way?"

"How do we get there?"

"The car's outside. I drove down from London last night."

"You must be exhausted."

"No, I've had a sleep."

"Where are you staying?"

"At the hotel. Can you come? Now?"

"Of course."

"You'll need a coat."

Emma smiled at him. "If you can spare thirty seconds, I'll get one."

When she had gone, her footsteps clattering away down an uncarpeted passage, Robert lit a cigarette and stood, looking about him, intrigued not only by the oddly-shaped little house, but also because it represented the unfamiliar, domestic side of Ben Litton's stormy personality.

The blue front door had led them straight into the living-room, low ceilinged and darkly beamed. There was a huge window with a view of the sea, its deep sill crowded with indoor plants – geraniums and ivy and a Victorian jug full of pink roses. The floor was flagged with slate and scattered with bright rugs, and there were books and magazines everywhere, and a great deal of blue and white Spanish pottery. In a granite hearth, flush with the floor, a log fire smouldered, flanked by baskets of weathered driftwood, and over this hung the only picture in the room.

His professional eye had noticed this as soon as he came into the house, but now Robert went over to inspect it more closely. It was a large oil of a child on a donkey. She wore a red dress, carried a bunch of white daisies, wore a garland of them on her dark head. The donkey stood knee-deep in the lush grass of summer, and, far beyond, the sea and the sky were suffused by a haze of fine weather. The child's dangling feet were bare, her eyes pale in the brown bloom of her face.

Emma Litton, by her father. Robert wondered when it had been painted.

The wind rose, with a sudden witch's shriek, and flung a torrent of rain at the window. It was an eerie sound and he realised that this could be a lonely place to live, and wondered what Emma found to do on such a day. When she came back, carrying her coat and a pair of gumboots, which she proceeded to pull on, he asked her about this.

"Oh, I clean the house, and I cook things and I go and shop. It all takes quite a long time."

"And this afternoon? What were you doing this afternoon when I knocked on the door?"

Emma tugged at the gumboot. "I was ironing."

"And what about evenings? What do you do in the evenings?"

"I usually go out. I go for walks and things. I watch the gulls and the cormorants. I look at the sunset, pick up driftwood for the fire.''

''Alone? Haven't you got any friends?''

''Oh, yes, but the children who lived here when I was little have all grown up and gone away.''

It sounded bleak. On an impulse, Robert said, ''You could come back to London with me. Helen would love to have you.''

''Yes, I know she would, but it's hardly worth it, is it? After all, Ben'll be back any day now. It's only a matter of days.''

She began to pull on her coat. It was navy blue and, with her black stockings and gumboots, made her look like a schoolgirl.

''Have you had any word from Ben?'' Robert asked.

''From Ben? You must be joking.''

''I'm beginning to wish we'd never suggested he went back to America.''

''Why?''

''Because it doesn't seem fair on you.''

''Oh, heavens, I'm all right.'' She smiled. ''Shall we go?''

The Stevens's farm lay in a grey stretch of moor that swept down to the cliffs. Grey, lichened, sunk like a boulder into the land, it might have been simply another larger outcrop of granite. The lane which led down from the road wound deep between tall stone hedges, crowned with hawthorn and brambles. The car bumped and jolted down the track, crossed a small bridge, came to the first cottages, a flock of white geese, and finally the farmyard, shrill with the voice of a screaming cockerel.

Robert stopped the car and switched off the engine. The wind was dying, the rain seemed to have congealed into a sea-mist, thick as smoke. There were various farm sounds; cows lowing, hens clucking, the distant churning of a tractor.

''Now,'' said Robert, ''how do I find this man?''

''He lives in the loft of that barn . . . you go up the stone steps to his door.'' The stone steps were already occupied by a number of wet hens, pecking for scraps of grain, and a bored-looking tabby cat. Below them, in the mud of the yard, a huge sow was rootling about. There was a strong smell of manure. Robert sighed. ''The things I am expected to do, and all in the name of Art.'' He opened the door of the car and began to get out. ''Do you want to come?''

''I think I'd be more use out of the way.''

''I'll try not to be too long.''

She watched him pick his way across the sodden farmyard, toe the pig aside, cautiously climb the steps. He knocked on the door, and then, when there was no reply, opened it and stepped inside. The door shut behind him. Almost at once another door opened, in the farmhouse this time, and the farmer's wife emerged, in boots and a raincoat to her ankles, and a black sou'wester. She carried a stout stick and came down the garden path, peering through the rain to see who was in the big green car.

Emma rolled down the window. ''Hello, Mrs Stevens. It's me.''

''Who?''

''Emma Litton.''

Mrs Stevens broke into a cackle of delighted astonishment, slapped her side, put her hand over her heart. ''Emma! Well, what a surprise you gave me. I haven't seen you since goodness knows how long. What are you doing here?''

''I came out with a man who wants to see Pat Farnaby. He's up there now.''

''Is your father home yet?''

''No, he's still in America.''

''On your own, are you?''

''That's right. How's Ernie?'' Ernie was Mr Stevens.

''He's lovely, but had to go into town today to see the dentist

about his plate. Agony, it gives him, he can scarcely bear
to keep it in his mouth. That's why I'm getting the cows in
for him . . ."

On an impulse Emma said, "I'll come with you . . ."

"Too wet for you."

"I've got boots . . . besides, I'd like the walk." She liked Mrs
Stevens, too, a woman who remained unquenchably cheerful
under all circumstances. They climbed a stile and started out
over the sodden fields. "You've been abroad, haven't you?"
said Mrs Stevens. "Yes, I thought you had. I never knew you
were home. Pity your Daddy had to go off like this. Still, can't
be helped, I suppose, him being the sort of man he is . . ."

The interview with Pat Farnaby was a difficult one, to say the
least of it. He was an intense young man, very pale and under-
nourished, with a shock of carroty hair and a beard to match.
His eyes were green and suspicious as a hungry cat's, and he
appeared to be very dirty. His abode was also dirty, but this
Robert had expected and, accordingly, ignored.

What he had not expected, though, was such antagonism.
Pat Farnaby did not like strangers walking in, uninvited and
unannounced, when he was working. Robert apologised and
explained that he had come on business, whereupon the young
man simply asked Robert what he was trying to sell.

Beating down his irritation, Robert tried another tack. With
some ceremony, he produced Marcus Bernstein's card. "Mr
Bernstein asked me to come and see you, perhaps to look at your
work, find out what your plans are . . ."

"I haven't any plans," said the artist. "I never make plans."
He treated the card as though it were contaminated and must
not be touched, so that Robert was forced to put it down on the
corner of a littered table.

"I saw your picture at the Gallery in Porthkerris, but it is only one picture."

"So what?"

Robert cleared his throat. Marcus was infinitely better at dealing with this sort of thing, and Marcus never lost his temper. It took time to cultivate such patience, Robert knew. His own was slipping away, like greasy rope between his fingers. He took a firm grip of it.

"I'd like to see some more of your work."

Pat Farnaby's pale eyes narrowed. "How did you find me?" he asked, sounding like a cornered criminal.

"They gave me your address at the Gallery. Emma Litton came with me to show me the way. Perhaps you know Emma."

"I've seen her around."

They seemed to be getting nowhere. In the silence that followed Robert let his eyes travel over the unsavoury studio. There were only the most sordid signs of human habitation; a bed like a disintegrating nest, a dirty frying pan, some nasty socks soaking in a bucket, an opened tin of beans, the jagged edge of the lid sticking up. But there were also many canvasses, stacked, scattered, propped on chairs, against walls. A potential treasure trove. Anxious beyond belief to inspect them, he dragged his eyes back to meet the cold unwinking stare of the artist.

He said at last, gently, "Mr Farnaby, I haven't all the time in the world."

Put to the test, Pat Farnaby's resistance cracked. He seemed, all at once, unsure of himself. Arrogance and rudeness were his only defences against the whims of a more sophisticated world. He scratched his head, frowned, made a face of resignation, and at last went to lift a random canvas and turn it to face the light.

"There's this," he said uncertainly, and backed away from it

95

to stand by Robert. As he did so, Robert took a new packet of cigarettes from his pocket and handed them across to the young man. In the silence that followed, Pat Farnaby cautiously slit the cellophane wrapper, took out a cigarette and lit it, and then, with the stealthy movements of a man who does not wish to be observed, slid the packet into his own trouser pocket.

An hour later Robert returned to the car. Emma, waiting for him, saw him come down the steps of the barn, pick his way across the farmyard. She leaned across to open the door for him, and as he got in beside her, asked, "How did you get on?"

"I think all right." He sounded cautious, but excited.

"Did he show you his work?"

"Most of it."

"And it's good?"

"I think so. We may be on the verge of something enormously important, but it's all in such an appalling mess that it's hard to be sure. Nothing's framed, there's no sequence or order . . ."

"I was right, wasn't I? He's a real oddball?"

"Crazy," said Robert. He grinned at her. "But a genius."

He turned the car in the yard and headed back up the lane towards the road. He was whistling tunelessly through his teeth and Emma sensed, beneath his excitement, the satisfaction of a job well done.

She said, "You'll want to speak to Marcus now."

"I said I'd telephone right away." He eased his cuff from the face of his watch, checked on the time. "A quarter past six. He said he'd wait in the Gallery till seven and then go home."

"If you like, you can drop me at the crossroads and I'll walk home."

"Now, why should I do that?"

"I haven't got a telephone, and you'll want to hurry back to the hotel."

He smiled. "It's not as urgent as all that. And if it hadn't been for you, I'd probably still be looking for Pat Farnaby. The least I can do is to take you home."

They were on the moor now, high above the sea. The wind had eased off considerably, veering round to the west, and ahead the sky seemed to be opening and breaking up, and there were unexpected scraps of blue, growing larger every moment, and watery fingers of sunlight. Emma said, "It's going to be a lovely evening," and as she spoke was conscious that she did not want Robert to go back to the hotel and leave her to spend it on her own. He had blown, unexpectedly, into the gloomy day, given it shape and purpose, filled with companionship of a shared venture, and now she did not want it to end.

She said, "When are you going back to London?"

"Tomorrow morning. Sunday. Back in the Gallery Monday morning. It's been a full weekend."

So there was only this evening. She imagined him telephoning Marcus from the phone by his bed. Then he would have a bath, perhaps a drink, go down for dinner. On Saturday evenings The Castle Hotel held little dinner dances; there was a band in white mess jackets and a patch of floor cleared for dancing. Deeply influenced by Ben, Emma had been brought up to regard such functions as unbearably genteel and boring, but tonight she felt that it would be fun to let Ben's rigid opinions go to the devil. She yearned for the starched white table-cloths, the last year's hit tunes, the ritual of the wine list, the souped-up glamour of pink-shaded lights.

Beside her Robert spoke unexpectedly, interrupting her train of thought.

"When did your father paint the picture of you on the donkey?"

"Why did you suddenly ask that?"

"I was thinking about it. It's enchanting. You look so solemn and important."

"That's the way I felt, solemn and important. I was six, and it was the only painting he ever did of me. The donkey was called Mokey. He used to carry us up and down to the beach along with all the picnic baskets and things."

"Have you always lived in the cottage?"

"Not always. Just since Ben married Hester. Before that we used to stay anywhere – in boarding-houses, or with friends. Sometimes we just camped in the studio. It was rather fun. But Harriet said she had no intention of living like a gipsy, so she bought the cottages and converted them."

"She did a good job."

"Yes, she was clever. But Ben has never thought of that house as home. His home is his studio and when he's in Porthkerris, he spends as little time as possible in the cottage. I think its associations with Hester slightly get him down. He's always expecting her to walk in and tell him that he's late for something, or that he's tracking mud on to the floor, or he's putting paint on the sofa cushions . . ."

"The creative instinct seems to thrive in disorder."

Emma laughed. "Do you suppose, that when you and Marcus have made Pat Farnaby rich and famous, he will still want to roost with Mrs Stevens's chickens?"

"That remains to be seen. But if he does come to London, there's no doubt that somebody will have to scrub him down and comb the dust of ages out of that scrofulous beard. Still . . ." He stretched luxuriously, arching his back against the leather seat. "It'll be worth it."

They had crested the hill and were now running down the long road that led to Porthkerris. The sea, in the calm evening light, had turned the translucent blue of butterfly wings; the tide was out, and the great bay an arc of newly-washed sand. The rain had left everything sparkling and fresh, and as the moors and the fields fell behind them, and they drove down through the narrow streets, Emma saw windows flung open to the fresh evening air, and caught, from tiny stamp-sized gardens, the heady smells of roses and lilac.

And there were other smells, too. Saturday evening smells, of fish frying and cheap scent. And there were people strolling the pavements in their best clothes, a smattering of early summer visitors, and boys and girls, hand in hand, headed for the cinema and the little cafés that lined the harbour road.

Stopped at the crossroads by the point-duty policeman, Robert observed them.

"What does young love do in Porthkerris on Saturday night, Emma?"

"It depends on the weather."

The policeman waved them on.

"What are we going to do?" asked Robert.

"We?"

"Yes. You and I. Do you want to be taken out for dinner?"

For a mad moment Emma wondered if she had been yearning aloud. "Well . . . I . . . you don't have to feel you have to . . ."

"I don't feel I have to. I want to. I'd like to. Where shall we go? My hotel? Or would you hate that?"

"No . . . of course . . . I wouldn't hate it . . . ."

"Perhaps you've got some amusing little Italian place you like better."

"There aren't any amusing little Italian places in Porth-kerris."

"No, I was afraid there wouldn't be. So it'll have to be the palm court and the central heating."

"There's a band too," said Emma, feeling she should warn him. "On Saturday nights. And people dance."

"You make it sound indecent."

"I thought perhaps you disliked that sort of thing. Ben does."

"I don't dislike it at all. Like most things, it can be quite fun if you do it with the right person."

"I never thought of it that way."

Robert laughed and looked again at his watch. "Half past six. I'll take you home, then go back to the hotel and change, and speak to Marcus, and then come back for you. Would half past seven be time enough?"

"I'll give you a drink," said Emma. "There's a bottle of Uncle Remus's Genuine Ole Rye Whisky that Ben was given ten years ago, and it's still not been opened. I've always longed to see what was inside."

But Robert was unenthusiastic. "Perhaps I'd better just make a martini."

At the hotel he collected his key, and three messages with it.

"When did these come?"

"The times are noted, sir. Three forty-five, five o'clock, half past five. A Mr Bernstein, telephoning from London. He says to call him the moment you come in."

"I was going to do that anyway, but thanks."

Frowning a little, for such impatience was foreign to Marcus, Robert went upstairs to his room. The copious telephone calls were disturbing. He wondered if Marcus had heard rumours that some other Gallery was after the young artist. Or perhaps he had had second thoughts about Farnaby's work, and wanted to cancel the whole thing.

In his room, the curtains had been drawn, the bed turned down, the fire turned on. He sat on the bed, and picked up the receiver and gave the number of the Gallery. He took the three telephone messages out of his pocket and put them in a neat row on top of the bedside table. *Mr Bernstein would like you to call him. Mr Bernstein called, will ring later. Mr Bernstein . . .*

"Kent 3778. Bernstein Galleries."

"Marcus . . ."

"Robert, thank God I've got you at last. Did you get my message?"

"Three of them. But I said I would call you about Farnaby."

"This isn't about Farnaby. This is much more important. This is about Ben Litton."

There was a dress, seen in Paris, wildly expensive, coveted, and finally bought. It was black, sleeveless, very plain. "But when will you wear such a dress?" Madame Duprés had asked, and Emma, basking in the luxury of possession, had replied, "Oh, some time. Some special time."

There had never been such an occasion until tonight. Now, with her hair coiled high and pearl earstuds set in her ears, Emma drew the black dress carefully over her head, zipped it up and fastened the tiny belt, and her reflection in the mirror reassured her that all those thousands of francs had been well spent.

When Robert came, she was in the kitchen, struggling with a trayful of ice-cubes for the martinis that he had promised to make. She heard his car, the slam of the door, the gate open and shut and his footsteps as he ran down the steps, and in a panic, she tumbled the ice into a glass dish and went to let him in, and found that the sullen day had turned into a clear and perfect night, jewel-blue and scattered with stars.

In surprise, she said, "What a beautiful night."

"Amazing, isn't it? After all that wind and rain Porthkerris is looking like Positano." He came into the house and Emma closed the door behind him. "There's even a moon rising over the sea to complete the illusion. All we need now is a guitar and a tenor singing 'Santa Lucia'."

"Perhaps we'll find one."

He had changed into a dark grey suit, a starched shirt with an impeccable collar and a gleam of white cuff, linked with gold, showing at his wrist. His tawny hair was once more tamed and smoothly brushed, and he brought with him the crisp, lemony smell of aftershave.

"Do you still want to make a martini? I've got everything ready, I was just trying to get the ice . . ." She went back to the kitchen, raising her voice to talk through the open door. "The gin and the martini are on the table and a lemon. Oh, and you'll need a knife to cut the lemon with."

She opened a drawer and found one, pointed and very sharp, and she carried the knife and the bowl of ice back into the living-room. "What a pity Ben isn't here. He adores martinis, only he can never remember the right proportions and he always drowns them with lemon . . ."

Robert made no reply to this. It occurred then to Emma that he had made no effort to make himself at home. He had done nothing about their drinks, he had not even lit himself a cigarette, and this in itself was unusual, for he was normally the most relaxed and composed of men. But now there was a definite constraint about him, and with a sinking heart, Emma wondered if he was already regretting the evening they were to spend together.

She went to put the lemon down beside the empty glasses, told herself she was imagining things, turned to swiftly smile at him. "Now, what else do you need?"

"Not another thing," said Robert, and put his hands into his trouser pockets. *Not the gesture of a man who is about to make a martini.* In the fire a burning log settled and broke, sending up a shower of sparks.

Perhaps it was the telephone call that had upset him. "Did you speak to Marcus?"

"Yes, I did. As a matter of fact, he'd been trying to get me on the telephone most of the afternoon."

"And of course you were out. Was he pleased when you told him about Pat Farnaby?"

"He wasn't calling about Farnaby."

"He wasn't?" Suddenly she was afraid. "Is it bad news?"

"No, of course not, but you may not be very pleased. It's about your father. You see, he called Marcus this morning, from the States. He wanted Marcus to tell you that yesterday, in Queenstown, he and Melissa Ryan were married."

Emma realised that she was still holding the knife, that it was very sharp and that she might cut herself with it, so she set it down, very carefully alongside the lemon . . .

Married. The word conjured up a hysterical image of a wedding; of Ben with a white flower in the button-hole of his sagging corduroy jacket; of Melissa Ryan in her pink wool suit, misted in white veiling and paper confetti; of demented church bells jangling their message out across the verdant Virginia countryside that Emma had never seen. It was like a nightmare.

She realised that Robert Morrow was still talking, his voice even and calm. ". . . Marcus feels that in some obscure way, he is to blame. Because he thought the private view was a good idea, and because he was with them in Queenstown – he saw them together all the time, and he never had the faintest inkling that this was going to happen."

Emma remembered Marcus's description of the beautiful

house, saw Ben caged by Melissa's money, a pacing tiger with all his creative impulses smothered by luxury; and she realised that she had underestimated Melissa Ryan in imagining that Ben would be put off by having to fight for what he wanted. She had not appreciated how much he would want it.

Suddenly, she was angry. "He should never have gone back to America. There was no need. He simply wanted to be left alone and to get on with his painting."

"Emma, nobody made him go."

"It isn't as though the marriage will last. Ben's never stayed faithful to a woman longer than six months, and I can't see Melissa Ryan standing for that."

Robert said mildly, "Perhaps this time it will work, and it will last."

"But you saw them together that day they met. They couldn't keep their eyes off each other. If she had been old and ugly, nothing would have dragged him away from Porthkerris."

"But she wasn't old and ugly. She's very beautiful, and highly intelligent and very rich. And if it hadn't been Melissa Ryan, very soon it would have been somebody else, and what is more . . ." he went on, swiftly, before Emma could interrupt, ". . . you know as well as I do that that is true."

She said bitterly, "But at least we would have had more than a month together."

Hopelessly, Robert shook his head. "Oh, Emma, let him go."

His tone infuriated her. "He's my father. What's wrong in wanting to be with him?"

"He's not a father, any more than he's a husband or a lover or a friend. He's an artist. As that dedicated maniac we went to see this afternoon is an artist. They have no time for our values or standards. Everything, and everybody else, has to take second place."

"*Second* place? I wouldn't mind taking second place, or third, or fourth. But I've always come at the bottom of a long list of priorities. His painting, his love affairs, his perpetual shunting about all over the world; even Marcus, and you. You're all more important to Ben than ever I was."

"Then leave him alone. Think about something else for a change. Chuck all this, leave it behind. Get yourself a job."

"I've done all those things. I've been doing them for the past two years."

"Then come back to London with me tomorrow and stay with Marcus and Helen. It'll get you away from Porthkerris, give you time to get used to the idea of Ben being married again, decide what you want to do next."

"Perhaps I've already decided."

It was there, in the back of her mind. Like watching the revolving stage from the darkened auditorium of a theatre. One set moves out of sight and as it does the new scenery comes slowly on to the stage. A different set. Another room, perhaps. Another view from another window. "But I don't want to come to London."

"And this evening?"

Emma frowned. She had forgotten. "This evening?"

"We're having dinner together."

She felt that she could not bear it. "I really would rather not . . ."

"It'll do you good . . ."

"No it won't. And I've got a headache . . ." It was an excuse, made-up, and it was with astonishment that she realised it was true. A pain that felt like the start of a migraine, with her eyeballs dragged by wires into the back of her head; the thought of food, chicken in gravy, ice-cream, was nauseous. "I couldn't come. I couldn't."

105

Robert said gently, "It isn't the end of the world," and the old, comforting cliché was somehow more than Emma could take. To her horror, she began to cry. She covered her face with her hands pressing her fingertips into her thudding scalp, trying to stop, knowing that crying would make it worse, that she would be blinded with pain, that she would be sick . . .

She heard him say her name, and in two strides he had covered the space between them, and he put his arms around her, cradling her, letting her cry all over the immaculate grey lapels of his good suit. And Emma did not try to move away, but stayed still, tightly clenched against her own grief, rigid and unresponsive and hating him for what he had done to her.

7

Jane Marshall, her hand curved round a half full tumbler of Scotch-on-the-rocks, said, ". . . so what happened then?"

"Nothing happened. She didn't want to come out to dinner, and she looked as though she was going to have a bilious attack, so I put her to bed, and gave her a hot drink and an aspirin, and then I went back to the hotel and had dinner on my own. Then, the next morning, the Sunday, I went down to the cottage to say goodbye before I drove back to London. She was up and about, rather pale, but she seemed to be all right."

"Did you try again to make her come back with you?"

"Yes, I did, but she was adamant. So we said goodbye, and I left her. And since then there has been no word."

"But you can surely find out where she is?"

"There is no way of finding out. There's no telephone, never has been. Marcus wrote, of course, but Emma seems to have inherited Ben's built-in aversion to answering letters. There hasn't been another word."

"But this is crazy. In this day and age . . . there must be someone who can tell you . . ."

"There's no one. No one Emma ever talked to. There was no daily woman, coming in to clean, she did it all herself. That was the big reason for going back to Porthkerris in the first place, so that she could keep house for Ben. Of course, after two weeks of frigid silence, Marcus could stand it no longer, and put through a telephone call to the landlord of the Sliding Tackle, which was the pub Ben used to frequent, but Ben had been gone for six weeks, anyway, and Emma never went near the place.''

"Then you'll have to go down to Porthkerris and ask around.''

"Marcus isn't prepared to do that.''

"Why not?''

"For reasons. Emma isn't a child. She's been hurt, and Marcus respects the fact that if she wants to be left alone, he has no right to interfere. He's asked her to come to London and live with Helen and himself . . . anyway until she's found her feet again. He can scarcely do more. And there's another reason, too.''

"I know," said Jane. "It's Helen, isn't it?''

"Yes, it is,'' said Robert, hating to admit it. "Helen has always resented the hold Ben has over Marcus. There have been times when she would gladly have seen Ben at the bottom of the ocean. But she's accepted it because she had to, because wet-nursing Ben's career is part of Marcus's job, and without Marcus to keep him, more or less on the rails, God knows what would have happened to Ben Litton.''

"And now she doesn't want him to start killing himself over Emma.''

"Precisely.''

Jane rocked her glass, letting the ice clink against its side. She said, "And you?''

He looked up. "What about me?''

"Do you feel involved?''

"Why do you ask that?''

"You sound involved.''

"I scarcely know the girl."

"But you're worried about her."

He considered this. "Yes," he said at last. "Yes, I suppose I am. God knows why."

His glass was empty. Jane laid down her own drink, and got up to take his glass and pour him another whisky. From behind him, busy with ice, she said, "Why don't *you* go down to Porthkerris and find out?"

"Because she isn't there."

"She isn't . . . ? You know? But you never told me that."

"After the abortive telephone call to the Sliding Tackle, Marcus got the wind up. He rang the local police, and they found out a few facts and called us back. Cottage closed up, studio closed up, Post Office told to keep all mail until further notice." He reached up to take the fresh drink that Jane handed him over the back of the sofa. "Thanks."

"And her father . . . ? Does he know?"

"Yes, Marcus wrote and told him. But you can't expect Ben to get unduly excited. After all, he's still in the throes of what is virtually a honeymoon, and Emma's been sculling round Europe on her own since she was fourteen. Don't forget, that this is not a normal father-daughter relationship."

Jane sighed. "It most certainly isn't."

Robert grinned at her. She was a comfortingly down-to-earth person and it was for this reason that, on an impulse, he had dropped in this evening for a drink on his way home from work. Usually, the double life he led with Marcus Bernstein, working with him at the Gallery, as well as living in the same house, offered no strain at all. But just now, things were difficult. Robert had come back from a business trip to Paris, to find Marcus on edge, and unable to concentrate for very long on anything but the problem of Emma Litton. After discussing it with him, Robert realised that Marcus blamed himself for what had happened, and refused to be talked out of his guilt. Helen, on the other hand, was unsympathetic, and determined that he should not get himself more deeply involved in the whole sorry business, and for the moment the tensions had got on top of them, and split the ménage at Milton Gardens from top to bottom.

The situation was not improved by the weather. After a cool spring, London had suddenly been caught up in the throes of a veritable heatwave. The early mornings broke in a pearl-like mist which gradually dissolved into day after day of baking sun. Girls went to work in sleeveless dresses, men shed their jackets and sat at their desks in shirt-sleeves. The parks at lunch-time were filled with recumbent picnickers; shops and restaurants sprouted striped awnings, windows were flung open to the smallest breeze, and in the streets, parked cars frizzled and pavements glared, and melted tar stuck to the soles of shoes.

The heat, like some monstrous epidemic, had invaded even the quiet, pond-green recesses of the Bernstein Gallery. All day long there had been an endless stream of visitors and prospective clients, for the trans-Atlantic tourist season had started, and this was apt to be their busiest time. And at the end of it all, Robert, driving home, had found himself longing for a new face, a cool drink, and some conversation that had nothing to do with Artists, be they Renaissance, Impressionist or Pop.

Jane Marshall sprang immediately to mind.

Her little house was in a narrow mews between Sloane Square and Pimlico Road. As he turned the car into the street, and eased down over the cobbles, he gave a double toot on the horn, and she appeared at the open upstairs window, her hands on the sill, her fair hair falling over her face as she leaned out to see who it was.

"Robert! I thought you were still in Paris."

"I was till two days ago. Have you got such a thing as a long, cool, alcoholic drink for an exhausted working man?"

"Of course I have. Hold on. I'll come down and let you in."

Her tiny house had always charmed him. Originally a coach-man's cottage, it had a steep, narrow staircase, which led straight up to the first floor. Here there was an open hall-way, a sitting-room, and a kitchen, and upstairs again, in the slope-roofed loft, her bedroom and bathroom. As such it was inadequate enough, but since she had started her interior decorating business, it had become a joke. The sitting-room she had turned into a workroom, but still the bales of fabric, the fringing and the cushions, and the small bits of bric-à-brac she so cleverly picked up, overflowed into every available corner of space, rendering it all as gay and colourful as a patchwork quilt.

She was delighted to see him. She had spent the morning with a tiresome woman who wanted her entire house in St John's Wood done up in cream, which she called "Redecorating in Magnolia." And then there had been a session with a young and rising actress who demanded something startling for her new flat.

"She sat here for hours, showing me pictures of the sort of thing she had in mind. I tried to tell her she should get a bulldozer in, not an interior decorator, but she wouldn't listen. These people never do. Whisky?"

"That," said Robert, collapsing on the sofa in front of the open window, "is the nicest thing anybody has said to me all day."

She poured two drinks, made sure he was supplied with cigarettes and an ash-tray, and then settled herself composedly down to face him. She was a very pretty girl. Her blonde hair was straight and thick, cut in a curve to her chin. Her eyes were green, her nose tip-tilted, her mouth sweet, but implacable. Her broken marriage had left certain scars upon her character and she was not always the most tolerant of people, but there was a directness about her that he found as refreshing as a drink of cold water, and she always looked delicious.

Now he said, "I came here with the express purpose of not talking shop. How did we get on to the subject of Ben Litton anyway?"

"I brought it up. I was intrigued. Every time I saw Helen, she kept dropping maddening hints and then refusing to say more. She feels strongly about this, doesn't she?"

"Only because, in his day, Ben Litton has run poor Marcus ragged."

"Does she know Emma?"

"She hasn't seen her since she went to Switzerland six years ago."

"It's difficult," said Jane, "to be fair about people if you don't know them very well."

"It's sometimes difficult to be fair even if you do. And now . . ." He leaned forward to stub out his cigarette. "Let's drop the subject and make a tacit agreement not to mention it again. Are you doing anything this evening?"

"Not a thing."

"Then why don't we go and find somewhere with a roof garden or a terrace, and have a quiet dinner together?"

"I'd like that," said Jane.

"I'll call Helen and tell her I'm not coming back . . ."

"In that case . . ." She stood up. "I shall go and have a shower and change. I shan't be long."

"There isn't any hurry."

"Make yourself at home . . . get yourself another drink. There are cigarettes here, and an evening paper somewhere if you care to look for it . . ."

She went up the stairs. He heard her moving about, high heels tapping on the polished floor. She sang under her breath, slightly out of tune. He put down his glass and went into her living-room, and ran her telephone to earth at last, beneath a bundle of flowered chintzes, and called Helen to say he would not be home for dinner. Then he went back to pour the third drink of the evening, and loosened his tie, and flopped once more on the sofa.

The whisky had revived him slightly, and beneath its clean cold bite, his tiredness had changed from end-of-the-day fatigue to a pleasant lassitude. The paper protruded from beneath a cushion, and he pulled it out, and then saw that it was not the *Evening Standard*, but the *Stage*.

"Jane."

"Hello!"

"I didn't know you took the *Stage*."

"I don't."

"Well it's here."

"Is it?" She didn't sound particularly interested. "Dinah Burnett must have left it behind. You know she's the actress who needs the bulldozer."

He opened it aimlessly. "Wanted One All Round Girl Dancer. Why does she have to be all round? Why can't she be all square?"

"Search me."

He turned to the Repertory page. They were doing Shakespeare at Birmingham, a restoration revival at Manchester, and at Brookford, staging the première of a new play . . .

Brookford.

The name leapt at him from the page like a bullet. Brookford. He sat up, slapped the paper into shape, and read the whole item.

*

113

Brookford Rep's summer season opens this week with the world première of *Daisies on the Grass*, a comedy in three acts by local writer Phyllis Jason. This light but well-knit play stars actress Charmian Vaughan in the lead role of Stella. Other parts are supplementary, but John Rigger, Sophie Lambart and Christopher Ferris all help to bring the mirthful suspense to its climax, and Sara Rutherford is charmingly natural as the bride. Tommy Childers' production is fast and furious, and the set, by scenic artist Brian Dare, evoked a spontaneous applause from the enthusiastic first-night audience.

Christopher Ferris.

He laid the paper carefully down, and reached for a cigarette, and lit it. Christopher Ferris. He had forgotten Christopher.

But now, out of a jumble of memories, he heard Emma's voice again, that first day, when he had given her lunch at Marcello's.

Did you know about Christopher? Quite by chance Christopher and I met up again in Paris. And he came this very morning and saw me off at Le Bourget.

And he remembered – facing her across the table – being suddenly wise, and knowing the reason for her smile and the bloom of her skin and the brightness of her eyes.

And later, in the draughty studio at Porthkerris, the subject of Christopher had, fleetingly, come up again, sandwiched between other more important items of discussion. *He'll be at Brookford by now*, Emma had said. *In the thick of rehearsals.*

He stood up and went to the foot of the stairs.

"Jane."

"Hello!"

"How nearly ready are you?"

"I'm just doing my face."

"Where's Brookford?"

"In Surrey."

"How long will it take us to get there?"

"Brookford? Oh, about forty-five, fifty minutes."

He glanced at his watch. "If we leave right away, or as near as we can . . . we shouldn't be too late."

Jane appeared at the head of the stairs, with a mirror in one hand and an eyeliner brush in the other.

"Late for what?"

"We're going to the theatre."

"I thought we were going out for dinner."

"Later, perhaps we will. But first we're going to Brookford, to see a well-knit comedy called *Daisies on the Grass* . . ."

"Have you gone out of your mind?"

". . . by local writer Phyllis Jason."

"You have gone out of your mind."

"I'll explain on the way down. Be a darling and hurry."

As they roared down the M4 Jane said, "You mean that nobody knows about this young man except you."

"Emma didn't tell Ben, because he'd never liked Christopher anyway – Helen says he was jealous of the boy."

"And Emma didn't tell Marcus Bernstein."

"I don't think so."

"But she told you."

"Yes, she told me. She told me that very first day. And why the devil I didn't think of him before I cannot imagine."

"Is she in love with him?"

"I wouldn't know. She's certainly very fond of him."

"Do you think we'll find her at Brookford?"

"If we don't, then I'll bet even money that Christopher Ferris will know where she is." Jane did not reply. After a little, he added, his eyes still fixed on the speeding road, "I'm sorry about this. I promised the subject wasn't to be raised again, and here I am whisking you off to the wilds of darkest Surrey.''

''Why,'' asked Jane, ''are you so anxious to find Emma?''

''Because of Marcus. I should like to set Marcus's mind at rest.''

''I see.''

''Because if Marcus's mind is at rest, then Helen will relax and life will be a great deal more comfortable for all of us.''

''Well, that's fair enough . . . Look, I think we should turn off here.''

The Brookford Repertory Theatre took some finding. They cruised up and down the High Street, then asked directions from a tired-looking policeman in shirt-sleeves. He sent them a half a mile from the centre of town, and, off a back street, up a cul-de-sac, they found the large brick edifice, looking more like a mission hall than anything else, but for the word THEATRE written above the door in neon letters, deadened by the hot evening light.

Outside, by the pavement, were parked a couple of cars, and alongside them, with their feet in the gutter, sat two small girls playing with a broken perambulator.

There were posters.

WORLD PREMIERE
DAISIES ON THE GRASS
by PHYLLIS JASON
A comedy in Three Acts
Produced by
TOMMY CHILDERS

Jane stood, taking in this inauspicious façade. ''So much for the living theatre.''

Robert put his hand under her elbow. ''Come along now.''

They went up a flight of stone steps, and into a small foyer, with a cigarette kiosk on one side, and a box office on the other. In the box office a girl sat knitting.

"I'm afraid the show's started," she said, as Robert and Jane appeared on the other side of the glass.

"Yes, we thought it would have. But we'll have a couple of tickets anyway."

"What price?"

"Oh . . . well – stalls."

"That's fifteen shillings. But you'll have to wait till the second act."

"Is there anywhere we could get a drink?"

"The bar's upstairs."

"Thank you very much." He took the tickets and his change. "I expect you know all the people who work here."

"Well, yes . . ."

"Christopher Ferris . . ."

"Oh, is he a friend of yours?"

"Well, a friend of a friend. The thing is, I wondered if he has his sister here . . . at least, she's his step-sister. Emma Litton."

"Emma's working here."

"She's *working* here. In the theatre?"

"That's right. As ASM – Assistant Stage Manager. Our last girl suddenly went off ill with an appendix, and Emma said she'd come and help out. Of course," her voice became professional ". . . Mr Childers usually likes someone in the job who's had a bit of stage training, you know, RADA, or a bit of experience somewhere, so that they double up in small parts. But as she was here, and didn't have anything to do, he let her have the job. Just until the regular girl's better."

"I see. Do you think we'd be able to see her?"

117

"Well, after the show, yes. But Mr Childers won't have anyone back stage until it's over."

"That's all right. We can wait. Thank you very much."

"Not at all. It's a pleasure."

They went upstairs to a second, larger foyer with a bar in the corner, and sat there, drinking lager and talking to the barman until a light spatter of applause announced the end of the first act. The lights went up, the doors opened, and a small stream of people emerged for refreshment. Jane and Robert waited until the first curtain bell, and then went into the auditorium themselves, buying a couple of programmes on their way, and being shown to their seats by an eager young girl in a nylon overall. Attendance that night was certainly sparse, and Jane and Robert were the only two people sitting in the third row. Jane looked about her with a professional eye.

"I think it was once a mission hall," she decided. "Nobody would have built anything so ugly as a theatre. But I must say, they have done it up quite imaginatively, and the lighting and the colours are good. What a shame they don't get better audiences . . ."

The curtain at last went up on the second act. "The lounge hall of Mrs Edbury's house in Gloucestershire" said the programme note, and there it was, complete with french windows, staircase, settee, table with drinks, table with telephone, low table with magazines (for leading lady to pick up and idly flick through in moments when she did not know what to do with her hands?) and three doors.

"Draughty house," murmured Jane.

"It's better when they shut the french windows."

But the french windows had to be open, for in bounced the *ingénue* (*Sara Rutherford is charmingly natural as the bride*),

118

flung herself on the settee and burst into tears. Jane's profile was alert with delighted disbelief. Robert settled more deeply into his seat.

It was a terrible play. Even if they had seen the first act, and so been able to unravel the tangled skein of the plot, it would still have been a terrible play. It bristled with clichés, with stock characters (there was even a comic charlady), with contrived exits and entrances, and with telephone calls. There were eight of these in the course of the second act alone.

When the curtain came down, Robert said, "Let's go and have another drink. I could do with a double brandy after that."

"I'm not going to move," said Jane. "I'm not going to break the spell. I haven't seen a play like this since I was seven. And the set makes me positively nostalgic. But there's one thing, Robert, that sticks out like a sore thumb."

"What's that?"

"Christopher Ferris is very, very good . . ."

He was, too. When he had shambled on stage, as the vague young university student who was eventually to win the heroine from her stockbroker fiancé, *Daisies on the Grass* showed its first, faint spark of life. His lines were not better than anyone else's, but his timing was impeccable, and he managed to make them funny or sad, or wryly charming. For the part he wore corduroys, a sagging sweater and horn-rimmed spectacles, but even these could not disguise his elegance and his good looks and the natural long-legged grace with which he moved.

". . . and he's not merely very good, he's very attractive," Jane went on. "I can see why his step-sister was so pleased to bump into him again in Paris. I wouldn't mind bumping into him myself."

The third act had the same set, but now it was night. Blue moonlight shone through the open window, and down the stairs came the little bride, carrying a suitcase, tiptoeing, all ready to run away or elope or whatever it was she'd spent the last hour in deciding to do. Robert couldn't remember. He was waiting for Christopher to come back on stage. When he did, Robert simply watched him the entire time, detachedly, absorbed and full of admiration. By now, he had the audience, small as it was, in the palm of his hand. As Robert watched, so they watched. Christopher scratched the back of his head and they laughed. He took off his spectacles to kiss the girl, and they laughed again. He put them back on to say goodbye for ever, and there was silence, and then people began to blow their noses. And when it was all over, and the cast lined up for the curtain call, the applause was long, and real, and it was all for Christopher.

"What do we do now?" asked Jane.

"It's not closing time for another ten minutes. Let's go and find a drink."

They went back to the bar. The barman said, "Well, how did you enjoy the show, sir?"

"Well, I don't know . . . I . . ."

Jane was braver. "We thought it was terrible," she said, but quite politely. "And I've fallen in love with Christopher Ferris."

The barman grinned. "Quite something, isn't he? Pity you had to come tonight, when the audience was so thin on the ground as it were. Mr Childers did hope, Miss Jason being local and all that jazz, that this play would bring them in. But you can't fight a heatwave."

"Do you usually have good houses?" Jane wanted to know.

"They go up and down. Now, last show we did was *Present Laughter* . . . that fairly filled the place up."

"It's a good play," said Robert.

"What part did Christopher Ferris have?" asked Jane.

"Now, let me see. Oh, I know, he was the young playwright.

You know, the one that bounces round on the chairs and eats biscuits. Ronald Maule he's called in the play. Oh, very funny, Christopher Ferris was in that part. Brought the house down, he did . . .'' Wiping away at his tumblers, he glanced up at the clock. ''I'm afraid I'll have to ask you to drink up, sir . . . closing time . . .''

''Yes, of course. By the way, how do we get back stage? We want to see Emma Litton.''

''You can just go down the auditorium, sir, go through the door at the right of the stage. But watch out for Mr Collins the Stage Manager. He doesn't exactly relish visitors.''

''Thanks,'' said Robert. ''And good night.''

They went back into the theatre. The curtains had been drawn back, and the stage was revealed once more, but without footlights the set looked less inspiring than ever. On stage a young boy was struggling with the sofa, trying to heave it to one side, and someone, somewhere, had left a door open, so that the whole theatre was swept with a stuffy draught of used-up air. The programme girl was going round, slapping up the empty seats and collecting empty chocolate boxes and cigarette cartons in a trash can.

''There is nothing,'' said Jane, ''so depressing as an empty theatre.''

They started to walk down towards the stage. As they approached, Robert realised that it was not a boy who struggled, single-handed with the heavy sofa, but a girl, dressed in an old blue sweater and jeans.

When he was close enough, he said, ''I wonder if you can help me . . . ?''

She turned to look at him, and Robert, with the shock of sheer disbelief, found himself face to face with Emma Litton.

8

After a second's gaping silence, Emma stopped trying to move the sofa, and straightened up. He thought that she seemed much taller and thinner, the cold stage light was not flattering, her wrists hung like sticks from her rolled-up sleeves. But the worst thing was her hair. She had cut off her hair, and now her head seemed small and vulnerable, furred like the pelt of an animal.

There was the animal feel of watchfulness about her, too. A scarey look as though she waited for him to make the first move, to say the first word, before she knew which way to jump. He slid his hands into his pockets, in a deliberate attempt to both look and feel casual, and he said, "Hello, Emma."

She gave the ghost of a smile. She said, "This sofa feels as though it's been stuffed with lead and lost its castors in the process."

"Isn't there anyone who can help you?" He came forward to the edge of his side of the stage, so that he was looking up at her. "It looks very heavy."

"Yes, there'll be someone in a moment." She did not seem to know what to do with her hands. She rubbed them on the seat of her jeans as though they were dirty, and then folded her arms. It was a curiously defensive movement, and made her shoulder-bones jut forward beneath the thin cotton of her shirt. ''What are you doing here?''

''We came down to see *Daisies on the Grass* . . . We drove down from town. This is Jane Marshall. Jane, this is Emma.''

They smiled, nodded at each other, murmured how do you do? Emma turned back to Robert. ''Did . . . did you know I was here?''

''No, but I knew Christopher was, and I thought you might be.''

''I've been working for a couple of weeks. It gives me something to do.''

Robert made no comment on this, and, perhaps disconcerted by his silence, Emma suddenly sat down on the sofa that she was meant to be shifting. Her hands hung listlessly between her knees. After a little, she said, ''Did Marcus send you?''

''No. We just came to call. Make sure you're all right . . .''

''I'm all right.''

''What time are you finished here . . . ?''

''I'll be about half an hour. I have to clear the stage for rehearsal tomorrow morning. Why?''

''I thought we might have all gone to some hotel or other, for a sandwich and a drink. Jane and I haven't had any dinner . . .''

''Oh, how kind!'' She did not sound enthusiastic. ''Well . . . the thing is . . . that I usually leave something in the oven at the flat . . . a casserole or something. Johnny and Chris never eat anything otherwise. We'll have to go back or it'll burn.''

''Johnny?''

''Johnny Rigger. He was the fiancé. You know, the other man. He lives with Christo . . . and me.''

''I see.''

There was another silence. Emma, discomfited, struggled with her more hospitable instincts. ''I would ask you to come back, if you'd like to, but there's nothing but a few cans of beer . . .''

"We like beer," said Robert promptly.

"And the flat's in a dreadful mess. There never seems to be time to clean it properly. Not now that I'm working, I mean."

"We don't mind. How do we get there?"

"Well . . . have you got a car?"

"Yes. It's outside."

"Yes . . . well. If you go out and wait, Christo and I will join you later. If that's all right. And then we can show you where it is."

"Splendid. How about Johnny?"

"Oh, he'll be along later."

"We'll wait for you."

He took his hands out of his pockets and turned, and he and Jane walked back up the slight slope of the auditorium. As they reached the double doors, and Robert held one half open for Jane to go through, all hell seemed to break loose on stage.

"Where the devil is that Litton girl?" Robert was in time to see Emma scramble off the sofa as though someone had set off a firework, and try once more to move the cumbersome thing. A small man with a black beard shot on stage, looking like the worst-tempered sort of pirate. "Look, ducky, I asked you to move the bloody sofa, not to go to sleep on it. God, I'll be thankful to see that other girl back and you safely out of this place . . ." One either had to go and knock him down, or withdraw. For Emma's sake Robert withdrew.

The door swung shut behind him, but as they crossed the foyer, the voice could still be heard ". . . She's a moron, we all know, but no one could be as crassly stupid as you . . ."

"Charming," said Jane, as they went down the stairs. Robert

did not reply, because, until the white-hot blaze of anger with which he had been suddenly consumed, died down, he was not capable of saying anything. "That must be Mr Collins, the stage manager. Not a very nice man to work for."

They reached the street door, and went down the steps and crossed the pavement and got into the car. It was dark now, a soft, bloomy dusk had descended upon the town, but the heat of the day still lingered, held by the narrow confines of the street, by sunbaked stone and paving. Above them the Theatre sign shone brightly, but as they got into the car, someone from inside the building turned it off. The evening's entertainment was over. Robert reached for his cigarettes, gave Jane one and lit it, and then took one for himself. After a moment he felt a little calmer.

He said, "She's cut off all her hair."

"Has she? What was it like before?"

"Long and silky and dark."

"She doesn't want us to go tonight. You know that, don't you?"

"Yes, I know that. But we must. We don't need to stay long."

"And I hate beer."

"I'm sorry. Perhaps someone will make you some coffee."

". . . It isn't even as though it's a job that requires any sort of brain. The most idiotic creature straight out of RADA could do it more competently than you."

Collins was letting fly, unloading the day's tensions and frustrations in a flood of invective that was directed solely at Emma. He hated her. It had something to do with Christopher; with the fact that her father was both successful and famous. At first, she had tried sticking up for herself, but now she knew better than to try and stem this venomous flood. With Collins, you couldn't win. She simply listened, got on with her work, tried not to let him see how deeply he could upset her.

"... you got this job because I have to have someone to help me ... God help me. You didn't get it because Chris shoved his oar in, and you didn't get it because some fool is willing to pay twenty thousand for a Ben Litton of red spots on a blue background. I've got more sense than that, as by now you have no doubt found out. So don't start thinking you can loll around entertaining your toffee-nosed friends ... and the next time they condescend to visit our humble little show, tell them to bloody well wait till we've finished, will you? Now come on, get that sofa out of the bloody way ..."

It was nearly eleven before at last he let her go, and then she found Christo waiting for her in Tommy Childers' office. The door was open and she heard them talking, and she knocked and put her head in and said, "I'm ready now. I'm sorry I was so long."

Christo stood up. "That's all right." He stubbed out his cigarette. "Good night, Tommy."

" 'Night, Chris."

"Thanks for everything."

"That's OK, old chap ..."

They went downstairs towards the stage door. He put his arm around her as they went. Their warm bodies touched, it was too hot for such contact, but she found it comforting. Outside, in the little alley that led down to the street, he stopped by the dustbins to light another cigarette.

He said, "You were long enough. Collins playing up?"

"He was furious because Robert Morrow's here."

"Robert Morrow?"

"He's in Bernstein's, with Marcus. He's Marcus's brother-in-

127

law. I told you. He came down to see the show . . . He's brought a girl with him.''

Christo stood looking down at her. ''To see the show or to see you?''

''I think to see us both.''

''He can't try to take you back. Say you're under age or anything?''

''Of course not.''

''Then that's all right.''

''Yes, I suppose it is. But, you see, like a fool, I asked them back to the flat. At least, I didn't mean to ask them, but somehow I did, and they're coming. They're waiting for us now, in the car. Oh, Christo, I am sorry.''

He laughed. ''*I* don't mind.''

''They won't stay long.''

''I don't mind if they stay all night. Don't look so tragic.'' He took her in his arms, and kissed her cheek. She thought that if only the evening, the day, the endless day, could end right here and now, she would be well content. She was afraid of Robert. She was too tired to fence with him, to answer questions, to try and evade those watchful grey eyes. She was too tired to compete with his friend, who was blonde and pretty and almost indecently cool-looking in her sleeveless navy-blue dress. She was too tired to tidy the flat for them, to shovel clothes and scripts and empty glasses out of sight, to open beer cans, and make coffee, and get Christo's dinner out of the oven.

Christo rubbed his chin against her cheek. ''What's wrong?'' he asked gently.

''Nothing.'' He did not like her to say she was tired. He was never tired. He did not know what the word meant.

He said, in her ear, ''It's been a good day, hasn't it?''

''Yes, of course.'' She drew away from him. ''A good day.''

With their arms entwined, they went down the alley towards the street. Robert heard their voices, and got out of the car to meet them. They came towards him, in and out of the patches of light flung by the street lamps. They walked like lovers, Emma trailing a sweater, Christo with a bulky script under one arm and a cigarette between his fingers. When they reached the car, they stopped. "Hello," said Christopher, smiling.

"Christo, this is Robert Morrow, and Miss Marshall . . ."

"Mrs Marshall," Jane corrected sweetly, leaning over the back of the front seat. "Hello, Christopher."

"Sorry we've been so long," said Christo " . . . Emma's only just told me you were here. And she was having her nightly set-to with Collins, so we've all been fairly occupied. I believe you're coming back to have a can of beer, or something. I'm afraid we've got nothing stronger."

"That's OK," said Robert. "If you can tell us the way . . ."

"Of course."

The flat was in the basement of a row of daunting Victorian houses that had once seen better days. They were much gabled, and decorated with fancy brick work and stained windows, but the street itself was dismal, and the curtains of bow-windowed front rooms sagged sadly and were not always very clean. Worn stone steps led down to an area where there were dustbins and one or two dead geraniums in pots, and, as they descended, there was a scream of fury from a frustrated cat, and a black, rat-like form shot up the stairs between their legs. Jane let out a small scream of fright.

"It's all right," said Emma. "It's only a cat."

Christo opened the door, and went ahead, turning on cold overhead lights, for the flat was a furnished one, and not supplied with lamps. Johnny had started making a couple out of Chianti bottles but had got no further than buying adaptors and a pair of fancy shades. The rooms of the flat had been sketchily converted, and it was still sadly obvious that their original intentions had been kitchens, larders, and wash-houses. An old range had been torn from the wall, and the resultant void filled with shelves, which no one had ever bothered to paint, and which acted as a catch-all for books, shoes, scripts, cigarettes, letters and a pile of old magazines. There was a divan which had been covered with an orange curtain and piled with thinly-filled cushions, but remained stubbornly a bed. There were one or two rickety kitchen chairs and a folding table, and the flagged floor was sparsely covered by an elderly carpet which had long since lost all colour and most of its pile. The walls had been whitewashed, but there were oozing damp stains like maps, and the corners of a bull-fighting poster, stuck to the bricks, was already beginning to curl. There was the smell of mice and dry rot, and, even on this hot summer evening, the very airlessness was clammy, like the inside of a cave.

Christo dropped his script on a table and went to open the window which was protected with iron bars, like a prison.

"Let's have some air. We have to keep the place shut up because of the cats, they get in anywhere. What would you like to drink? . . . There is beer, if Johnny hasn't drunk it all . . . or perhaps you'd like coffee. Have we got any coffee, Emma . . . ?"

"There's some instant coffee. I don't get the other sort, because there's nothing to make it in. Do sit down . . . sit on the bed. Sit anywhere. There are some cigarettes . . ." She found them, a box of fifty, handed them round, searched for an ash-tray while Robert lit them. There was no ash-tray, so she went down the flagged passage to the kitchen for a couple of saucers. The sink was full of dirty dishes, and for a moment she could not think when they had used them, when she had last been here, from what back-log of history they dated. Pinned down, remembered, the morning seemed three weeks away. No day had ever lasted for longer. And now, it was past eleven o'clock at night, and still it was not over. Still, the boys had to be given their supper, the kettle boiled for coffee, the can-opener found.

She found two clean saucers and took them back to the others. Christo had put on a record. He could do nothing, not even talk, without perpetual background music. It was Ella Fitzgerald and Cole Porter.

Every time we say good-bye
I die a little.

They were talking about *Daisies on the Grass*. ". . . if you can breathe life into a script like that," Jane was saying to Christopher, ". . . I'm sure you're going to go far." She was laughing. Emma put down the ash-tray, and Jane looked up. "Thank you . . . is there anything I can do?"

"No, nothing. I'll just go and get some glasses. Would you like beer, or would you rather have coffee?"

"Would coffee be too much trouble?"

"No, not at all . . . I'd like coffee too . . ."

Back in the kitchen, she closed the door, so that they would not hear her clattering dishes, and tied on an apron, and put a kettle on to boil. When she lit the gas, it always backfired and frightened her out of her wits. She found a tray and cups and saucers, the tin of coffee, sugar, the cans of beer in a box beneath the sink. There were black beetles on the floor and Johnny had not emptied the trash can. She picked it up to take it out to the dustbin, but as she did so the door behind her opened, and she turned to face Robert Morrow.

He looked at the bucket. "Where are you taking that?"

"Nowhere," said Emma, furious at being caught. She turned to sling it back under the sink again, but he caught her arm and took it from her, looking with distaste at the mixture of old tea-leaves and of opened tins, and wet paperbags.

"Where does this go?"

Defeated, Emma told him. "In the dustbin. By the door. Where we came in."

He bore it off, down the passage, looking ridiculous, and Emma went back to the sink, and wished that he had not come. He didn't belong in Brookford; at the theatre; here, in the flat. She didn't want him to be sorry for her. For after all, there was nothing to be sorry about. She was happy, wasn't she? She was with Christo, and that was all that mattered, and how they managed their affairs had nothing whatever to do with Robert.

She prayed that he and his immaculate friend would be gone by the time Johnny Rigger returned.

When he came back with the empty bucket, she was clattering dishes, trying to give the impression that she was being busy. She half-turned over her shoulder and said coolly, "Thank you. I shan't be a moment," hoping that he would take the hint and leave her alone.

But it was no good. He shut the door, put the trash can down on the floor, and taking Emma by the shoulders, turned her round to face him. He wore an unrumpled and cool-looking suit, a blue shirt, and a dark tie, and Emma had the dish-mop in one hand and a plate in the other, and had to make herself look up and meet those probing grey eyes.

She said, "I wish you hadn't come. Why did you come?"

"Marcus has been worried about you." He took the dish-mop and the plate from her and leaned over to tip them back into the cluttered sink. "Perhaps you should have let him know where you were."

"Well, now you can tell him, can't you? And, Robert, I've got a lot to do, and there's just not room for two people in this kitchen . . ."

"Isn't there?" He was smiling. He settled himself on the edge of the table, and now his face was on a level with hers. He said, "You know, this evening, when I first saw you in the theatre I didn't know it was you. Why did you cut your hair?"

He could be very disarming. Emma put up a hand to stroke the stubbly nape of her neck. "When I started working at the theatre, it was such a nuisance. It got in the way, and then it was so hot, and it was always being splashed with paint when I was doing scenery. And there's nowhere here to wash it, and even if I did wash it, it took hours to dry." She hated talking about her hair. She missed it; missed its weight and familiarity and the soothing therapy of brushing it each night. "So one of the girls in the theatre cut it off for me." It had lain on the Green Room carpet like skeins of brown silk and Emma had felt like a murderer.

"Do you like working in the theatre?"

She thought of Collins. "Not much."

"Do you have to . . . ?"

"No, of course not. But Christo's there all day, you see, and there's nothing much to do here, on my own. Brookford's terribly dull. I didn't know such dull places even existed. So when this other girl went ill with appendicitis, Christo fixed it for me to go and help out."

"What will you do when she comes back?"

"I don't know. I haven't thought."

Behind her, the kettle boiled over. Emma turned swiftly to put out the gas, and lift the kettle on to the tray, but Robert said, "Not just yet."

She frowned. "I was going to make coffee."

"Coffee can wait. Let's get everything sorted out first."

Emma's face closed up. "There's nothing to sort out."

"Yes, of course there is. And I want to be able to tell Marcus what happened. For instance, how did you get hold of Christopher?"

"I rang him up – early that Sunday morning. I went to the call box and rang him up. They were having a dress rehearsal, so he was at the theatre. You see, he'd already asked me to come to Brookford and be with him, but I couldn't, because of Ben."

"You'd already spoken to him that morning, when I came to say goodbye?"

"Yes."

"And you never told me?"

"No, I didn't tell you. I wanted to start something quite new, a whole new life, without anybody knowing."

"I see. So you rang Christopher . . ."

"Yes, and that night he borrowed Johnny Rigger's car, and he came down to Porthkerris and brought me back here. We closed up the cottage together, and we left the key of the studio at the Sliding Tackle."

"The landlord didn't know where you were."

"I didn't tell him where I was going."

"Marcus phoned him."

"Marcus shouldn't have. Marcus isn't responsible for me any more. I'm not a little girl now."

"What Marcus feels is not simply responsibility, Emma, but a real fondness and you should realise that. Have you heard from Ben?"

"Yes, I had a letter on that Monday morning, before I left Porthkerris. And one from Melissa, too . . . asking me to go out and visit them."

"And did you write back?"

Emma shook her head. "No." She was ashamed of this, and swiftly looked down, to fiddle with a jagged thumbnail.

"Why not?"

She shrugged. "I don't know. I suppose I thought I'd be in the way."

"I should have thought that even being in the way was preferable to this . . ." His gesture embraced the littered kitchen, the whole seedy flat.

It was not the most fortunate of remarks. "What's wrong with it?"

"It's not just this place, it's that crumby theatre, the lunatic with a beard who was yelling at you to move the sofa . . ."

"Well, you told me to get a job."

"Not this kind of a job. You have a good brain, you speak three languages, and you appear to be moderately intelligent. What sort of a job is it pushing furniture around a third class re . . . ?"

"*My real job is being with Christo!*"

After this outburst, there was a terrible silence. A car passed in the street outside. Christopher's voice came up the stone passage, backed by the soft-playing record. A cat started yowling.

Robert spoke at last. "Do you want me to tell your father that?"

Emma blazed once more into the attack. "I supposed that's why you came. Spying for Ben."

"I simply came to find out where you were and how you were."

"Be sure to give him all the ghoulish details. It doesn't matter to us, and he won't take any notice, anyway."

"Emma . . ."

"Don't forget, he is no ordinary, run-of-the-mill parent, as you are only too fond of telling me."

"*Emma, will you listen . . . !*"

The last word was scarcely out of his mouth, when the door behind him burst open and a slurred and cheerful voice broke in. "Well, what a nice little chat you two are having!"

Robert wheeled. In the open doorway stood the young man who had played the part of the stuffy stockbroker in *Daisies on the Grass*. Only now he was stuffy no longer, but quite simply very drunk, and to steady himself hung on to the top of the doorway, like a monkey swinging on a trapeze. His legs, buckling slightly, did nothing to dispel this impression.

"Hello, darling," he said to Emma. He let go of the door and weaved into the tiny kitchen, rendering it unbearably crowded. With the palms of his hands flat on the table, he leaned forward to kiss Emma. The kiss was loud and smacking, but did not come within six inches of her face.

"We've got callers," he observed. "And a bloody great car parked outside. It adds great tone to the neighbourhood." His legs buckled again, and for a second his weight was supported solely by his arms. He smiled expansively at Robert. "What's your name?"

"He's called Robert Morrow," said Emma shortly, "and I'll make you some coffee."

"I don't want coffee. I do not want coffee." He raised his fist to the words, and once more his legs let him down. This time Robert caught him, and hauled him upright.

"Thanks, old boy. Very civil of you. Emma, how about a little sustenance? Feed the inner man; you know the routine. I do hope you've asked this nice chap Robert to stay for dinner. There's also a toothsome blonde in the other room, chatting Christopher up to no mean tune. Know anything about her?"

Nobody bothered to answer him. Emma turned back to the cooker, took the lid off the kettle and put it on again. Johnny Rigger stared at her back and then at Robert, apparently waiting for life, with all its confusions, to be explained to him.

Robert could not trust himself to speak. He yearned to pick up this shambling drunk by the scruff of his neck and chuck him somewhere; preferably in the dustbin, where he had just dumped the unsavoury contents of the trash can. Then he would come back to deal with Emma in the same way, flinging her into the back of his car, driving her to London, to Porthkerris, to Paris – anywhere, away from this terrible basement, from the theatre, from the depressing suburban town.

He stared at her stubborn back view, willing her to turn round and face up to him. But she did not move, and her thin neck, and her shorn head, and the droop of her shoulders, all of which, he knew, should touch on his sympathy, did nothing but infuriate him.

He said, at last, formally, "This is simply a waste of everybody's time. I think Jane and I should go."

Emma accepted this in silence, but Johnny was full of protests. "Oh, you must stay, old chap. Stay and have something to eat . . ."

But Robert had pushed past him and was already halfway down the flagged passage. He found the other two deep in conversation, and quite unaware of any sort of drama. Christopher was saying, "Yes, it's a wonderful play. And what a part! You can build on to it, yet never overload it, never interfere in any way with production . . ."

(And he remembered bitterly the old crack about actors. "Now, let's talk about *you*, my friend. What did *you* think of my performance?")

"I trust you're not discussing *Daisies on the Grass*."

Christopher looked round. "Good God, no! *Present Laughter*. What's Emma doing?"

"Your friend has just arrived back."

"Johnny? Yes, we just saw him tottering by."

"He's drunk."

"He quite often is. We fill him up with black coffee and shovel him into his bed. He's right as rain in the morning. Most unfair, really."

"Is there any particular reason why he should have to be here with you and Emma?"

Christopher raised his eyebrows. "Every reason." His voice was cool. "It's his flat. He got here first. I was second. Emma made a very cosy third."

There was a pause in the conversation. Jane, sensing the worst sort of conflict, broke tactfully in.

"Robert, it is getting late . . ." She picked up her bag and her gloves, and got up off the divan. ". . . Perhaps we should be going."

"But you haven't had your coffee. Or beer, or anything. What is Emma doing?"

"Doing her best to prop up Mr Rigger," Robert told him. "I suggest you go and help her. His legs don't seem to be at their most reliable."

Christopher, shrugging, acknowledged this. He uncurled his length from the low chair in which he had been sitting, and stood up. "Well, if you really feel you have to go . . ."

"I think we should. Thank you for . . ."

The words died out. There was nothing to thank him for. Christopher looked amused and Jane once again came to Robert's rescue.

". . . thank you for your wonderful performance this evening. We won't forget it." She held out her hand. "Goodbye."

"Goodbye. And goodbye, Robert."

"Goodbye, Christopher." And then he had to make himself say it. "Look after Emma."

They drove with unlawful speed back to London. On the motorway the needle of the speedometer crept up and up. Eighty, ninety, a hundred . . .

Jane said, "You're going to get into trouble."

"I already am," said Robert shortly.

"Did you have a row with Emma?"

"Yes."

"I thought you were looking a little fraught. What was it about?"

"Snooping. And moralising. And interfering. And trying to make a basically intelligent girl see the smallest glimmer of sense. She looked awful, too. She looked ill."

"She'll be all right."

"Last time I saw her, she was brown as a gipsy, with hair to her waist and a sort of bloom about her, like a delicious ripe fruit." He remembered the pleasure of kissing her goodbye. "Why do people have to do such dreadful things to themselves?"

"I don't know," said Jane. "Perhaps because of Christopher."

"How did you get on with him? I mean, apart from falling in love with him."

She ignored this. "He is clever. He is single-minded. He is ambitious. I think he will go far. But alone."

"You mean, without Emma."

"I'd say that."

Even at one in the morning London was alive with lights and traffic. They turned down into Sloane Street, circled Sloane Square, took the narrow road that led to Jane's mews. Outside

139

her little house, he killed the engine of the Alvis, and it was very quiet. Street lamps shone on to the cobbles, on to the gleaming bonnet of the car, on to Jane's blonde and shining head. Robert was suddenly very tired. He began to reach for a cigarette, but Jane was there first. She put the cigarette into his mouth and lit it for him. In that instant her eyes became large and mysteriously shadowed, and there was a small and beguiling shadow, like a smudge, below the curve of her lower lip.

She snapped out the lighter. He said, "It's been a bloody awful evening. And I'm sorry."

"It always makes a change. It was interesting."

He pulled off his cap and dropped it on to the back seat. "Do you suppose," he said, "that they're living together?"

"Darling, I wouldn't know."

"But she's in love with him."

"I would say so."

For a little they were silent. Then Robert stretched, flexing himself after the long drive. He said, "We never got any dinner, did we? I don't know about you, but I'm hungry."

"If you want, I'll cook you scrambled eggs. And pour you a big cold Scotch-on-the-rocks."

"You're twisting my arm . . ."

They laughed, quietly. Night time laughter, he thought. Pillow laughter. He put his left hand up and around her neck, slid his fingers up into her hair, and leaned forward to kiss her mouth. She tasted sweet and fresh and cool. Her lips parted, and he threw his cigarette away, and pulled her tightly and closely into his arms.

After a little, he took his mouth from hers. "What are we waiting for, Jane?"

"One thing."

He smiled. "What's that?"

"Me. I don't want to start something that isn't ever going to be finished. I don't want to be hurt again. Even for you, Robert, and God knows how fond I am of you."

He said, "I won't hurt you," and meant it, and kissed the shadow under her mouth.

"And please," she said, "no more Littons."

He kissed her eyes, and the end of her short nose. "It's a promise. No more Littons."

He let her go then, and they got out of the car, and closed the doors as quietly as they had laughed together. And Jane found her key, and Robert took it from her and opened the door, and they went in, and Jane turned on the light, and started up the narrow stairs, and Robert closed the door, gently, behind them.

9

One of the delights of the big old house in Milton Gardens was living there in the summer. At the end of a warm and stuffy June day, and after the frustrations of a snail's-pace, petrol-laden journey back down the Kensington High Street, it was a positive physical pleasure to come in through the front door and slam it with happy finality behind you. The house always felt cool. It smelt of flowers and wax-polish, and in June the chestnut trees were out and so thick with leaves and pink and white blossom that the surrounding terraces of houses were shrouded from sight, sounds of all traffic were muffled, and only the occasional aeroplane, passing overhead, broke the evening calm.

Today was a classic example of this particular relief. There was thunder about, and since morning the temperature had steadily risen as the storm clouds gathered. Beneath this doom-like atmosphere, the city sweltered. By now the parks were dusty and the trampled grass turning brown, and the air about as refreshing as a draught of used bath-water. But here, at home, Helen had the sprinklers working on the lawn, and a gust of sweet, damp air swept through the open door at the end of the hall, and greeted Robert as he came indoors.

He dropped his hat on the hall chair, picked up his letters, called ''Helen?''

She wasn't in the kitchen. He went down the hall and out of the door and down the steps to the terrace and found her there, with a tea-tray and a book – unread – and a basket of mending. She wore a sleeveless cotton dress and a faded pair of espadrilles, and the sun had brought freckles out, big as paint spots, across her nose.

He came across the grass towards her, shedding the jacket of his suit.

She said, "You have caught me, doing nothing."

"And very nice too." He slung the jacket over the back of a painted wrought-iron chair, and collapsed beside her. "What a day! Anything left in that teapot?"

"No, but I can make you some more."

"Why don't I?" said Robert automatically, but without notable enthusiasm.

She did not reply to this hypothetical question, simply got up and took the teapot indoors. There was a plate of biscuits, and he took one and began to eat it, pulling his tie loose with the other hand. Beneath the sprinklers the lawn lay thick and green. It needed cutting again. He leaned back and shut his eyes.

It was now six weeks since he had been to Brookford to find Emma Litton, and in all that time there had been no word from her. After some discussion with Marcus and Helen he had written to Ben, telling him that Emma was staying with Christopher Ferris, whom she had re-met in Paris. That she was working in the Repertory Theatre in Brookford. That she was well. He could not, in truth, say more. Surprisingly, Ben had acknowledged this, not directly, to Robert, but as a scribbled footnote to a letter to Marcus. The purpose of the letter itself was purely business, typewritten on the impressive engraved paper of the Ryan Memorial Museum of Fine Arts. The retrospective Litton Exhibition was now over. In every way it had been a resounding success. Now, the new exhibition – a posthumous collection of drawings of a Puerto Rican genius who had lately died in dismal circumstances in a Greenwich Village garret, was well under way, and he and Melissa were taking the opportunity of a trip to Mexico. He intended to start painting again. He did not know when he would be returning to London. He remained, always, Marcus's Ben. And then, under the signature, and in Ben's own indecipherable scrawl:

Had a letter from R. Morrow. Please thank him. Emma always fond of Christopher. Only hope his manners have improved.

Marcus showed this to Robert. "I don't know what you expected," he said, dryly, "but this is what you have got."

So it was over. For the first time Robert found himself in whole-hearted agreement with his sister Helen. The Littons were brilliant, unpredictable and charming. But they refused to conform to any pre-set behaviour pattern and they would not help themselves. So they were impossible.

To his surprise, he found that Emma was easy to forget. He could put her out of his mind as ruthlessly as an old trunkful of junk, relegated to the darkest recesses of some distant, dusty attic. And his life immediately became so full that the void left by her going was, almost at once, filled by more worthwhile pursuits.

At the Gallery, they were furiously busy. His days were a round of prospective clients, foreign visitors, and eager young artists carrying folios which bulged with their unsalubrious paintings. Would Bernstein mount an exhibition for them? Would Bernstein back this flame of new talent? The answer was usually, No, Bernstein's would not, but Marcus was a kindly man, and it was a house rule that no young man was returned to Glasgow or Bristol or Newcastle, or wherever it was he lived, without a good meal in his stomach, and the price of his return fare in the pocket of genuinely work-stained jeans.

Robert found that his vitality leapt to meet these demands, and, running at full speed, his energy could not – or would not – slow down. He could not bear to find himself doing nothing, and deliberately filled his leisure time with extraneous diversions, and a surprising number of them were involved with Jane Marshall.

The fact that their working hours did not always coincide put him off not at all. Sometimes he would call in for a drink at her little house, on the way home from the Gallery, and find her still in an apron, sewing braid on to yards of curtain, or working out the intricacies of a scalloped pelmet on graph paper. Sometimes she was out of town, and then he would fill the evening with furious physical labour, digging the garden or mowing the lawn.

One weekend he and Jane went down to Bosham, where Jane's brother had a small cottage, and kept a catamaran moored out on the choppy waters of the Hard. They sailed all Sunday and there was a stiff breeze and a bright, burning sun, and at the end of the day, sleepy with all the fresh air, they sat in the village pub and drank draught bitter and played shove ha'penny, and drove back to London very late, with the roof of the Alvis down, and wind blowing scraps of cloud across the face of the stars.

Once more Helen started saying, "I think you should marry her."

Robert ignored the nudging suspicion that he was behaving badly, and only said, "Perhaps I will."

"But when? What are you waiting for?"

He did not answer because he did not know. He only knew that this was not the time to plan; or assess; or to start to analyse the feelings that he had for Jane.

Now, he was disturbed, by Helen, returning with his tea-tray. She set it down, and the iron table grated on the pavings as she pulled it towards him. She said, "Marcus phoned at lunch-time."

Marcus had had to return to Scotland. The whisky-loving Scottish baronet, who had been so anxious to part with his art treasures, was being balked by his son, who would presumably inherit the heirlooms and did not want them sold out of hand. Or, if they were to be sold, he wanted three times as much for them as his thirsty father was prepared to ask. After a great deal of expensive telephoning, Marcus had reluctantly decided that another visit must be paid north of the border. Business must always come before personal comforts and preferences, and if, to lay his hands on those pictures, he had to sleep in damp beds and icy rooms and eat appallingly-cooked food, then he was ready to do so.

"How is he getting on?"

"He was reserved. No doubt speaking from some soaring baronial hall, with the old Laird listening from one end of the room, and the young Laird listening from the other."

"Has he got the pictures?"

"No, but he will. If not all, then some of them . . ." She went away from him, across the grass, to move the sprinkler. "The Raeburn he is determined on," she said, over her shoulder. "He'll go to any price."

Robert poured his tea, and began to read the evening paper. When Helen came back, he handed it to her open at a middle page.

"What's this?" she asked.

"That girl. Dinah Burnett . . ."

"Who is she?"

"You should know her face by now. She's a young actress with an efficient publicity agent. Every time you open a paper or a magazine, there's a picture of her perched on a piano, or cuddling a kitten or something equally obnoxious."

Helen made a comic face at the thrusting, sexy photograph, and read the caption aloud.

Dinah Burnett, the red-head who made such an impact on the TV series *Detective*, is in rehearsal now for the new Amos Monihan play *The Glass Door*, her first serious stake in legitimate theatre. "I'm scared," she told our special reporter. "But so very proud to have been chosen for this wonderful play." Miss Burnett is twenty-two and comes from Barnsley.

"I didn't know there was a new Amos Monihan play on the stocks. Who's producing?"

"Mayo Thomas."

"Then she must be good. Extraordinary, what talent can lurk behind really very stupid faces. But why did you suddenly show this to me?"

"No reason, really. Just that Jane's doing up a flat for her. At first it was going to be a pretty modest affair, but as soon as she got this part, she reckoned she'd moved in with the big-time spenders; you know, mirror bathrooms and white mink bedcovers."

"Very nice," said Helen. She tossed the paper back into his lap but he was too hot and lazy to catch it, so it slipped from his knee and fell to the ground. After a little, Helen began, in a

desultory fashion, to gather the tea things together. She picked
up the tray and started indoors.

"How about dinner?" she asked. "You going to Jane's or
are you staying here?"

"I'm going to Jane's."

"That's fine. I'll eat a piece of cheese. It's too hot to cook,
anyway."

When she had gone, he lit a cigarette and sat, listening to
the pigeons, and watching the shadows lengthen over the grass.
The cool and the quiet were like a benediction. The cigarette
finished, he got up and went back into the house, and upstairs to
his own flat, where he showered and shaved, and changed into
jeans and a cool shirt. As he was pouring the first drink of the
evening, the telephone rang. He filled the tumbler halfway up
with soda, and went to his desk to answer it. It was Jane.

"Robert?"

"Yes."

"Darling, it's me. Look I just wanted to warn you, don't get
here till about eight . . ."

"Why, are you entertaining a lover?"

"Wish I were. No, it's Dinah Burnett, she's had a new idea
for her bathroom, God rot her soul, and she wants to come along
after rehearsals and talk about it."

"For a girl who is so proud about being in the blasted play,
her mind does harp on material things, doesn't it?"

"So you've been reading the evening paper. That blurb
makes me ill."

"I can't think why she didn't bother to mention that she was
doing up a flat, and had chosen well-known interior decorator,
twenty-seven-year-old Jane Marshall, 34, 26, 36, to help her.
Were you expecting to be taken out for dinner, because I'm not
dressed accordingly."

"Of course not, it's much too hot. I've got some cold chicken; I thought I'd make a salad."

"And I shall subscribe a frosty bottle of wine."

"Delicious."

"Till eight, then."

"Yes, eight." He was on the point of putting down the receiver when she said again, "Don't come before," and then rang off. Mildly puzzled, he put down the receiver and then decided that he must have imagined a certain urgency in her voice. He went to find ice for his drink.

Deliberately, he was a little late, but even so, when he drew up outside Jane's house, there was a small blue Fiat still parked by her door. He gave his double toot on the horn and got out of the car, carrying the bottle of wine, and almost at once the front door opened and Jane stood there, in a faded pair of pink cotton trousers and a sleeveless top. Her hair fell across her cheek and she looked, for Jane, mildly distraught, making flapping gestures with her hand, and pointing upstairs.

He was amused. He came to kiss her. "What is it?"

She took the bottle of wine from him. "She's still here. She won't go. She won't stop talking. And now you've come, nothing's going to shift her."

"We'll say we're going out, and that we're late already."

"I suppose it's worth a try." They had been talking in whispers. Now she said in clear and social tones, "I wasn't sure if it was you or not. Come along up."

He followed her up the narrow, steep stairs. "Dinah, this is Robert Morrow . . ." Casually she introduced them, before going into the kitchen with the wine. He heard the big fridge door open and shut as she put it away.

Dinah Burnett sat on Jane's big sofa by the open window, with her legs curled up beneath her, looking as though she was expecting a photographer, or an interviewer, or a prospective lover. She was a beautiful girl, ripe and colourful, and it occurred to Robert that no photograph could do her full justice. She had auburn hair and pale green eyes, and skin like an apricot, and was built on proportions that are normally described as ''lavish''. She wore a short shift dress in a green to match her eyes, and it might have been designed to display as much as possible of her smooth, well-rounded arms and endless legs. Her feet were thrust into wooden sandals, her wrists jangled with gold bracelets and in her ears, gleaming through the profusion of hair, were enormous gold hoop ear-rings. Her teeth were white and even, and her black lashes long and black as soot, and it was hard to believe that she had started life in Barnsley.

''How do you do,'' said Robert. They shook hands. ''I've just been reading all about you in the evening paper.''

''Wasn't it a dreadful photograph?'' She still had an endearing trace of a Yorkshire accent. ''I look like a broken-down barmaid. But still, I suppose it's better than nothing.''

She smiled at him, all her feminine charm rising to the bait of a new and attractive man, and Robert, flattered and warmed by her friendliness, settled himself at the other end of the sofa. She went on, ''I shouldn't really be here at all, but Jane's doing up this new flat for me, and today I found this American magazine with a fabulous bathroom and I just had to bring it along, after rehearsals, and show it to her.''

''How's the play going?''

''Oh, it's most exciting.''

''What's it about?''

''Well, it's . . . .''

At this juncture Jane reappeared from the kitchen and briskly interrupted. ''How about a drink? Dinah, Robert and I are actually going out, but there's just time for a drink before you go.''

''Oh, that's sweet of you. If you're sure. I'd love a glass of beer.''

''How about you, Robert?''

''Sounds very nice, let me get it . . .''

''No, that's all right. I'm up.'' She snapped the top off a beer bottle, and poured a glass expertly, with no head to it. ''Dinah, Robert's an art dealer, he works in Bernstein's in Kent Street.''

''Oh, are you really?'' said Miss Burnett, looking wide-eyed and interested, but not very much wiser. ''Do you sell pictures and stuff. . . ?''

''Well, yes . . .''

Jane brought Dinah's beer across, pulled up a small table and set the glass down.

''Robert is a very high-powered man,'' she said. ''He's always dashing off to Paris or Rome, to pull off enormous deals, aren't you, Robert?'' She went back to her drink tray. ''Dinah, you should get him to look out for a picture for the new flat. You need something modern over that fireplace and you never know, it might be an investment. Something to sell when they run out of good parts for you.''

''Don't talk about running out. I've only just started. Besides, wouldn't it be very expensive?''

''Not as expensive as that American bathroom.''

Dinah smiled engagingly. ''But, I always feel a bathroom's terribly important.''

Jane had poured two more drinks, now she brought them over, and handed one to Robert. Then settled herself in the chair opposite the sofa, and faced them both across the low table.

''Well, it's your flat, ducky,'' she said.

Her voice was a little acid. Robert said quickly, ''You still haven't told me about the new play . . . *The Glass Door*. When are you opening?''

''Wednesday. This Wednesday as ever is. At the Regent Theatre.''

''We must try and get seats, Jane.''

''Yes, of course,'' said Jane.

''The thought of a first night makes me sick with nerves. You see, it's my first shot at the living theatre, as it were, and if it wasn't for Mayo being such a fabulous producer I'd have dropped out weeks ago . . .''

''You still haven't told us what it's about.''

''Well, it's . . . oh, I don't know. It's about this young man, from an ordinary, working-class family. And he writes a book and it's a best seller, and he becomes a sort of celebrity – you know, on television and such. And then he gets mixed up with the film people, and all the time, he's getting richer, and nastier, and he's drinking and having affairs, and generally living it up. And then, of course, in the end, the whole racket falls round his ears like a pack of cards and he finishes up, right where he started, in his mother's house, in the kitchen, with his old typewriter and a blank sheet of paper. It sounds corny, I know, but it's moving and real and the dialogue is out of this world.''

''Do you think it's going to go?''

''I don't see how it can fail. But then I'm prejudiced.''

''What part do you play?''

''Oh, I'm just one of the many girls. But I'm different, because I get pregnant.''

''Charming,'' murmured Jane.

''But it isn't sordid, not a bit,'' Dinah assured her. ''When I first read the script I didn't know whether to laugh or cry. Real life, I suppose.''

"Yes." Jane finished her drink, and put down the empty glass and looked at her watch. She said, pointedly, "Robert, I'm going up to change. We mustn't be late. We'll keep everybody waiting." She stood up. "You'll excuse me, Dinah, won't you?"

"Of course I will, and thank you for being so sweet about the bathroom. I'll ring you up and let you know what I've decided."

"Yes, you do that."

When she had gone upstairs, Dinah smiled once more, confidingly, at Robert. "I hope I'm not keeping you. I will go when I've finished my drink, but I live in such a dump just now, it's depressing. And it's so hot, isn't it? I wish it would thunder. It would be so much cooler if only it would thunder."

"It will this evening, I'm sure. Tell me, how did you get this part?"

"Well, Amos Monihan, you know, he wrote the play – he'd seen me on TV in *Detective*, and he rang Mayo Thomas and said he thought I'd be right for the part. So I had an audition. That's all really."

"And who plays the lead? The young man. The writer?"

"This is the gamble. The backers wanted a big name, somebody famous. But Mayo had found this new boy – he'd seen him in some provincial rep, and somehow, he convinced the man with the money to give him a try."

"So you have an unknown in the lead?"

"That's about it," said Dinah. "But, believe me, he's good."

She finished her drink. Upstairs Jane was moving about in her bedroom, going to and fro, opening and shutting drawers. Robert got up to retrieve the empty glass. "Would you like the other half?"

"No, really, I won't. I mustn't keep you any longer . . ."

She stood up, pulling down her dress, and tossing her long hair away from her neck. She called up the stair. "I'm off. Goodbye, Jane!"

"Oh, goodbye." Jane sounded more friendly now that her visitor was actually on her way out.

Dinah started downstairs, and Robert followed her, intending to politely see her off the premises. Over her bright head, he leaned forward to unsnib the latch of Jane's front door. Outside, the mews slumbered in the hot airless evening.

He said, "I'll keep my fingers crossed for Wednesday."

"Bless you."

They went out into the street. He opened the door of the Fiat for her. He said, "What's he called, this young actor?"

Dinah slid into the driving-seat, revealing more leg than was good for anybody's blood pressure.

She said, "Christopher Ferris."

He thought, *So that's why Jane didn't want me to meet you.*

"Christopher Ferris? I know him."

"Do you? How funny."

"At least . . . I knew his sister."

"I don't know anything about his family."

"He's never mentioned her? Emma?"

"Never a word. But then, chaps don't usually talk about their sisters, do they?"

She laughed, and slammed the car door shut, but the window was down, and Robert leaned his elbow on it, like a salesman with a foot in the door.

He said, "I'd like to wish him luck."

"I'll give him a message for you tomorrow."

"Could I ring him up?"

"Well, I suppose you could, but calls aren't exactly welcome when we're working." And then she had a bright idea. "Tell you what, I've got his home number somewhere. I had to ring up for Mayo, once, and leave a message.''

She picked her bag off the other seat, and started to delve. She brought out a script, a purse, a scarf, a bottle of sun oil, a diary. She leafed through the diary. "Here it is, Flaxman 8881. Do you want me to write it down for you?"

"No. I'll remember."

"He might be there now . . . I don't know what he does in his spare time." She smiled again. "Fancy you knowing him. It's a small world, isn't it?"

"Yes. It's a small world."

She started up her engine. "Well, it's been fun meeting you. Cheerio."

He stood back. "Goodbye."

The little car roared away down the mews, and he watched it go. At the junction at the end of the narrow street it paused for a moment, then shot away, turned left and was gone, the sound of its engine swallowed into the anonymous grumble that was London traffic.

He went back into the house, closed the door, went upstairs. There was no sound from the bedroom.

"Jane."

She began immediately to move about, as though occupied.

"Jane."

"What is it?"

"Come here."

"But I'm not . . ."

"Come down here."

After a moment, she appeared at the head of the stairs, wrapped in a thin dressing-gown. "What is it?"

"It's Christopher Ferris," said Robert.

She stared down at him, her expression closed and suddenly implacable.

"What about him?"

"You knew he was in this play. That he's been in London all this time."

She came down the stairs towards him. When her face was on a level with his, she said coolly, "Yes, I knew."

"But you never told me. Why not?"

"Perhaps because I don't believe in stirring up muddy ponds. Besides, you promised. No more Littons."

"This has nothing to do with that promise."

"Then what are you getting so hot and bothered about? Look, Robert, I think I feel about this business much the same way as your sister Helen. Bernstein's act, in a professional capacity, for Ben Litton, and after that, their commitments to the family should end. I know about Emma and the sort of life she's led and I'm sorry for her. I went to Brookford with you, and I saw that creepy little theatre and that dreadful flat. But she is adult, and, as you said yourself, highly intelligent . . . What if Christopher is in London? That doesn't mean Emma has been abandoned. It's a part of his job, and she'll accept it as such, I'm sure."

"That still doesn't explain why you never told me."

"Perhaps because I knew all along that you'd start running round in circles like a demented sheepdog. Imagining the worst, nagged by responsibility, simply because the wretched girl is Ben Litton's daughter. Robert, you *saw* her. She doesn't want to be helped. And if you try, you'll just be interfering . . ."

He said slowly, "I don't know if you're trying to convince me, or yourself."

"You fool, I'm trying to make you see the truth."

"The truth is that, as far as we know, Emma Litton is alone, living in a damp basement with a paralytic drunk."

157

"Isn't that what she chose to do?"

She flung the question at him, and then, before he could reply, pushed past him and went to the trolley and began fiddling about with empty glasses and beer-bottle tops in a feeble pretence at tidying up. He watched, with a great sadness, her back view, the smooth bell of hair, the tiny waist, the small, capable hands. She was unrelenting.

He said gently, "Dinah Burnett gave me Christopher's number. Perhaps it would be better if I rang him from here."

"Do whatever you like." She carried the glasses through to the kitchen. Robert picked up her phone and dialled the remembered number. Jane came back to collect up the empty bottles.

"Hello." It was Christopher.

"Christopher, this is Robert Morrow speaking. You remember, I came down to Brookford . . ."

"To see Emma. Yes, of course. How splendid! How did you know where to find me?"

"Dinah Burnett gave me your number. She also told me about *The Glass Door*. Congratulations."

"You can save them till we see what the critics have to say."

"Still, it's a great effort. Look, I was wondering about Emma."

Christopher's voice turned cautious. "Yes?"

Jane had come back from the kitchen and now stood by the window, her arms folded, looking down into the street.

"Where is she?"

"In Brookford."

"In the flat. With your friend?"

"My friend? Oh, Johnny Rigger? No, he left. He came to rehearsals drunk one morning and the producer slung him out. Emma's on her own."

Carefully controlling his temper, Robert said, "You never thought of ringing up Marcus Bernstein or myself and telling us this?"

"Well, I would have, but before I left Brookford, Emma made me promise not to. So, you see, I couldn't." While Robert, in seething silence, tried to accept this excuse, Christopher went on, sounding suddenly much younger and not so sure of himself. "I tell you what I did do, though. I felt a bit of a heel leaving her like that . . . so I wrote to Ben."

"You wrote to *who*?"

"Her father."

"But what the hell could he do? He's in America . . . he's in Mexico . . ."

"I didn't know he was in Mexico, but I wrote to him care of Bernstein's, and put please forward on the envelope. You see, I felt *someone* should know what had happened."

"And Emma? Is she still working in the theatre?"

"She was when I left. You see, there was really no point her coming up to London with me. I rehearse dawn to dusk as it is, and we'd never have seen each other. Besides, if *The Glass Door* folds up after a week, then I'll need my old Brookford job back again. Tommy Childers is very kindly keeping it open for me. So we decided it would be better if Emma stayed down there."

"And if *The Glass Door* runs for two years?"

"I don't know what would happen then. But right now, I'll be honest with you, things are a bit tricky. This house I'm living in – it belongs to my mother. I'm living with my mother. You can see, what with things being the way they are, it is a bit tricky."

"Yes," said Robert. "Yes, I can see . . . as you say, it's tricky."

*

He put down the receiver. Jane, not turning from the window, said, "What's so tricky?"

"He's living with Hester, his mother. And she's obviously refusing to let a Litton darken her door. Silly old bitch. And the drunk flatmate has had the sack, so Emma's on her own. And, to ease his conscience, Christopher has written to Ben Litton to tell him what has happened. And I should like to tie the lot of them together with one great big millstone, and consign them all to a bottomless lake."

"I knew this would happen," said Jane. She turned, then, to face him, her arms still rigidly folded, and he saw that she was not only angry, but deeply upset. "It could be good, this thing between us . . . you know that, don't you, as well as I do. And that's why I didn't tell you about Christopher, because I knew, that if you knew, it would be the end of everything."

He wished he could say *It doesn't have to be the end*, but it was impossible.

"In a way, Robert, all this time, you did keep your promise. You never mentioned Emma. But she was never out of the back of your mind."

Now that it was said, and out in the open, he saw that this was true. He said, hopelessly, "Only because in some extraordinary way, I am involved with her."

"If you are involved with her, it's because you want to be. And it's not good enough, Robert. Not for me. I won't settle for second best. I'd rather go without. I hoped I'd made that clear. With me, it has to be all or nothing at all. I can't go through it all again."

He understood. But could only say that he was sorry.

"I think . . . perhaps, you'd better go."

Her arms were still folded, a barrier against him. There was no way to say goodbye. He could not kiss her. He could not lightly say, ''It's been fun'' in the best traditions of drawing-room comedy. And he could never forgive her for trying to keep him from Emma.

He said, ''I'll go now.''

''Yes, do that.'' But as he started downstairs, she remembered something. ''You left the wine.''

''Forget about the wine,'' said Robert.

10

The song was over. The lights were dimmed. Charmian as Oberon moved forward for her final speech. The taped Mendelssohn music – for the meagre proportions of the Brookford Rep did not allow space for an orchestra – stole out across the dark cave of the auditorium and evoked for Emma, sitting at the prompt desk – all the distilled magic of a summer night.

> Now until the break of day
> Through this house each fairy stray . . .

It was the end of the first week of *A Midsummer Night's Dream*. The financial fiasco of *Daisies on the Grass* had driven the management to a production of Shakespeare which, although it entailed double the work for everybody, ensured an Arts Council grant and full houses, composed mostly of school children and students.

By now Emma was no longer working for Collins, the stage manager. There was a new ASM, a young girl fresh from drama school, dedicated, tough and seemingly immune to Collins' barbed tongue. She was on-stage now, in the grey velvet tunic and silvered wings of Cobweb, the fairy, for the huge cast of *The*

Dream demanded that every member of the company should be called in and given a part.

Because of this, Tommy Childers had asked Emma to come back and lend a hand with the back-stage activities. During the past fortnight she had coped with a number of jobs; helping in the wardrobe, working in the scenery store; typing scripts, and all the time nipping out for sandwiches and cigarettes, and making endless pots of tea.

Tonight, she had been given the job of prompter, and had spent the evening with her eyes glued to the prompt copy, terrified of losing her place, of missing a cue, of letting somebody down. But now, as the play drew to its close, and, knowing the rest of it by heart, she allowed her concentration to relax a little, and indulged in the luxury of watching the stage.

Charmian wore a crown of emerald leaves, a silver tabard and silver tights on her long, slim legs. The audience, caught by the old magic of the words, stayed breathless, spellbound.

Trip away; make no stay;
Meet me all by break of day.

To eke out the cramped wing space on either side of the stage, Tommy Childers had had built a ramp which led down from the stage and into the centre aisle of the auditorium. Now Oberon and Titania, hand-in-hand, and followed by a retinue of fairies, made their exit down this ramp, running, with the draperies flying like exuberant wings, off the lighted stage, and down into the darkness; swift and quiet; up the aisle and out of the double doors at the back with such an airy suddenness that they were gone almost without a sound, without a trace.

And then it was left to Sara Rutherford, playing Puck, as

a tilt-eared teenager, with the stage to herself and a single spotlight.

If we shadows have offended,
Think but this, and all is mended.

She had a little pipe. When she got to "So good night unto you all," she played on it the single thread of notes that was the theme of the Mendelssohn music.

Then, triumphant, "Give me your hands, if we be friends, and Robin shall restore amends." And darkness, and curtain, and applause.

All over. Emma let out a sigh of relief that nothing had gone wrong, shut the prompt copy and sat back in her chair. The cast were surging back on stage for the first curtain call. As he went past her, the boy who played Nick Bottom leant over to whisper,

"Tommy asked me to tell you – there's some chap waiting to see you. He's been sitting in the Green Room for half an hour, but Tommy's put him in his office. Thought it might be a bit more private for you. Better go and see what it's all about."

"To see me? But who is it?"

But Bottom was already on stage. The curtain swept up, there was a fresh burst of applause, and smiles and bows and curtsies . . .

Emma's first thought was that it was Christo. But if it was Christo, why hadn't he said? She went down the wooden steps and along the cat-walk that led to the landing at the head of the stage door stairs. Ahead, down a short passage, the Green Room door stood ajar, showing a glimpse of sagging velvet sofa, the old playbills framed on the walls. Tommy Childers's office led off this passage. The door was shut.

Behind her, the applause died down, and then rose again for the second curtain call.

She opened the door.

It was a tiny room, scarcely bigger than a cupboard; scarcely big enough to contain the desk, and a couple of chairs and a filing cabinet. He sat behind the desk, in Tommy's chair, behind Tommy's personal and private chaos of scripts and letters and programme proofs and production notes. The wall behind him was thumb-tacked with stage photographs. Someone had made him a cup of tea, but he had not deigned to drink it, and it stood before him, horribly cold, untouched. He wore pearly-grey trousers, a russet corduroy jacket, a dark blue cotton shirt and a chrome yellow tie, loosely tied, so that his top button showed. He was browner than ever, and he looked about ten years younger, and almost indecently attractive.

He was smoking an American king-size cigarette, and an ashtray full of butts was indicative of the length of time he had been waiting for Emma. When she came through the door, he turned his head to look at her, resting his elbow on the desk, his chin on his thumb. His eyes, through the veil of cigarette smoke, remained dark and shadowed and quite unreadable.

He said, sounding mildly irritated, "What have you been doing?" and Emma was too stunned to do anything but tell him.

"Prompting."

"Well, come along in and shut the door."

She did as she was told. The applause from the auditorium was closed away. She found that her heart was thudding, but whether this was due to shock, or pleasure, or a certain apprehension it was impossible to know. She said at last, feebly, "I thought you were in America."

"I was, this morning. Flew back today. And yesterday . . . at least I suppose it was yesterday, these International date lines

and clocks being changed complicate life to an alarming degree
. . . I was in Mexico. Yes; yesterday. Acapulco.''

Emma felt for a chair, lowered herself gently on to it before
her legs gave way.

"Acapulco?"

"Do you know that the aeroplanes that fly to Acapulco are
all painted different colours? And as you go south, the air
hostesses do a sort of uniform strip tease. Fascinating.'' He
continued to survey her. "Emma, there's something different
about you. That's it, you've cut your hair. What a good idea!
Turn around and let me see the back.'' She did so, swivelling her
head cautiously, and watching him out of the corner of her eye.
"Much better. Never knew you had such a good shape to your
head. Have a cigarette.''

He pushed the packet across the desk. Emma took one, and he
lit it for her, leaning forward, cupping the flame with his familiar
and beautiful hands. As he shook out the match he said, casually,
"A great many letters have been winging their way across the
Atlantic. None of them written by you.''

It was a rebuke. "No. I know.''

"Difficult to understand. Not that I minded in particular –
though I must say, as it was about the first letter I'd ever written
you, it would have been pleasant to get a reply. But with Melissa
it was different. She wanted you to come out to the States, and
be with us, if only for a short visit. You've always been rather
good about these things. What happened?''

"I don't know. I suppose I was . . . disappointed because you
didn't come home. And the idea of your being married took a
bit of time to get used to. And then, by the time I got round to
accepting it . . . it had become too late to answer your letters. And
every day that passed made it worse; made it more impossible.
I never knew that if you did something you weren't particularly

proud of . . . it became progressively more difficult to undo it again.'' He did not comment on this. Simply continued to smoke, to watch her. ''You said a great many letters. Who else did you hear from?''

''Well, I heard from Marcus, of course. That was business. And then a rather stilted, formal affair from Robert Morrow. Saying that he'd been here to see some play or other, and had had a drink with you and Christopher. I couldn't gather, however, whether he had come specifically to see the play or to see you.''

''Yes. Well . . .''

''As soon as we realised that you were still alive and apparently occupied and with no intention of visiting us, Melissa and I set off in our coloured aeroplane for Mexico where we stayed with a mad old film star who lives in a house full of parakeets. Then, yesterday, we flew back to Queenstown, and what should I find waiting for me but yet another letter.''

''From Robert?''

''No. From Christopher.''

She could not help it. ''From *Christopher*?''

''He must be an exceptionally talented young man. A London production, so soon, with so little experience. Of course, I always knew that he'd make a flagrant success of his life. Either that or end up in prison . . .''

But even this provocation could not divert her. ''You mean *Christopher*? Wrote to *you*?''

''Said in that tone of voice, it sounds insulting.''

''But why?''

''One can only imagine that he felt mildly responsible.''

''But . . .'' An idea was forming. A suspicion so wonderful that, if it was not true, then it must be scotched immediately. ''But you didn't come home because of that letter? You came home to paint. To go back to Porthkerris and paint again?''

"Well, of course, taking the long view, I have. Mexico was inspiring. They have an extraordinary pink that keeps recurring in their buildings, and their pictures, and their very clothes . . ."

"Perhaps you'd had enough of Queenstown, and America," she persisted. "You've never been much good at staying in any one place for more than a couple of months. And, of course, you'll have to see Marcus. And start thinking about a new exhibition."

He stared at her blankly. "Why this catalogue of motives?"

"Well, there has to be some reason."

"I've just told you. I came to see you."

She did not want the cigarette he had given her. She leaned forward and stubbed it out, and then clasped her hands in her lap, the palms pressed tight together, the fingers interlaced. Misinterpreting her silence, Ben looked aggrieved. "I don't think, Emma, that you quite understand the situation. I literally flew in from Mexico, read Christopher's letter, kissed Melissa goodbye and flew out again. Didn't even have time to change my shirt. I then subjected myself to another twelve hours of flying, the tedium broken only by a series of uneatable meals, all of which tasted like plastic. Do you think I endure such tortures simply to talk to Marcus Bernstein about another exhibition?"

"But Ben . . ."

He was, however, well away, and in no mood to be interrupted.

"And, once arrived, do I go to Claridges, where Melissa has thoughtfully cabled in advance and reserved me a room? Do I indulge in a bath, or a drink, or a decent meal? No. I climb into the slowest taxi-cab this side of the Atlantic, and drive, through unspeakable rain, to Brookford" (he said the word as though it were something distasteful), "where, after interminable incorrect directions, I eventually run the repertory theatre to earth.

The taxi is at this moment outside, ticking up a monumental fare. And if you don't believe me, you can go and look.''

''I believe you,'' said Emma, quickly.

''And then, when you do deign to appear, all you can talk about is Marcus Bernstein and some hypothetical exhibition. Do you know something? You're an ungrateful brat. A typical example of the modern generation. You don't deserve to have a father.''

She said, ''But I've been alone before. For years I've been alone. In Switzerland and Florence and Paris. You never came to see me then.''

''You didn't need me then,'' said Ben flatly. ''And I knew what you were doing, and who you were with. This time, when I read that letter from Christopher, I knew the first, faint stirrings of concern. Perhaps because Christopher, of all people, would never have written if he hadn't been concerned himself. Why didn't you tell me you'd met him in Paris?''

''I thought you wouldn't be pleased.''

''It depends on what sort of a person he's turned into. Has he changed very much from the small boy who lived with us at Porthkerris?''

''He looks the same . . . but he's tall . . . he's a man now. Single-minded and ambitious and, perhaps, a little self-centred. And with all the charm in the world.'' Talking about him, to Ben, was like having a weight lifted from her shoulders. Emma smiled. She said, ''And I adore him.''

Ben, accepting this, returned the smile. ''You sound like Melissa, talking about Ben Litton. It seems that young Christopher and I have, after all, much in common. It's ironic that we should have wasted so many years in detesting each other. Perhaps I should make his acquaintance again. This time, we might get on a little better.''

"Yes, I think you might."

"Melissa is joining me in a week or two. Coming down to Porthkerris."

"Living at the cottage?" said Emma, unbelieving.

Ben was amused. "Melissa? At the cottage? You must be joking. A suite has already been reserved at The Castle Hotel. I shall lead the life of a goldfish in a bowl, but perhaps, as I get older, the sybaritic existence is beginning to reveal its charms."

"But didn't she mind? Your coming home like that? Kissing her and leaving her without even taking time to change your shirt?"

"Emma, Melissa is a clever woman. She doesn't try to pin a man down or to possess him. She knows that the best way to hold on to someone you love is to . . . very gently . . . let him go. Women take a long time to learn this. Hester never did. How about you?"

"I'm learning," said Emma.

"The extraordinary thing is, I believe you are."

By now, darkness had fallen. This had happened, unheeded, while they talked, the dusk deepening imperceptibly until Ben's face, across the tiny distance that separated them, was simply a blur, his hair a wing of white. There was a lamp on the desk, but neither of them reached out to turn it on. The twilight enclosed them, the shut door kept the rest of the world out. They were the Littons; a family; together.

As they talked, the backstage shell of the theatre had rung with routine sounds. The last curtain call. Voices; Collins swearing at some unfortunate electrician. Hurrying feet, running upstairs to the dressing-rooms, anxious to be away, to be free of costumes and make-up, to catch buses, to go home, to cook food and wash stockings and, perhaps, to make love. Footsteps passed to and fro, in and out of the Green Room, *Darling, have you got a cigarette? Where's Delia? Has anybody seen Delia? There wasn't a phone call for me, was there?*

The sounds thinned out, as in twos and threes they left the theatre. Down the stone stairs, out of the banging door, into the narrow alley. A car started up. Somewhere a man started to whistle.

Behind Emma the door was abruptly opened, and the soft darkness split with an oblong of yellow light.

"Sorry to interrupt you . . ." It was Tommy Childers . . . "Wouldn't you like some illumination?" He snapped on the switch, and Ben and Emma were transfixed, blinking, like a couple of sleepy owls. "I just wanted something off my desk, before I go home."

Emma stood up, pulling her chair out of the way.

"Tommy, did you know this was my father?"

"I wasn't sure," said Tommy, smiling at Ben. "I thought you were in America."

"Everybody thought I was in America. Even my wife did until I said goodbye to her. I hope we haven't inconvenienced you, sitting here for so long in your office."

"Not at all. The only thing is the night-watchman's getting a bit edgy about the stage door. I'll tell him you'll shut it, Emma."

"Yes, of course."

"Well . . . Good night, Mr Litton . . ."

Ben heaved himself to his feet. "I had thought of taking Emma to London with me tonight. You wouldn't have any objections to that?"

"None at all," said Tommy. "She's been working like a slave for the past two weeks. Do her good to have a few days off."

Emma said, "I don't know why you ask Tommy, when you haven't even asked me."

"I don't ask you things," Ben said. "I tell you."

Tommy laughed. He said, "In that case, I expect you'll be going to the first night."

Ben remained vague. "First night?"

Dryly, Emma enlightened him. "He means Christopher's private view. On Wednesday."

"So soon? I shall probably be back in Porthkerris by then. We shall have to see."

"You should try and make it," said Tommy. They shook hands. "It's been splendid meeting you. And Emma . . . I'll see you sometime . . ."

"Maybe next week if *The Glass Door* folds up . . ."

"It won't," said Tommy. "If what Chris did to *Daisies on the Grass* is anything to go by, it'll run as long as *The Mousetrap*. Don't forget to shut the door."

He went away, downstairs; they heard his footsteps fade down the alley below the window, out into the street. Emma sighed. She said, "I think we should go. The night-watchman gets traumas if he thinks the place isn't properly locked up. And that taxi driver of yours will either give up hope of ever seeing you again, or else die of old age."

But Ben had once more settled himself into Tommy's chair. "In a moment," he said. "There's just one more thing." He tapped a fresh cigarette from the American packet. "I wanted to ask you about Robert Morrow."

He had the most disconcertingly calm voice. It never changed or varied its inflections so that you were continuously being taken unawares. Every nerve in Emma's body leapt in warning, but she only said, casually enough, "What about him?"

"I always had a . . . strong feeling about that young man."

173

She tried being flippant. "You mean, apart from admiring the shape of his head."

He ignored this. "I asked you once if you liked him, and you said, 'I suppose so. I scarcely know him.'"

"What of it?"

"Do you know him any better now?"

"Well, yes, I suppose I do."

"When he came to Brookford that time, he wasn't simply visiting the theatre, was he? He came to see you."

"He came to find me. That isn't quite the same thing."

"But he took the trouble to find you. I wonder why."

"Perhaps he was prompted by the famous Bernstein sense of responsibility."

"Stop fencing."

"What do you want me to say?"

"I want you to tell me the truth. And to be honest with yourself."

"What makes you think I haven't?"

"Because a light has gone out of your eyes. Because I left you at Porthkerris, blooming and brown as a gipsy. Because of the way you sit, the way you talk, the way you look." He lit the cigarette then, broke the match, and dropped it meticulously into the ash-tray. "Perhaps you forget I've been watching people, dissecting their personalities, painting them, for more years than you've been alive. And it's not Christopher who's made you unhappy. You've as good as told me that yourself."

"Perhaps it was you."

"Rubbish? A father? Angry, maybe. Hurt and resentful. Never heart-broken. Tell me about Robert Morrow. What went wrong?"

The little room was suddenly unbearably stuffy. Emma got up and went to the window, and opened it wide, leaning her elbow on the sill, and breathing in great draughts of cool, rain-washed air.

She said, "I suppose I never bothered to understand what sort of a person he really was."

"I don't understand."

"Well . . . meeting him, for the first time, the way I did. That started everything off on the wrong foot. I never thought of him as a person with a private life, and a private existence, and likes and dislikes . . . and lovers. He was just part of Bernstein's, as Marcus is part of Bernstein's. Simply there to look after us. To arrange exhibitions, and cash cheques and reserve hotel accommodation, and make sure that life, for the Littons, at least, runs on oiled wheels." She turned to frown at her father, puzzled by her own revelation. "How *could* I have been so moronic?"

"You probably inherited it from me. What put an end to this happy illusion?"

"Oh, I don't know. Things. He came down to Porthkerris to look at Pat Farnaby's pictures, and he asked me to go out to Gollan with him, because he didn't know the way. And it was raining, and very stormy, and he had a big thick sweater on, and we laughed about things. I don't know, but it was nice. And we were going to have dinner together, but he . . . well . . . anyway, I had a headache, so I didn't go after all. And then I came to Brookford to be with Christo, and I didn't think about Robert Morrow any more until that evening when he came to the theatre. I was clearing the stage, and suddenly he spoke, just behind me, and I turned round and he was there. And he had this girl with him. She's called Jane Marshall, and she's an interior decorator, or something very talented. She's pretty, and successful, and they seemed so much a couple. Do you know what I mean? Contained and self-sufficient and . . . together. And I felt as though someone had slammed a door in my face and left me out in the cold.''

She turned from the window then, and came back to the desk and sat on it, with her back to her father, and picked up a rubber band and began to play with it, snapping it like a catapult through her fingers.

''And they came back to the flat, for a beer or a coffee or something, and everything was hideous, and Robert and I had a horrible row, and he just walked out without saying goodbye and took Jane Marshall with him. And drove back to London, and, one imagines . . .'' she tried desperately to keep her voice light, ''. . . lived happily ever after. Anyway, I haven't seen him since.''

''Is that why you wouldn't let Christopher tell him that you were on your own?''

''Yes.''

''Is he in love with this girl?''

''Christo thought he was. Christo thought she was gorgeous. He said that if Robert didn't marry her, he ought to have his head examined.''

''And what was the row about?''

Emma could scarcely remember. In retrospect, it jarred as painfully as a gramophone record, played backwards, at full pitch. An exchange of shouted words, meaningless, hurtful, regretted.

''Oh, everything. You. And not answering your letter. And Christo. I think he imagines Christo and I are madly in love, but by the time we'd got round to that I was so angry I didn't bother to disillusion him.''

''Perhaps that was a mistake.''

''Yes, perhaps it was.''

''Do you want to stay here, at Brookford?''

"There's nowhere else to go."

"There's Porthkerris."

Emma turned to smile down at him. "With you? At the cottage?"

"Why not?"

"A thousand reasons. Running home to Daddy never solved anything. Besides, you can't run away from the inside of your own head."

He was on his way at last, and the self-delusion and the restlessness of the past six weeks were over. The Alvis – like a home-bound hunter – streamed west, out over the Hammersmith fly-over and on to the M4. Robert settled her permanently in the fast outer lane, and kept her speedometer prudently, carefully down to seventy, for the frustration, at this stage, of being stopped by a police patrol would be almost more than he could bear. As he approached Heathrow Airport, the first rumble of thunder broke the heavy, quiet air, and he stopped in at the first lay-by and put up the hood. He was only just in time. As he moved out into the road again, the sullen evening erupted like a volcano. The wind, with staggering abruptness, swept up from the west, bearing towering black thunderheads before it, and when the rain came it was a positive explosion of water, sheets of it, like a monsoon downpour, against which the windscreen-wipers could scarcely compete. In seconds, the surface of the road was awash, reflecting the livid streaks of forked lightning which split the sky.

It occurred to him that perhaps it would be wise to stop, and wait until the worst of the storm was over, but by now his sense of relief at doing what he had for weeks been subconsciously wanting to do, was stronger than any ideas of caution. So he went on, and the huge cambered curve of the motorway pouted

177

up towards him, and roared beneath his wheels, and was flung away in a wave of water; already a thing of the past; rejected and forgotten, along with his own feeble uncertainties.

He found the theatre closed. By the light of the street lamp, he was able to read the posters. A MIDSUMMER NIGHT'S DREAM. Unlit, deserted, the place looked gloomy as the mission hall it had once been. The door was barred and bolted; all the windows dark.

He got out of the car. It was cooler now, and he reached into the back seat and took out a sweater that had been lying there since the Bosham weekend, and pulled it on over his shirt. He slammed the door shut, and then saw the solitary taxi, waiting at the pavement's edge, the driver slumped over his wheel. He might have been dead.

"Is there anyone in there?"

"Must be, Guv-nor. I'm waiting for a fare."

Robert walked down the pavement, as far as the narrow lane, down which, so long ago, Emma and Christopher had come, walking like lovers, with their arms about each other. On this side of the sombre building a first-floor window blazed with uncurtained light. He went down the shadowed alley, tripped over a dustbin, found an open door. Inside, a flight of stone stairs led upwards, illuminated palely from a light which burned on the first-floor landing. He was assailed by the stale theatre smell of grease-paint, oil-paint, musty velvet. From above came the murmur of voices and he went upstairs, towards it, and found the short passage, and the door marked PRODUCER'S OFFICE, ajar, and edged with bright light.

He pushed the door open and the voices ceased abruptly, and he found himself on the threshold of a tiny, crowded office, looking down into the astonished faces of Ben and Emma Litton.

Emma sat on the desk, with her back to her father, facing

Robert. She wore a short dress, cut simply as an overall, and her long legs were bare and brown. The room was so small that as he stood there in the doorway, he was only an arm's length from her. If he wanted he could reach out and touch her. He thought that she had never looked so beautiful.

His relief and pleasure at seeing Emma was so great that the unexpectedness of Ben Litton's appearance became insignificant. Ben himself was equally unsurprised. He simply raised his dark eyebrows and said:

"Well, bless my soul, see who's turned up now."

Robert put his hands in his pockets, and said, "I thought . . ."

Ben held up a hand. "I know. You thought I was in America. Well, I'm not; I'm in Brookford. And the sooner I get out of the place and back to London, the better."

"But when did you . . . ?"

But Ben was stubbing out his cigarette, standing up, ruthlessly interrupting. "You didn't by any chance notice a taxi-cab at the front of the theatre, did you?"

"Yes, I did. The driver looked as though he had become fossilised to the wheel."

"Poor fellow. I must go and put his mind at rest."

"I've got my car," said Robert. "If you like I'll drive you back to London."

"Even better. I can pay the man off." Emma had not moved. Now, Ben edged his way around the desk, and Robert stood aside to let him out of the door.

"By the way, Robert, Emma's coming too. Will you have room for her?"

"But of course." In the doorway, they eyed each other. Then Ben gave a satisfied nod. "Splendid," he said. "I'll wait outside for you both."

*

"Did you know he was coming?"

Emma shook her head.

"Did it have anything to do with the letter Christopher wrote to him?"

Emma nodded.

"He flew back, today, from the States, to make sure you were all right?"

Emma nodded again, her eyes shining. "He'd been in Mexico with Melissa. But he came straight here. Even Marcus doesn't know he's in the country. He didn't even go to London. He took a taxi from the airport to Brookford. And he wasn't angry about Christopher, and he says if I want I can go back to Porthkerris with him."

"And are you?"

"Oh, Robert, I can't go on, all my life, making the same mistakes. And it was Hester's mistake, too. We both wanted Ben to conform to our ideas of a nice reliable husband, and a kind domestic father. And it was as realistic as trying to cage a panther. And when you come to think of it, how dull caged panthers are! Besides, Ben isn't my problem any longer. He's Melissa's."

Robert said, "So what price now, coming at the bottom of a long list of priorities?"

Emma made a face at him. "You know, Ben once said that you had a noble head, and that you should grow a beard and then he would paint you. But if I tried to paint you it would be with a great big balloon coming out of your mouth with I TOLD YOU SO written on it."

"I never said that to anyone in the whole of my life. And I certainly didn't come all the way down here tonight to say it."

"What did you come to say?"

"That if I'd known you were on your own, I'd have been here

weeks ago. That if I can get two seats for Christo's first night, I want you to come with me. That I'm sorry about shouting at you, that last time I was here.''

''I shouted too.''

''I hate having rows with you, but in some extraordinary way, being away from you is a thousand times worse. I kept telling myself that it was simply something that was over, and best forgotten. But all the time you were never out of the back of my mind. Jane knew. She told me this evening, she'd known all along.''

''Jane . . . ?''

''I'm ashamed to say I've been running Jane round in demented circles trying to keep myself from squaring up to the horrible truth.''

''But it was because of Jane that I made Christopher promise not to ring you up. I thought . . .''

''And it was because of Christopher that I didn't come back to Brookford.''

''You thought we were having an affair, didn't you?''

''Wasn't that what I was meant to think?''

''But you silly man, Christopher's my brother.''

Robert took her head between his hands, and put his thumbs beneath her chin and turned her face up to his. Just before he kissed her, he said, ''And how the hell was I supposed to know that?''

When they got back to the car, there was no sign of Ben, but he had left a message for them, tucked between the windscreen-wiper and the wind-shield. ''Like a parking ticket,'' said Emma.

It was an unconventional letter, written on a sheet of car-tridge paper torn from Ben's sketch book, and headed by two thumbnail sketches – two profiles turned to face each other.

There was no mistaking her own determined chin and Robert's formidable nose.

"It's us. It's for both of us. Read it aloud."

Robert did so. "*The cabby seemed morose at the thought of returning to London on his own, so I decided to accompany him. I shall be at Claridges, but would prefer not to be disturbed before noon tomorrow.*"

"But if I'm not to go to Claridges before noon, where am I meant to go?"

"You're meant to come home with me. To Milton Gardens."

"But I haven't any things. I haven't even got a toothbrush."

"I will buy you a toothbrush," said Robert, and kissed her, and then went on reading the letter. "*By then I should have caught up on my sleep and had time to cool the champagne, and will be ready to celebrate anything you may have to tell me.*"

"The wily old brute! He knew, all along."

"*My love, and God bless you both. Ben.*"

After a little while, Emma said, "Is that all?"

"Not quite." He handed her the letter and Emma saw, beneath Ben's signature, a third little drawing. A wing of white hair, a brown face, a pair of dark and cruelly observant eyes.

"Self-portrait," said Robert. "Ben Litton by Ben Litton. It must be unique. One day, we might sell it for thousands of pounds."

My love and God bless you both.

"I shan't ever want to sell it," said Emma.

"Nor I. Come on, my darling, it's time to go home."

ROSAMUNDE PILCHER

The Day of
the Storm

HODDER

1

It all started on a Monday at the end of January. A dull day at a dull time of the year. Christmas and the New Year were over and forgotten and yet the new season had not started to show its face. London was cold and raw, the shops filled with empty hope and clothes "for cruising". The trees in the park stood lacy and bare against low skies, the trodden grass beneath them dull and dead, so that it was impossible to believe that it could ever again be carpeted with drifts of purple and yellow crocus.

It was a day like any other day. The alarm woke me to darkness, but a darkness made paler by the wide expanse of the uncurtained windows, and through them I could see the top of the plane tree, illuminated by the orange glow of distant street lights.

My room was unfurnished, except for the sofa bed on which I lay, and a kitchen table which I was going to strip of paint when I had the time, and polish with a coat of beeswax. Even the floor was bare, boards stretching to the wainscotting. An orange box did duty as a bedside table, and a second one filled in for a chair.

I put out a hand and turned on the light and surveyed the desolate scene with the utmost satisfaction. It was mine. My first home. I had moved in only three weeks ago but it belonged entirely to me. With it, I could do as I pleased. Cover the white walls with posters or paint them orange. Sand the bare floor or stripe it in colour. Already I had started to acquire a proprietary interest in junk and antique shops, and could not pass one without scanning the window for some treasure that I might be able to afford. This was how the table had come into my possession, and I already had my eye on an antique gilt mirror, but had not yet plucked up the courage to go into the shop and find out how much it was going to cost. Perhaps I would hang it in the centre of the chimney breast, or on the wall opposite the window, so that the reflections of the sky and the tree would be caught, like a picture, within its ornate frame.

These pleasant imaginings took some time. I looked again at the clock, saw that it was growing late, and climbed out of bed to pad, barefooted, across the floor and into the tiny kitchen, where I lit the gas and put the kettle on to boil. The day had begun.

The flat was in Fulham, the top floor of a small terrace house which belonged to Maggie and John Trent. I had met them only at Christmas, which I had spent with Stephen Forbes and his wife Mary and their large family of untidy children, in their large and untidy house in Putney. Stephen Forbes was my boss, the owner of the Walton Street bookshop where I had been working for the past year. He had always been enormously kind and helpful towards me and when he found out, from one of the other girls, that I would be on my own for Christmas, he and Mary had immediately issued a firm invitation – more an order, really – that I should spend the three days with them. There was plenty of space, he insisted vaguely, a room in the attic, a bed in Samantha's room, somewhere, but I wouldn't mind, would I? And I could always help Mary baste the turkey and pick all those torn bits of tissue paper off the floor.

Considering it from this angle, I finally accepted, and had a wonderful time. There's nothing like a family Christmas when there are children everywhere and noise and paper and presents, and a pine-smelling Christmas tree, glittering with baubles and crooked home-made decorations.

On Boxing Night, with the children safely in bed, the Forbeses threw a grown-up party, although we still seemed to continue playing childish games, and Maggie and John Trent came to this. The Trents were young marrieds, she the daughter of an Oxford don, whom Stephen had known well in his undergraduate days. She was one of those laughing, cheerful, out-going people, and after she had arrived the party went with a swing. We were introduced but we didn't manage to talk until a game of charades, when we found ourselves side by side on a sofa, trying to guess, from the most incoherent gestures, that Mary was trying to act to us, in dumb show, the title of a film. "*Rose Marie!*" somebody yelled, for no apparent reason.

"*Clockwork Orange!*"

Maggie lit a cigarette and sank back on the sofa, defeated. "It's beyond me," she said. She turned her dark head to look at me. "You work in Stephen's shop, don't you?"

"Yes."

"I'll come in next week and spend all my Christmas book tokens. I've been given dozens."

"Lucky girl."

"We've just moved into our first house, so I want lots of coffee table stuff so that all our friends think I'm wildly intelligent . . ." Then somebody shouted, "Maggie, it's your turn," and she said "Cripes," and shot to her feet, and went stalking off to find out what she was going to have to act. I can't remember what it was, but watching her make a cheerful fool of herself, my heart warmed to her, and I hoped that I would see her again.

*

I did, of course. True to her word, she came into the shop a couple of days after the holiday wearing a sheepskin coat and a long purple skirt, and carrying a bulging handbag stuffed with book tokens. I wasn't serving anybody at that particular moment and I came out from behind a neat stack of shiny-jacketed novels and said, "Hello."

"Oh, good, there you are. I was hoping I'd find you. Can you help me?"

"Yes, of course."

Together, we chose a cookery book, a new autobiography which everybody was talking about, and a marvellously expensive volume of Impressionist paintings for the legendary coffee table. All this came to a little more than the book tokens did, so she groped around in that handbag and took out a cheque book in order to pay for the balance of the amount.

"John'll be furious," she told me happily, writing out the amount with a red felt pen. The cheque was yellow and the effect quite gay. "He says we're spending far too much money as it is. There." She turned it over to write her address. "Fourteen Bracken Road, SW6." She said it aloud in case I couldn't read her writing. "I haven't got used to writing it yet. We've only just moved in. Terribly exciting, we've bought it freehold, believe it or not. At least our parents chipped in with the deposit and John managed to con some building society or other into giving us a loan for the rest. But of course because of this, we've got to let the top floor to help pay the mortgage, but still, I suppose it'll all work out." She smiled. "You'll have to come and see it."

"I'd like to." I was wrapping her parcel, being meticulous about matching the paper and folding the corners.

She watched me. "You know, it's terribly rude, but I don't know your name. I know it's Rebecca, but Rebecca what?"

"Rebecca Bayliss."

"I suppose you don't know of a nice peaceful individual who wants an unfurnished flat?"

I looked at her. Our thoughts were so close I scarcely had to speak. I tied the knot on the parcel and snapped the string. I said, "How about me?"

"You? But are you looking for somewhere to live?"

"I wasn't until a moment ago. But I am now."

"It's only a room and a kitchen. And we have to share the bath."

"I don't mind if you don't. And if I can afford the rent. I don't know what you're asking."

Maggie told me. I swallowed and did a few mental calculations and said, "I could manage that."

"Have you got any furniture?"

"No. I've been living in a furnished flat with a couple of other girls. But I can get some."

"You sound as though you're desperate to get out."

"No, I'm not desperate, but I'd like to be on my own."

"Well, before you decide you'd better come and see it. Some evening, because John and I both work."

"*This* evening?" It was impossible to keep my impatience and excitement out of my voice and Maggie laughed.

"All right," she said. "This evening," and she picked up the beautifully wrapped parcel of books and prepared to depart.

I suddenly panicked. "I . . . I don't know the address . . ."

"Yes you do, silly, it's on the back of the cheque. Get a twenty-two bus. I'll expect you about seven."

"I'll be there," I promised.

Jolting slowly down the Kings Road in the bus I had to consciously damp down my enthusiasm. I was out to buy a pig in a poke. The flat might be totally impossible, too big, too small or inconvenient in some unimagined way. Anything was better than being disappointed. And indeed, from the outside, the little house was entirely unremarkable, one of a row of red brick villas, with fancy pointing around the doors and a depressing tendency towards stained glass. But inside Number 14 was bright with fresh paint and new carpets and Maggie herself in old jeans and a blue sweater.

"Sorry I look such a mess but I've got to do all the housework, so I usually change when I get back from the office. Come on, let's go up and see it . . . put your coat on the banisters, John's not home yet, but I told him you were coming and he thought it was a frightfully good idea . . ."

Talking all the time, she led the way upstairs and into the empty room which stood at the back of the house. She turned on the light. "It faces south, out over a little park. The people who had the house before us built an extension on underneath, so you've got a sort of balcony on its roof." She opened a glass door and we stepped together out into the cold dark night, and I smelt the leaf-smell of the park, and damp earth, and saw, ringed by lamplight from the streets all around, the stretch of empty darkness. A cold wind blew suddenly, gustily, and the black shape of the plane tree rustled and then the sound was lost in the jet roar of an aeroplane going overhead.

I said, "It's like being in the country."

"Well, next best thing perhaps." She shivered. "Let's go in before we freeze." We stepped back through the glass door, and Maggie showed me the tiny kitchen which had been fashioned out of a deep cupboard, and then, halfway down the stairs, the bathroom, which we would all share. Finally, we ended up downstairs again in Maggie's warm, untidy sitting-room, and she found a bottle of sherry and some potato crisps which she swore were stale, but tasted all right to me. "Do you still want to come?" she asked.

"More than ever."

"When do you want to move in?"

"As soon as possible. Next week if I could."

"What about the girls you're sharing with just now?"

"They'll find someone else. One of them has a sister who's coming to London. I expect she'll move into my room."

"And what about furniture?"

"Oh . . . I'll manage."

"I expect," said Maggie comfortably, "your parents will come up trumps, they usually do. When I first came to London, my mother produced the most wonderful treasures out of the attic and the linen cupboard and so . . ." Her voice died away. I watched her in rueful silence, and she finally laughed at herself. "There I go again, opening my mouth and putting my foot in it. I'm sorry. I've obviously said something idiotically tactless."

"I haven't got a father, and my mother's abroad. She's living in Ibiza. That's really why I want somewhere of my own."

"I am sorry. I should have known, you spending Christmas with the Forbeses . . . I mean, I should have guessed."

"There's no reason why you should guess."

"Is your father dead?"

She was obviously curious, but in such an open and friendly way that all at once it seemed ridiculous to close up and shut up the way I usually did when people began asking me questions about my family.

"I don't think so," I said, trying to sound as though it didn't matter. "I think he lives in Los Angeles. He was an actor. My mother eloped with him when she was eighteen. But he soon got bored with domesticity, or perhaps he decided that his career was more important than raising a family. Anyway, the marriage lasted only a few months before he upped and left her, and then my mother had me."

"What a terrible thing to do."

7

"I suppose it was. I've never thought very much about it. My mother never talked about him. Not because she was particularly bitter or anything, just that when something was over and in the past, she usually forgot it. She's always been like that. She only looks forward, and always with the utmost optimism."

"But what happened after you were born? Did she go back to her parents?"

"No. Never."

"You mean, nobody sent a telegram saying 'Come back all is forgiven'?"

"I don't know. I honestly don't know."

"There must have been the most resounding row when your mother ran off, but even so . . ." Her voice trailed away. She was obviously unable to understand a situation which I had accepted with equanimity all my life. ". . . what sort of people would do a thing like that to their daughter?"

"I don't know."

"You must be joking!"

"No. I honestly don't know."

"You mean you don't know your own grandparents?"

"I don't even know who they are. Or perhaps who they were. I don't even know if they're still alive."

"Don't you know anything? Didn't your mother ever say anything?"

"Oh, of course . . . little scraps of the past used to come into her conversation but none of it added up to anything. You know how mothers talk to their children, remembering things that happened and things they used to do when they were little."

"But – Bayliss." She frowned. "That's not a very usual name. And it rings a bell somehow but I can't think why. Haven't you got a single clue?"

I laughed at her intensity. "You talk as though I really

wanted to know. But you see, I don't. If you've never known grandparents, then you don't miss them.''

"But don't you wonder . . ." she groped for words ". . . where they *lived*?''

"I know where they lived. They lived in Cornwall. In a stone house with fields that sloped down to the sea. And my mother had a brother called Roger but he was killed during the war.''

"But what did she do after you were born? I suppose she had to go out and get a job.''

"No, she had a little money of her own. A legacy from some old aunt or other. Of course, we never had a car or anything, but we seemed to manage all right. She had a flat in Kensington, in the basement of a house that belonged to some friends. And we stayed there till I was about eight, and then I went to boarding school, and after that we sort of . . . moved around . . .''

"Boarding schools cost money . . .''

"It wasn't a very grand boarding school.''

"Did your mother marry again?''

I looked at Maggie. Her expression was lively and avidly curious, but she was kind. I decided that, having gone so far, I may as well tell her the rest.

"She . . . wasn't exactly the marrying type . . . But she was always very, very attractive, and I don't remember a time when there wasn't some adoring male in attendance . . . And once I was away at school, I suppose there wasn't much reason to go on being circumspect. I never knew where I was going to spend the next set of holidays. Once it was in France, in Provence. Sometimes in this country. Another time it was Christmas in New York.''

Maggie took this in, and made a face. "Not much fun for you.''

"But educational." I had long ago learned to make a joke of it. "And just think of all the places I've seen, and all the extraordinary places I've lived in. The Ritz in Paris once, and another time a gruesomely cold house in Denbighshire. That was a poet who thought he'd try sheep farming. I've never been so glad in my life when that association came to an end."

"She must be very beautiful."

"No, but men think she is. And she's very gay and improvident and vague, and I suppose you'd say utterly amoral. Maddening. Everything is 'jokey'. It's her big word. Unpaid bills are 'jokey' and lost handbags and unanswered letters, they're all 'jokey'. She has no idea of money and no sense of obligation. An embarrassing sort of person to live with."

"What's she doing in Ibiza?"

"She's living with some Swedish man she met out there. She went out to stay with a couple she knew, and she met this guy and the next thing I knew I had a letter saying that she was going to move in with him. She said he was terribly Nordic and dour but he had a beautiful house."

"How long is it since you've seen her?"

"About two years. I eased out of her life when I was seventeen. I did a secretarial course and took temporary jobs, and finally I ended up working for Stephen Forbes."

"Do you like it?"

"Yes. I do."

"How old are you?"

"Twenty-one."

Maggie smiled again, shaking her long hair in wonderment. "What a lot you've done," she said, and she did not sound in the least bit sorry for me but even slightly envious. "At twenty-one I was a blushing bride in a beastly busty white wedding dress and an old veil that smelt of mothballs. I'm not really a trad. person, but I've got a mother who is, and I'm very fond of her so I usually used to do what she wanted.''

I could imagine Maggie's mother. I said, resorting to the comfort of clichés, because I couldn't think of anything else to say, ''Oh, well, it takes all sorts,'' and at that moment we heard John's key in the lock and after that we did not bring up the subject of mothers and families again.

It was a day like any other day, but it had a bonus attached to it. Last Thursday I had worked late with Stephen, trying to complete the last of the January stocktaking, and in return he had given me this morning off so that I had until lunchtime to my own devices. I filled it in cleaning the flat (which took, at most, no more than half an hour), doing some shopping and taking a bundle of clothes to the launderette. By eleven thirty all this domesticity was completed so I put on my coat and set off, in a leisurely way, for work, intending to walk some of the way, and maybe stand myself an early lunch before getting to the shop.

It was one of those cold, dark, damp days when it never really gets light. I walked, through this gloom, up into the New Kings Road, and headed west. Here, every other shop seems to sell either antiques or second-hand beds or picture frames, and I thought I knew them all, but all at once I found myself outside a shop which I had not noticed before. The outside was painted white, the windows framed in black, and there was a red and white awning pulled out as protection against the imminent drizzle.

I looked up to see what the shop was called and read the name TRISTRAM NOLAN picked out in neat black Roman capitals over the door. This door was flanked by windows filled with delectable odds and ends and I paused to inspect their contents, standing on the pavement bathed in brightness from the many lights which burned within. Most of the furniture was Victorian, re-upholstered and restored and polished. A buttoned sofa with a wide lap and curly legs, a sewing box, a small picture of lap dogs on a velvet cushion.

I looked beyond the windows and into the shop itself, and it was then that I saw the cherrywood chairs. They were a pair, balloon backed, with curved legs and seats embroidered with roses.

I craved them. Just like that. I could picture them in my flat, and I wanted them desperately. For a moment I hesitated. This was no junk shop and the price might well be more than I could afford. But after all, no harm could be done by asking. Before I could lose my nerve, I opened the door and went in.

The shop was empty, but the door opening and closing had rung a bell, and presently there was the sound of someone coming down the stairs, the woollen curtain that hung over the door at the back of the shop was drawn aside and a man came into view.

I suppose I had expected someone elderly and formally attired, in keeping with the ambience of the shop and its contents, but this man's appearance rocked all my vague, preconceived notions. For he was young, tall and long-legged, dressed in jeans – faded to a soft blue and clinging like a second skin – and a blue denim jacket, equally old and faded, with the sleeves turned back in a businesslike way to reveal the checked cuffs of the shirt he wore beneath it. A cotton handkerchief was knotted at his neck and on his feet he wore soft moccasins, much decorated and fringed.

That winter the most unlikely people were drifting around London dressed as cowboys, but somehow this one looked real, and his worn clothes appeared as genuine as he was. We stood and looked at each other, and then he smiled and for some reason he took me unawares. I don't like being taken unawares, and I said "Good morning" with a certain coolness.

He dropped the curtain behind him and came forward, soft footed. ''Can I help you?''

He may have looked like a genuine, dyed-in-the-wool American, but the moment he opened his mouth it was clear that he was no such thing. For some reason this annoyed me. The life I had led with my mother had left me with a thick streak of cynicism about men in general, and phoneys in particular, and this young man, I decided then and there, was a phoney.

''I . . . I was going to ask about these little chairs. The balloon-back ones.''

''Oh, yes.'' He came forward to lay his hand on the back of one. The hand was long and shapely, with spade-tipped fingers, the skin very brown. ''There's just the pair of them.''

I stared at the chairs, trying to ignore his presence.

''I wondered how much they were.''

He squatted beside me to search for a price ticket and I saw his hair fell thick and straight to his collar, very dark and lustrous.

''You're in luck,'' he told me. ''They're going very cheap because the leg of one has been broken and then not very professionally repaired.'' He straightened up suddenly, surprising me by his height. His eyes were slightly tip-tilted, and a very dark brown, with an expression in them that I found disconcerting. He made me uncomfortable and my antipathy for him began to turn to dislike. ''Fifteen pounds for the pair,'' he said. ''But if you'd like to wait and pay a little more, I can get the leg reinforced, and perhaps a small veneer put over the joint. That would make it stronger and it would look better too.''

''Isn't it all right now?''

''It would be all right for you,'' said the young man, ''. . . but if you had a large fat man for dinner, he'd probably end up on his backside.''

There was a pause while I regarded him – I hoped coldly.

His eyes were brimming, with a malicious amusement which I had no intention of sharing. I did not appreciate the suggestion that the only men who would ever come and have dinner with me would necessarily be large and fat.

I said at last, "How much would it cost me to have the leg repaired?"

"Say five pounds. That means you get the chairs for a tenner each."

I worked this out, and decided that I could just afford them.

"I'll take them."

"Good," said the young man and put his fists on his hips and smiled amiably, as though this were the end of the transaction.

I decided he was utterly inefficient. "Do you want me to pay for them now, or to leave a deposit . . .?"

"No, that doesn't matter. You can pay for them when you collect them."

"Well, when will they be ready?"

"In about a week."

"Don't you want my name?"

"Not unless you want to give it to me."

"What happens if I never come back?"

"Then I expect they'll be sold to someone else."

"I don't want to lose them."

"You won't," said the young man.

I frowned, angry with him, but he only smiled and went to the door to open it for me. Cold air poured in, and outside the drizzle had started and the street looked dark as night.

He said, "Goodbye," and I managed a frosty smile of thanks and went past him, out into the gloom, and as I did so I heard the bell ring as he shut the door behind me.

The day was, all at once, unspeakable. My pleasure in buying the chairs had been wrecked by the irritation which the young man had generated. I did not usually take instant dislikes to people and I was annoyed not only with him, but with myself, for being so vulnerable. I was still brooding on this when I walked down Walton Street and let myself into Stephen Forbes's bookshop. Even the comfort of being indoors and the pleasant smell of new paper and printers' ink did nothing to dispel my wretched mood.

The shop was on three levels, with new books on the ground floor, second-hand books and old prints upstairs, and Stephen's office in the basement. I saw that Jennifer, the second girl, was busy with a customer, and the only other person visible was an old lady in a tweed cape engrossed in the Gardening section, so I headed for the little cloakroom, unbuttoning my coat as I went, but then I heard Stephen's heavy, unmistakable footsteps coming up from downstairs, and for some reason I stopped to wait for him. The next moment he appeared, tall, stooping and spectacled, with his usual expression of vague benevolence. He wore dark suits that always managed to appear as though in need of a good press, and already, at this early hour, the knot of his tie had begun to slip down, revealing the top button of his shirt.

"Rebecca," he said.

"Yes, I'm here . . ."

"I'm glad I've caught you." He came to my side speaking low-voiced, so as not to disturb the customers. "There's a letter for you downstairs; it's been forwarded on from your old flat. You'd better nip down and collect it."

I frowned. "A letter?"

"Yes. Airmail. Lots of foreign stamps. It has, for some reason, an air of urgency about it."

My irritation, along with all thoughts of new chairs, was lost in a sudden apprehension.

"Is it from my mother?"

"I don't know. Why don't you go and find out?"

15

So I went down the steep, uncarpeted stairs to the basement, lit, on this dark day, by long strip-lights let into the ceiling. The office was marvellously untidy – as usual – littered with letters and parcels and files, piles of old books, and cardboard boxes and ashtrays which nobody ever remembered to empty. But the letter was on the middle of Stephen's blotter and instantly visible.

I picked it up. An airmail envelope, Spanish stamps, an Ibizan postmark. But the writing was unfamiliar, pointed and spiky, as though a very fine pen had been used. It had been sent to the old flat, but this address had been crossed out and the address of the bookshop substituted in large, girlish, handwriting. I wondered how long the letter had lain on the table by the front door, before one of the girls realised that it was there and had taken the trouble to forward it on to me.

I sat down in Stephen's chair and slit the envelope. Inside, two pages of fine airmail paper, and the date at the head was the third of January. Very nearly a month ago. My mind sounded a note of alarm and, suddenly frightened, I began to read.

Dear Rebecca,

 I hope you do not mind me calling you by your Christian name, but your mother has spoken to me of you a great deal. I am writing because your mother is very ill. She has been unwell for some time and I wished to write to you before but she would not let me.

 Now, however, I am taking matters into my own hands, and with the doctor's approval I am letting you know that I think you should come out to see her.

 If you can do this, perhaps you will cable me the number of your aeroplane flight so that I can be at the airport to meet you.

 I know that you are working and it may not be easy to

16

make this trip, but I would advise you to waste no time.
I am afraid that you will find your mother very changed,
but her spirit is still high.

   With good wishes.
   Sincerely,
   Otto Pedersen.

I sat in unbelief, and stared at the letter. The formal words told
me nothing and everything. My mother was very ill, perhaps
dying. A month ago I had been asked to waste no time but to
go to her. Now it was a month later, and I had only just got
the letter and perhaps she was already dead – and I had never
gone. What would he think of me, this Otto Pedersen whom I
had never seen, whose name, even, I had not known until this
moment?

2

I read the letter again, and then again, the flimsy pages rustling in my hands. I was still there, sitting at his desk, when Stephen finally came downstairs to find me.

I turned to look up at him over my shoulder. He saw my face and said, "What is it?"

I tried to tell him, but could not. Instead I thrust the letter at him, and while he took it, and read it, I sat with my elbows on his desk, biting my thumbnails, bitter and angry, and fighting a terrible anxiety.

He was soon finished reading. He tossed the letter down on the desk between us, and said, "Did you know she was ill?"

I shook my head.

"When did you last hear from her?"

"Four, five months ago. She never wrote letters." I looked up at him and said, furiously, choked by the great lump in my throat, "That was nearly a *month* ago. That letter's been lying in the flat, and nobody bothered to send it to me. She may be dead by now and I never went, and she'll think I simply didn't care!"

"If she had died," said Stephen, "then we'd have surely heard. Now, don't cry, there isn't time for that. What we have to do is get you out to Ibiza with all convenient speed, and let . . ." he glanced down at the letter again ". . . Mr Pedersen know you're arriving. Nothing else matters."

I said, "I can't go," and my mouth began to grow square and my lower lip tremble as though I were a ten-year-old.

"Why can't you go?"

"Because I haven't got enough money for the fare."

"Oh, my dear child, let me worry about that . . ."

"But I can't let you . . ."

"Yes, you can, and if you get all stiff-necked about it then you can pay me back over the next five years and I'll charge you interest, if it'll make you feel happier, and now for God's sake don't let's mention it again . . ." He was already reaching for the directory, behaving in an altogether efficient and un-Stephen-like fashion. "Have you got a passport? And nobody's going to clamp down on you for smallpox injections or anything tiresome like that. Hello? British Airways? I want to make a reservation on the first plane to Ibiza." He smiled down at me, still fighting tears and temper, but already feeling a little better. There is nothing like having a large and kindly man to take over in times of emotional stress. He picked up a pencil and drew a sheet of paper towards him and began to make notes. "Yes. When? Fine. Can we have a reservation, please? Miss Rebecca Bayliss. And what time does it get to Ibiza? And the flight number? Thank you so much. Thank you. Yes, I'll get her to the airport myself."

He put down the receiver and surveyed, with some satisfaction, the illegible squiggles his pencil had made.

"That's it, then. You fly tomorrow morning, change planes at Palma, get to Ibiza about half past seven. I'll drive you to the airport. No, don't start arguing again, I wouldn't feel happy unless I saw you actually walk on to the aeroplane. And now we'll cable Mr Otto Pedersen . . ." he picked up the letter again ". . . at the Villa Margareta, Santa Catarina, and let him know that you're coming." He smiled down at me with such cheerful reassurance that I was suddenly filled with hope.

I said, "I can't ever thank you . . ."

"I don't ever want you to," said Stephen. "It's the least I can do."

I flew the next day, in a plane half-filled with hopeful winter holiday tourists. They even carried straw hats against an improbably blazing sun, and their faces, as we stepped out into a steady drizzle at Palma, were disappointed but resolutely cheerful, as though, for certain, tomorrow would be better.

The rain never ceased, all the four hours I waited in the transit lounge, and the flight out of Palma was bumpy with thick, wet clouds. But as we rose above them and headed out across the sea, the weather brightened. The clouds thinned and broke, disclosing an evening sky of robin's egg blue, and far below the crumpled sea was streaked with the pink light of the setting sun.

It was dark when we landed. Dark and damp. Coming down the gangway beneath a sky full of bright southern stars, there was only the smell of petrol, but as I walked across the puddled tarmac towards the lights of the terminal building I felt the soft wind in my face. It was warm and smelt of pines, and was evocative of every summer holiday I had ever spent abroad.

At this quiet time of the year the plane had not been full. It did not take long to get through Customs and Immigration, and – my passport stamped – I picked up my suitcase and walked into the Arrivals Lounge.

There were the usual small groups of waiting people standing about or sitting hunched apathetically on the long plastic banquettes. I stopped and looked about me, waiting to be identified, but could see nobody who looked in the least like a Swedish writer come to meet me. And then a man turned from buying a newspaper at the bookstall. Across the room our eyes met, and he folded the newspaper and began to walk towards me, pushing his paper into his jacket pocket as though it were no longer of any use to him. He was tall and thin, with hair that

21

was either blond or white – it was impossible to tell in the bright, impersonal electric light. Before he was halfway across the polished floor I smiled tentatively, and as he approached he said my name, ''Rebecca?'' with a question mark at the end of it, still not entirely certain that it was I.

''Yes.''

''I'm Otto Pedersen.'' We shook hands and he gave a formal little bow as he did so. His hair, I saw then, was pale blond, turning grey, and his face was deeply tanned, thin and bony, the skin dry and finely wrinkled from long exposure to the sun. His eyes were very pale, and more grey than blue. He wore a black polo-necked sweater and a light oatmeal-coloured suit with pleated pockets, like a safari shirt, and a belt which hung loose, the buckle swinging. He smelt of aftershave and looked as clean as if he had been bleached.

Having found each other, it was suddenly difficult to find anything to say. All at once we were both overwhelmed by the circumstances of our meeting and I realised that he was as unsure of himself as I. But he was also urbane and polite, and dealt with this by taking my suitcase from me and asking if this was all my luggage.

''Yes, that's all.''

''Then let us go to the car. If you like to wait at the door, I will fetch it and save you the walk . . .''

''I'll come with you.''

''It's only across the road, in the car park.''

So we went out together, into the darkness again. He led me to the half empty car park. Here, he stopped by a big black Mercedes, unlocked it, and tossed my case on to the back seat. Then he held the door open so that I could get in before coming around to the front of the car to settle himself beside me.

''I hope you had a good journey,'' he said, politely, as we left the terminal behind us and headed out into the road.

"It was a little bumpy in Palma. I had to wait four hours."

"Yes. There are no direct flights at this time of the year."

I swallowed. "I must explain about not answering your letter. I've moved flats, and I didn't get it till yesterday morning. It wasn't forwarded to me, you see. It was so good of you to write, and you must have wondered why I never replied."

"I thought something like that must have happened."

His English was perfect, only the precise Swedish vowel sounds betraying his origins, and a certain formality in the manner in which he expressed himself.

"When I got your letter I was so frightened . . . that it would be too late."

"No," said Otto. "It is not too late."

Something in his voice made me look at him. His profile was knife sharp against the yellow glow of passing street lights, his expression unsmiling and grave.

I said, "Is she dying?"

"Yes," said Otto. "Yes, she is dying."

"What is wrong with her?"

"Cancer of the blood. You call it leukaemia."

"How long has she been ill?"

"About a year. But it was only just before Christmas time that she became so ill. The doctor thought that we should try blood transfusions, and I took her to the hospital for this. But it was no good, because as soon as I got her home again, she started this very bad nose bleed, and so the ambulance had to come and take her back to hospital again. She was there over Christmas and only then allowed home again. It was after that I wrote to you."

"I wish I'd got the letter in time. Does she know I'm coming?"

"No, I didn't tell her. You well know how she loves surprises, and equally how she hates to be disappointed. I thought there was a chance that something would go wrong and you wouldn't be on the plane.'' He smiled frostily, "But of course you were.''

We stopped at a crossroads to wait for a country cart to pass in front of us, the feet of the mule making a pleasant sound on the dusty road, and a lantern swinging from the back of the cart. Otto took advantage of the pause to take a cheroot from the breast pocket of his jacket and light it from the lighter on the dashboard. The cart passed, we moved on.

"How long is it since you have seen your mother?''

"Two years.''

"You must expect a great change. I am afraid you will be shocked, but you must try not to let her see. She is still very vain.''

"You know her so well.''

"But of course.''

I longed to ask him if he loved her. The question was on the tip of my tongue, but I realised that at this stage of our acquaintance it would be nothing but impertinence to ask such an intimate and personal thing. Besides, what difference did it make? He had met her and wanted to be with her, had given her a home, and now, when she was so ill, was cherishing her in his own apparently unemotional manner. If that wasn't love, then what was?

After a little, we began to talk of other things. I asked him how long he had lived on the island, and he said five years. He had come first in a yacht and had liked the place so well that he had returned the next year to buy his house and settle here.

"You're a writer . . .''

"Yes, but I am also a Professor of History.''

"Do you write books on history?''

"I have done so. At the moment I am working on a thesis concerned with the Moorish occupation of these islands and southern Spain.''

I was impressed. As far as I could remember, none of my mother's previous lovers had been even remotely intellectual.

"How far away is your house?"

"About five miles now. The village of Santa Catarina was quite unspoiled when I first came here. Now, however, large hotel developments are planned and I fear it will become spoiled like the rest of the island. No, that is wrong. Like some parts of the island. It is still possible to be entirely remote if you know where to go and have a car or perhaps a motor boat."

It was warm in the car and I rolled down the window. The soft night air blew in on my face and I saw that we were in country now, passing through groves of olives, with every now and then the glimmering light of a farmhouse window shining beyond the bulbous, spiked shapes of prickly pear.

I said, "I'm glad she was here. I mean, if she has to be ill and die, I'm glad it's somewhere like this, in the south, with the sun warm and the smell of pines."

"Yes," said Otto. And then, precisely as ever, "I think that she has been very happy."

We drove on in silence, the road empty, telegraph poles rushing to meet the headlights of the car. I saw that now we were running parallel to the sea, which spread to an invisible, dark horizon and was dotted here and there with the lights of fishing boats. Presently there appeared ahead of us the neon-lighted shape of a village. We passed a sign reading SANTA CATARINA and then were driving down the main street; the air was filled with the smell of onions and oil and grilling meat. Flamenco music flung itself at us from open doorways, and dark faces, filled with absent curiosity, turned to watch us pass. In a moment we had left the village behind us, and had plunged forward into the darkness which lay beyond, only to slow down almost immediately to negotiate a steep corner which led up a narrow lane between orchards of almond trees. The headlights bored into the darkness, and ahead I saw the villa, white and square, pierced by small, secretive windows and with a lighted lantern swinging over the great, nailed front door.

Otto braked the car and switched off the engine. We got out, Otto taking my suitcase from the back seat and leading the way across the gravel. He opened the door and stood aside and I walked in ahead of him.

We were in a hallway, lit by a wrought-iron chandelier and furnished with a long couch covered in a bright blanket. A tall blue and white jar stood by the door containing a selection of ivory-handled walking sticks and sun umbrellas. As Otto closed the front door, another opened ahead of us and a small, dark-haired woman appeared, wearing a pink overall and flat, worn slippers.

"Señor."

"Maria."

She smiled, showing a number of gold teeth. He spoke to her in Spanish, asking a question to which she replied and then, turning, introduced me to her.

"This is Maria, who takes care of us. I have told her who you are . . ."

I held out my hand and Maria took it: we made friends by smiling and nodding. Then she turned back to Otto and spoke some more. Presently he handed her my suitcase, and she withdrew.

Otto said, "Your mother has been asleep but she is awake now. Let me take your coat."

I unbuttoned it, and he helped me off with it and laid it across the end of the couch. Then he went across the floor towards yet another door, motioning me to follow. I did, and was suddenly nervous, afraid of what I was going to find.

It was the salon of the house into which he led me. A long low-ceilinged room, whitewashed like the rest of the house, and furnished with a pleasing mixture of modern Scandinavian and antique Spanish. The tile floor was scattered with rugs, there were a great many books and pictures, and in the centre of the room a round table was laid out, seductively, with neatly ordered magazines and newspapers.

A wood fire burned in a great stone fireplace, and in front of this was a bed, with a low table alongside, holding a glass of water and a jug, a few pink geraniums in a mug, some books and a lighted lamp.

This lamp and the flicker of flames provided the only light in the room, but from the door I could see the narrow shape which humped the pink blankets and the attenuated hand and arm which was extended as Otto came forward to stand on the hearth-rug.

"Darling," she said.

"Lisa." He took the hand and kissed it.

"You haven't been long after all."

"Maria says you have slept. Do you feel ready for a visitor?"

"A visitor?" Her voice was a thread. "Who?"

Otto glanced up at me, and I moved forward to stand beside him. I said, "It's me. Rebecca."

"Rebecca. Darling child. Oh, how blissfully jokey." She held out both arms to me, and I knelt down beside the bed to kiss her; her body gave me no resistance or support at all, so thin was she, and when I touched her cheek it felt papery beneath my lips. It was like kissing a leaf that has long since been wrenched by the wind from its parent tree.

"But what are you doing *here*?" She looked over my shoulder at Otto, and then back at me again. She put on the pretence of a frown. "You didn't *tell* her to come?"

"I thought you would like to see her," said Otto. "I thought it would cheer you up."

"But darling, why didn't you tell me?"

I smiled. "We wanted it to be a surprise."

"But I wish I'd known, then I could have looked forward to seeing you. That's what we always used to think, before Christmas. Half the fun was anticipation." She let me go and I sat back on my heels. "Are you going to stay?"

"For a day or so."

"Oh, how utterly perfect. We can have the most gorgeous gossips. Otto, does Maria know she's staying?"

"Of course."

"And what about dinner tonight?"

"It's all arranged . . . we'll have it together, in here, just the three of us."

"Well, let's have something now. A little drinkey. Is there any champagne?"

Otto smiled. "I think I can find a bottle. In fact, I think I remembered to put one on ice for just such an occasion."

"Oh, you clever man."

"Shall I get it now?"

"Please, darling."

She slid her hand in mine and it was like holding chicken bones. "And we'll drink to being together."

He went away to fetch the champagne and we were alone. I found a little stool and pulled it up so that I could sit close to her. We looked at each other, and she could not stop smiling. The dazzling smile and the bright dark eyes were still the same, so was the dark hair that spread like a stain over the snowy pillowcase. Otherwise her appearance was horrifying. I had never known anyone could be so thin and still be alive. And to make it more unreal, she was not pale and colourless but quite brown, as though she still spent most of the day lying in the sun. But she was excited. It seemed she could not stop talking.

"So sweet of the darling man to know how much I would

28

love to see you. The only thing is, I'm so boring just now, I don't feel like doing anything, he should have waited until I'm better and then we could have had some fun together, and gone swimming and out in the boat and had picnics and things.''

I said, "I can come again."

"Yes, of course you can." She touched my face with her hand as though needing this contact to reassure her that I was really there. "You're looking gorgeous, do you know that? You've got your father's colouring, with those big grey eyes, and that corn-coloured hair. Is it corn, or is it gold? And I love the way you're doing it." Her hand travelled to the single plait which fell forward, like a rope over my right shoulder. "It makes you look like something out of a fairy story; you know, those old-fashioned books with the magical pictures. You're very pretty."

I shook my head. "No. I'm not."

"Well, you look it, and that's the next best thing. Darling, what are you doing with yourself? It's such ages since I wrote or heard from you. Whose fault was that? Mine, I suppose, I'm hopeless at writing letters."

I told her about the bookshop and the new flat. She was amused by this. "What a funny person you are, building a little nest for yourself without anybody to share it with. Haven't you met anybody yet you want to marry?"

"No. Nor anyone who wants to marry me."

She looked malicious. "What about the man you work for?"

"He's married, he's got a charming wife and a brood of children."

She giggled. "That never bothered me. Oh, darling, what a dreadful mother I was to you, trailing you round in that reprehensible fashion. It's a wonder you haven't collected the most ghastly selection of neuroses or hang-ups or whatever they

29

call them these days! But you don't look as though you have, so perhaps it was all right after all.''

''Of course it was all right. I just grew up with my eyes open and that was no bad thing.'' I added, ''I like Otto.''

''Isn't he divine? So correct and punctilious and *northern*. And so blazingly intelligent . . . So lucky he doesn't want me to be intelligent too! He just likes having me make him laugh.''

Somewhere, in the middle of the house, a clock struck seven, and as the last note chimed Otto came back into the room carrying a tray with the champagne bottle in a bucket of ice, and three wine glasses. We watched as he expertly loosened the cork and the golden foaming wine spilled into the three glasses, and we each took one and raised them, all of us smiling because it was suddenly a party. My mother said, ''Here's to the three of us and happy times. Oh, so divinely jokey.''

Later, I was shown to my bedroom, which was either simply luxurious or luxuriously simple, I couldn't decide which. A fitted bathroom led off it, so I showered, and changed into trousers and a silk shirt, and brushed my hair and replaited it, and returned to the salon. I found Otto and my mother waiting for me, Otto also changed for the evening, and Mother wearing a fresh bedjacket of powder blue with a silk shawl embroidered with pink roses flung across her knees, its long fringe brushing the floor. We had another drink and then Maria served dinner on a low table by the fire. My mother never stopped talking – it was all about the old days when I was growing up, and I kept thinking that Otto would be shocked, but he wasn't shocked at all, he was curious and much amused and kept asking questions and prompting my mother to tell us more.

''. . . and that dreadful farm in Denbighshire . . . Rebecca, do you remember that terrible house? We nearly died of cold and the fire smoked whenever we lit it. That was Sebastian,'' she explained for Otto's benefit. "We all thought he was going to be a famous poet, but he wasn't any better at writing poetry than he was at sheep farming. In fact, if anything, worse. And I couldn't think how on earth I could leave him without hurting his feelings and then luckily Rebecca got bronchitis so I had the most perfect excuse."

"Not so lucky for Rebecca," suggested Otto.

"It certainly was. She hated it just as much as I did; anyway he had a horrible dog that was always threatening to bite her. Darling, is there any more champagne?"

She ate hardly anything, but sipped glass after glass of the icy wine while Otto and I worked our way steadily through Maria's delicious, four-course dinner. When it was finished, and the dishes cleared away, my mother asked for some music, and Otto put a Brahms concerto on the record-player, turned very low. Mother just went on talking, like a toy that has been overwound and will only stop whirring senselessly around the floor when it finally breaks.

Presently, saying that he had work to do, Otto excused himself and left us, first building up the fire with fresh logs and making sure that we had everything we needed.

"Does he work every evening?" I asked, when he had gone.

"Nearly always. And in the mornings. He's very punctilious. I think that's why we've got on so well because we're so different."

I said, "He adores you."

"Yes," said my mother, accepting this. "And the best bit is that he never tried to turn me into someone else; he just accepted me, with my wicked ways and my lurid past." She touched my plait again. "You're growing more like your father . . . I always thought you looked like me, but you don't, you look like him now. He was very handsome."

"You know, I don't even know what his name was."

31

"Sam Bellamy. But Bayliss is a much better name, don't you think? Besides, having you all on my own like that, I always felt you were my child and nobody else's."

"I wish you'd tell me about him. You never have."

"There's so little to tell. He was an actor, and too good-looking for words."

"But where did you meet him?"

"He came down to Cornwall with a Summer Stock company doing open-air Shakespeare. It was all terribly romantic, dark blue summer nights and the damp, dewy smell of the grass, and that divine Mendelssohn music and Sam being Oberon.

> Through the house give glimmering light
>   By the dead and drowsy fire;
> Every elf and fairy sprite
>   Hop as light as bird from brier.

It was magical. And falling in love with him was part of the magic."

"Was he in love with you?"

"We both thought he was."

"But you ran away with him, and married him . . ."

"Yes. But only because my parents left me with no alternative."

"I don't understand."

"They disliked him. They disapproved. They said I was too young. My mother said why didn't I marry some nice young man who lived locally, why didn't I settle down and stop making an exhibition of myself? And if I married an actor, what would people say? I sometimes thought that was all she cared about, what people would say. As if it could possibly matter what anybody said."

It was, unbelievably, the first time I had ever heard her

mention her mother. I said, cautiously prompting, "Didn't you like her?"

"Oh, darling, it's so long ago. It's so difficult to remember. But she stifled and repressed me. I sometimes felt she was trying to choke me with conventions. And Roger had been killed and I missed him so dreadfully. Everything would have been different if Roger had been there." She smiled. "He was so nice. Almost too nice. A real BV right from the very start."

"What's a BV?"

"Bitches' victim. He always fell in love with the most impossible girls. And finally he married one. A little blonde doll, with dolly hair and dolly china blue eyes. My mother thought she was sweet. I couldn't stand her."

"What was she called?"

"Mollie." She made a face as though the very word tasted bad.

I laughed. "She can't have been as bad as all that."

"I thought she was. So maddeningly tidy. Always cleaning out her handbag or putting trees into her shoes, or sterilising the baby's toys."

"She had a baby then?"

"Yes, a little boy. Poor child, she insisted on calling him Eliot."

"I think that's a nice name."

"Oh, Rebecca, it's sickening." It was obvious that nothing Mollie had done could find favour in my mother's eyes. "I always felt sorry for the child, being saddled with such a dreadful name. And somehow he lived up to it, you know how people do, and after Roger was killed the poor scrap was worse than ever, always hanging round his mother's neck and having to have a light on in his room at night."

"I think you're being very unkind."

She laughed. "Yes, I know, and it wasn't his fault. He

probably would have turned into quite a personable young man if his mother gave him half a chance.''

"I wonder what happened to Mollie?''

"I don't know. I don't particularly care, either." My mother could always be cruelly off-hand. "It's like a dream. Like remembering dream people. Or perhaps . . ." her voice trailed away ". . . perhaps they were real and I was the dream.''

I felt uncomfortable, because this was too near the truth that I was trying to keep at bay. I said quickly, "Are your parents still alive?''

"My mother died that Christmas we spent in New York. Do you remember that Christmas? The cold and the snow and all the shops full of the sound of 'Jingle Bells'? By the end of that Christmas I felt I never wanted to hear that damned tune again. My father wrote to me, but of course the letter didn't reach me until months later by which time it had followed me half round the world. And then it was really too late to write and say anything. Besides, I'm so useless about writing letters. He probably thought I simply didn't care.''

"Didn't you ever write?''

"No.''

"Didn't you like him either?'' It seemed a sorry state of affairs.

"Oh, I adored him. He was wonderful. Terribly good-looking, attractive to women, frightfully fierce and frightening. He was a painter. Did I ever tell you that?''

A painter. I had imagined everything, but never a painter. "No, you never said.''

"Well, if you'd had any sort of education at all you'd probably have guessed. Grenville Bayliss. Doesn't that mean anything to you at all?''

I shook my head sadly. It was terrible never to have heard of a famous grandfather.

"Well, why should it? I was never any good at trailing you round art galleries or museums. Come to think of it, I was never much good at anything. It's a wonder you've turned out so well on a solid diet of maternal neglect."

"What did he look like?"

"Who?"

"Your father."

"How do you imagine him?"

I considered the question and came up with Augustus John. "Bohemian, and bearded and rather leonine . . ."

"Wrong," said my mother. "He wasn't like that at all. He started off his life in the Navy, and the Navy left an indelible stamp on him. You see, he didn't decide to be a painter until he was nearly thirty, when he threw up a promising career and enrolled at the Slade. It nearly broke my mother's heart. And moving to Cornwall and setting up house at Porthkerris simply added insult to injury. I don't think she ever forgave him for being so selfish. She'd adored queening it in Malta, and probably fancied herself as wife to the Commander-in-Chief. I must say, he was tailor-made for the part, very blue-eyed and imposing and terrifying. He never lost what was known in those days as a quarter-deck manner."

"But you weren't terrified of him?"

"No. I loved him."

"Then why didn't you go home?"

Her face closed up. "I couldn't. I wouldn't. Terrible things had been said, by all of us. Old resentments and old truths had all come boiling up, and threats were made and ultimatums handed out. And the more they opposed me, the more determined I became, and the more impossible it was, when the time came, to admit that they'd been right, and I'd been wrong, and I'd made a hideous mistake. And if I had gone home, I would never have got away again. I knew that. And you wouldn't have belonged to me any more, you'd have belonged to your grandmother. I couldn't have borne that. You were such a precious little thing.'' She smiled and added rather wistfully, ''And we did have fun, didn't we?''

''Yes, of course we did.''

''I would have liked to go back. Sometimes I very nearly did. It was such a lovely house. Boscarva it was called, and it was rather like this villa, standing square on a hill above the sea. When Otto first brought me here, it reminded me of Boscarva. But here it's warm and the winds are gentle; there, it was wild and stormy, and the garden was honeycombed with tall hedges to shelter the flower beds from the sea winds. I think the wind was the thing that my mother most hated. She used to seal all the windows and shut herself indoors, playing bridge with her friends or doing needlepoint.''

''Didn't she ever do things with you?''

''Not really.''

''But who looked after you?''

''Pettifer. And Mrs Pettifer.''

''Who were they?''

''Pettifer had been in the Navy, too; he looked after my father and cleaned the silver and sometimes drove the car. And Mrs Pettifer did the cooking. I can't tell you how cosy they were. Sitting by the kitchen fire with them making toast and listening to the wind battering at the windows, knowing that it couldn't get in . . . it made you feel so safe. And we used to read fortunes from the teacups . . .'' Her voice trailed off, memories uncertain now. And then, ''No, that was Sophia.''

''Who was Sophia?''

She did not reply. She was staring at the fire, her expression far away. Perhaps she had not heard me. She said at last, ''After my mother died I should have gone back. It was naughty of me to stay away, but I was never over-endowed with what is known

36

as moral fibre. But, you know, there are things at Boscarva that belong to me.''

''What sort of things?''

''A desk, I remember. A little one, with drawers down the side, and a lid that opened up. I think it's called a davenport. And some jade that my father brought home from China and a Venetian looking-glass. They were all mine. On the other hand, I moved around so much that they would just have been a nuisance.'' She looked at me, frowning a little. ''But perhaps you don't think they are a nuisance. Have you got any furniture in this flat of yours?''

''No. Practically none.''

''Then perhaps I'll see if I can get hold of them for you. They must still be at Boscarva, provided the house hasn't been sold or burned down or something. Would you like me to try and get hold of them?''

''More than anything. Not just because I need furniture, but because they belonged to you.''

''Oh, darling, how sweet, too jokey the way you long for roots, and I could never bear to have any. I always felt they would just tie me down in one place.''

''And I always feel that they would make me belong.''

She said, ''You belong to me.''

We stayed talking until the early hours of the morning. About midnight, she asked me to refill her water-jug, and I found my way into the deserted kitchen and did this for her, and realised then that Otto, with gentle tact, had probably taken himself quietly off to bed, so that we could be together. And when at last her voice grew tired and her words began to trail off in a blur of exhaustion, I said that I was sleepy too, which I was, and I stood up, cramped from sitting, stretched, and put more logs on the fire. Then I took away her second pillow so that she lay, ready for sleep. The silken shawl had slipped to the

floor, so I picked this up and folded it and laid it on a chair.
It remained only to stoop and kiss her, turn off the lamp, and
leave her there in the firelight. As I went through the door, she
said, as she always used to say when I was a little girl, ''Good
night, my love. Goodbye until tomorrow.''

The next morning I was awake early, aware of sunshine
streaming through the gaps in the shutters. I got up and went
to open them, and saw the brilliant Mediterranean morning. I
stepped out through the open windows on to the stone terrace
which ran the length of the house and saw the hill sloping down
to the sea, maybe a mile distant. The sand-coloured land was
veiled in pink, the first tender blossoms of the almond trees. I
went back into my room, dressed, and went out again – across
the terrace, down a flight of steps, and through the ordered,
formal garden. I vaulted a low stone wall, and walked on in the
direction of the sea. Presently, I found myself in an orchard,
surrounded by almond trees. I stopped and looked up at a froth
of pink blossom and beyond it a pale and cloudless blue sky.

I knew that each flower would bear a precious fruit which,
when the time came, would be frugally cropped, but even so I
could not resist picking a single spray, and I was still carrying
this when an hour or so later, having walked to the sea and
back, I retraced my steps up the hill towards the villa.

It was steeper than I had realised. Pausing for breath, I looked
up at the house, and saw Otto Pedersen standing on the terrace
watching my progress. For an instant we both stood still; then he
moved and started down the steps, and came down the garden
to meet me.

I went on more slowly, still holding the spray of blossom.
I knew then. I knew before he came close enough for me to
see the expression on his face, but I went on, up through the
orchard, and we met at last by the little dry-stone wall.

He said my name. That was all.

I said, "I know. You don't have to tell me."

"She died during the night. When Maria went in this morning to wake her . . . it was all over. It was so peaceful."

It occurred to me that we were not doing much to comfort each other. Or maybe there was no need. He put out a hand to help me over the wall, and kept my hand in his as we walked together up through the garden to the house.

She was buried, according to Spanish law, that very day, and in the little churchyard in the village. There was only the priest present, and Otto and Maria and myself. When it was all over, I put the spray of almond blossom on to her grave.

I flew back to London the next morning, and Otto drove me to the airport in his car. For most of the time we travelled in silence, but as we approached the terminal he suddenly said, "Rebecca, I don't know whether this has any significance, but I would have married Lisa. I would have married her, but I already have a wife in Sweden. We do not live together, and have not done so for a number of years, but she will not divorce me because her religion will not allow it."

"You didn't need to tell me, Otto."

"I wanted you to know."

"You made her so happy. You took such care of her."

"I am glad that you came. I am glad that you saw her."

"Yes." There was, all at once, a terrible lump in my throat, and my eyes filled and brimmed with painful tears. "Yes, I am glad too."

In the terminal, my ticket and my luggage checked, we stood and faced each other.

"Don't wait," I said. "Go now. I hate goodbyes."

"All right . . . but first . . ." He felt in his jacket pocket and took out three fine, worn silver bracelets. My mother had worn

39

them always. She had been wearing them that last night. "You must have these." He took my hand and slipped them on to my wrist. "And this." Out of another pocket came a folded wad of British notes. He pressed it into my palm and closed my fingers over it. "They were in her handbag . . . so you must have them."

I knew they hadn't been in her handbag. She never had any money in her handbag except a few coppers for the next telephone call, and some dog-eared bills, long overdue. But there was something in Otto's face that I couldn't refuse, so I took the money and kissed him, and he turned on his heel, without a word.

I flew back to London in a state of miserable indecision. Emotionally I was empty, drained even of grief. Physically I found that I was exhausted but I could neither sleep nor face the meal that the stewardess offered me. She brought me tea and I tried to drink that, but it tasted bitter and I left it to grow cold.

It was as though a long-locked door had been opened, but only a crack, and it was up to me to open it wide, although what lay behind it was dark and fraught with uncertainty.

Perhaps I should go to Cornwall and seek out my mother's family, but the glimpses I had been given of the set-up at Porthkerris were not encouraging. My grandfather would be very old, lonely and probably bitter. I realised that I had made no arrangement with Otto Pedersen about letting him know that my mother was dead, and so there was the hideous possibility that if I went to see him, I should be the one who would have to break the news. As well, I blamed him a little for having let his daughter make such a mess of her life. I knew that she was impulsive and thoughtless, and stubborn too, but surely he could have been a little more positive in his dealings with her. He could have sought her out, offered to help, inspected me, his grandchild. But he had done none of these things, and surely this would always stand like a high wall between us.

And yet, I longed for roots. I did not necessarily want to live with them, but I wanted them to be there. There were things at Boscarva that had belonged to my mother, and so now belonged to me. She had wanted me to have them, had said as much, so perhaps I was under an obligation to go to Cornwall and claim them as my own, but to go only for this reason seemed both soulless and greedy.

I leaned back and dozed and heard again my mother's voice. *I was never frightened of him. I loved him. I should have gone back.*

And she had said a name – Sophia – but I had never found out who Sophia was.

I slept at last and dreamed that I was there. But the house in my dream had no shape or form and the only real thing about it was the sound of the wind, battering its way inland, fresh and cold from the open sea.

I was in London by the early afternoon, but the dark day had lost its shape and meaning, and I could not think what I was meant to do with what remained of it. In the end I got a taxi and went to Walton Street to seek out Stephen Forbes.

I found him upstairs, going through a box of books out of an old house which had just been sold up. There was no one else with him, and as I appeared at the top of the stairs he stood up and came towards me, thinking that I was a potential customer. When he saw that I was not, his manner changed.

"Rebecca! You're back."

I stood there, with my hands in my coat pockets.

"Yes. I got in about two." He watched me, his face a question. I said, "My mother died, early yesterday morning. I was just in time. I had an evening with her, and we talked and talked."

"I see," said Stephen. "I'm glad you saw her." He cleared some books from the edge of a table, and leaned against it,

ROSAMUNDE PILCHER

folding his arms and eyeing me through his spectacles. He said,
"What are you going to do now?"

"I don't know."

"You look exhausted. Why not take a few days off?"

I said again, "I don't know."

He frowned. "What don't you know?"

"I don't know what to do."

"What's the problem?"

"Stephen, have you ever heard of an artist called Grenville
Bayliss?"

"Heavens, yes. Why?"

"He's my grandfather."

Stephen's face was a study. "Good Lord. When did you find
that out?"

"My mother told me. I'd never heard of him," I had to admit.

"You should have."

"Is he well known?"

"He was, twenty years ago when I was a boy. There was a
Grenville Bayliss over the dining-room fireplace in my father's
old house in Oxford. Part of my growing up, one might say. A
grey stormy sea and a fishing boat with a brown sail. Used to
make me feel seasick to look at it. He specialised in seascapes."

"He was a sailor. I mean, he'd been in the Royal Navy."

"That follows."

I waited for him to go on, but he was silent. I said at last,
"What am I to do, Stephen?"

"What do you want to do, Rebecca?"

"I never had a family."

"Is it so important?"

"Suddenly it is."

"Then go and see him. Is there any reason not to?"

"I'm frightened."

"Of what?"

42

"I don't know. Of being snubbed, I suppose. Or ignored."

"Were there dreadful family rows?"

"Yes. And cuttings-off. And never darken my door again. You know the sort of thing."

"Did your mother suggest that you went?"

"No. Not in so many words. But she said there were some things that belonged to her. She thought I should have them."

"What sort of things?"

I told him. "I know it's nothing very much. Perhaps not even worth making the journey for. But I'd like to have something that belonged to her. Besides . . ." I tried to turn it into a joke ". . . they might help to fill up some of the blank spaces in the new flat."

"I think collecting your possessions should be a secondary reason for going to Cornwall. Your first should be making friends with Grenville Bayliss."

"Supposing he doesn't want to make friends?"

"Then no harm has been done. Except possibly a little bruising to your pride, but that won't kill you."

"You're rail-roading me into this," I told him.

"If you didn't want my advice, then why did you come to see me?"

He had a point. "I don't know," I admitted.

He laughed. "You don't know much, do you?" and when at last I smiled back, he said, "Look. Today's Thursday. Go home and get some sleep. And if tomorrow's too soon, then go down to Cornwall at the weekend. Just go. See how the land lies, see how the old boy is. It may take a few days, but that doesn't matter. Don't come back to London until you've done all you can. And if you can get hold of your own bits and pieces, well and good, but remember that they're of secondary importance."

"Yes. I'll remember."

He stood up. "Then push off," he said. "I've got enough to do without wasting my time running a private Tell Auntie column on your account."

"Can I come back to work when all this is over?"

"You better had. I can't manage without you."

"Goodbye then," I said.

"Au revoir," said Stephen, and as if on an afterthought, leaned forward to give me a clumsy kiss.

"And Good Luck!"

I had already spent enough money on taxis, so, still carrying my case, I walked up to the bus stop and waited until one came, and lurched my way back to Fulham. Gazing, unseeing, out of the window at the grey, crowded streets, I tried to make some plans. I would go to Cornwall, as Stephen suggested, on Monday. At this time of year it shouldn't be difficult to get a seat on the train or find somewhere to stay when I finally got to Porthkerris. And Maggie would keep an eye on my flat.

Thinking of the flat made me remember the chairs I had bought before I had gone to Ibiza. That day seemed a lifetime ago. But if I did not claim them then they would be sold as the disagreeable young man had threatened. With this in mind, I got off the bus a few stops before my own so that I could call into the shop and pay for the chairs and thus be certain that they would be waiting for me when I returned.

I had steeled myself to do business once more with the young man in the blue denims, but as I let myself in and the bell rang with the opening and the closing of the door, I saw with some relief that it was not he who stood up from behind the desk at the back of the shop, but another man, older, with grey hair and a dark beard.

He came forward, taking off a pair of horn-rimmed spectacles, as I thankfully put down my suitcase.

"Good afternoon."

"Oh, good afternoon. I came about some chairs I bought last Monday. Cherrywood, balloon-back ones."

"Oh, yes, I know."

"One of them had to be repaired."

"It's been done. Do you want to take them with you?"

"No. I've got a suitcase. I can't carry them. And I'm going away for a few days. But I thought if I paid for them now, perhaps you'd keep them until I got back."

"Yes, of course." He had a charming, deep voice, and when he smiled his rather saturnine face lit up.

I began to open my bag. "Will it be all right if I write you a cheque? I've got a Banker's Card."

"That's all right . . . would you like to use my desk? And here's a pen."

I began to write. "Who shall I make it out to?"

"To me. Tristram Nolan."

I was gratified to know that it was he who owned this pleasant shop and not my mannerless, cowboy friend. I wrote the cheque and crossed it, and handed it to him. He stood, head down, reading it, and took so long that I thought I must have forgotten something.

"Have I put the date?"

"Yes, that's perfect." He looked up. "It's just your name. Bayliss. It's not very common."

"No. No it's not."

"Are you any relation to Grenville Bayliss?"

Having his name flung at me, just now, was extraordinary and yet not extraordinary at all, in the same way that a name, or a relevant item of news, will spring at you, unbidden, from a page of close print.

I said, "Yes, I am." And then because there was no reason why he shouldn't know, "He's my grandfather."

"Extraordinary," he said.

I was puzzled. "Why?"

"I'll show you." He laid my cheque down on his desk and went to pull out from behind a drop-leafed sofa table a large, sturdy oil painting in a gilt frame. He held it up, balancing one corner on his desk, and I saw that it was by my grandfather. His signature was in the corner, and the date below it, 1932.

"I've only just bought it. It needs cleaning, of course, but I think it's very charming."

I stepped closer to inspect it, and saw sand dunes in an evening light, and two young boys, naked, bent over a collection of shells. The work was perhaps old-fashioned, but the composition charming – the colouring delicate and yet somehow robust – as though the boys, vulnerable in their nakedness, were still tough, and creatures to be reckoned with.

"He was good, wasn't he?" I said, and could not hide the note of pride in my voice.

"Yes. A marvellous colourist." He put the picture back. "Do you know him well?"

"I don't know him at all. I've never met him."

He said nothing, simply stood, waiting for me to enlarge on this odd statement. To fill the silence I went on. "But I've decided that perhaps it's time I did. In fact, I'm going to Cornwall on Monday."

"But that's splendid. The roads will be empty at this time of the year, and it's a lovely drive."

"I'm going by train. I haven't got a car."

"It will still be a pleasant journey. I hope the sun shines for you."

"Thank you very much."

We moved back to the door. He opened it, I picked up my suitcase. "You'll look after my chairs for me?"

"Of course. Goodbye. And have a good time in Cornwall."

3

But the sun did not shine for me. Monday dawned grey and depressing as ever and my faint hopes that the weather would improve as the train rocketed westwards soon died, for the sky darkened with every mile and the wind got up and the day finally dissolved into pouring rain. There was nothing to be seen from the streaming windows; only the blurred shapes of hills and farmsteads, and every now and then the clustered roofs of a village flashed by, or we raced through the half-empty station of some small anonymous town.

By Plymouth, I comforted myself, it would be different. We would cross the Saltash Bridge and find ourselves in another country, another climate, where there would be pink-washed cottages and palm trees and thin winter sunshine. But of course all that happened was that the rain fell even more relentlessly; as I stared out at flooded fields and leafless wind-torn trees, my hopes finally died and I began to be discouraged.

It was nearly a quarter to five by the time we reached the junction which was the end of my journey, and the dark afternoon had sunk, already, into twilight. As the train slowed down alongside the platform, I saw an incongruous palm tree, silhouetted like a broken umbrella against the streaming sky, and the falling rain shimmered and danced in front of the lighted sign which said "St Abbotts, change for Porthkerris". The train finally stopped. I shouldered my rucksack and opened the heavy door which was instantly torn out of my grasp by the wind. The sudden impact of strong cold air, driven inland over the dark sea, made me gasp, and with some idea of making haste I picked up my bag and jumped out on to the platform. I followed the general exodus of travellers up and over the wooden bridge to the station building on the far side. Most of the other passengers seemed to have friends to meet them, or else walked through the ticket office in a purposeful fashion, as though knowing that a car was waiting for them on the far side. Blindly, I followed them, feeling very new and strange but hoping that they would lead me to a taxi. But when I came out into the station yard, there were no taxis. I stood about, hopeful of being offered a lift, but too shy to ask for one, until the tail light of the last car, inevitably, disappeared up the hill in the direction of the main road and I was forced to return to the ticket office for help and advice.

I found a porter, stacking hen coops in a smelly parcels office.

"I'm sorry, but I have to get to Porthkerris. Would there be a taxi?"

He shook his head slowly, without hope, and then said, brightening slightly, "There's a bus. Runs every hour." He glanced up at the slow-ticking clock high on the wall. "But you've just missed one, so you'll 'ave to wait some time."

"Can't I ring up for a taxi?"

"Isn't much call for taxis at this time of the year."

I let my heavy rucksack slip to the floor and we gazed at each other, both defeated by the enormity of the problem. My wet feet were slowly congealing. As we stood there, there came, above the noise of the storm, the sound of a car, driven very fast down the hill from the road.

I said, raising my voice slightly in order to make my point, "I must get a taxi. Where could I telephone?"

"There's a box just out there . . ."

I turned to go in search of it, trailing my rucksack behind me, and as I did so I heard the car stop outside in the yard; a door slammed, footsteps ran, and the next moment a man appeared, banging the door open and shut against the icy wind. He shook himself like a dog before crossing the floor and disappearing through the open door of the Parcels Office.

I heard him say, "Hello, Ernie. I think there's a parcel here for me. From London."

" 'Ullo, Mr Gardner. That's a dirty night."

"Filthy. The road's awash. That looks like it . . . that one over there. Yes, that's it. Want me to sign for it?"

"Oh, yes, you'll 'ave to sign. 'Ere we are . . ."

I imagined the slip of paper, smoothed on a table top, the stub of a pencil taken from behind Ernie's ear. And for the life of me I could not remember where I had heard that voice before, nor why I knew it so well.

"That's great. Thanks very much."

"You're welcome."

The telephone, the taxi, forgotten for the moment, I watched the door, waiting for him to reappear. When he did, carrying a large box stuck with red GLASS labels, I saw the long legs, the blue denims drenched in mud to the knee, and a black oilskin, beaded and running with rivulets of water. He was bareheaded, his black hair plastered to his skull, and he saw me for the first time and stopped dead, holding the parcel in front of him like an offering. In his dark eyes was first a flicker of puzzlement, and then recognition. He began to smile. He said, "Good God!"

It was the young man who had sold me the two little cherrywood chairs.

I stood open-mouthed, feeling obscurely that someone had played me a mean and unfair trick. If ever I was in need of a friend it was at this moment, and yet fate had chosen to send me possibly the last person on earth I ever wanted to see again. And that he should see me thus, drenched and desperate, was somehow the last straw.

His smile widened. "What a fantastic coincidence. What are you doing here?"

"I've just got off the train."

"Where are you going?"

I had to tell him. "To Porthkerris."

"Is someone coming for you?"

I very nearly lied and told him "yes." Anything to get rid of him. But I was always a useless fibber, and he would be bound to guess the truth. I said, "No," and then I went on, trying to sound competent, as though I could take good care of myself, "I'm just going to phone for a taxi."

"It'll take hours. I'm going to Porthkerris, I'll give you a ride."

"Oh, you don't need to bother . . ."

"No bother, I'm going anyway. Is that all your luggage?"

"Yes, but . . ."

"Come on then."

I still hesitated, but he seemed to consider the matter already settled, going over to the door to open it, and holding it open with his shoulder, waiting for me to follow. So eventually I did, edging past him, and out into the fury of the dark evening.

In the dim light I saw the Mini pick-up, parked, with the sidelights burning. Letting the door slam behind him, he crossed over to this, and gently loaded his parcel into the back, and then took my rucksack from me, and heaved this in too, covering the two bundles in a cursory fashion with an old piece of tarpaulin. I stood watching him, but he said, "Go on, get in, there's no point us both getting wet through," so I did as I was told, settling myself in the passenger seat with my bag jammed between my legs. Almost at once he had joined me, shutting his door with an almighty slam, and switching on the engine as though there were not a moment to be lost. We roared up the hill away from the station, and the next moment had turned on to the main road and were heading for Porthkerris.

He said, "Tell me more, now. I thought you lived in London."

"Yes, I do."

"Have you come down for a holiday?"

"Sort of."

"That sounds good and vague. Are you staying with friends?"

"Yes. No. I don't know."

"What does that mean?"

"Just that. It means I don't know." This sounded rude but it couldn't be helped. I felt as though I had no control over what I was saying.

"Well, you'd better make up your mind before you get to Porthkerris, otherwise you'll be spending the night on the beach."

"I . . . I'm going to stay in a hotel. Just for tonight."

"Well, that's great. Which one?"

I sent him an exasperated look and he said, reasonably enough, "Well, if I don't know which one, I can't take you there, can I?"

He seemed to have me cornered. I said, "I haven't booked in to any hotel. I mean, I thought I could do that when I arrived. There *are* hotels, aren't there?"

"Porthkerris is running with them. Every other house is a hotel. But at this time of the year most of them are closed."

"Do you know some that are open?"

"Yes. But it depends what you want to pay."

He glanced at me sideways, taking in my patched jeans,

scuffed shoes, and an old fur-lined leather coat that I had worn for warmth and comfort. At the moment this garment looked and smelt like a wet dog.

"We go from one extreme to the other. The Castle, up on the hill, where you change for dinner, and dance the foxtrot to a three-piece orchestra, right down to Mrs Kernow who does Bed and Breakfast at Number Two, Fish Lane. Mrs Kernow I can recommend. She looked after me for three months or more before I got into my own place, and her prices are very reasonable."

I was diverted. "Your own place? You mean you live here?"

"I do now. Have done for the last six months."

"But . . . the shop in the New Kings Road . . . where I bought the chairs?"

"I was just helping out for a day or so."

We came to a crossroads, and, slowing down, he turned to look at me. "Have you got the chairs yet?"

"No. But I've paid for them. They'll still be there when I get back."

"Good," said the young man.

We drove for a little in silence. Through a village, and up over a wild bit of country high above the sea; then the road leaned down again, and there were trees on either side of us. Through these, through twisted trunks and branches tortured by the wind, there presently appeared, far below us, the twinkling lights of a little town.

"Is that Porthkerris?"

"It is. And in a moment you're going to have to tell me if it's to be The Castle or Fish Lane."

I swallowed. The Castle was out of the question, obviously, but if I went to Fish Lane I would necessarily place myself under an obligation to this managing person. I had not come to Porthkerris for any other reason than to see Grenville Bayliss, and I had an uncomfortable feeling that if I once got involved with this man he would stick like a burr.

I said, "No, not The Castle . . ." meaning to suggest some other, more modest establishment, but he cut me short.

"That's great," he said, with a grin. "Mrs Kernow of Fish Lane it is, and you won't regret it."

My first impression of Porthkerris, in the dark and the gusty rain, was confused to say the least of it. The town was, on this unsalubrious evening, nearly empty of people; the deserted streets gleamed wetly with reflected light, and the gutters ran with water.

At a great speed, we plunged down into a warren of baffling lanes and alleys, at one time emerging out on to the road which circled the harbour, only to turn back once more into the maze of cobbled roads and uneven, haphazard houses.

We turned at last into a narrow street of grey terrace houses, with front doors opening flush on to the pavement.

All was seemly and respectable. Lace curtains veiled windows, and there could be glimpsed statuettes of girls with dogs, or large green pots containing aspidistras.

The car slowed at last and stopped.

"We're here." He switched off the engine, and I could hear the wind and, above its whine, the nearby sound of the sea. Great breakers thundered up on to the sand, and there was the long hiss of the retreating waves.

He said, "You know, I don't know your name."

"It's Rebecca Bayliss. And I don't know yours."

"Joss Gardner . . . it's short for Jocelyn, not Joseph." With this useful bit of information he got out of the car and rang a bell in a door and, while waiting for an answer, went to retrieve my rucksack from underneath the tarpaulin. As he heaved it out, the door opened and he turned and was illuminated in a shaft of warm light which streamed from inside the house.

"Joss!".

"Hello, Mrs Kernow."

"What are you doing here?"

"I've brought you a visitor. I said you were the best hotel in Porthkerris."

"Oh, my soul, I don't belong to take visitors at this time of the year. But come along in now, out of the rain, what weather isn't it? Tom's down at the Coastguard lodge, been some sort of a warning up from the Trevose way, but I don't know, I haven't heard no rockets . . ."

Somehow we were all inside and the door shut and there was scarcely room for the three of us to stand in the narrow hall.

"Come along in by the fire . . . it's nice and warm, I'll get you a cup of tea if you like . . ." We followed her into a tiny, cluttered, cosy parlour. She knelt to poke the fire to life and add more coal, and for the first time I was able to take a good look at her. I saw a small, bespectacled lady, quite elderly, wearing bedroom slippers and a pinafore over her good brown dress.

"We don't really want tea," he told her. "We just want to know if you can give Rebecca a bed – for a night or so."

She stood up from the fireplace. "Well, I don't know . . ." She looked at me doubtfully, and what with my appearance and the dog-smelling coat I didn't blame her for being doubtful.

I started to open my mouth, but Joss sailed in before I could say a word. "She's highly respectable and she won't run away with the spoons. I'll vouch for her."

"Well . . ." Mrs Kernow smiled. Her eyes were pretty, a very pale blue. "The room's empty, so she may as well have it. But I can't give her supper tonight, not expecting anybody, I haven't anything in the house but a couple of little pasties."

"That's all right," said Joss. "I'll feed her."

I started to protest, but once again I was overborne. "I'll leave her here to get settled in and unpacked, and then I'll be back about . . ." he glanced at his watch ". . . seven thirty, to pick her up. That all right?" he flung casually in my direction. "You're an angel, Mrs Kernow, and I love you like a mother." He put an arm around her and kissed her. She looked delighted; then he gave me a final, cheerful grin, said, "See you," and so departed. We heard his car roaring away down the street.

"He's a lovely boy," Mrs Kernow informed me. "I had him living here three months or more . . . now come along, pick up your little bag and I'll show you your room. 'Course it'll be cold, but I've got an electric fire you can have, and the water in the tank's nice and hot if you want a bath . . . I always say you feel so mucky coming off those dirty trains . . ."

The room was as tiny as all the other rooms in this little house, furnished with an enormous double bed which took up nearly all the space. But it was clean and, presently, warm, and after Mrs Kernow had shown me where to find the bathroom she went back downstairs and left me to myself.

I went to kneel by the low window and draw back the curtains. The old frames had been jammed tight shut against the wind by rubber wedges, and the dark glass streamed with rain. There was nothing to be seen, but I stayed there anyway, wondering what I was doing in this little house, and trying to work out why Joss Gardner's sudden reappearance in my life had left me with this unexplained feeling of unease.

4

I needed defences. I needed to build up my confidence and my self-esteem, disliking the role of rescued waif in which I had suddenly found myself. A hot bath and a change of clothes went a long way towards restoring my composure. I did my hair, made up my eyes, splashed on the last of a bottle of expensive scent and was halfway towards being in charge again. I had already unpacked a dress from the ubiquitous rucksack and hung it hopefully to shed its wrinkles; now I put it on, a dark cotton with long sleeves, and dark stockings, very fine, and shoes with heels and old-fashioned buckles which I had found, long back, on a stall in the Portobello Road . . . As I fastened my pearl ear-rings I heard, over the rattle and bang of the gusty wind, the sound of Joss Gardner's little van, tyres drumming on the cobbles, coming up the street. It screeched to a noisy halt outside the door, and the next moment I heard his voice downstairs, calling first for Mrs Kernow and then for me.

I continued, slowly, to screw the fastening of the last ear-ring. I picked up my bag, and then my leather coat. This I had draped near the electric fire in the hope that it would dry off, but it hadn't. The heat had merely emphasised the smell of a spaniel come in from a wet walk, and it still weighed heavy as lead. Lugging it over my arm, I went down the stairs.

"Hallo, there." Joss, in the hall, looked up at me. "Well, what a transformation. Feel better now?"

"Yes."

"Give me your coat . . ."

He took it from me intending to help me on with it, and instantly became a comic weightlifter, sagging at the knees with the sheer bulk of it.

"You can't wear this, it'll drive you into the ground. Anyway it's still wet."

"I haven't got another." Still toting the coat, he started to laugh. My self-esteem began to drain away and some of this must have showed on my face, because he suddenly stopped laughing and shouted for Mrs Kernow. When she appeared, with an expression both exasperated and loving on her face, he bundled my coat into her arms, told her to dry it for me, unbuttoned and removed his own black oilskin and laid it, with a certain grace, around my shoulders.

Beneath it he wore a soft grey sweater, a cotton scarf knotted at the neck. "Now," he said, "we are ready to go." He opened the door, on to a curtain of rain.

I protested, "But you'll get wet," but he only said "Scuttle" so I scuttled, and he scuttled too, and the next instant we were back in the van, scarcely wet at all, with the doors banged tight and shut against the storm, although small puddles of rain on my seat and at my feet gave rise to the suspicion that this staunch vehicle was no longer as watertight as it had once been. But he started the noisy engine and we were away, and with the volume of water both outside and inside the car it was a little like being taken for a fast ride in a leaky motor boat.

I said, "Where are we going?"

"The Anchor. It's just round the corner. Not very smart. Do you mind?"

"Why should I mind?"

"You might mind. You might have wanted to be taken to The Castle."

"You mean to foxtrot to a three-piece orchestra?"

He grinned. He said, "I can't foxtrot. Nobody ever learned me."

We flashed down Fish Lane, around a right-angled corner or two, beneath a stone archway and so out into a small square. One side of this was formed by the low, uneven shape of an old inn. Warm light shone from behind small windows spilled from a crooked doorway and the Inn sign over the door swung and creaked in the wind. There were four or five cars already parked outside, and Joss inserted the van neatly into a tidy space between two of them, turned off the engine, said, "One, two, three, run," and we both got out and sprinted the short distance between the car and the shelter of the porch.

There Joss shook himself slightly, brushed the rain from the soft surface of his sweater, took the oilskin off my shoulders and opened the door for me to go ahead of him.

It was warm inside, and low-ceilinged and smelt the way old pubs have always smelt. Of beer and pipe smoke and musty wood. There was a bar, with high stools, and tables around the edge of the room. Two old men were playing darts in a corner.

The barman looked up and said, "Hi, Joss." Joss put the oilskin up on a coat hook, and led me across the room to be introduced.

"Tommy, this is Rebecca. Rebecca, this is Tommy Williams. He's been here man and boy; anything you want to know about Porthkerris, or the people who live here, you come and ask Tommy."

We said, "How do you do." Tommy had grey hair and a lot of wrinkles. He looked as though he might be a fisherman in his spare time. We sat ourselves on two stools, and Joss ordered a Scotch and soda for me and a Scotch and water for himself, and while Tommy fixed these the two men began to talk, falling comfortably into conversation the way men in pubs always seem to.

"How are things going with you?" That was Tommy.

"Not too bad."

"When are you opening up?"

"Easter, maybe, with a bit of luck."

"Place finished is it?"

"More or less."

"Who's doing the carpentry?"

"Doing it myself."

"That'll save you something."

My attention wandered. I lit a cigarette and looked around me, liking what I saw. The two old men playing darts; a young couple, jeaned and long-haired, crouched over a table and a couple of pints of bitter, discussing, with avid and intense concentration – existentialism? Concrete painting? How they were going to pay the rent? Something. But it mattered, intensely, to both of them.

And then a party of four, older, expensively dressed, the men self-consciously casual, the women unwittingly formal. I guessed they were staying at The Castle, and out of boredom with the weather, perhaps, had come down the town for a spot of slumming. They seemed uncomfortable, as though they knew they looked out of place, and could scarcely wait to get back to the padded velvet comfort of the big hotel on the hill.

My eyes moved on around the room, and it was then that I caught sight of the dog. He was a beautiful dog, a great red setter, his coat handsome and shining, his tail a silken plume of copper fur against the grey flags of the floor. He sat very still, close to his master, and every now and then the tail would move slightly in a thump of approval, a private applause.

Intrigued, I inspected the man who appeared to own this

enviable creature, and found him almost as interesting as the dog. Sitting, with an elbow on the table top, and his chin resting on his fist, he presented to me a clear and unblurred profile, almost as though he were posing for my inspection. His head was well shaped, and his hair had that thick silver-fox look of a person who has started to go grey early in life. The single eye which his profile allowed me was deep-set, and darkly shadowed, the nose was long and aquiline, the mouth pleasant, the chin strongly formed. And, from the length of his wrist, emerging from a checked shirt cuff and the sleeve of a grey tweed jacket, and the way he disposed of his legs beneath the little table, I guessed that he was tall, probably over six feet.

As I watched him, he laughed suddenly at something his companion had said. This drew my attention to the other man, and I felt a shock of surprise, because, for some reason, they did not match. Where the one was slender and elegant, the other was short, fat, red of face, and dressed in a tight-fitting navy blue blazer and a shirt collar that looked as though it were about to strangle him. It was not overly warm in the pub, but there was a shine of sweat on the ruddy brow, and I saw that the dark hair had been barbered with some ingenuity, so that a long oiled lock was combed up and over, concealing what would otherwise have been a totally bald head.

The man with the dog was not smoking, but the fat man suddenly crushed out his own cigarette in the brimming ash-tray on the table, as though emphasising some point that he was making, and almost instantly reached into his pocket for a silver case and another cigarette.

But the man with the dog had decided that it was time to go. He took his hand from his chin, pushed back his shirt cuff to consult his watch, and then finished his drink. The fat man, apparently anxious to comply with the other's arrangements, hastily lit the cigarette and then tossed back his whisky. They began to get

61

up, pushing back their chairs with a hideous scraping sound. The dog stood up, his tail swooping in exultant circles.

Standing, one so short and fat and the other so tall and slim, the two men looked more ill-assorted than ever. The thin one reached for a raincoat which had been lying across the back of his chair and slung it over his shoulders like a cloak, and then turned towards us, heading for the door. For an instant I was disappointed, because full face, his finely drawn good looks did not live up to the promise of that intriguing profile. And then I forgot about being disappointed, because he suddenly saw Joss. And Joss, perhaps sensing his presence, stopped talking to Tommy Williams and turned to see who was standing behind him. For an instant they both looked disconcerted, and then the tall man smiled, and the smile etched lines down his thin brown cheeks and creased up his eyes, and it was impossible not to be warmed by such charm.

He said, "Joss. Long time no see." His voice was pleasant and friendly.

"Hi," said Joss, not getting off his stool.

"I thought you were in London."

"No. Back again."

The creaking swing of the door caught my attention. The other man, the fat man, had quietly left. I decided that he had an urgent appointment and thought no more about it.

"I'll tell the old boy I've seen you."

"Yes. Do that."

The deep-set eyes moved in my direction, and then away again. I waited to be introduced, but nothing happened. For some reason this lack of manners on Joss's part was like a slap in the face.

At last, "Well, see you around," said the tall man, and moved off.

"Sure," said Joss.

"Night, Tommy," he called to the barman as he pushed the door open and let the dog out ahead of him.

"Good night, Mr Bayliss," said the barman.

I felt my head jerk around as though someone had pulled a string. He had already disappeared, leaving the door swinging behind him. Without thinking, I slipped off the stool to go after him, but a hand caught my arm and restrained me, and I turned to find Joss holding me back. For a surprising second our eyes clashed, and then I shook myself free. Outside I heard a car start up. Now it was too late.

I said, "Who is he?"

"Eliot Bayliss."

Eliot. Roger's boy. Mollie's child. Grenville Bayliss's grandson. My cousin. My family.

"He's my cousin."

"I didn't know that."

"You know my name. Why didn't you tell him? Why did you stop me going after him?"

"You'll meet him soon enough. Tonight it's too late and too wet and too dark for family reunions."

"Grenville Bayliss is my grandfather, too."

"I thought there was probably some connection," said Joss coolly. "Have another drink."

By now I was really angry. "I don't want another drink."

"In that case, let's go and eat."

"I don't want to eat either."

I thought that I truly didn't want to. I didn't want to spend another moment with this boorish and overbearing young man. I watched him finish his drink and get down off his stool, and for an instant I thought that he was actually going to take me at my word; was going to drive me back to Fish Lane and there dump me, un-nourished. But, luckily, he did not call my bluff, simply paid for the drinks, and without a word led the way through a door at the far end of the bar, which gave on to a flight of stairs and a small restaurant. I followed him because there didn't seem to be anything else to do. Besides, I was hungry.

Most of the tables were already occupied, but a waitress saw Joss and recognised him and came over to say good evening, and led us to what was obviously the best table in the room, set in the narrow alcove of a jutting bay window. Beyond the window could be seen the shapes of rain-washed roofs, and beyond them again the liquid darkness of the harbour, a-shimmer with reflections from the street lamps on the quay and the riding lights of fishing boats.

We faced each other. I was still deeply angry and would not look at him. I sat, drawing patterns with my finger on the table mat, and listened to him ordering what I was to eat. Apparently I was not even to be allowed the right of making my own choice. I heard the waitress say, "For the young lady, too?" as though even she were surprised by his cursory behaviour, and Joss said, "Yes, for the young lady, too," and the waitress went off, and we were alone.

After a little I looked up. His dark gaze met mine, unblinking. The silence grew, and I had the ridiculous feeling that he was waiting for me to apologise to him.

I heard myself say, "If you won't let me talk to Eliot Bayliss, perhaps you'll talk about him."

"What do you want to know?"

"Is he married?" It was the first question that came into my head.

"No."

"He's attractive." Joss acknowledged this. "Does he live alone?"

"No, with his mother. They have a house up at High Cross, six miles or so from here, but about a year ago they moved into Boscarva, to be with the old man."

"Is my grandfather ill?"

"You don't know very much about your family, do you?"

"No." I sounded defiant.

"About ten years ago Grenville Bayliss had a heart attack. That's when he stopped painting. But he always appears to have had the constitution of an ox, and he made a miraculous recovery. He didn't want to leave Boscarva, and he had this couple to take care of him . . ."

"The Pettifers?"

Joss frowned. "How do you know about the Pettifers?"

"My mother told me." I thought of the long-ago tea parties by the kitchen fire. "I never imagined they'd still be there."

"Mrs Pettifer died last year, so Pettifer and your grandfather were left on their own. Grenville Bayliss is eighty now, and Pettifer can't be far behind him. Mollie Bayliss wanted them to move up to High Cross and sell Boscarva, but the old man was adamant, so in the end she and Eliot moved in with him. Without noticeable enthusiasm, I may add." He leaned back in his chair, his long clever hands resting on the edge of the table. "Your mother . . . was she called Lisa?" I nodded.

"I knew Grenville had a daughter who'd had a daughter, but the fact that you call yourself Bayliss threw me slightly."

"My father left my mother before I was born. She never used his name."

"Where's your mother now?"

"She died – just a few days ago. In Ibiza." I repeated, "Just a few days ago," because all at once it seemed like a lifetime.

"I'm sorry." I made some sort of vague gesture, because there weren't any words. "Does your grandfather know?"

"I don't know."

"Have you come to tell him?"

"I suppose I may have to." The idea of doing so was daunting.

"Does he know you're here? In Porthkerris?"

65

I shook my head. "He doesn't even know me. I mean we've never met. I've never been here before." I made the final admission. "I don't even know how to find his house."

"One way and another," said Joss, "you're going to give him something of a shock."

I felt anxious. "Is he very frail?"

"No, he's not frail. He's fantastically tough. But he's getting old."

"My mother said he was frightening. Is he still frightening?"

Joss made a gruesome face, doing nothing to comfort me. "Terrifying," he said.

The waitress brought our soup. It was oxtail, thick and brown and very hot. I was so hungry that I ate it right down to the bottom of the bowl without saying another word. As I finally laid down my spoon, I looked up and saw that Joss was laughing at me.

"For a girl who didn't want to eat, you haven't done so badly."

But this time I did not rise. I pushed the empty bowl away, and leaned my elbows on the table.

"How is it that you know so much about the Bayliss family?" I asked him.

Joss had not bolted his soup as I had. Now, he was taking his time, buttering a roll, being maddeningly slow.

"It's easy," he said. "I do a certain amount of work up at Boscarva."

"What sort of work?"

"Well, I restore antique furniture. And don't gape in that unattractive fashion, it does nothing for you."

"*Restore antique furniture?* You must be joking."

"I'm not. And Grenville Bayliss has a houseful of old and very valuable stuff. In his day he made a lot of money, and he invested most of it in antiques. Now, some of the things are in a shocking state of repair, not that they haven't been polished to within an inch of their lives, but then years ago he put in central heating and that wrecks old furniture. Drawers shrink and veneers curl and crack, and legs fall off chairs. Incidentally . . ." he added, diverted by the memory ". . . it was I who mended your cherrywood chair."

"But how long have you been doing this?"

"Let's see, I left school when I was seventeen, and I'm twenty-four now, so that makes it about seven years."

"But you had to *learn* . . ."

"Oh, sure. I did joinery and carpentry first, four years of it at a trade school in London, and then when I'd got that under my belt, I apprenticed myself for another couple of years to an old cabinet-maker down in Sussex. I lived with him and his wife, did all the dirty jobs in the workshop, learned everything I know."

I did a few sums. "That's only six years. You said seven."

He laughed. "I took a year off in the middle to travel. My parents said I was becoming parochial. My father has a cousin who runs a cattle ranch up in the Rockies, south-west Colorado. I worked as a ranch hand nine months or more." He frowned. "What are you grinning about?"

I told him. "That first time I saw you, in the shop . . . you looked like a ranch hand . . . you looked real. And somehow it annoyed me that you weren't."

He smiled. "And you know what you looked like?"

I cooled off. "No."

"The head girl of a nicely run orphanage. And that annoyed *me*."

A small clash of swords, and once more we were on opposite sides of the fence.

I eyed him with dislike as he cheerfully finished his soup; the waitress came to take away the empty plates, and to set down a carafe of red wine. I had not heard Joss ordering the

wine, but now I watched him pour two full glasses and I saw
the long spade-tipped fingers; I liked the idea of them working
with wood and old and beautiful things, turning and measuring
and oiling and coaxing into shape. I picked up the glass of wine
and against the light it glowed red as a ruby. I said, ''Is that
all you're doing in Porthkerris? Restoring Grenville Bayliss's
furniture?''

''Good God, no. I'm opening a shop. I managed to rent these
premises down on the harbour six months or so ago. I've been
here, off and on, ever since. Now, I'm trying to get it into some
sort of order before Easter, or Whitsun, or whenever the summer
business really starts.''

''Is it an antique shop?''

''No, modern, furniture, glass, textiles. But antique restoring
goes on in the background. I mean I have a workroom. I also
have a small pad on the top floor which is where I now live,
which is why you were able to take over my room at Mrs
Kernow's. One day when you've decided that I'm trustworthy
you can climb the rickety stairs and I'll show it to you.''

I ignored this fresh little sally.

''If you work down here, what were you doing in that shop
in London?''

''Tristram's? I told you, he's a friend; I drop in and see him
whenever I'm up in town.''

I frowned. There were so many coincidences. Our lives
seemed to be tied up in them, like a parcel well-knotted with
ends of string. I watched him finish his wine and once more
was visited with the unease which I had known earlier in the
evening. I knew I should ask him a thousand questions, but
before I could think of one the waitress arrived at our table
once more, bearing steaks and vegetables and fried potatoes and
dishes of salad. I drank some wine and watched Joss, and when
the waitress had gone I said, ''What does Eliot Bayliss do?''

"Eliot? He runs a garage up at High Cross, specialises in highly-powered second-hand cars, Mercedes, Alfa Romeos. If you've got the right sort of cheque book he can supply you with practically anything."

"You don't like him, do you?"

"I never said I didn't like him."

"But you don't."

"Perhaps it would be nearer the mark to say he doesn't like me."

"Why?" He looked up, his eyes dancing with amusement. "I haven't any idea. Now why don't you eat up your steak before it gets cold."

He drove me home. It was still raining and I was, all at once, deathly tired. Outside Mrs Kernow's door Joss stopped the car, but left the engine running. I thanked him and said good night and began to open the door, but before I could do so he had reached across and stopped me. I turned to look at him.

He said, "Tomorrow. Are you going to Boscarva?"

"Yes."

"I'll take you."

"I can go alone."

"You don't know where the house is, and it's a long climb up the hill. I'll pick you up in the car. About eleven?"

Arguing with him was like arguing with a steamroller. And I was exhausted. I said, "All right."

He opened the door for me and pushed it open.

"Good night, Rebecca."

"Good night."

"I'll see you in the morning."

5

The wind did not drop during that night. But when I woke,
the little window of my room at Mrs Kernow's gave me sight
of a square of pale blue traversed by ballooning white clouds
travelling at some speed. It was very cold, but bravely I got
up and dressed and went downstairs in search of Mrs Kernow.
I found her outside in the little yard at the back of the house,
pegging out her washing on a line. At first, battling with flailing
sheets and towels, she didn't see me, but when I appeared
between a shirt and a modest lock-knit petticoat she gave a
great start of surprise. Her own astonishment amused her, and
she shook with shrill laughter, as though the two of us were a
double act on the halls.

"You gave me some shock. I thought you were still asleep!
Comfortable were you? That dratted wind's still around the
place, but the rain's stopped, thank heaven. Want your breakfast
do you?"

"A cup of tea, perhaps."

I helped her peg out the rest of the washing and then she picked
up her empty basket and led the way back indoors. I sat at the
kitchen table and she boiled a kettle and began to fry bacon.

"Have a good supper last night did you? Go to The Anchor?
Tommy Williams keeps a good place there, always packed,
winter and summer. I heard Joss bring you home. He's a

lovely boy. I missed him when he moved out. Still, I go down sometimes to his new place, clean it up a bit for him, bring his washing home and do it here. Sad, a young man like that on his own. All wrong somehow, not having someone to take care of him.''

"I should think Joss could take care of himself.''

"It's not right a man doing woman's work.'' Mrs Kernow obviously did not believe in Women's Lib. "Besides, he's busy enough working for Mr Bayliss.''

"Do you know Mr Bayliss?''

"Everyone knows he. Lived here nearly fifty years now. One of the old ones, he is. And some lovely painter he was before he took ill. Used to have an exhibition every year, and all sorts used to come down from London, famous people, everybody. 'Course, lately we don't see so much of him. He can't walk up and down the hill like he used to, and it's a bit of a business Pettifer getting that great car down these narrow lanes. Besides, in the summer, you can't move for traffic and visitors. The place is teeming with them. Sometimes you'd think half the population of the country is jammed into this little town.''

She flipped the bacon on to a warm plate and set it in front of me. "There now, eat that up before it gets cold.''

I said, "Mrs Kernow, Mr Bayliss is my grandfather.''

She stared at me, frowning. "Your grandfather?'' Then, "Whose child are you?''

"Lisa's.''

"Lisa's child.'' She reached for a chair and slowly sat down upon it. I saw that I had shocked her. "Does Joss know?''

It seemed irrelevant. "Yes, I told him last night.''

"She was a lovely little girl.'' She stared into my face. "I can see her in you . . . except that she was so dark and you're fair. We missed her when she went, and never came back. Where is she now?''

I told her. When I had finished she said, "And Mr Bayliss doesn't know you're here?"

"No."

"You must go now. Right away. Oh, I wish I could be there to see the old man's face. He worshipped your mother . . ."

A tear gleamed. Quickly, before we were both awash with sentiment, I said, "I don't know how to get there."

Trying to tell me, she confused the two of us so much that finally she found an old envelope and the stub of a pencil and drew a rough map. Watching her I remembered Joss's promise to come at eleven o'clock and take me to Boscarva in his ramshackle van, but suddenly it seemed a much better idea to go at once, on my own. Besides, last night I had been altogether too meek and compliant. It would do Joss's boundless ego no harm to arrive here and find me already gone. The thought of this happening cheered me considerably and I went upstairs to fetch my coat.

Outside I was instantly buffeted by the wind which tunnelled down the narrow street like the draught in a chimney. It was a cold wind, smelling of the sea, but when the sun burst out from behind the racing clouds the brightness was dazzling, full of glare, and overhead gulls screamed and floated, their wings white sails against the blue of the sky.

I walked and soon I was climbing. Up narrow, cobbled streets, between haphazard lines of houses. Up flights of steps, and leaning alleys. The higher I went the stronger became the wind. As I climbed the town dropped below me, and the ocean revealed itself, dark blue, streaked with jade and purple and flecked with white horses. It spread to the horizon where the sky took over, and below me the town and the harbour shrank to toy-size, to insignificance.

I stood looking at it, catching my breath, and all at once a funny thing happened. For this new place was not new to me at

73

all, but totally familiar. I felt at home, as though I had returned to somewhere I had known all my life. And though I had scarcely thought of my mother since making the decision to come to Porthkerris, she was suddenly beside me, climbing the steep streets, long-legged, breathless, and warm with exertion as I was.

I was comforted by this sense of *déjà vu*. It made me feel less lonely and much more brave. I went on and was glad I had not waited for Joss. His presence was disturbing, but I could not for the life of me decide why. He had, after all, been quite open with me, answering questions, giving perfectly believable reasons for his every action.

It was obvious that there was no love lost between himself and Eliot Bayliss, but I could easily understand this. The two young men would have nothing in common. Eliot, albeit unwillingly, was living at Boscarva. He was a Bayliss and the house was, for the time being, his home. On the other hand Joss's occupation in the house would give him the freedom to come and go in his own time. Be found, unexpectedly, at odd hours of the day, perhaps when his presence was neither convenient nor welcome. I imagined him on easy terms with everybody, sometimes getting in the way, and worst of all, blithely unaware of the trouble he was causing. A man like Eliot would resent this and Joss, in return, would react to his resentment.

Busy with these thoughts and the exertion of climbing, I did not observe my surroundings, but now the road levelled off beneath my feet, and I stopped to look around and take my bearings. I was on top of the hill, that was for sure. Behind and below me lay the town; ahead stretched the rugged coastline, curving away into the distance. It bordered a green country, patchworked with small farms and miniature fields, traversed by deep valleys, thick with hawthorn and stunted elm, where narrow streams channelled their way down to the sea.

I looked about me. This too was country. Or a year ago it

had been. But since then a farm, perhaps, had been bought out, the bulldozers brought in, old hedges demolished, the rich earth torn up and flattened, and a new housing estate was in the process of being erected. All was raw, stark and hideous. Cement mixers churned, a lorry ground through a sea of mud, there were piles of brick and concrete, and in front of it all, like a proud banner, a hoarding which announced the man responsible for this carnage.

ERNEST PADLOW
DESIRABLE DETACHED HOUSES
FOR SALE
Apply Sea Lane, Porthkerris
Telephone Porthkerris 873

The houses were certainly detached, but only just. Scarcely three feet lay between them, and one window stared straight into another.

My heart mourned for the lost fields and the lost opportunities. As I stood there, mentally redesigning the entire project, a car came up the hill behind me, and drew to a halt in front of the hoarding. It was an old Jaguar, navy blue, and the man who stepped out of it, shutting the door behind him with a resounding thump, wore a workman's donkey jacket and carried a clip board and a lot of papers which fluttered in the wind. He turned and saw me, hesitated for only a second and then walked towards me, trying to flatten his hair down over his bald head.

"Morning." His smile was familiar as though we were old friends.

"Good morning."

I had seen him before. Last night. At The Anchor. Talking to Eliot Bayliss.

He glanced up at the hoarding.

"Thinking of buying a house for yourself?"

"No."

"You should. Get a good view up here."

I frowned. "I don't want a house."

"Be a good investment."

"Are you the foreman?"

"No." He glanced, with some pride, up at the hoarding which reared above us. "I'm Ernest Padlow."

"I see."

"Lovely site this . . ." He looked around at the devastation with some satisfaction. "Lot of people after this site, but the old girl who owned the land was a widow, and I managed to charm her into letting me have it."

I was surprised. As he spoke he reached for and lit himself a cigarette; he did not offer me one, his fingers were stained with nicotine and he seemed to me the most uncharming man I had ever met.

He turned his attention back to me. "Haven't seen you around, have I?"

"No."

"Visiting?"

"Yes, perhaps."

"It's better out of season. Not so crowded."

I said, "I'm looking for Boscarva."

Caught unawares, the bonhomie slid from his manner. His eyes were sharp as pebbles in his florid face. "Boscarva? You mean old Bayliss's place?"

"Yes."

His expression became wily. "Looking for Eliot?"

"No."

He waited for me to enlarge on this. When I didn't he tried to make a joke of it. "Well, I always say, least said, soonest mended. You want Boscarva, you go down that little lane. About

76

half a mile. You'll see the house down towards the sea. It's got a slate roof, a big garden round it. You can't miss it.''

''Thank you.'' I smiled politely. ''Goodbye.''

I turned and began to walk, feeling his eyes on my back. Then he spoke once more and I turned back. He was smiling, all friends again.

''You want a house, make up your mind quickly. They're selling like hot cakes.''

''Yes, I'm sure. But I don't want one. Thank you.''

The lane led downhill towards the great blue bowl of the sea, and now I was truly in the country, in a farmland of fields grazed by sweet-faced Guernseys. Wild violets and primroses grew in the grassy hedges, and the sun came out and turned the rich grass to emerald. Presently, I came around a corner and saw the white gates, set between low dry-stone walls; a driveway curved down, out of sight, and there were high hedges of escallonia and elm trees, tortured to unnatural shapes by the relentless winds.

I could not see the house. I stood at the open gates and looked down the drive, my courage seeping away like bathwater after the plug has been pulled out. I could not think what I was meant to do, nor what I was going to say once I had done it.

My mind was, unexpectedly and mercifully, made up for me. Down by the house, out of sight, I heard a car start up and come at some speed up the drive towards me. As it approached, a low-slung open sports car of some age and style, I stood aside to let it flash past between the gate posts and up the hill in the direction from which I had come, but still there was time to see the driver and the great red setter sitting up on the back seat, with the deliriously joyful expression of any dog being taken for a ride in an open car.

I thought that I had not been noticed but I was wrong. A moment later the car stopped with a screech of brakes and a shower of small stones flung from the back wheels. Then it went into reverse, and returned, with scarcely less speed back to the spot where I stood. It stopped, the engine was killed, and Eliot Bayliss, leaning an arm on the driving wheel, surveyed me across the empty passenger seat. He was bare-headed and wore a sheepskin car coat, and his expression was one of amusement, perhaps intrigue.

"Hello," he said.

"Good morning." I felt a fool, bundled in my old coat, with the wind blowing stray strands of hair over my face. I tried to push them away.

"You look lost."

"No. I'm not."

He continued to regard me, frowning slightly. "I saw you last night, didn't I? At The Anchor? With Joss."

"Yes."

"Are you looking for Joss? As far as I know he's not arrived yet. That is, if he's decided to come today."

"No. I mean I'm not looking for him."

"Then who – " asked Eliot Bayliss gently, "are you looking for?"

"I . . . I wanted to see old Mr Bayliss."

"It's a little early for that. He doesn't usually appear till mid-day."

"Oh." I had not thought of this. Some of my disappointment must have shown in my face, for he went on, in the same gentle and friendly voice, "Perhaps I could help. I'm Eliot Bayliss."

"I know. I mean . . . Joss told me last night."

A small frown appeared between his eyebrows. He was obviously and naturally puzzled by my relationship with Joss.

"Why did you want to see my grandfather?" And when I did not reply, he suddenly leaned across to open the door of the car and said, with cool authority, "Get in."

I got in, closing the door behind me. I could feel his eyes

on me, the shapeless coat, the patched jeans. The dog leaned forward to nuzzle my ear; his nose was cold and I reached over my shoulder to stroke the long, silky ear.

I said, "What's he called?"

"Rufus. Rufus the Red. But that doesn't answer my question, does it?"

I was saved by another interruption. Another car. But this time it was the Post Office van, rattling scarlet and cheerful, down the lane towards us. It stopped, and the postman rolled down the window to say to Eliot, good naturedly, "How can I get down the drive and deliver the letters if you park your car in the gateway?"

"Sorry," said Eliot, unperturbed, and he got out from behind the driving wheel and went to take a handful of mail and a newspaper from the postman. "I'll take it – it'll save you the trip."

"Lovely," said the postman. "Be nice if everyone did my job for me," and with a grin and a wave he went on his way, presumably to some outlying farmstead.

Eliot got back into the car.

"Well," he said, smiling at me. "What am I going to do with you?"

But I scarcely heard him. The pile of mail lay loosely in his lap, and on the top was an airmail envelope, postmarked Ibiza, and addressed to Mr Grenville Bayliss. The spiky handwriting was unmistakable.

A car is a good place for confidences. There is no telephone and you can't be unexpectedly interrupted. I said, "That letter. The one on the top. It's from a man called Otto Pedersen. He lives in Ibiza."

Eliot, frowning, took up the envelope. He turned it over and read Otto's name on the back. He looked at me. "How did you know?"

"I know his writing. I know him. He's writing to . . . to your grandfather to tell him that Lisa is dead. She died about a week ago. She was living with Otto in Ibiza."

"Lisa. You mean Lisa Bayliss?"

"Yes. Roger's sister. Your aunt. My mother."

"You're Lisa's child?"

"Yes." I turned to look directly at him. "I'm your cousin. Grenville Bayliss is my grandfather, too."

His eyes were a strange colour, greyish-green, like pebbles washed by some fast-moving stream. They showed neither shock nor pleasure, simply regarded me levelly without expression. He said at last, "Well I'll be damned."

It was hardly what I expected. We sat in silence because I could think of nothing to say, and then, as though coming to a sudden decision, he tossed the pile of mail into my lap, started the car up once more, and swung the wheel around so that once more we were facing the drive.

"What are you doing?" I asked.

"What do you think? Taking you home of course."

Home. Boscarva. We came around the curve of the drive and it was there, waiting for me. Not small, but not large either. Grey stone, smothered in creeper, grey slate roof, a semicircular stone porch with the door open to the sunshine, and inside a glimpse of red tiles, a clutter of flowerpots, the pinks and scarlets of geranium and fuchsia. A curtain fluttered at an open upstairs window and smoke plumed from a chimney. As we got out of the car the sun came out from behind a cloud and, caught in the spread arms of the house, sheltered from the north wind, it was suddenly very warm.

"Come along," said Eliot and led the way, the dog at his heels. We went through the porch and into a dark, panelled hallway illuminated by the big window on the turn of the stairs. I had imagined Boscarva as being a house of the past, sad and nostalgic, filled with the chill of old memories. But it wasn't like that at all. It was vital, humming with a sense of activity. There were papers lying on the table, a pair of gardening gloves, a dog's lead. From beyond a doorway came the kitchen sounds of voices and the clatter of crockery. From upstairs a vacuum-cleaner hummed. And there was a smell compounded of scrubbed stone and old polished floors, and years of woodfires.

Eliot stood at the foot of the staircase and called, "Mamma." But when there was no answer, only the continued hum of the vacuum-cleaner, he said, "You'd better come this way." We went down the hall and through a door which led into a long, low drawing-room, palely panelled and sensuous with the brightness and scent of spring flowers. At one end, in a fireplace of carved pine and Dutch tiles, a newly lit fire flickered cheerfully, and three tall windows, curtained in faded yellow silk, faced out over a flagged terrace, and beyond the balustrade of this I could see the blue line of the sea.

I stood in the middle of this charming room as Eliot Bayliss closed the door and said, "Well, you're here. Why don't you take your coat off?"

I did so. It was very warm. I laid it over a chair where it looked like some great, dead creature.

He said, "When did you get here?"

"Last night. I caught the train from London."

"You live in London?"

"Yes."

"And you've never been here before?"

"No. I didn't know about Boscarva. I didn't know about Grenville Bayliss being my grandfather. My mother never told me till the night before she died."

"How does Joss come into it?"

"I . . ." It was too complicated to explain. "I'd met him in

London. He happened to be at the junction when my train got in. It was a coincidence.''

''Where are you staying?''

''With Mrs Kernow in Fish Lane.''

''Grenville's an old man. He's ill. You know that, don't you?''

''Yes.''

''I think . . . this letter from Otto Pedersen . . . we'd better be careful. Perhaps my mother would be the best person . . .''

''Yes, of course.''

''It was lucky you saw the letter.''

''Yes. I thought he would probably write. But I was afraid that I would have to break the news to you all.''

''And now it's been done for you.'' He smiled, and all at once he looked much younger . . . belying those strange-coloured eyes and the thick silver-fox hair. ''Why don't you wait here and I'll go and find my mother and try to put her in the picture. Would you like a cup of coffee or something?''

''Only if it's not a nuisance.''

''No nuisance. I'll tell Pettifer.'' He opened the door behind him. ''Make yourself at home.''

The door closed softly, and he was gone. Pettifer. *Pettifer had been in the Navy too, he looked after my father and sometimes drove the car and Mrs Pettifer did the cooking.* So my mother had told me. And Joss had told me that Mrs Pettifer had died. But in the old days she had taken Lisa and her brother into the kitchen and made hot buttered toast. She had drawn the curtains against the dark and the rain, and made the children feel safe and loved.

Alone, I inspected the room where I had been left to wait. I saw a glass-doored cabinet filled with Oriental treasures, including some small pieces of jade, and wondered if these were the ones that my mother had mentioned to me. I glanced around, thinking that perhaps I might find the Venetian mirror and the davenport desk as well, but then my attention was caught by the picture over the mantelpiece, and I went to look at it, all else forgotten.

It was a portrait of a girl, dressed in the fashion of the early 1930s, slender, flat-chested, her white dress hanging straight to her hips, her dark, bobbed hair revealing with enchanting innocence the long, slender neck. She sat, in the picture, on a tall stool, holding a single long-stemmed rose, but you could not see her face, for she was looking away from the artist, out of some unseen window, into the sunshine. The effect was all pink and gold, with sunlight filtering through the thin stuff of her white dress. It was enchanting.

Behind me the door opened suddenly and I turned, startled, as an old man came into the room, stately, bald-headed, a little stooped, perhaps; treading cautiously. He wore rimless spectacles and a striped shirt with an old-fashioned hard collar, and over it all a blue and white butcher's apron.

"Are you the young lady wanting a cup of coffee?" He had a deep, lugubrious voice, and this, with his sombre appearance, made me think of a reliable undertaker.

"Yes, if it's not too much trouble."

"Milk and sugar?"

"No sugar. Just a little milk. I was looking at the portrait."

"Yes. It's very pleasing. It's called 'Lady Holding a Rose'."

"You can't see her face."

"No."

"Did my . . . Did Mr Bayliss paint it?"

"Oh yes. That was hung in the Academy, could have been sold a hundred times over, but the Commander would never part with it." As he said this, he carefully took off his spectacles, and was now staring at me intently. His old eyes were pale. He said, "For a moment, when you spoke, you reminded me of someone else. But you're young and she'd be middle-aged by now. And her hair was dark as a blackbird. That's what Mrs Pettifer used to say. Dark as a blackbird's wing.''

I said, ''Eliot didn't tell you?''

''What didn't Mr Eliot tell me?''

''You're talking about Lisa, aren't you? I'm Rebecca. I'm her daughter.''

''Well.'' Fumbling a little he put his spectacles back on again. A faint gleam of pleasure showed on his gloomy features. ''I was right then. I'm not often wrong about things like that.'' And he came forward, holding out a horny hand. ''It's a real pleasure to meet you . . . A pleasure that I never thought I should have. I thought you'd never come. Is your mother with you?''

I wished that Eliot had made it a little easier for me.

''My mother's dead. She died last week. In Ibiza. That's why I'm here.''

''She died.'' His eyes clouded. ''I'm sorry. I'm really sorry. She should have come back. She should have come home. We all wanted to see her again.'' He took out a copious handkerchief and blew his nose. ''And who . . .'' he asked ''. . . is going to tell the Commander?''

''I think . . . Eliot's gone to fetch his mother. You see, there's a letter for my grandfather in the post, it came this morning. It's from Ibiza, from the man who was . . . taking care of my mother. But if you think that wouldn't be a very good idea . . .''

''What I think won't make no difference,'' said Pettifer. ''And whoever tells the Commander, it's not going to lessen his sorrow. But I'll tell you one thing. You being here will help a lot.''

''Thank you.''

He blew his nose again and put away his handkerchief.

''Mr Eliot and his mother . . . well, this isn't their home. But it was either the old Commander and me moving up to High Cross or them coming here. And they wouldn't be here if the doctor hadn't insisted. I told them we could manage all right, the Commander and me. We've been together all these years . . . but there, we're neither of us as young as we used to be, and the Commander, he had this heart attack . . ."

"Yes, I know . . ."

"And after Mrs Pettifer passed on, there wasn't anyone to do the cooking. Mind, I can cook all right, but it takes me a good part of my time taking care of the Commander, and I wouldn't want to see him going about the place looking shabby."

"No, of course not . . ."

I was interrupted by the slam of a door.

A hearty male voice called, "Pettifer!" and Pettifer said, "Excuse me a moment, Miss," and went out to investigate, leaving the door open behind him.

"Pettifer!"

I heard Pettifer say, with what sounded like the greatest satisfaction, "Hello, Joss."

"Is she there?"

"Who, here?"

"Rebecca."

"Yes, she's right here, in the sitting-room . . . I was just going to get her a cup of coffee."

"Make it two would you, there's a good chap. And black and strong for me."

His footsteps came down the hall, and the next moment he was there, framed in the doorway, long-legged, black-haired, and it was obvious – angry.

"What the hell do you think you're doing?" he demanded.

I could feel my hackles rising, like a suspicious dog. Home, Eliot had said. This was Boscarva, my home, and whether I was here or not was nothing to do with Joss.

"I don't know what you're talking about."

"I went to pick you up and Mrs Kernow told me you'd already left."

"So?"

"I told you to wait for me."

"I decided not to wait."

He was silent, fuming, but finally appeared to accept this inescapable fact.

"Does anyone know you've arrived?"

"I met Eliot at the gate. He brought me here."

"Where's he gone?"

"To find his mother."

"Have you seen anyone else? Have you seen Grenville?"

"No."

"Has anyone told Grenville about your mother?"

"A letter came by this morning's post, from Otto Pedersen. But I don't think he's seen it yet."

"Pettifer must take it to him. Pettifer must be there when he reads it."

"Pettifer didn't seem to think that."

"I think it," said Joss.

His apparently outrageous interference left me without words, but as we stood glaring at each other across the pretty patterned carpet and a great bowl of scented narcissus, there came the sound of voices and footsteps down the uncarpeted staircase and along the hall towards us.

I heard a woman's voice say, "In the sitting-room, Eliot?"

Joss muttered something that sounded unprintable, and marched over to the fireplace where he stood with his back to me, staring down into the flames. The next instant, Mollie appeared in the doorway, hesitated for a moment and then came towards me, hands outstretched.

"Rebecca." (So it was to be a warm welcome.) Eliot,

following behind her, closed the door. Joss did not even turn round.

I worked it out that by now Mollie must be over fifty, but this was hard to believe. She was plump and pretty, her fading blonde hair charmingly coiffed, her eyes blue, her skin fresh and lightly scattered with freckles which helped to create this astonishing illusion of youth. She wore a blue skirt and cardigan and a creamy silk blouse; her legs were slim and shapely and her hands beautifully manicured, decorated with pale pink fingernails, and many rings and fine gold bracelets. Scented, immaculately preserved, she made me think of a charming little tabby cat, curled precisely in the centre of her own satin cushion.

I said, "I'm afraid this is something of a shock."

"No, not a shock, but a surprise. And your mother . . . I'm so dreadfully sorry. Eliot's told me about the letter . . ."

At this Joss swung around from the fireplace."

"Where is the letter?"

Mollie turned her gaze upon him, and it was impossible to guess whether this was the first time she had realised he was there, or whether she had seen him and simply decided to ignore him.

"Joss. I didn't think you were coming this morning."

"Yes. I just got here."

"You know Rebecca, I believe."

"Yes, we've met." He hesitated, seeming to be making an effort to pull himself together. Then he smiled, ruefully, turned to lean his broad shoulders against the mantelpiece and apologised. "I'm sorry. And I know it's none of my business, but that letter that came this morning . . . where is it?"

"In my pocket," said Eliot, speaking for the first time. "Why?"

"It's just that I think Pettifer should be the one to break the news to the old man. I think Pettifer is the only person to do it."

This was greeted by silence. Then Mollie let go of my hands and turned to her son.

"He's right," she said. "Grenville's closest to Pettifer."

"That's all right by me," said Eliot but his eyes, on Joss, were cold with antagonism. I did not blame him. I felt the same way myself – I was on Eliot's side.

Joss said again, "I'm sorry."

Mollie was polite. "Not at all. It's very thoughtful of you to be so concerned."

"None of my business, really," said Joss. Eliot and his mother waited with pointed patience. At last he took the hint, heaved his shoulders away from the mantelpiece, and said, "Well, if you'll excuse me, I'll go and get on with some work."

"Will you be here for lunch?"

"No, I can only stay a couple of hours. I'll have to get back to the shop. I'll pick up a sandwich at the pub." He smiled benignly at us all, not a trace of his former temper showing. "Thanks all the same."

And so he left us, modest, apologetic, apparently cut down to size. Once more the young workman, an employee, with a job to do.

6

Mollie said, "You must forgive him. He's not always the most tactful of men."

Eliot laughed shortly. "That's the understatement of the year."

She turned to me, explaining, "He's restoring some of the furniture for us. It's old and it had got into bad repair. He's a marvellous craftsman, but we never know when he's going to arrive or when he's going to go!"

"One day," said her son, "I shall lose my temper with him and punch his nose into the back of his neck." He smiled at me charmingly, his eyes crinkling, belying the ferocity of his words. "And I'm going to have to go too. I was late as it was, now I'm bloody late. Rebecca, will you excuse me?"

"Of course. I'm sorry, I'm afraid it was my fault. And thank you for being so kind . . ."

"I'm glad I stopped. I must have known how important it was. I'll see you . . ."

"Yes, of course you will," said Mollie quickly. "She can't go away now that she's found us."

"Well I'll leave the two of you to fix everything up . . ." He made for the door, but his mother interrupted gently.

"Eliot." He turned. "The letter."

"Oh yes, of course." He took it from his pocket, the fateful letter, a little crumpled now, and handed it to Mollie. "Don't let Pettifer make too big a meal of it. He's a sentimental old chap."

"I won't."

He smiled again, saying goodbye to both of us. "See you at dinner."

And he was gone, whistling up his dog as he went down the hall. We heard the front door open and shut, his car start up. Mollie turned to me.

"Now," she said, "come and sit by the fire and tell me all about it."

I did so, as I had already told Joss and Mrs Kernow, only this time I found myself stumbling a little when I got to the bit about Otto and Lisa living together, as though I were ashamed of it, which was a thing which I had never been. As I talked and Mollie listened, I tried to work this out, and to understand why my mother had disliked her so much. Perhaps it was simply a natural antipathy. It was obvious that they would never have had anything in common. And my mother had never had much tolerance for women who bored her. Men, now, were different. Men were always amusing. But women had to be very special for my mother to be able to tolerate their company. No, it could not all have been Mollie's fault. Sitting across the fireside from her, I resolved that I would be friends with her, and perhaps compensate, in a small way, for the short shrift she had received from Lisa.

"And how long are you going to be able to stay in Porthkerris? Your job . . . do you have to get back?"

"No. I seem to have been given a sort of indefinite leave."

"You'll stay here, with us?"

"Well, I've got this room with Mrs Kernow."

"Yes, but you'd be much better here. There's not a lot of space, that's the only thing; you'll have to sleep up in the attic, but it's a dear little room if you don't mind the sloping ceilings

and you manage not to bump your head. You see, Eliot and I
seem to have filled up the guest rooms, and as well I've got
my niece staying for a few days. Perhaps you'll make friends
with her. It'll be nice for her to have someone young about the
place."

I wondered where the niece was. "How old is she?"

"Only seventeen. It's a difficult age, and I think that her
mother felt it would be a good thing if she was out of London for
a little. They live there, you see, and of course she has so many
friends, and there is so much going on . . ." She was obviously
finding it difficult to find the right words ". . . Anyway, Andrea's
down here for a week or two to have a little change, but I'm
afraid she's rather bored."

I imagined myself at seventeen, in the unseen Andrea's
shoes, staying in this warm and charming house, cared for by
Mollie and Pettifer, with the sea and the cliffs on my doorstep,
the countryside inviting long walks, and all the secret crooked
streets of Porthkerris waiting to be explored. To me it would
have been heaven, and impossible to be bored. I wondered if I
would have very much in common with Mollie's niece.

"Of course," she went on, "as you've probably gathered,
Eliot and I are only here because Mrs Pettifer died and really
the two old men couldn't manage on their own. We've got Mrs
Thomas, she comes in each morning to help do the housework,
but I do all the cooking, and keep the place as bright and pretty
as I can."

"The flowers are so lovely."

"I can't bear a house without flowers."

"What about your own house?"

"My dear, it's empty. I shall have to take you up to High
Cross one day to show it to you. I bought a pair of old cottages
just after the war and converted them. Even though I shouldn't
say so, it is very charming. And, of course, it's so handy for

Eliot's garage; as it is, living here, he seems to be perpetually on the road.''

''Yes, I suppose so.''

I could hear footsteps coming down the hall again; in a moment the door opened, and Pettifer edged around it, cautiously, carrying a tray laden with all the accoutrements of mid-morning coffee, including a large silver pot with steam drifting from its spout.

''Oh, Pettifer, thank you . . .''

He came forward, stooped with the weight of the tray, and Mollie got up to fetch a stool and place it swiftly beneath the tray so that the old man could put it down before it tilted so sharply that everything on it went hurtling to the floor.

''That's splendid, Pettifer.''

''One of the cups was for Joss.''

''He's upstairs working. He must have forgotten about the coffee. Never mind, I'll drink it for him. And, Pettifer . . .'' He straightened, slowly, as though all his old joints were aching. Mollie took the letter from Ibiza off the mantelpiece where she had placed it for safety. ''We thought, all of us, that perhaps it would be the best if you told the Commander about his daughter and then gave him this letter. It would be best, we thought, coming from you. Would you mind?''

Pettifer took the thin blue envelope.

''No, Madam. I'll do it. I'm just on my way up now to get the Commander up and dressed.''

''It would be a kindness, Pettifer.''

''That's all right, Madam.''

''And tell him that Rebecca is here. And that she's staying. We'll have to make up the bed in the attic but I think she'll be quite comfortable.''

Again a gleam came into Pettifer's face. I wondered if he ever really smiled, or whether his face had dropped permanently into those lugubrious lines and a cheerful expression had become physically impossible.

"I'm glad you're staying," he said "The Commander will like that."

When he'd gone, I said, "You'll have a lot to do. Shouldn't I go, and get out from under your feet?"

"You'll have to collect your things from Mrs Kernow anyway. I wonder how we could manage that? Pettifer could take you, but now he'll be occupied with Grenville and I must speak to Mrs Thomas about your room and then start thinking about lunch. Now what are we going to do?" I could not imagine. I was certainly not going to be able to carry all my belongings up the hill from the town. But luckily Mollie answered her own question. "I know. Joss. He can take you and bring you back up the hill in his van."

"But isn't Joss working?"

"Oh, for once we'll interrupt him. It's not often he's asked to put himself out – I'm sure he won't mind. Come along, we'll go and find him."

I had thought that she would take me to some forgotten outhouse or shed where we would find Joss, surrounded by wood shavings and the smell of hot glue, but to my surprise, she led me upstairs, and I forgot about Joss, because these were my first impressions of Boscarva, where my mother had been brought up, and I didn't want to miss a thing. The stairs were uncarpeted, the walls half panelled and then darkly papered above and hung with heavy oil paintings. All was at variance with the pretty, feminine sitting-room which we had left downstairs. On the first-floor landing passages led to left and right, there was a tallboy of polished walnut, and bookcases heavy with books, and then we went on again, up the stairs. Here was red drugget, white paint, again the passages led away to either side, and Mollie took the right-hand one. At the end of this passage was an open door, and from behind it the sound of voices, a man's and a girl's.

She seemed to hesitate and then her footsteps quickened, determined. Her back view became, all at once, formidable. With me following she went down the passage and through the door, and we were in an attic which had been converted, by means of a skylight, to a studio, or perhaps a billiard room, for against one wall was a massive, leather-seated sofa with oaken arms and legs. Now, however, this cold and airy room was being used as a workshop, with Joss in the middle of it, surrounded by chairs, broken picture frames, a table with a crooked leg, some scraps of leather, tools and nails, and a gimcrack gas ring on which reposed an unsavoury-looking glue pot. Wrapped in a worn blue apron, he was carefully fitting beautiful scarlet hide over the seat of one of the chairs, and as he did this, was being entertained by a young and female companion, who turned, disinterested, to see who had come into the room, and was so breaking up this cosy *tête-à-tête*.

Mollie said, "Andrea!" And then, less sharply, "Andrea, I didn't realise you were up."

"Oh, I've been up for hours."

"Did you have any breakfast?"

"I didn't want any."

"Andrea, this is Rebecca. Rebecca Bayliss."

"Oh, yes," she turned her eyes on to me. "Joss has been telling me all about you."

I said, "How do you do." She was very young and very thin, with long seaweedy hair that hung on either side of her face, which was pretty, except for her eyes which were pale and slightly protuberant, and not improved by a great deal of clumsy mascara. She wore, inevitably, jeans, and a cotton tee-shirt which did not look entirely clean and which revealed, with no shadow of a doubt, the fact that she wore nothing beneath it. On her feet were sandals which looked like surgical boots that had been striped in green and purple. There was a leather bootlace around her neck upon which hung a heavy silver cross of vaguely Celtic design. Andrea, I thought. So bored with Boscarva. And it made me uncomfortable to think that she and Joss had been discussing me. I wondered what he had said.

Now, she did not move, but stayed where she was, legs straddled, leaning against a heavy old mahogany table.

"Hi," she said.

"Rebecca's going to stay here," Mollie told them. Joss looked up, his mouth full of tacks, his eyes bright with interest, a lock of black hair falling over his forehead.

"Where's she going to sleep?" asked Andrea. "I thought we were a full house."

"In the bedroom along the passage," her aunt told her crisply. "Joss, would you do a favour for me?" He spat the tacks neatly into his palm and stood up, pushing his hair back with his wrist. "Would you take her, now, down to Mrs Kernow, and tell Mrs Kernow that she's coming here, and then help her with her suitcases and bring her back up to Boscarva again? Would that be very inconvenient?"

"Not at all," said Joss, but Andrea's face assumed an expression of bored resignation.

"It's a nuisance, I know, when you're busy, but it would be such a help . . ."

"It's no trouble." He laid down his little hammer and began to untie the knot of his apron. He gazed at me. "I'm getting quite used to carting Rebecca about."

And Andrea gave a snort, whether of disgust or impatience it was impossible to tell, sprang to her feet and marched out of the room, leaving the impression that we had been lucky to escape without a monumentally slammed door.

*

And so I was back where I started, with Joss, crammed into the ramshackle little van. We drove in silence away from Boscarva, through Mr Padlow's building estate, and on to the slope of the hill that led down to the town.

It was Joss who broke the silence.

"So, it all worked out."

"Yes."

"How do you like your family?"

"I haven't met them all yet. I haven't met Grenville."

He said, "You'll like him," but the way he said it, he made it sound, "You'll like *him*."

"I like them all."

"That's good."

I looked at him. He wore his blue denim jacket, a navy polo-necked sweater. His profile was impassive. I felt it would be easy to be maddened by him.

"Tell me about Andrea," I said.

"What do you want to know about Andrea?"

"I don't know. I just want you to tell me."

"She's seventeen, and she thinks she's in love with some guy she met at Art School, and her parents don't approve so she's been rusticated with Auntie Mollie. And she's bored stiff."

"She seems to have taken you into her confidence."

"There's no one else to talk to."

"Why doesn't she go back to London?"

"Because she's only seventeen. She hasn't got the money. And I think she hasn't quite got the courage to stand up to her parents."

"What does she do with herself all day?"

"I don't know. I'm not there all day. She doesn't seem to get up until lunch-time, and then she sits around watching television. Boscarva's a house of old people. You can't blame her for being bored."

I said, without thinking, "Only the boring are bored." This had once been drummed into me by a wise and well-meaning headmistress.

"That," said Joss, "sounds uncomfortably sanctimonious."

"I didn't mean it to."

He smiled. "Were you never bored?"

"Nobody who lived with my mother was ever bored."

He sang, "You may have been a headache, but you never were a bore."

"Exactly."

"She sounds great. Exactly my sort of female."

"That's what most men thought about her."

When we got to Fish Lane Mrs Kernow was out, but Joss seemed to have a key. We let ourselves in and I went upstairs to pack my rucksack while Joss wrote Mrs Kernow a note to explain the new arrangements.

"How about paying her?" I asked as I came downstairs, bumping the rucksack behind me.

"I'll fix that when I next see her. I've told her so in the note."

"But I can pay for myself."

"Of course you can, but let me do it for you." He took my rucksack and went to open the door, and there did not seem to be opportunity for further argument.

Once more my belongings were heaved into the back of the little truck, once more we headed for Boscarva, only this time Joss took me round by the harbour road.

"I want to show you my shop . . . I mean, I just want to show you where it is. Then if you want to get hold of me for any reason, you'll know where to find me."

"Why should I want to get hold of you?"

"I don't know. You might need wise counselling; or money; or just a good laugh. There it is, you can't miss it."

It was a tall narrow house, boxed in between two short fat houses. Three storeys high with a window on each floor, and the ground floor still in a state of reconstruction, with new wood unpainted and great circles of whitewash splashed over the plate glass of the shop window.

As we flashed past it, tyres rattling on the cobbles, I said, "That's a good position, you'll get all the visitors coming in to spend their money."

"That's what I hope."

"When can I see it?"

"Come next week. We'll be more or less straight then."

"All right. Next week."

"It's a date," said Joss, and turned the corner by the church. He put the little truck into second gear and we roared up the hill with a noise like a badly tuned motor bicycle.

Back at Boscarva, it was Pettifer who, hearing our arrival, emerged from the front door as Joss lifted my rucksack from the back of the truck.

"Joss, the Commander's downstairs and in his study. He said to bring Rebecca in to see him just as soon as you arrived."

Joss looked at him. "How is he?"

Pettifer ducked his head. "Not too bad."

"Was he very upset?"

"He's all right . . . now you leave that rucksack, and I'll carry it upstairs."

"You'll do no such thing," said Joss, and for once I was glad that he was being his usual bossy self. "I'll take it up. Where's she sleeping?"

"In the attic . . . the other end from the billiard room, but the Commander did say, right away."

"I know," Joss grinned, "and naval time is five minutes beforehand. But there's still time to take the girl up to her room, so stop fussing, there's a good man."

Leaving Pettifer still mildly protesting, I followed him up the two flights of stairs that I had already climbed this morning. The sound of the vacuum had stopped, but there was the smell of roasting lamb. I realised then that I was very hungry and my mouth watered. Joss's long legs sped ahead of me, and by the time I reached the slope-ceilinged bedroom which was to be mine, he had set down the rucksack and gone to fling wide the dormer window, so that I was met by a blast of cold, salty air.

''Come and look at the view.''

I went to stand beside him. I saw the sea, the cliffs, the gold of bracken and the first yellow candles of gorse. And below was the Boscarva garden which, because of the stone balustrade of the terrace, I had not been able to see from the drawing-room window. It had been built in a series of terraces, dropping down the slope of the hill, and at the bottom, tucked into a corner of the garden wall, was a stone cottage with a slate roof. No, not a cottage, perhaps a stable, with a commodious loft above it.

I said, ''What's that building?''

''That's the studio,'' Joss told me. ''That's where your grandfather used to paint.''

''It doesn't look like a studio.''

''From the other side it does. The entire north wall is made of glass. He designed it himself, had it built by a local stonemason.''

''It looks shut up.''

''It is. Locked and shuttered. It hasn't been opened since he had his heart attack and stopped painting.''

I shivered suddenly.

''Cold?'' asked Joss.

''I don't know.'' I moved away from the window, undoing my coat, dropping it over the end of the bed. The room was white, the carpet dark red. There was a built-in wardrobe, shelves full of books, a washbasin. I went over to wash my hands, turning the soap beneath the warm water. Over the basin was a mirror which gave me back a reflection both dishevelled and anxious. I realised then how nervous I was of meeting Grenville for the first time, and how important it was that he should get a good impression of me.

I dried my hands, went to unbuckle my rucksack, and found a brush and comb. "Was he a good painter, Joss? Do you think he was a good artist?"

"Yes. The old school, of course, but magnificent. And a marvellous colourist."

I pulled the rubber band from the end of my plait, shook the coils free, and went back to the mirror to start brushing. Over my reflected shoulder I could see Joss watching me. He did not speak while I brushed and combed and finally re-plaited my hair. As I fastened the ends, he said, "It's a wonderful colour. Like corn."

I laid down the brush and comb. "Joss, we mustn't keep him waiting."

"Do you want me to come with you?"

"Please."

I realised then that this was the first time I had ever had to ask him to help me.

I followed him downstairs, down the hall and past the sitting-room, to a door which stood at the end of the passage. Joss opened it and put his head around.

He said, "Good morning."

"Who's that? Joss? Come along in . . ." The voice was higher pitched than I had imagined, more like the voice of a much younger man.

"I've brought someone to see you . . ."

He opened the door wide, and put his arms behind me to propel me gently forward into the room. It was a small room, with french windows leading out on to a paved terrace and a secret garden, warm with trapped sunshine, and enclosed by dense hedges and escallonia.

I saw the fire flickering in the grate; the panelled walls covered either with pictures or books; the model, on the mantelpiece, of an old-fashioned naval cruiser. There were photographs in silver frames, a table littered with papers and magazines, and a blue and white Chinese bowl filled with daffodils.

As I entered, he was already heaving himself – with the aid of a stick – out of a red leather armchair, which stood half turned towards the warmth of the fire. I was amazed that Joss did nothing to help him, and I began to say, "Oh, please don't bother . . ." but by then he was on his feet and erect, and a pair of blue eyes surveyed me calmly from beneath jutting brows and bristling white eyebrows.

I realised then that I had steeled myself to finding him pathetic in some way, old, infirm, perhaps a little shaky. But Grenville Bayliss, at eighty, was formidable. Very tall, very upright, starched and barbered, smelling faintly of Bay Rum, he was a credit to his servant Pettifer. He wore a dark blue blazer, of naval cut, neatly creased grey flannels, and velvet slippers with his initials embroidered in gold. He was also very tanned, his bald head brown as a chestnut beneath the thinning strands of white hair, and I imagined him spending much time in that little sunny secret garden, reading his morning paper, enjoying a pipe, watching the gulls and the white clouds scudding across the sky.

We looked at each other. I wished that he would say something but he simply looked. I hoped that he liked what he saw, and was glad I had taken the time to brush my hair. And then he said, "I've never been in this situation before. I'm not quite sure how we're meant to greet each other."

I said, "I could give you a kiss."

"Why don't you do that?"

So I did, stepping forward and raising my face, and he stooped slightly and my lips touched the smooth clean skin of his cheek.

"Now," he said, "why don't we sit down? Joss, come and sit down."

But Joss excused himself, said that if he didn't start work soon then he would have done nothing all day. But he stayed long enough to help the old man back into his chair, and pour us both a glass of sherry from the decanter on the side table, and then he said, "I'll leave you. You'll have a lot to talk about," and with a cheerful wave of his hand, slipped away. The door closed quietly behind him.

Grenville said, "I believe you know him quite well."

I pulled up a stool so that I could sit and face him. "Not really. But he's been very kind, and . . ." I tried to think of the right word. "Convenient. I mean, he always seems to be there when people need him."

"And never when they don't?" I was not sure if I could entirely agree with this. "He's a clever boy, too. Doing up all my furniture."

"Yes I know."

"Good craftsman. Lovely hands." He laid down his sherry glass, and once more I was subjected to that piercing blue stare. "Your mother died."

"Yes."

"Had a letter from this Pedersen fellow. He said it was leukaemia."

"Yes."

"Did you meet him?"

I told him about going to Ibiza and the night I had spent with Otto and my mother.

"He was a decent chap, then? Good to her?"

"Yes. He was immensely kind. And he adored her."

"Glad she ended up with somebody decent. Most of the chaps she picked on were just a lot of bounders."

I smiled at the old-fashioned word. I thought of the sheep-farmer, and the American in his Brooks Brothers shirts, and wondered how they would have liked being called bounders. They probably wouldn't even have known what it meant.

I said, "I think she sometimes got a little carried away."

A gleam of humour showed in his eyes. "You seem to have adopted a fairly worldly attitude?"

"Yes. I did. Long ago."

"She was a maddening woman. But she'd been the most enchanting little girl it was possible to imagine. I painted her often. I've still got one or two canvases of Lisa as a child. I'll have to get Pettifer to look them out, show them to you. And then she grew up and everything changed. Roger, my son, was killed in the war, and Lisa was always at loggerheads with her mother, rushing off in her little car, never coming home at night. Finally she fell in love with this actor fellow, and that was it."

"She really *was* in love with him."

"In love." He sounded disgusted. "That's an overrated expression. There's a lot more to life than just being in love."

"Yes, but you have to find that out for yourself."

He looked amused. "Have you found it out?"

"No."

"How old are you?"

"Twenty-one."

"You're mature for twenty-one. And I like your hair. You don't look like Lisa. You don't look like your father either. You look like yourself." He reached for his sherry glass, raised it carefully to his mouth, took a sip, and then replaced the glass on the table by his chair. In such cautious actions did he betray his age and his infirmity.

He said, "She should have come back to Boscarva. At any

time we would have welcomed her. Come to that, why didn't *you* come?''

''I didn't know about Boscarva. I didn't know about you until the night before she died.''

''It was as though she'd put the past out of her life. And when her mother died and I wrote to tell her, she never even replied.''

''We were in New York that Christmas. She didn't get your letter till months later. And then it seemed too late to write. And she was so bad at writing letters.''

''You're standing up for her. You don't resent the fact that she kept you from this place? You could have been brought up here. This could have been your home.''

''She was my mother. That was the important thing.''

''You seem to be arguing with me. Nobody argues with me nowadays. Not even Pettifer. It gets very dull.''

Once more I was fixed with that blue stare. ''Have you met Pettifer? He and I were in the Navy together about a century ago. And Mollie and Eliot? Have you met them?''

''Yes.''

''They shouldn't be living here at all, of course, but the doctor insisted. Doesn't make that much difference to me, but it's hard luck on poor Pettifer. And Mollie's got a niece here as well, dreadful child with sagging breasts. Have you seen her?''

I managed not to giggle. ''Yes, for a moment.''

''A moment would be too long. And Boscarva. What do you think of Boscarva?''

''I love it. What I've seen of it, I love.''

''The town's creeping out over the hill. There was a farm at the top, belonged to an old lady called Mrs Gregory. But this builder fellow talked her into selling up to him and now they've bulldozed the fields flat as a pancake and they're putting up houses nineteen to the dozen.''

"I know. I saw them."

"Well, they can't come any further, because the farm at the back of this place and the fields on either side of the lane belong to me. Bought them when I bought Boscarva, back in 1922. Wouldn't like to tell you how little it cost me. But a bit of land around you gives you a feeling of security. Remember that."

"I will."

He frowned. "What's your name again? I've forgotten it already."

"Rebecca."

"Rebecca. And what are you going to call me?"

"I don't know. What do you want me to call you?"

"Eliot calls me Grenville. You call me Grenville too. It sounds more friendly."

"All right."

We drank our sherry, smiling, content with each other. Then, from the back of the house, came the sound of a gong being struck. Grenville put down his glass and got painfully to his feet, and I went to open the door for him. Together, we went down the passage towards the dining-room and family lunch.

7

Exhaustion hit me at the end of that long, eventful day, and unfortunately in the middle of dinner. Luncheon had been a sustaining, homely meal, eaten at a round table set in the bay window of the big dining-room. This had been laid with a simple checked cloth, and everyday china and glass, but dinner was a different affair altogether.

The long, polished table in the middle of the room was set for the five of us, with fine linen mats, and old silver and glass sparkling in the candlelight.

Everybody, it seemed, was expected to change in honour of this apparently nightly ritual. Mollie came downstairs in a brocade housecoat the colour of sapphires, which emphasised the brightness of her eyes. Grenville wore a faded velvet dinner-jacket and Eliot a pale flannel suit in which he looked as elegant as a greyhound. Even Andrea, probably under much protest, had put on a different pair of trousers and a blouse of broderie anglaise which looked as though it could have done with a press, or a wash, or maybe both. Her lank hair was tied back with a scrap of velvet ribbon, the expression on her face continued to be one of resentful boredom.

Not in the habit of attending formal dinner parties, I had nevertheless packed a garment which would obviously have to appear every evening as long I stayed in this house, for I had no other. It was a caftan of soft brown jersey wool, with silver embroidery at the neck and the wrists of the flowing sleeves. With it, I wore my silver bracelets and a pair of hoop ear-rings which my mother had given me for my twenty-first birthday. Their weight, on this occasion, gave me odd comfort and confidence, two things which I badly needed.

I did not want to have dinner with my newly acquired family. I did not want to have to make conversation, to listen, to be intelligent and charming. I wanted to go to bed and be brought something undemanding, like Bovril or a boiled egg. I wanted to be alone.

But there was soup and duckling, and red wine, dispensed by Eliot. The duckling was rich and the room very warm. As the meal slowly progressed I felt more and more strange, disembodied, light-headed. I tried to concentrate on the flames of the candles in front of me, but as I stared at them they separated and repeated themselves, and the voices around me became blurred and unintelligible, like the hum of conversation heard from a distant room. Instinctively, I pushed my plate away from me, knocked over the wineglass, and watched, in hopeless horror, as the red wine spread amongst the shattered splinters of glass.

In a way the accident was a blessing, for they all stopped talking and looked at me. I must have gone quite pale, for Eliot was on his feet in an instant and at my side . . .

"Are you all right?"

I said, "No, I don't think I am. I'm sorry . . ."

"Oh, my dear." Mollie flung aside her napkin and pushed back her chair. From across the table Andrea eyed me with chill interest.

"The glass . . . I'm so sorry . . ."

From the head of the table Grenville spoke. "It doesn't matter about the glass. Leave the glass. The girl's exhausted. Mollie, take her up and put her to bed."

108

I tried to protest, but not very hard. Eliot drew back my chair and helped me to my feet, his hands firm beneath my elbows. Mollie had gone to open the door, and cooler air moved in from the hall – already I felt better, as though, perhaps, after all, I was not going to faint.

As I passed Grenville, I said, "I'm sorry," for the third time. "Forgive me. Good night." I bent and kissed him, and left them all. Mollie closed the door behind us and came upstairs with me. She helped me undress and get into bed, and I was asleep before she had even turned off the light.

I slept for fourteen hours, waking at ten o'clock. I had not slept so late for years, and beyond my window the sky was blue and the cold bright northern light reflected from the sloping white-painted walls of my room. I got up, pulled on a dressing-gown and went and had a bath. Dressed, I felt wonderful, apart from the sinking sensation of shame at my behaviour the night before. I hoped they had not all thought that I was drunk.

Downstairs, I finally ran Mollie to earth in a little pantry, arranging a great mass of purple and pink polyanthus in a flowered bowl.

"How did you sleep?" she asked at once.

"Like the dead. I'm sorry about last night . . ."

"My dear, you were tired out. I'm sorry I didn't realise before. You'll want some breakfast."

"Just coffee."

She took me into the kitchen and heated coffee while I made some toast. "Where is everybody?" I asked.

"Eliot's at the garage, of course, and Pettifer's taken the car to Fourbourne to do some shopping for Grenville."

"What can I do? There must be something I can do to help."

"Well . . ." she debated. I looked at her. This morning she wore a cashmere sweater the colour of caramel and a slender tweed skirt. Immaculately made up, with every strand of hair in place, she seemed almost inhumanly neat. "You could go and fetch the fish for me in Porthkerris. The fishmonger rang up to say he'd got some halibut and I thought we'd have it for dinner. I could lend you my little car. Do you drive?"

"Yes, but couldn't I walk down? I like walking and it's such a lovely morning."

"Of course, if you want to. You could take the short cut over the fields and along the cliff. I know . . ." she appeared to be suddenly struck by inspiration ". . . take Andrea with you, and then she can show you the way, and show you where the fish shop is. Besides, she never takes any exercise if she can possibly help it and a walk would do her good." She made Andrea sound like a lazy dog. I did not particularly relish the idea of Andrea's company for the entire morning but I was sympathetic to Mollie, being encumbered by this unengaging girl, so I said that I would do as she suggested, and when I had finished my breakfast went in search of Andrea whom Mollie had last seen out on the terrace.

I found her bundled in a rug, lying on a long cane chair in a patch of sunshine, and peevishly regarding the view, like a seasick passenger on a liner.

"Will you walk down to Porthkerris with me?" I asked her.

She fixed me with her protuberant stare. "Why?"

"Because Mollie's asked me to go and pick up some fish and I don't know where the shop is. Besides, it's a lovely morning, and she thought we might go down to the cliffs."

She considered my suggestion, said, "All right," uncoiled herself from the rug and stood up. She wore the same dirty jeans as yesterday and a vast black and white sweater which reached below her narrow hips. We went back to the kitchen to fetch a basket and then set out, by way of the terrace and the sloping garden, down in the direction of the sea.

At the bottom of the garden, stone steps led up and over the wall, and Andrea went ahead of me, but paused because I wanted to inspect the studio from this new angle. It was, as Joss had said, locked and shuttered, and somehow desolate, and the great window on the north wall had been closed off by tightly-drawn curtains so that not a chink presented itself to any inquisitive passer-by.

Andrea stood on the top of the wall, her gaze following mine.

"He never paints now," she told me.

"I know."

"I can't think why. There's nothing wrong with him." She jumped, hair flying, down off the wall, and totally disappeared. I took a last look at the studio and then followed her and we took a trodden path that led down through small, irregular fields, and came out at last, through the hazard of some waist-high gorse bushes, to a stile, and so on to the cliff path.

This was obviously a favourite walk with visitors to Porthkerris, for there were seats set in sheltered view points, and litter bins for rubbish, and notices warning people not to go too near the edge of the cliff which was likely to collapse.

Andrea instantly went to the very edge and peered over. Gulls wheeled and screamed all around her, the wind tore at her hair and the baggy sweater, and from far below came the distant thunder of surf on rocks. She flung her arms wide and teetered slightly as though about to fall over the edge, but when she saw that I didn't care whether she committed suicide or not, she returned to the path, and in single file we walked on, Andrea in front.

The cliff curved and the town came into view in front of us, the low grey houses nestled around the sweep of the bay and climbing the steep hill to the moor behind. We went through a gate, and were now on to a proper road, and so able to walk side by side.

Andrea became conversational.

"Your mother's just died, hasn't she?"

"Yes."

"Aunt Mollie was telling me about her. She said she was a tart."

Painfully, I remained serene. It would have been instant victory for Andrea if I had been anything else.

"She didn't really know her. They hadn't seen each other for years."

"Was she a tart?"

"No."

"Mollie said she lived with men."

I realised then that Andrea was not merely trying to needle me, she was genuinely curious, and there was envy there as well.

I said, "She was very gay and very loving and very beautiful."

She accepted this. "Where do you live?"

"In London. I've got a little flat."

"Do you live alone, or with somebody?"

"No, I live alone."

"Do you go to parties and things?"

"Yes, if someone asks me and I want to go."

"Do you work? Do you have a job?"

"Yes. In a bookshop."

"God, how grim."

"I like it."

"Where did you meet Joss?"

Now, I thought, we're getting down to business, but her face was empty of expression.

"I met him in London . . . he mended a chair for me."

"Do you like him?"

"I don't know him well enough to dislike him."

"Eliot hates him. So does Aunt Mollie."

"Why?"

"Because they don't like having him around the place all the time. And they treat him as though he should call them Sir and Madam, and of course he doesn't. And he talks to Grenville and makes him laugh. I've heard them talking."

I imagined her creeping up to closed doors, listening at keyholes.

"That's nice, if he makes the old man laugh."

"He and Eliot had a terrible row once. It was about some car that Eliot had sold to a friend of Joss's and Joss said it wasn't roadworthy and Eliot called him an insolent, interfering bastard."

"Did you listen in to that one as well?"

"I couldn't help hearing. I was in the loo and the window was open and they were out on the gravel by the front door."

"How long have you been staying at Boscarva?" I asked, curious to know how long it had taken her to dig all these skeletons out of the family cupboards.

"Two weeks. It seems like six months."

"I should have thought you'd have loved coming down."

"For heaven's sake, I'm not a child. What am I meant to do with myself. Go bucket and spading on the beach?"

"What do you do in London?"

She kicked a pebble, viciously, hating Cornwall. "I was at an art school, but my parents *didn't approve* . . ." she put on a mealy voice ". . . of my friends. So they took me away and sent me here."

"But you can't stay here for ever. What are you going to do when you go back?"

"That's up to them, isn't it?"

I felt a twinge of pity for her parents, even parents who had somehow raised such an obnoxious child.

"I mean, isn't there anything you *want* to do?"

"Yes, just get away, be on my own, do my own thing. Danus, this fabulous chap I went around with, he had a friend who was running a pottery on the Isle of Skye, and he wanted me to go and help . . . It sounded super, you know, living in a sort of commune, and right away from everybody . . . but my grotty mother shoved her great oar in and spoiled it all."

"Where's Danus now?"

"Oh, he went to Skye."

"Has he written to tell you about it?"

She tossed her head, fiddled with her hair, would not meet my eye. "Yes, actually, long letters. Reams of them. He still wants me to go there, and I'm going to, just as soon as I'm eighteen and they can't stop me any more."

"Why don't you just go back to art school first, and get some sort of a qualification . . . that'd give you time . . ."

She turned on me. "You know something? You talk like all the rest of them. How old are you anyway? You sound like someone with one foot in the grave."

"It's crazy to wreck your life before it's even started."

"It's my life. Not yours."

"No, it's not my life."

Having thus stupendously quarrelled, we continued our walk into the town in silence, and when Andrea did speak again, it was to say, "That's the fish shop," and wave a hand in its direction.

"Thank you." I went in to collect the halibut but she stayed, pointedly, outside on the cobbled pavement. When I emerged again, she had gone, only to appear the next moment from a paper-shop next door, where she had been buying a lurid magazine called *True Sex*.

"Shall we go back now?" I asked her. "Or do you want to do more shopping?"

"I can't shop, I haven't any money. Only a few pence."

I was suddenly, irrationally, sorry for her. "I'll stand you a cup of coffee if you'd like one."

She looked at me with sudden delight and I thought she was going to gleefully accept my modest offer, but instead she said, "Let's go and see Joss."

I was taken unawares. "Why do you want to go and see Joss?"

"I just do. I often go and see him when I come down to the town. He's always pleased to see me. He made me promise always to go and see him if I'm down here."

"How do you know he'll be there?"

"Well, he's not at Boscarva today, so he must be at the shop. Have you been there? It's super, he's got a sort of pad on the top floor, just like something out of a magazine, with a bed that's a sort of sofa and masses of cushions and things, and a log fire. And at night . . ." her voice became dreamy "it's all closed-in and secret, and there's nothing but firelight."

I tried not to gape. "You mean . . . you and Joss . . ."

She shrugged, tossing her hair. "Once or twice, but nobody knows. I don't know why I told you. You won't tell the others, will you?"

"But don't they . . . doesn't Mollie . . . ask questions?"

"Oh, I tell her I'm going to the cinema. She doesn't seem to mind me going to the cinema. Come on, let's go and see Joss . . ."

But after this revelation, nothing would have induced me to go near Joss's shop. I said, "Joss will be working, he won't want to be interrupted. And anyway there isn't time. And I don't want to go."

"You said there was time for coffee, why isn't there time for Joss?"

"Andrea, I told you, I don't want to go."

She began to smile. "I thought you liked Joss."

"That's not the point. He doesn't want us under his feet every time he turns round."

"Do you mean me?"

"I mean *us*." I was beginning to be desperate.

"He always wants to see me. I know he does."

"Yes, I'm sure," I said gently. "But let's go back to Boscarva."

I reminded myself that from the very start I had not liked Joss. Despite his concern and apparent friendliness he had always left me with that strange sensation of disquiet, as though someone were creeping up behind my back. Yesterday I had begun to forget this initial antipathy, even to like him, but after Andrea's confidences it was not hard to whip back to life my first distrust of the man. He was too good-looking, too charming. Andrea could be a liar, but she was no fool; she had pigeon-holed the rest of the family with disconcerting accuracy, and even if there was only a grain of truth in what she said about Joss, I wanted to have no part of it.

If I had known him and liked him better, I would have taken him aside and taxed him with what she had said. As it was, he held no importance for me. Besides, I had other things to think about.

Grenville did not come down for lunch that day.

"He's tired," Mollie told us. "He's having a day in bed. Perhaps he'll join us for dinner. Pettifer's going to take him up a tray."

So the three of us ate lunch together. Mollie had changed into a neat woollen dress and a double string of pearls. She was going, she said, to play bridge with friends in Fourbourne. She hoped that I would be able to occupy myself.

I said that of course I would be perfectly all right. Across the table, we smiled at each other and I wondered if she had really told Andrea that my mother was a tart, or if this was simply Andrea's interpretation of some vague euphemistic explanation that Mollie had given her. I hoped it was the latter, but still I wished that Mollie had not found it necessary to discuss Lisa with Andrea. She was dead now, but once she had been funny and enchanting and full of laughter. Why couldn't she be remembered that way?

As we sat around the table, the day outside changed its face. A wind got up from the west, and with great speed a bank of grey cloud sped over the blue sky, obliterating the sunshine, and presently it started to rain. It was in this rain that Mollie set off for her bridge party, driving her little car, and saying that she would be home about six. Andrea, perhaps exhausted by her morning's exercise, but more likely bored to death with my company, disappeared up to her bedroom with her new magazine. Alone, I stood at the foot of the stairs, wondering how to amuse myself. The silence of the gloomy afternoon was broken only by the ticking of the grandfather clock and small, occupied sounds which came from the direction of the kitchens, and which, investigated, proved to be Pettifer, seated at a wooden table in his pantry and cleaning silver.

He looked up as I put my head around the door.

"Hello. I didn't hear you."

"How's my grandfather?"

"Oh, he's all right. Just a bit weary after all the excitement of yesterday. We thought it would be better if he had a day with his toes up. Has Mrs Roger gone?"

"Yes." I pulled up a chair and sat opposite him.

"Thought I heard the car."

"Do you want me to help you?"

"That'd be very kind . . . those spoons there need a good rub up with the shammy. Don't know how they get so marked and stained. But, there, I do know. It's this damp sea air. One thing silver really hates it's damp sea air.'' I began to rub at the thin worn bowl of the spoon. Pettifer looked at me over the top of his glasses. "Funny to have you sitting there after all these years. Your mother used to spend half her life in the kitchen . . . When Roger went off to boarding school there wasn't anyone else for her to talk to. So she used to come and spend her time with Mrs Pettifer and me. Taught her to make fairy cakes, Mrs Pettifer did, and how to play two-handed whist. We had great times. And on a day like this, she used to make toast at the old range . . . mind, that's gone now, we've got a new one and good thing too . . . but that old range was cosy, with the fire burning behind the bars, and all the brass knobs polished up lovely.''

"How long have you been at Boscarva, Pettifer?"

"Ever since the Commander bought it, back in 1922. That was the year he left the Navy, decided to be a painter. Old Mrs Bayliss didn't like that. For three months or more she wouldn't even talk to him.''

"Why did she mind so much?"

"She'd been with the Navy all her life. Her father was the Captain of the *Imperious* when the Commander was First Lieutenant. That was how they met. They were married in Malta. A lovely wedding with an arch of swords and all. Being with the Navy meant a lot to Mrs Bayliss. When the Commander said he was going to leave they parted brass rags good and proper, but she couldn't make him change his mind. So we left Malta, for good and all, and the Commander found this house, and then we all moved down here.''

"And you've been here ever since?"

"More or less. The Commander enrolled at the Slade, and that meant working in London, so he had this little *pied-à-terre*, just off St James's it was, and when he went up to

London I went too, to keep an eye on him, and Mrs Pettifer stayed here with Mrs Bayliss and Roger. Your mother wasn't born then.''

"But, when he'd finished at the Slade . . .?''

"Well, then he came back for good. And built the studio. That was when he was painting at his best. Lovely stuff he did then, great seascapes, so cold and bright you could smell the wind, feel the salt on your lips.''

"Are there many of his pictures in this house?''

"No, not many. There's the fishing boat over the dining-room fireplace, and one or two little black and white drawings along the upstairs passage. He's got three or four in his study, and then there's a couple in the room where Mrs Roger sleeps.''

"And the one in the drawing-room . . .''

"Oh, yes, that one of course. 'Lady Holding a Rose.' ''

"Who was she?''

He did not reply; was, perhaps, preoccupied with his silver, rubbing away at a fork as though determined to flatten the pattern.

"Who was she? The girl in the picture?''

"Oh,'' said Pettifer. "That was Sophia.''

Sophia. Ever since my mother had fleetingly mentioned her I had wanted to know about Sophia and now here was Pettifer bringing up her name as though it were the most natural thing in the world.

"She was a girl who used to model for the Commander. I think she first worked for him in London when he was a student, and then she used to come down here sometimes during the summer months, take lodgings in Porthkerris and work for any artist who was ready and able to pay her.''

"Was she very beautiful?''

"Not my idea of a beauty. But lively, and what a talker! She was Irish, she'd come from County Cork.''

"What did my grandmother think of Sophia?"

"Their paths never crossed, any more than your grandmother would have had social dealings with the butcher or the girl who did her hair."

"So Sophia never came to Boscarva?"

"Oh, yes, she used to come and go. She'd be down at the studio with the Commander, and then he'd get tired, or lose his patience with her, and call it a day, and she'd come up the garden and through the back door calling out, 'Any chance of a cup of tea?' and because it was Sophia, Mrs Pettifer always had the kettle on."

"She used to tell fortunes from teacups."

"Who told you that?"

"My mother."

"That's right, she did. And wonderful things she told us were going to happen to us all. 'Course, they didn't, but it was fun listening to her, just the same. She and your mother were great friends. Sophia used to take her down to the beach and Mrs Pettifer would pack a picnic. And if it was stormy weather they'd go for long walks up on the moor."

"But what was my grandmother doing all this time?"

"Oh, playing bridge or mah-jong most afternoons. She had a very select circle of friends. She was a nice enough lady, but not really interested in children. Perhaps if she'd been more interested in Lisa when she was a child, they'd have had more in common when Lisa grew up, and maybe your mother wouldn't have run off like that, breaking all our hearts."

"What happened to Sophia?"

"Oh, she went back to London, she got married and she had a baby, I think. Then, in 1942, she was killed in the Blitz. The baby was down in the country and her husband was overseas, but Sophia stayed in London because she was working in a hospital there. We didn't hear about it for a long time, till long after it happened. Mrs Pettifer and I felt as though a light had gone out of our lives.''

''And my grandfather?''

''He was sorry, of course. But he hadn't seen her for years. She was just a girl who'd once worked for him.''

''Are there any more pictures of her?''

''There's pictures of Sophia in provincial art galleries up and down the country. There's one in the gallery in Porthkerris if you want to go and look at that. And there's a couple upstairs in Mrs Roger's bedroom.''

''Could we go and look at them now?'' I sounded eager and Pettifer looked surprised, as though I were suggesting something faintly indecent. ''I mean Mrs Bayliss wouldn't mind, would she?''

''Oh, she wouldn't mind. I don't see why not . . . come on.''

He got laboriously to his feet, and I followed him upstairs and along the first-floor passage to the bedroom over the drawing-room, which was large and furnished in a very feminine fashion with old-fashioned Victorian furniture and a faded pink and cream carpet. Mollie had left it painfully neat. The two little oil paintings hung side by side between the windows, one of a chestnut tree with a girl lying in its shade, the other of the same girl hanging out a line of washing on a breezy day. They were scarcely more than sketches, and I was disappointed.

''I still don't know what Sophia looks like.''

Pettifer was about to reply when, from the depths of the house, came the ringing of a bell. He cocked his head, like a dog listening. ''That's the Commander, he's heard us talking through the wall. Excuse me a moment.''

I followed him out of Mollie's room and closed the door behind me. He went on down the passage a little way and opened a door, and I heard Grenville's voice.

''What are you two muttering about in there?''

"I was just showing Rebecca the two pictures in Mrs Roger's room . . ."

"Is Rebecca there? Tell her to come in . . ."

I went in, past Pettifer. Grenville was not in bed, but sitting in a deep armchair with his feet propped up on a stool. He was dressed, but there was a rug over his knees and the room was cheered by the flicker of a fire. Everything was very neat and ship-shape and smelt of the Bay Rum he put on his hair.

I said, "I thought you were in bed."

"Pettifer got me up after lunch. I get bored stiff lying in bed all day. What have you been talking about?"

"Pettifer was showing me some of your pictures."

"I expect you think they're very old-fashioned. They're going back to realism now, you know, these young artists. I knew it would come. You'll have to have one of my pictures. There are racks of them in the studio that have never been sorted out. I closed the place up ten years ago, and I haven't been there since. Pettifer, where's the key?"

"Put safely away, sir."

"You'll have to get the key off Pettifer, go down and nose around, see if there's anything you'd like. Got anywhere to hang it?"

"I've got a flat in London. It needs a picture."

"I thought of something else sitting here. That jade in the cabinet downstairs. I brought it back from China years ago, gave it to Lisa. Now, it belongs to you. And a mirror that her grandmother left her – where's that, Pettifer?"

"That's in the morning-room, sir."

"Well, we'll have to get it down, give it a clean. You'd like that, wouldn't you?"

"Yes, I would." I felt greatly relieved. I had been wondering how to bring up the subject of my mother's possessions, and now, without any prompting, Grenville had done it for me. I hesitated and then, striking while the iron was hot, mentioned the third thing. ". . . and there was a davenport desk."

"Hm?" He fixed me with his ferocious stare. "How do you know?"

"My mother told me about the jade and the mirror, and she said there was a davenport desk." He continued to glare at me. I wished all at once that I had said nothing. "I mean, it doesn't matter, it's just that if nobody did want it . . . if it wasn't being used . . ."

"Pettifer, do you remember that desk?"

"Yes, I do, sir, now you come to mention it. It was up in the other attic bedroom, but I can't remember having seen it lately."

"Well, look for it some time, there's a good fellow. And put another bit of wood on the fire . . ." Pettifer did so. Grenville, watching him, said suddenly, "Where is everybody? The house is quiet. Only the sound of the rain."

"Mrs Roger's out to a bridge party. I think Miss Andrea's in her room . . ."

"How about a cup of tea?" Grenville cocked an eye at me. "You'd like a cup of tea, wouldn't you? We haven't had the chance of getting to know each other. Either you're keeling over in the middle of dinner, or I'm too old and infirm to get out of bed. We make a fine pair, don't we?"

"I'd like to have tea with you."

"Pettifer will bring up a tray."

"No," I said. "I will. Pettifer's legs have been up and down these stairs all day. Let's give him a rest."

Grenville looked amused. "All right. You bring it up, and let's have a good big plateful of hot buttered toast."

I was to wish, many times over, that I had never brought up the subject of the davenport desk. Because it could not be found. While Grenville and I ate our tea, Pettifer began to look for it.

By the time he came to take the tray away, he had combed the house from top to bottom, and the desk was nowhere.

Grenville scarcely believed him. "You've just missed it. Your eyes are getting as old as mine."

"I could scarcely miss seeing a desk." Pettifer sounded aggrieved.

"Perhaps," I said, trying to be helpful, "it was sent away to be mended or something . . ." They both looked at me as though I were a fool, and I hastily shut up.

"Would it be in the studio?" Pettifer ventured.

"What would I do with a desk in the studio? I painted there, I didn't write letters. Didn't want a desk cluttering the place up . . ." Grenville was getting quite agitated. I stood up, "Oh, it'll turn up," I said in my best, soothing voice, and picked up the tea-tray to carry it downstairs. In the kitchen I was joined by Pettifer, upset by what had happened.

"It's not good for the Commander to get worked up about anything . . . and he's going to go after this like a terrier after a rat. I can tell."

"It's all my fault. I don't know why I ever mentioned it."

"But I remember it. I just can't remember having seen it lately." I began to wash the cups and saucers and Pettifer picked up a tea towel in order to dry them. "And there's another thing. There was a Chippendale chair that used to go with it . . . mind, they didn't match, but the chair always sat in front of that desk. It had a tapestry seat, rather worn, birds and flowers and things. Well, that's gone, too . . . but I'm not going to tell the Commander that and neither are you."

I promised that I wouldn't. "Anyway," I said, "it doesn't matter to me one way or the other."

"No, but it matters to the Commander. Artistic he may have been, but he had a memory like an elephant and that's one thing he hasn't lost." He added gloomily, "I sometimes wish he had."

That evening when I went downstairs, changed once more into the brown and silver caftan, I found Eliot in the drawing-room, alone except for that inevitable companion, his dog. Eliot sat by the fire with a drink and the evening paper, and Rufus was stretched, like some glorious fur, on the hearth-rug. They looked companionable, caught in the light of the lamp, but my appearance disturbed the peaceful scene, and Eliot stood up, dropping the paper behind him on the seat of the chair.

"Rebecca. How are you?"

"I'm all right."

"I was afraid last night that you were going to be ill."

"No, I was just tired. I slept till ten o'clock."

"My mother told me. Would you like a drink?"

I said that I would and he poured me some sherry and I went to crouch by the fire and fondle the dog's silky ears.

As Eliot brought me my drink I asked, "Does he go everywhere with you?"

"Yes, everywhere. To the garage, to the office, out to lunch, into the pubs, anywhere I happen to be going. He's a very well-known dog in this part of the world."

I sat on the hearth-rug, and Eliot subsided once more into his chair and picked up his drink. He said, "Tomorrow I have to go over to Falmouth, see a man about a car. I wondered if you'd like to come with me, see a bit of the country. Does that appeal to you?"

I was surprised by my own pleasure at this invitation. "I'd love it."

"It won't be very exciting. But perhaps you can amuse yourself for an hour or two while I'm doing business, and then we'll stop at a little pub I know on the way home. They serve delicious sea food. Do you like oysters?"

"Yes."

"Good. So do I. And then we'll come home by High Cross, and you can see where we normally live, my mother and I."

"Your mother told me about it. It sounds charming."

"Better than this mausoleum . . ."

"Oh, Eliot, it's not a mausoleum . . ."

"I was never much of a one for Victorian relics . . ."

Before I could protest further, we were joined by Grenville. At least, we heard him coming, step by step downstairs; heard him talking to Pettifer, the high-pitched voice and the low growl; heard them coming down the hall, the tap of Grenville's stick on the polished wood.

Eliot made a small face at me and went to open the door, and Grenville moved in, like the prow of some great, indestructible ship ... .

"That's all right, Pettifer, I can manage now." I had got up from the hearth-rug, wanting to help push forward the chair which he had used the night before, but this seemed to madden him. He was obviously not in a good mood.

"For God's sake, girl, stop fussing around. Do you think I want to sit *in* the fire, I'll burn to death sitting there . . ."

I edged the chair back to its original position and finally Grenville reached it and sank into it.

"How about a drink?" Eliot asked him.

"I'll have a whisky . . ."

Eliot looked surprised ". . . Whisky?"

"Yes, a whisky. I know what that fool of a doctor said but tonight I'm having a whisky."

Eliot said nothing, just nodded his head in patient acquiescence and went to pour the drink. As he did so Grenville leaned round the edge of the chair and said, "Eliot, have you seen that davenport desk around the place?" and my heart sank into my shoes.

"Oh, Grenville, don't start that again . . ."

"What do you mean, start that again? We've got to find the damned thing. I told Pettifer just now, got to go on looking till we've found it."

Eliot came back with the glass of whisky. He drew up a table and set the glass within Grenville's reach.

"What davenport desk?" he asked patiently.

"Little davenport desk, used to be in one of the bedrooms. Belonged to Lisa and now it belongs to Rebecca. She wants it. She's got a flat in London, wants to put it there. And Pettifer can't find it, says he's been through the house with a toothcomb, can't find it. You haven't seen it, have you?"

"I've never set eyes on it. I don't even know what a davenport desk is."

"It's a little desk. Got drawers down the side. Bit of tooled leather on the top. They're rare now, I believe. Worth a lot of money."

"Pettifer's probably put it somewhere and forgotten."

"Pettifer doesn't forget things."

"Well, perhaps Mrs Pettifer did something with it and forgot to tell him."

"I've already *said*; he doesn't forget things."

We were joined at this moment by Mollie, who appeared, smiling determinedly, as though she had heard the angry voice raised beyond the closed door, and was about to spread oil on troubled waters.

"Hello, everybody, I'm afraid I'm a little late. I had to go and do some very exciting things to that delicious piece of halibut Rebecca bought for me this morning. Eliot, dear . . ." she kissed him, apparently seeing him for the first time that evening. "And Grenville . . ." she stooped to kiss him too ". . . you're looking more rested." Then, before he could contradict her, she smiled across the top of his head at me. "Did you have a good afternoon?"

"Yes, thank you. How was the bridge?"

"Not too bad. I won twenty pence. Eliot darling, I'd love a drink. Andrea's just coming. She won't be a moment . . ." But she finally ran out of defensive small talk, and Grenville instantly opened fire. "We've lost something," he told her.

"What have you lost? Your cuff-links again?"

"We have lost a davenport desk."

It was becoming ludicrous.

"You've *lost* a davenport desk?"

For her benefit, Grenville went through the whole rigmarole. On being told that it was I who had precipitated this crisis, Mollie looked at me with some reproach, as though she thought this a poor way to return her hospitality and kindness. I was inclined to agree with her.

"But it must be somewhere." She took her glass from Eliot, drew up a stool and sat, all ready to work the whole thing out. "It must have been put somewhere for safety."

"Pettifer has looked for it."

"Perhaps he hasn't seen it. I'm sure he should get his glasses changed. Perhaps it's been put somewhere and he's forgotten."

Grenville thumped the arm of his chair with a balled fist. "Pettifer does not forget things."

"In fact . . ." said Eliot coolly ". . . he forgets things all the time."

Grenville glared at him. "And what does that mean?"

"Nothing personal. Just that he's getting older."

"I suppose you're blaming Pettifer . . ."

"I'm not blaming anybody . . ."

"You just said he's too old to know what he's doing. If he's too old what the hell do you think I am?"

"I never said that . . ."

"You blamed *him* . . ."

Eliot lost his patience. "If I was going to blame anybody,"

he said, raising his voice almost to the pitch of Grenville's, "I'd ask a few questions of your Joss Gardner." There was a pause after he'd come out with this. And then, in a more controlled, reasonable voice, he went on. "All right, so nobody wants to accuse another man of stealing. But Joss is in and out of this house all the time, in and out of all the rooms. He knows what's in this place better than anybody. And he's an expert, he knows what it's worth."

"But why should Joss take a desk?" asked Mollie.

"A valuable desk. Don't forget that. It's rare and it's valuable, Grenville just said so. Perhaps he needed the money. To look at him he could do with a bit of extra cash. And he's an expert. He's up and down to London all the time. He'd know where to sell it."

He stopped, abruptly, as though realising that already he had said too much. He finished his whisky, and went, without speaking, to pour himself a second glass.

The silence became uncomfortable. To break it, Mollie said, briefly, "I don't think that Joss . . ."

"Just a lot of poppycock," Grenville interrupted her savagely.

Eliot set down the whisky bottle with a thump.

"How do you know? How do you know anything about Joss Gardner? He turns up, like a hippy, out of nowhere, says he's going to open a shop, and the next thing you've opened up the house to him and given him the job of patching up all the furniture. What do you know about Joss? What do any of us know about him?"

"I know that I can trust him. I was trained to judge a man's character . . ."

"You could be wrong . . ."

Grenville raised his voice and rode over Eliot's, ". . . and it would be no bad thing if you were to take a few lessons in choosing your companions."

Eliot's eyes narrowed. "What does that mean?"

"It means that if you want to be made a fool of, try doing business with that little shyster Ernest Padlow."

If I could have escaped at that moment, I would. But I was caught, jammed into the corner behind Grenville's chair.

"What do you know about Ernest Padlow?"

"I know you've been seen around with him . . . drinking in bars . . ."

Eliot shot a glance at me, and then said, under his breath, "That bastard Joss Gardner."

"It wasn't Joss who told me, it was Hargreaves, at the bank. He came up for a glass of sherry the other day. And Mrs Thomas came in to do my fire this morning, she'd seen you with Padlow, up at that gimcrack nightmare he calls a housing estate."

"Back-stairs gossip."

"You hear the truth from truthful people. It doesn't matter in which direction they live. And if you think I'm selling up my land to that jumped-up little beachsweeper, you're wrong . . ."

"It won't always be your land."

"And if you're so sure it will be yours, all I can say is, don't count your chickens before they're hatched. Because you, dear boy, are not my only grandchild."

And at this dramatic moment, like a nicely stage-managed play, the door opened and Andrea appeared to tell us that Pettifer had told her to tell us that dinner was ready.

8

It was hard to sleep that night. I tossed and turned, fetched
a glass of water, paced the floor, looked out of the window,
climbed back into bed and tried once more to compose myself,
but always, when I closed my eyes, the evening came back to
me like a film played over and over, voices drummed in my
ears, and would not be stilled.

*All right, so nobody wants to accuse another man of stealing.
What do any of us know about Joss?*

*If you want to be made a fool of, try doing business with that
little shyster Ernest Padlow. And if you think I'm selling my
land to that jumped-up little beachsweeper, you're wrong . . .*

It won't always be your land . . .

. . . you, dear boy, are not my only grandchild.

Dinner had been a gruesome meal. Eliot and Grenville had
scarcely spoken a word from beginning to end. Mollie, to
make up for their silence, had kept up a patter of meaningless
conversation to which I had tried to respond. And Andrea had
watched us all, a gleam of triumph in her round, seeking eyes,
while Pettifer trod heavily to and fro, removing dishes, handing
round a lemon soufflé rich with whipped cream, which nobody
seemed to want.

When at last it was over, they had all dispersed. Grenville
to his bedroom, Andrea to the morning-room from whence we

131

presently heard the blare of the television set. Eliot, with no explanations, put on a coat, whistled up his dog and banged out of the front door. I guessed he had gone to get drunk and didn't entirely blame him. Mollie and I ended up in the drawing-room, one on either side of the fire. She had some tapestry and seemed quite prepared to sit and sew in silence, but this would have been unbearable. I said, plunging straight in with the apology which I felt I owed her, "I am sorry about this evening. I wish I'd never mentioned that desk."

She did not look at me. "Oh, it can't be helped."

"It was just that my mother had mentioned it to me, and when Grenville spoke about the jade and the mirror, well, it never occurred to me that I'd start such a storm in a teacup."

"Grenville's a strange old man. He's always been stubborn about people, he'll never see that there can be two sides to every situation."

"You mean about Joss . . ."

"I don't know why he's so taken with Joss. It's frightening. It's as though Joss were able to exert some hold over him. Eliot and I never wanted him in and out of the house this way. If Grenville's furniture needed to be repaired, surely he could have come and fetched it in his van and taken it down to his workshop, like any other tradesman would do. We tried to talk Grenville out of it, but he was adamant, and, after all, this is his house. It isn't ours."

"But it will be Eliot's one day."

She sent me a cold look.

"After this evening, one wonders."

"Oh, Mollie, I don't want Boscarva, Grenville would never leave a place like this to me. He just said that to win a point; perhaps it was the first thing that came into his head. He didn't mean it."

"He hurt Eliot."

"Eliot will understand. You have to make allowances for old people."

"I'm tired of making allowances for Grenville," said Mollie, viciously snapping at a strand of wool with her silver scissors. "My life has been disrupted by Grenville. He and Pettifer could have come and lived at High Cross; that's what we wanted. The house is smaller and more convenient and it would have been better for everybody. And Boscarva should have been made over to Eliot years ago. As it is, death duties are going to be exorbitant. Eliot is never going to be able to afford to keep it going. The whole situation is *so* unrealistic."

"I suppose it's hard to be realistic when you're eighty and you've lived in a place most of your life."

She ignored this. "And all that land, and the farm. Eliot is simply trying to make the best of it all, but Grenville won't see that. He's never shown any interest, never encouraged Eliot in any way. Even the garage at High Cross, Eliot got that going entirely on his own. At the beginning, he asked his grandfather to help, but Grenville said he wasn't going to have anything to do with second-hand cars, and there was a row, and finally Eliot borrowed the money from someone else, and he's never asked his grandfather for a shilling since that day. You'd think he'd deserve some credit for that."

She was pale with anger on Eliot's account – a little tigress, I thought, fighting for her cub, and I remembered my mother's low opinion of the way in which she had possessed and molly-coddled the young Eliot. Perhaps neither of them had ever grown out of the habit.

To change the subject I told her about Eliot's invitation for the next day. "He said he'd take me into High Cross on the way home."

But Mollie was only momentarily diverted. "You must go in and see the house, Eliot's got the key. I go up most weeks to make sure everything's all right, but really I get so depressed having to leave my darling little house and come back to this gloomy place . . .'' and then she laughed at herself wryly. ''It's getting me down, isn't it? I must try to pull myself together. But really I'll be glad when it's all over.''

When it's all over. That meant when Grenville finally died. I didn't want to think about him dying any more than I wanted to think about Joss coupled with the unsavoury Andrea; any more than I wanted to think about Joss helping himself to a davenport desk and a Chippendale chair, heaving them into the back of his little truck, and selling them to the first dealer who made him a good offer.

What do you know about Joss? What do any of us know about him?

For my part I wished I knew nothing. I turned in bed, thumped at the pillows, and waited, without much hope, for sleep.

It rained in the night, but the next morning it was still and clear, the sky a pale, washed blue, everything wet and shining, translucent in the cool spring light. I leaned out of the window and smelt the dampness, mossy and sweet. The sea was flat and blue as a sheet of silk, gulls drifted lazily over the rim of the cliff, a boat moved out from the harbour, heading for distant fishing-grounds, and so still was the air that I could hear the distant chug of its engine.

My spirits rose. Yesterday was over, today would be better. I was glad to be getting out of the house, away from Mollie's reproach and Andrea's unsettling presence. I bathed and dressed and went downstairs and found Eliot in the dining-room, eating bacon and eggs, and looking – I was thankful to see – cheerful.

He looked up from the morning paper. ''I wondered,'' he said, ''if I was going to have to come and wake you up. I thought perhaps you'd forgotten.''

''No, I didn't forget.''

"We're the first down. With any luck we'll be out of the house before anyone else appears." He grinned, ruefully, like a repentant boy. "The last thing I want on a beautiful morning like this is recriminations."

"It was all my fault, mentioning that stupid desk. I said I was sorry last night to your mother."

"It'll all blow over," said Eliot. "These little differences of opinion always do." I poured myself a cup of coffee. "I'm just sorry that you were involved."

We left straight after breakfast, and there was a marvellous feeling of relief to be in his car, with Rufus perched on the back seat, and to be escaping. The car roared up the hill away from Boscarva; the wet road was blue with reflected sky, and the air smelt of primroses. As we climbed up and over the moor, the view spread and dipped before us – there were hills topped by ancient cairns and standing stones, and tiny forgotten villages, tucked into the folds of unexpected valleys where little rivers ran, and ancient clumps of oak and elm stood clustered by narrow, hump-backed bridges.

But I knew that we could not enjoy our day together, that we could not be entirely at ease, until I had made my peace with him.

I said, "I know that it'll blow over, and that perhaps it *wasn't* important, but we have to talk about last night."

He smiled at me, glancing sideways. "What do we have to say?"

"Just that, what Grenville said about having another grandchild. He didn't mean it. I know he didn't mean it."

"No, perhaps he didn't. Perhaps he was just trying to set us against each other, like a pair of dogs."

"He'd never leave me Boscarva. Never in a thousand years. He doesn't even know me, I've only just come into his life."

"Rebecca, don't give it another thought. I'm not going to."

"And, after all, if it is going to be yours one day, I don't see why you shouldn't start thinking about what you're going to do with it."

"You mean Ernest Padlow? What a lot of gossips those old people are, carrying tales and making mischief. If it isn't the bank manager it's Mrs Thomas, and if it isn't Mrs Thomas it's Pettifer."

I made myself sound casual. "Would you sell the land?"

"If I did I could probably afford to live at Boscarva. It's time I set up on my own."

"But . . ." I chose my words tactfully ". . . but wouldn't it be rather . . . spoiled . . . I mean, living there with rows of Mr Padlow's little houses all round you?"

Eliot laughed. "You've got entirely the wrong end of the stick. This wouldn't be a building estate like the one at the top of the hill. This would be high-class stuff, two-acre lots, very high specifications as to the style and the price of the houses built on them. No cutting down of trees, no despoiling of the amenities. They'd be expensive houses for expensive people, and there wouldn't be a lot of them. How does that sound to you?"

"Have you told Grenville this?"

"He won't let me. He won't listen. He's not interested and that's it."

"But surely if you explained . . ."

"I've been trying to explain things to him all my life and I've never got anywhere. And now, is there anything else you want to discuss?"

I considered. I certainly didn't want to discuss Joss. I said, "No."

"In that case shall we forget about last night and enjoy ourselves?"

It seemed a good idea. We smiled at each other. "All right,"

I said at last. We crossed a bridge and came to a steep hill, and Eliot changed down, expertly, with the old-fashioned gear stick. The car purred up the savage slope, its long, elegant bonnet seeming to point straight to the sky.

We got to Falmouth about ten o'clock. While Eliot attended to his business I was turned loose to explore the little town. Facing south, sheltered from the north wind, with gardens already filled with camellias and scented daphne bushes, it made me think of some Mediterranean port, and this illusion was strengthened by the blue of the sea on that first warm spring day, and the tall masts of the yachts which lay at anchor in the basin.

I felt, for some reason, impelled to shop. I bought freesias for Mollie, tightly in bud with their stalks wrapped in damp moss so that they would not wither before I got home, a box of cigars for Grenville, a bottle of fruity sherry for Pettifer, a record for Andrea. The sleeve portrayed a transvestite group with sequined eyelids. It seemed to me to be right up her street. And for Eliot . . . I had noticed that his watch strap was wearing thin. I found a narrow strap in dark crocodile, very expensive, exactly right for Eliot. Then I bought a tube of toothpaste for myself, because I needed one. And for Joss . . .? Nothing for Joss.

Eliot picked me up, as we had arranged, in the lounge of the big hotel in the middle of town. We drove very fast out of the town and through Truro, and down into the little maze of lanes and wooded creeks that lay beyond until we came to a village called St Endon, where there were white cottages, palm trees and gardens full of flowers. The road wound down towards the creek, and at the very bottom was a little pub, right on the water's edge, with the high tide lapping at the wall below the terrace. Kittiwakes perched along the top of it, their eyes bright and friendly, unlike the greedy, wild gulls of Boscarva.

We sat out in the sunshine, drinking sherry, and I gave Eliot his present, then and there; he seemed inordinately delighted, ripping off the old watch strap right away and fitting on the new, shining leather one, adjusting the little clips with the blade of his penknife.

"What made you think of giving me that?"

"I noticed your old one was worn. I thought perhaps that you might lose your watch."

He leaned back in his chair, watching me across the table. It was so warm that I had pulled off my sweater and rolled up the sleeves of my cotton shirt. He said, "Did you buy presents for everybody?"

I was embarrassed. "Yes."

"I thought you had a lot of parcels. Do you always buy presents for people?"

"It's nice to have people to buy presents for."

"Isn't there anyone in London?"

"Not really."

"No one special?"

"There's never been anyone special."

"I can't believe it."

"It's true." I could not think why I was confiding in him this way. Perhaps it had something to do with the warmth of the day, surprising me by its beneficence, lowering all my guards. Perhaps it was the sherry. Perhaps it was simply the intimacy of two people who had weathered such a storm as the row that had taken place last night. Whatever the reason, it was easy that day to talk to Eliot.

"Why. is that?" he asked.

"I don't know. It may have something to do with the way I was brought up . . . my mother lived with one man after another, so I lived with them too. And there's nothing like living at close quarters with people to destroy that marvellous illusion of romance."

We laughed. "That could be a good thing," said Eliot. "But

it could be a bad thing, too. You mustn't close up altogether. Otherwise nobody's ever going to get near you.''

''I'm all right.''

''Are you going back to London?''

''Yes.''

''Soon?''

''Probably.''

''Why not stay for a bit?''

''I don't want to wear out my welcome.''

''You won't do that. And I've hardly spoken to you. Anyway, how can you go back to London and leave all this behind you . . .?'' His gesture included the sky, the sun, the quiet, the lap of water, the promise of the coming spring.

''I can, because I have to. I've a job to get back to and a flat that needs painting, and a life to pick up and start all over again.''

''Can't that wait?''

''Not indefinitely.''

''There's no reason to go.'' I did not reply. ''Unless,'' he went on, ''you were put off by what happened last night.'' I smiled and shook my head, because we had promised not to mention that again. He leaned on the table, his chin on his fist. ''If you really wanted a job you could get one here. If you wanted a flat of your own you could rent that too.''

''Why should I stay?'' But I was flattered at being so persuaded.

''Because it would be good for Grenville, and for Mollie, and for me. Because I think we all want you to stay. Particularly me.''

''Oh, Eliot . . .''

''It's true. There's something very serene about you. Did you know that? I noticed it that first evening I saw you before I even knew who you were. And I like the shape of your nose, and the sound of your laugh, and the way you can look marvellously ragamuffin one minute, in jeans and with your hair coming all unravelled, and then, the next minute, like a princess in a fairy story, with your plait over your shoulder and that stately gown you wear in the evenings. I feel as though I'm finding out new things about you every day. And this is why I don't want you to go. Not just yet."

I found that I could think of no rejoinder to this long speech. I was touched by it, and embarrassed too. But still, it was gratifying to be liked and admired, and even more gratifying to be told so.

Across the table, he began to laugh at me. "Your face is a picture. You don't know where to look and you're blushing. Come along, finish your drink and we'll go and eat oysters. I promise I'll not pay you any more compliments!"

We lingered over lunch in the small, low-ceilinged dining-room, eating at a table which wobbled so much on the uneven floor that Eliot was forced to prop up one of the legs with a scrap of folded paper. We ate oysters and steak and a fresh green salad and drank our way through a bottle of wine. We took our coffee back into the sunshine, and sat on the edge of the terrace wall, watching two boys, sunburned and barelegged, rig up a dinghy and take her sailing out on to the blue waters of the creek. We saw the striped sail fill with some mysterious, unfelt breeze, as the dinghy heeled and went away from us, around the tip of a wooded promontory. And Eliot said that if I stayed in Cornwall, he would borrow a boat and teach me to sail; we would go mackerel fishing from Porthkerris – in the summer he would show me all the tiny coves and secret places which the tourists never found.

At last it was time to go, and the afternoon wound itself in like a long, shining ribbon. I was sleepy and replete when he drove me slowly back to High Cross, taking the long road that led through forgotten villages and the heart of the country.

When we got to High Cross, I realised that it stood at the very summit of the peninsula, so that the village had two aspects, one north to the Atlantic, the other south to the Channel; it was like being on an island, swept with clean winds and ringed by the sea. Eliot's garage stood in the middle of the village street, a little back from the road, with a cobbled forecourt set about with tubs of flowers, and inside the glass-fronted showroom stood the gleaming, racy cars. Everything was very new and expensive-looking and immaculately kept. I wondered, as we crossed the forecourt towards the showrooms, how much Eliot had had to sink into such a venture, and why he had decided that it was a viable proposition to open such a specialised garage in this out-of-the-way spot.

He pulled one of the sliding glass doors aside and I went in, my feet making no sound on the highly polished rubber floors.

"Why did you decide to start your garage here, Eliot? Wouldn't it have been better in Fourbourne or Falmouth or Penzance?"

"Psychological selling, my dear. Get a good name for yourself and people will come from the ends of the earth to buy what you've got to sell." And he added with disarming candour, "Besides, I already owned the land, or at least my mother did, which was an excellent incentive to build the garage here."

"Are all these cars for sale?"

"Yes. As you can see we concentrate on continental and sports cars. We had a Ferrari in last week, but that was sold a couple of days ago. It had been crashed, but I've got this young mechanic working for me, and by the time he'd finished with it it was as good as new . . ."

I laid my hand on the gleaming yellow bonnet. "What's this?"

"A Lancia Zagato. And this is an Alfa Romeo Spyder, only two years old. Beautiful car."

"And a Jensen Interceptor . . ." That was one that I recognised.

"Come and see the workshop." I followed him through another sliding door at the back of the showroom and decided that this was more like my idea of a garage. Here was the usual clutter of dismantled engines, oil cans, long flexes trailing from the ceiling, naked bulbs, tool benches, old tyres and trolleys.

In the middle of all this a figure was stooped over the stripped-down engine of a skeletal car. He wore a welding mask which made him appear monstrous, and worked with the roaring blue flame of a welding gun. The noise of the gun was overlaid by non-stop blaring music from a surprisingly small transistor radio perched on a beam above him.

Whether or not he saw us coming was anybody's guess, but it was only when Eliot switched off the radio that he shut off his gun and straightened up, pushing the welding mask up and back off his face. I saw a thin, dark young man, oil-stained and in need of a shave, his hair long, his eyes sharp and bright.

"Hello, Morris," said Eliot.

"Hello."

"This is Rebecca Bayliss, she's staying at Boscarva."

Reaching for a cigarette, Morris looked my way and gave me a nod. I said, "Hello," just to be friendly, but got no more response. He lit his cigarette, then slipped the fancy lighter back into the pocket of his oily overalls.

"Thought you'd be coming in this morning," he told Eliot.

"I told you I was going over to Falmouth."

"Any luck?"

"A 1933 Bentley."

"What sort of condition?"

"Looked OK. A bit of rust."

"Get the old paint spray out. There was a chap in the other day, wanting one of them."

"I know, that's why I bought it. Thought we'd take the transporter over, tomorrow or the next day, pick her up."

They fell silent. Morris went to his transistor and turned it on again, if anything louder than before. I looked down at the confusion of engineering on which he had been working and finally asked Eliot what sort of a car it had originally been.

"A 1971 Jaguar XJ6 4.2 litre, if you really want to know. And it will be again when Morris has finished with it. This is another that was in a crash."

Morris came back to stand between us.

"What exactly are you doing to it?" I asked him.

"Straightening out the chassis, fixing the wheel alignment."

"What about the brake shoes?" said Eliot.

"It could have done with new brake shoes, but I fixed the old ones to cover us for the guarantee . . . and Mr Kemback rang up from Birmingham . . ."

They began to talk shop. I drifted away, deafened by the sound of rock, went back through the showroom and out into the forecourt where Rufus waited, with dignity and patience, behind the driving wheel of Eliot's car. Together we sat there until we were rejoined by Eliot. "Sorry about that, Rebecca; I wanted to check on another job. Morris is a good mechanic, but he gets shirty if he's expected to answer the telephone as well."

"Who's Mr Kemback? Another customer?"

"No, not exactly. He was down here last summer on holiday. He runs a motel, a garage, just off the M6. He's got quite a selection of old cars. Wants to start a museum, you know, a sort of sideline to the bacon-and-egg trade. He seems to want me to run it for him."

"You mean go and live in Birmingham?"

"Doesn't sound very tempting, does it? Anyway, that's it. Let's go and look at my mother's house."

We walked there, just a little way down the street, then up a short lane and through a double white gate, and the path sloped up to a long, low white house, which had been converted from two ancient thick-walled stone cottages. Eliot took a key out of his pocket and opened the door and inside it was cold, but not musty or damp. It was furnished like an expensive London flat, with pale, thick, fitted carpets and pale walls and sofas upholstered in mushroom-coloured brocade. There were a great many mirrors and little crystal bag chandeliers hanging from the low-beamed ceilings.

It was all charming, and just what I had imagined, and somehow wrong. A kitchen like an advertisement, a dining-room furnished with gleaming mahogany, upstairs there were four bedrooms and three bathrooms, a sewing-room and a linen cupboard of mammoth proportions, richly smelling of soap.

At the back of the house was a little patio, and then a long garden sloped up to a distant hedge. I looked at the patio and could see Mollie out there, entertaining her friends, with cane furniture set out on the flagstones, and martinis to drink, served from an expensive glass trolley.

I said, "It's a perfect house," and meant it. But I did not love it as I loved Boscarva. Perhaps because it was too perfect.

We stood in the elegant out-of-place drawing-room and eyed each other. Our day together seemed to have come to an end. Perhaps Eliot felt this too and wanted to postpone it, for he said, "I could put on a kettle and make you a cup of tea, only I know that there's no milk in the fridge."

"I think we should go home." I was surprised by an enormous yawn, and Eliot laughed at me. He took my shoulders between his hands. "You're sleepy."

"Too much fresh air," I answered. "Too much wine."

I tipped my head back to look up into his face, and we were very close. I could feel his fingers tighten over my shoulders.

He wasn't laughing any more, but his deep-set eyes held an expression as gentle as anything I had ever seen.

I said, "It's been a wonderful day . . ." but that was as far as I got, because he kissed me then, and for some time I was not able to say anything at all. When at last he drew away I was so shaken that all I could do was lean limply against him, wanting to cry, feeling a fool, knowing that the situation was fast slipping out of my control. My cheek was against his coat, and his arms around me held me so close that I could feel, like the throb of a drum, the solid beating of his heart.

Over the top of my head, I heard him say, "You mustn't go back to London. You mustn't ever go away again."

9

The shopping which I had done in Falmouth proved to be an unexpected blessing. I must have been inspired, for, without thinking, I provided exactly the small talking point we all needed to smooth over the embarrassment of the previous uncomfortable evening. Mollie was charmed with her freesias; she couldn't grow them at Boscarva, she explained, the winds were too cold, the garden too exposed. She paid me the compliment of arranging them with more artistry than one would have thought possible, and finally giving them the place of honour in the middle of the mantelpiece in the drawing-room. They filled the room with their rich romantic scent, and the cream and the violet and the deep pink drew one's eye, quite naturally, up to the portrait of Sophia. The flowers seemed to complement the glowing skin tones and the fragile shimmer of the white dress.

"Beautiful," said Mollie, standing back, but I could not be sure whether she was referring to the flowers or the portrait. "It was sweet of you to bring them. And did Eliot take you to see my house? So now you can understand how I feel about having to live in this great place." She regarded me thoughtfully, her eyes narrowed. "You know, I believe the day has done you good. I could even imagine you've caught the sun. You've got quite a good colour. The air must agree with you."

Pettifer accepted his sherry with dignity, but I could tell that he was pleased. And Grenville was wickedly delighted with his cigars, for the doctor had warned him against smoking and Pettifer had hidden his usual supply. I understood that he was parsimonious about doling them out. Grenville took and lit one instantly, puffing away with immense satisfaction and leaning back in his big chair like a man without a care in the world. Even with Andrea I had for once done the right thing. *"The Creepers!* How did you know they're my favourite group? Oh, I wish there was a record-player here, but there isn't and I left mine in London. Gosh, aren't they fabulous, groovy . . .?'' And then she came down to earth again, searching for the price tag. ''That must have cost you something.''

It was as though, with peace offerings, we had all formed an unspoken pact. Last night was never discussed. There was no mention of the davenport desk, of Ernest Padlow, of the possible sale of Boscarva Farm. There was no mention of Joss. After dinner Eliot set up a table, and Mollie got out the rosewood box containing the mah-jong set, and we played until bed-time, Andrea sitting with Mollie in order to learn the rules.

I caught myself thinking that, if a stranger were to come, unexpectedly, upon us, how he would be charmed by the picture we made, caught, like flies in amber, in the pool of light from the standard lamp, absorbed by our timeless occupation. The distinguished painter, mellow in the twilight of his years, surrounded by his family; the pretty daughter-in-law and the handsome grandson – and even Andrea, for once alert and interested, absorbed by the intricacies of the game.

I had played as a child with my mother, sometimes making up a foursome with two of her friends, and found myself comforted by the remembered touch of the ivory and bamboo tiles, by their beauty, and the satisfying sound they made, like sea pebbles disturbed by the tide, as we stirred them around in the middle of the table.

THE DAY OF THE STORM

At the start of each round we built the four walls, two tiles high, and closed them together into a tight square, "to keep the evil spirits out," we were told by Grenville, who had learned to play as a young sub-lieutenant in Hong Kong and knew all the traditional superstitions of the ancient game. I thought how easy it would be, how safe, if ghosts and doubts and skeletons-in-the-cupboard could be thus shut out and kept at bay.

The travel brochures and holiday posters of Porthkerris inevitably portrayed a place where the sea and the sky were always a bright and unsullied blue, the houses white with sunshine, the odd palm tree in the foreground lending that suggestion of Mediterranean glamour. The imagination was led, naturally, to visions of fresh lobster, eaten out of doors; artists with beards and paint-stained smocks; and weather-beaten fishermen, picturesque as pirates, sitting on bollards, smoking their pipes and discussing last week's catch.

But Porthkerris, in February, in a north-east gale, had no shred of connection with this nebulous paradise.

The sea, the sky, the very town were grey, the maze of baffling, narrow streets subjected to onslaughts of bitter wind. The tide was high; the waves broke against the sea wall and splashed across the road, misting the windows of the houses opposite with salt, and filling the gutters with yellow foam, like dirty soapsuds.

It was as though the place were under some sort of a siege. Shoppers were wrapped, buttoned, scarved in every sort of protective clothing, their faces half hidden by hoods or deep coat collars, their bodies bundled into ambiguity, so that men and women all looked alike, gumbooted and shapeless.

The sky was the colour of the wind, the air filled with flying flotsam, old leaves, twigs, scraps of paper, even tiles torn from roofs. In the shops, people forgot what they had come to buy, the talk was all of the weather, the wind, the damage the storm was going to do.

I had come, once more, to shop for Mollie, fighting my way down the hill in borrowed raincoat and rubber boots, because I felt safer on my feet than I would have driving Mollie's insubstantial car. Now that I was more familiar with the town I no longer needed Andrea to show me the way . . . anyway Andrea was still in bed when I left Boscarva, and for once I did not blame her. The day was not inviting and it was hard to believe that only yesterday I had been sitting out, in my shirtsleeves, basking in a sun as warm as May.

The last of the shopping completed, I emerged from the baker's as the clock in the tower of the Norman church struck eleven. Normally, under such conditions, I would have headed straight back up the hill to Boscarva, but I had other plans. With my head down, the heavy basket over one arm, I made for the harbour.

The Art Gallery, I knew, was housed in an old Baptist Chapel, somewhere in the maze of streets which lay to the north of the town. I had thought that I would simply go and look for it, but as I braved the harbour road, battling with alternate assaults of wind and spray, I saw the old fisherman's lodge which had been converted to a Tourist Information Bureau and decided that I would save myself both time and effort if I made a few enquiries.

Inside, I found an unenthusiastic girl huddled over a paraffin stove; booted and shivering, she looked like the sole survivor of some Arctic expedition. When I appeared she did not move from her chair but said, "Yes?" and stared at me through a pair of unbecoming spectacles.

I tried to feel sorry for her. "I'm looking for the Art Gallery."

"Which one did you want?"

"I didn't know there was more than one."

Behind me the door opened and shut and we were joined by a third person. The girl looked over my shoulder and a faint interest gleamed behind her pebble glasses.

"There's the Town Gallery and the New Painters," she said, much more lively.

"I don't know which I want."

"Perhaps," said a voice behind me, "I can help."

I swung around and Joss stood there, in rubber boots and a streaming black oilskin, a fisherman's cap jammed down on to his head. His face was wet with rain, his hands rammed into the deep pockets of the coat, his dark eyes glinting with amusement. One half of me could see exactly why the sluggish girl behind the counter had suddenly come to life. The other half was maddened by his extraordinary ability to turn up just when I was least expecting him.

I remembered Andrea. I remembered the desk and the chair. I said, coolly, "Hello, Joss."

"I saw you come in. What are you wanting to do?"

The girl chipped in. "She wants the Art Gallery."

Joss waited for me to enlarge on this and, thus cornered, I did so.

"I thought perhaps there might be some pictures of Grenville's there . . ."

"You're quite right, there are three. I'll take you . . ."

"I don't need to be taken, I just want to be told how to get there."

"I'd like to take you . . . here . . ." he removed my heavy basket from my arm, smiled at the girl and went to open the door. A howl of wind and a blast of spume-laden air poured in from the outside and a pile of leaflets flew and scattered from the counter all over the floor. Before we could do any more damage, I hurried out, and the door swung shut behind us. As though it were the most natural thing in the world, Joss took

151

my arm and we made our way down the middle of the cobbled road, Joss carrying on a cheerful conversation despite the fact that the wind tore the words from his mouth, and that, even with his arm in mine, it was taking all my efforts to progress at all.

"What on earth brings you down to the town on a day like this?"

"You're carrying it. Mollie's shopping."

"Couldn't you have brought the car?"

"I thought I might get blown off the road."

"I love it," he told me. "I love a day like this." He looked as though he loved it too, wind-whipped and wet and bursting with vitality. "Did you have a good day yesterday?"

"What do you know about yesterday?"

"I was up at Boscarva and Andrea told me you'd gone to Falmouth with Eliot. Don't imagine you can keep any secrets in this place. If Andrea hadn't told me, Pettifer would, or Mrs Thomas, or Mrs Kernow, or Miss Bright-Eyes in the Information Bureau. It's part of the fun of living in Porthkerris, everybody knows exactly what everybody else is up to."

"I'm beginning to realise that."

We turned away from the harbour and began to climb a steep cobbled hill. Houses closed in on either side of us, a cat flashed across the street and disappeared through a crack in a window. A woman in a pot-hat and a blue apron was scrubbing her steps. She looked up and saw us, and said, " 'Ullo, my lover," to Joss; her fingers were like a bunch of pink sausages, made so by the hot water and the cold wind.

At the end of the street, we found ourselves in a little square which I had not seen before. One side of this was taken up by a large barn-like structure, with arched windows set high along the wall. By the door was a sign, PORTHKERRIS ART GALLERY, and Joss let go of my arm, pushed open the door with his shoulder and stood aside to let me go ahead of him. Inside it was bitterly cold, draughty, totally empty. The white walls were hung with paintings, of all sorts and shapes and sizes, and two great abstract sculptures were marooned in the middle of the floor, like rocks exposed by an ebb tide. There was a table by the door, with neat stacks of catalogues and folders and copies of *The Studio*, but despite this window-dressing the gallery stayed thick with the atmosphere of joyless bygone Sundays.

"Now," Joss put down my basket and took off his cap, shaking it free of rain as a dog shakes its coat, "what do you want to see?"

"I want to see Sophia."

He glanced at me sharply with a sudden turn of his head, but in the same instant smiled and put his hat on his head again, pulling the peak down over his eyes, like a guardsman.

"Who told you about Sophia?"

I smiled sweetly. "Perhaps it was Mrs Thomas. Perhaps it was Mrs Kernow. Perhaps it was Miss Bright-Eyes in the Information Bureau."

"Insolence will get you nowhere."

"There *is* a portrait of Sophia here. Pettifer told me."

"Yes. It's over this way."

I followed him down the length of the floor, our rubber-booted footsteps sounding loud in the emptiness.

"There," he said. I stopped beside him and looked up, and she was there, sitting in a beam of lamplight with some sewing in her hands.

I stared at it for a long time and finally let out a long sigh of disappointment. Joss looked down at me from under the ridiculous peak of his cap.

"What's that sigh for?"

"You still can't see her face. I still don't know what she looks like. Why didn't he ever paint her face?"

"He did. Often."

"Well, I still haven't seen it. It's always the back of her head or her hands or else she's so small a part of the picture she doesn't have a face at all, just a blob."

"Does it matter what she looked like?"

"No, it doesn't matter. It's just that I want to know."

"How did you know about Sophia in the first place?"

"My mother told me about her. And then Pettifer, and the picture of her – the one at Boscarva in the drawing-room – is so charming and feminine, one feels she must have been beautiful. But Pettifer says that she wasn't beautiful at all. Just very charming and attractive." We looked again at the picture. I saw the hands, and the shine of lamplight on her dark hair. "Pettifer says that art galleries up and down the country have portraits of Sophia hanging on their walls. I shall just have to go on from Manchester to Birmingham, to Nottingham, to Glasgow, until I find one that isn't of the back of her head."

"What will you do then?"

"Nothing. Just know what she looks like."

I turned from my disappointment and began to walk back to the door where my laden basket waited for me, but Joss was there first, stooping to swing it up and out of my reach.

I said, "I must go back."

"It's only . . ." he consulted his watch ". . . half past eleven. And you've never seen my shop. Come back with me and let me show it off, and I'll make you a cup of coffee and drive you home. You can't possibly walk up the hill with this great weight on your arm."

"Of course I can."

"I won't let you." He opened the door. "Come along."

I couldn't go without the basket and he obviously wasn't going to give it up, so, resigned and reluctant, I went with him, pushing my hands into my pockets so that he could not take my arm. He seemed in no way put out by my ungraciousness, which in itself was disconcerting, but when we got back to the harbour and were once more in the teeth of the wind, I nearly lost my balance with the unexpectedness of it, and he laughed and pulled my hand out of my pocket, taking it in his own. It was hard not to be disarmed by this protective and forgiving gesture.

As soon as the shop came in view, the tall narrow house shouldering up between the two short fat ones, I saw that indeed changes had taken place. The window frames were now painted, the plate glass had been cleared, and a sign put up over the door. JOSS GARDNER.

"How does that look?" He was full of pride.

"Impressive," I had to admit.

He took a key out of his pocket and unlocked the door and we went into the shop. Packing cases stood about on the flagged floor, and around the walls, shelving was being erected in varying widths, up to the ceiling. In the centre of the room was another structure, rather like a child's climbing frame, and this had already been set out with modern Danish glass and china, cooking pots in bright colours, and brightly striped Indian rugs. The walls were white, the woodwork had been left in its natural state, and this and the grey floor provided a simple and effective background to the bright wares which he had to sell. At the back of the shop an open staircase rose to the upper floors, and beneath this was another door, ajar, leading down into what appeared to be a dark cellar. "Come upstairs . . ." He led the way.

I followed him. "What's that door there?"

"That's my workshop. It's in a dreadful mess, I'll show you that another time. Now this . . ." we emerged on to the first floor, and could scarcely move for baskets and wickerwork ". . . I haven't exactly got this straight but, as you can see, this is where you buy baskets for logs, clothes pegs, shopping, babies, laundry, anything you care to put in them.''

None of it was very spacious. The narrow house was just a glorified staircase with a landing on each floor.

''Up again. How are your legs? Now we come to the *pièce de résistance*, the owner's palatial living quarters.'' I passed a tiny bathroom squeezed into the turn of the stairs. And lagging behind Joss's long legs found myself remembering Andrea's yearning descriptions of his flat, and hoping it would not be the way she had described it to me, but entirely different, so that I would know that her imagination had taken control, and that she had made the whole thing up. *Just like something out of a magazine. With a bed that's a sort of sofa and masses of cushions and things and a log fire.*

But it was just the way she had said. As I came up the last stairs, my fleeting hope swiftly died. And there *was* something closed-in and secret about it, with the ceiling sloping down to the floor and a dormer window set into the gable with a seat below it. I saw the little galley, enclosed behind a counter, like a bar, and the old Turkish carpet on the floor, and the divan, red-blanketed, pushed against the wall. As she had said, it was scattered with cushions.

Joss had put down my basket and was already divesting himself of his wet clothes and hanging them on an old-fashioned cane hat-stand.

''Take your things off before you die of cold,'' he told me. ''I'll light a fire . . .''

''I can't stay, Joss . . .''

''No reason not to light the fire. And please, take off that coat.''

I did, unbuttoning it with frozen fingers, pulling off my damp woollen hat and shaking my plait down over my shoulder. While I hung these up beside Joss's things, he was busy at the fireplace, snapping twigs, balling paper, scraping together the ashes from some previous fire, lighting it all with a long taper. When it was crackling he took some pieces of driftwood, tar-soaked, from a basket by the fireplace, and stacked them round the flames. They spat, and spluttered, and swiftly caught. And the room, by firelight, sprang to life. He stood up and turned to face me.

"Now, what do you want? Coffee? Tea? Chocolate? Brandy and soda?"

"Coffee?"

"Two coffees coming up." He retired behind his counter, filled a kettle and lit the gas. As he collected a tray and cups, I went over to the window, knelt on the seat and looked down through the fury of the storm to the street below, washed by spray as the waves broke over the sea wall. The boats in the harbour bobbed about like demented corks, and huge herring gulls floated over their swinging mastheads, screaming at the wind. Absorbed in the task of making our coffee, Joss moved with economy from one side of the galley to the other, neat-fingered and self-sufficient as a single-minded yachtsman. So occupied, he appeared harmless enough, but the disconcerting point about Andrea's revelations was that they all seemed to contain an element of truth.

I had known Joss for only a few days, but already I had seen him in every sort of mood. I knew he could be charming, stubborn, angry, and downright rude. It was not difficult to imagine him as a ruthless and passionate lover, but it was distasteful to imagine him with Andrea.

He looked up suddenly and caught my eye. I was embarrassed, caught with my thoughts. I said, quickly, to divert us both, "In good weather you must have a lovely view."

"Clear out to the lighthouse."

"In the summer it must be like being abroad."

157

"In the summer it's like Piccadilly Underground at rush hour. But that only lasts for two months." He came out from behind his counter, carrying a tray with the steaming cups, the sugar bowl and the milk jug. The coffee smelt delicious. He pulled forward a long stool with his foot, set the tray at one end of it and himself at the other. Thus, we faced each other.

"I want to hear more about yesterday," said Joss. "Where did you go besides Falmouth?"

I told him about St Endon and the little pub by the water's edge.

"Yes, I've heard about it, but I've never been there. Did you get a good lunch?"

"Yes. And it was so warm that we sat out in the sunshine."

"That's the south coast for you. And what happened then?"

"Nothing happened then. We came home."

He handed me my cup and saucer. "Did Eliot take you to High Cross?"

"Yes."

"Did you see the garage?"

"Yes. And Mollie's house."

"What did you think of all those elegant, sexy cars?"

"I thought just that. That they were elegant and sexy."

"Did you meet any of the guys who work for him?"

His voice was so casual that I became wary.

"Who, for instance?"

"Morris Tatcombe?"

"Joss, you didn't ask me here for coffee at all, did you? You're pumping me."

"I'm not. I promise I'm not. It's just that I wondered if Morris was working for Eliot."

"What do you know about Morris?"

"Just that he's rotten."

"He's a good mechanic."

"Yes, he is. Everybody knows that, and it's the only good thing about him. But he's also totally dishonest and vicious to boot."

"If he's totally dishonest, why isn't he in jail?"

"He's already been. He's just come out."

This took the wind out of my sails, but I soldiered bravely on, sounding more sure of myself than I felt.

"And how do you know he's vicious . . .?"

"Because he picked a quarrel with me one night in a pub. We went outside and I punched him on the nose, and it was lucky for me I hit him first, because he was carrying a knife."

"Why are you telling me this?"

"Because you asked. If you don't want to be told things, you shouldn't ask questions."

"And what am I meant to do about it?"

"Nothing. Absolutely nothing. I'm sorry I brought it up. It was just that I'd heard Eliot had given him a job and I hoped it wasn't true."

"You don't like Eliot, do you?"

"I don't like him, I don't dislike him. He's nothing to do with me. But I'll tell you something. He picks bad friends."

"You mean Ernest Padlow?"

Joss sent me a glance that was full of reluctant admiration.

"You don't waste much time, I'll say that for you. You seem to know it all."

"I know about Ernest Padlow because I saw him with Eliot that first night when you gave me dinner at The Anchor."

"So you did. That's another rotten egg. If Ernest had his way the whole of Porthkerris would be bulldozed into car parks. There wouldn't be a house left standing. And we would all have to go up the hill and live in his fancy little semis which in ten years' time will be leaking, leaning, cracking up and generally bagging at the knees."

159

I did not reply to this outburst. I drank my coffee and thought how pleasant it would be to have a conversation without being instantly drawn into longstanding vendettas which had nothing to do with me. I was tired of listening to everybody I wanted to like running down the reputations of everybody else.

I finished my coffee, set down the cup and said, "I must get back."

Joss, with an obvious effort, apologised. "I'm sorry."

"Why?"

"For losing my temper."

"Eliot's my cousin, Joss."

"I know." He looked down, turning his cup in his hands. "But, without meaning to, I've become involved with Boscarva, too."

"Just don't take your prejudices out on me."

His eyes met mine. "I wasn't angry with you."

"I know." I stood up. "I must go," I said again.

"I'll drive you back."

"You don't have to . . ." But he paid no attention to my protest, just took my coat from its hook and helped me on with it. I pulled the wet woollen hat over my ears and picked up the heavy basket.

The telephone rang.

Joss, in his oilskin, went to answer it, and I started downstairs. I heard him call, just before he took the receiver off the hook, "Rebecca, wait for me. I won't be a moment . . ." and then, into the telephone, "Yes? Yes, Joss Gardner here . . ."

I went down to the ground floor and the shop. It was still raining. Upstairs I could hear Joss deep in conversation.

Bored with waiting for him, perhaps a little curious, I pushed open the door of the workshop, turned on the light, and went down four stone steps. There was the usual confusion, benches, woodshavings, scraps, tools, vices; over all hung the smell of glue, of new wood, of polish. There was also a clutter of old furniture, so dusty and ramshackle it was impossible to tell whether it was of any value or not. A chest of drawers missing all its handles, a bedside cupboard without a leg.

And then, at the very back of the room, in the shadows, I saw them. A davenport desk, in apparently perfect repair, and alongside it a chair in the Chinese Chippendale style, with a tapestry seat, embroidered in flowers.

I felt sick, as though I had been kicked in the stomach. I turned and went up the steps, turning off the light and closing the door, going through the shop and out into the bitter windblast of that wicked February day.

My workshop's in a dreadful mess, I'll show you that another time.

I walked and then found that I was running up towards the church, into a warren of little lanes where he would never find me. I was running, always uphill, encumbered by the shopping basket, heavy as lead, and my heart pounded in my chest and there was the taste of blood in my mouth.

Eliot had been right. It was too easy for Joss and he had simply taken his chance. It was my desk; it was *my* desk that he had taken, but he had taken it from Grenville's house, flinging the old man's trust and kindness back in his face.

I could imagine killing Joss, and it was easy. I told myself that I could never speak to him, could never bear to be near him again. I had never been so angry in my life. With him; but worse with myself, for having been taken in by his empty charm, for having been proved so totally wrong. I had never been so angry.

I stumbled on up the hill.

But if I was so angry, then why was I crying?

10

It was a long and exhausting climb back to Boscarva, and I have never found it possible to sustain extreme emotion for more than ten minutes. Gradually, fighting my way up the hill against the weather, I calmed down, wiped my tears away with my gloved hand, pulled myself together. In an apparently intolerable situation, there is nearly always something one can do, and long before I reached Boscarva I had decided what it was. I would go back to London.

I left the shopping basket on the kitchen table and went upstairs to my room, took off all my drenched clothes, changed my shoes, washed my hands, carefully re-plaited my hair; thus calmed I went in search of Grenville and found him in his study, sitting by the fire and reading the morning paper.

He lowered this and looked over the top of it as I came in.

"Rebecca."

"Hello. How are you this wild morning?" I sounded determinedly cheerful, like a maddening nurse.

"Full of aches and pains. The wind's a killer even if you never go out in it. Where've you been?"

"Down in Porthkerris. I had to do some shopping for Mollie."

"What time is it?"

"Half past twelve."

"Then let's have a glass of sherry."

"Is that allowed?"

"I don't give a damn if it's allowed or not. You know where the decanter is."

I poured two glasses, carried his over and set it carefully down on the table by his chair. I pulled up a stool and sat facing him. I said, "Grenvillè, I have to go back to London."

"What?"

"I have to go back to London." The blue eyes narrowed, the great jaw thrust out; I hastily made Stephen Forbes my scapegoat. "I can't stay away for ever. I've already been away from work nearly two weeks, and Stephen Forbes, the man I work for, he's been so good about it, I can't just go on taking advantage of his kindness and generosity. I've just realised that it's Friday already. I must go back to London this weekend. I must be back at work on Monday morning."

"But you've only just come." He was obviously thoroughly disgusted with me.

"I've been here three days. After three days fish and guests stink."

"You're not a guest. You're Lisa's child."

"But I still have commitments. And I like my job and I don't want to stop working." I smiled, trying to divert him. "And now I've found the way to Boscarva, perhaps I can come again, when I've got more time to spare, to spend with you."

He did not reply but sat, looking old and grumpy, staring into the fire.

He said dismally, "I may not be here then."

"Oh, of course you will be."

He sighed, took a slow, shaky mouthful of sherry, set down his glass, and turned to me, apparently resigned.

"When do you want to go?"

I was surprised, but relieved, that he had given in so easily.

"Perhaps tomorrow night. I'll get a sleeper. And then I can have Sunday to get myself settled into my flat."

"You shouldn't be living in a flat in London on your own. You weren't made for living alone. You were made for a man, and a home, and children. If I were twenty years younger and could still paint, that's how I'd show you to the world, in a field or a garden, knee-deep in buttercups and children."

"Perhaps it'll happen one day. And then I shall send for you."

His face was suddenly full of pain. He turned away from me and said, "I wish you'd stay."

I longed to say that I would, but there were a thousand reasons why I couldn't. "I'll come back," I promised.

He made a great and touching effort to pull himself together, clearing his throat, re-settling himself in his chair. "That jade of yours. We'll have to get Pettifer to pack it in a box, then you can take it with you. And the mirror . . . could you manage that on the train, or is it too big? You ought to have a car, then there would be no problems. Have you got a car?"

"No, but it doesn't matter . . ."

"And I suppose that desk hasn't . . ."

"It doesn't matter about the desk!" I interrupted, so loudly and so suddenly that Grenville looked at me in some surprise, as though he had not expected such bad manners.

"I'm sorry," I said quickly. "It's just that it really doesn't matter. I couldn't bear everybody to start quarrelling about it again. Please, for my sake, don't talk about it, don't think about it any more."

He regarded me thoughtfully, a long unblinking stare that made me drop my eyes.

He said, "You think I'm unfair to Eliot?"

"I just think that perhaps you never talk to each other, you never tell each other anything."

"He'd have been different if Roger hadn't been killed. He was a boy who needed a father."

"Couldn't you have done as a father?"

"Could never get near him for Mollie. He was never made to stick to anything. Always chopping and changing jobs and then he started that garage up three years ago."

"That seems to be a success."

"Second-hand cars!" His voice was full of unjustified contempt. "He should have gone into the Navy."

"Suppose he didn't want to go into the Navy?"

"He might have, if his mother hadn't talked him out of it. She wanted to keep him at home, tied to her apron strings."

"Oh, Grenville, I think you're being thoroughly old-fashioned and very unfair."

"Did I ask you for your opinion?" But already he was cheering up. A good argument was, to Grenville, like a shot in the arm.

"I don't care whether you asked for it or not, you've got it."

He laughed then, and reached forward to gently pinch my cheek. He said, "How I wish I could still paint. Do you still want one of my pictures to take back to London with you?"

I was afraid that he had forgotten. "More than anything."

"You can get the key of the studio from Pettifer. Tell him I said you could have it. Go and nose around, see what you can find."

"You won't come with me?"

Again the pain came into his face. "No," he said gruffly, and turned away to take up his sherry. He sat, looking down at the amber wine, turning the glass in his hand. "No, I won't come with you."

At lunch he broke the news to the others. Andrea, livid that I was going back to London while she had to stay in horrible, boring Cornwall, went into a sullen sulk. But the others were gratifyingly dismayed.

"But do you have to go?" That was Mollie.

"Yes, I really must. I've got a job to do and I can't stay away for ever."

"We really love having you here." She could be charming when she wasn't aggressive and possessive about Eliot, resentful of Grenville and Boscarva. I saw her again as a pretty little cat, but now I was aware of long claws hidden in the soft velvet paws, and I knew that she had no compunction about using them.

"I've loved it too . . ."

Pettifer was more outspoken. After lunch I went out to the kitchen to help him with the dishes, and he minced no words.

"What you want to go away for now, just when you're settling down and the Commander's getting to know you – well, it's beyond me. I didn't think you were that sort of a person . . ."

"I'll come back. I've said I'll come back."

"He's eighty now. He's not going to last for ever. How are you going to feel, coming back and him not here, but six feet under the ground and pushing up the daisies?"

"Oh, Pettifer, *don't*."

"It's all very well saying 'Oh, Pettifer, *don't*.' There's nothing I can do about it."

"I've got a job. I must go back."

"Sounds like selfishness to me."

"That's not fair."

"All these years he's not seen his daughter, and then you turn up and stay three days. What sort of a grandchild are you?"

I didn't reply because there was nothing to say. And I hated feeling guilty and being put in the wrong. We finished the dishes in silence, but when they were done and he was wiping down the draining board with a damp cloth, I tried to make my peace with him.

"I'm sorry. I really am. It's bad enough having to go without you making me feel a brute. And I will come back. I've said I will. Perhaps in the summer . . . he'll still be here in the summer, and the weather will be warm and we can do things together. Perhaps you could take us out in the car . . ."

My voice trailed away. Pettifer hung his cloth neatly over the edge of the sink. He said, gruffly, "The Commander said you were to have the key of the studio. Don't know what you'll find down there. A lot of dust and spiders, I should think."

"He said I could have a picture. He said I could go and choose one."

He slowly dried his worn, gnarled hands. "I'll have to find the key. It's put away for safe keeping. Didn't want it lying around where anyone could get their hands on it. There's a lot of good stuff down in the studio."

"Any time will do." I could not bear his disapproval. "Oh, Pettifer, don't be angry with me."

He melted then. "Oh, I'm not angry. Perhaps it's me who's being selfish. Perhaps it's me who doesn't want you to go."

I saw him suddenly, not as the ubiquitous Pettifer around whom this household revolved, but as an old man, nearly as old as my grandfather and probably as lonely. A stupid lump came into my throat and for a terrible moment I thought I was going to burst into tears, which would have made it the second time that day, but then Pettifer said, "And don't go choosing one of them nudes, they wouldn't be suitable," and the dangerous moment was behind me and we were smiling, friends again.

That afternoon Mollie lent me her car, and I drove the five miles to the railway junction and there bought myself a ticket back to London and reserved a sleeper for the night train on Saturday. The violence of the wind had dropped a little, but it was still wild and stormy, with trees down and devastation everywhere, smashed greenhouses, broken branches, and fields of early spring bulbs flattened by the gales.

I got home to find Mollie in the garden at Boscarva, bundled up against the weather (even Mollie could not look elegant on such a day) and trying to tie up and rescue some of the more fragile shrubs that grew around the house. When she saw the car, she decided to call it a day, for as I put it away and walked back towards the house I met her coming towards me, stripping off her gloves and tucking a strand of hair into her head-scarf.

"I can't bear it a moment longer," she told me. "I hate wind, it exhausts me. But that darling little daphne was being snapped to ribbons, and all the camellias have been burnt by this wind. It turns them quite brown. Let's go in and have a cup of tea."

While she changed I put the kettle on, and set out cups on a tray. "Where is everybody?" I asked her when she reappeared, miraculously neat once more, down to her pearls and her matching ear-rings.

"Grenville's having a nap and Andrea's up in her room . . ." she sighed. ". . . I must say, she really isn't the easiest of girls. If only she'd do something to amuse herself instead of skulking around in this tiresome manner. I'm afraid it's not doing her any good being down here, I didn't think it would, to be quite honest, but my poor sister was quite desperate." She looked around the comfortable kitchen. "This is cosy. Let's have our tea in here. The drawing-room's so draughty when the wind's from the sea, and we can scarcely draw the curtains at half past four in the afternoon . . ."

She was right, it was cosy in the kitchen. She found a cloth and laid the tea, setting out cakes and biscuits, sugar bowl and silver milk jug. Even for kitchen tea, it appeared, her standards were meticulous. She pulled up two wheel-back chairs, and was in the act of reaching for the teapot when the door opened and Andrea appeared.

"Oh, Andrea, dear, just in time. We're having kitchen tea today. Do you want a cup?"

"I'm sorry, I haven't got time."

This unexpectedly mannerly reply made Mollie look up sharply. "Are you going out?"

"Yes," said Andrea, "I'm going to the cinema."

We both stared at her like fools. For the impossible had happened – Andrea had suddenly decided to take much trouble with her appearance. She had washed her hair and tied it back off her face, found a clean polo-necked tee-shirt, and even, I was delighted to see, a bra to wear beneath it. Her Celtic cross hung around her neck on its thread of leather, her black jeans were neatly pressed, her clumpy shoes polished. Over her arm was a raincoat and a fringed leather handbag. I had never seen her look so presentable. And, best of all, the expression on her face was neither sulky nor malevolent, but . . . demure? Could one possibly describe Andrea as looking demure?

"I mean," she went on, "if that's all right by you, Auntie Mollie."

"Well, of course. What are you going to see?"

"*Mary of Scotland*. It's on at the Plaza."

"Are you going by yourself?"

"No, I'm going with Joss. He rang me while you were out gardening. He's going to give me supper afterwards."

"Oh," said Mollie, faintly. And then, feeling that further comment was expected of her, ". . . how are you going to get down there?"

"I'll walk down, and I expect Joss will drive me home . . ."

"Have you got some money?"

"I've got 50p. I'll be all right."

"Well . . ." But Mollie was defeated. "Have a good time."

"I will," she flashed us both a smile. "Goodbye."

The door swung to behind her.

"Goodbye," said Mollie. She looked at me. "Extraordinary," she said.

I was concentrating on my cup of tea. "Why so extraordinary?" I said casually.

"Andrea and . . . Joss. I mean he's always been quite polite to her, but . . . to ask her out . . .?"

"You shouldn't sound so surprised. She's attractive when she cleans herself up and bothers to smile. Probably she smiles at Joss all the time."

"You think it's all right, letting her go? I mean I do have responsibilities . . .?"

"Honestly, I don't see how you could have stopped her going. Anyway she's seventeen, she's not a child. She can surely look after herself by now . . ."

"That's just the trouble," said Mollie ". . . That's always been the trouble with Andrea."

"She'll be all right."

She would not be all right, and I knew this, but I could not disillusion Mollie. Besides, what did it matter? It was no business of mine if Joss chose to spend his evenings making firelit love to an adolescent nymphomaniac. They were two of a kind. They deserved each other. They were welcome to each other.

When we had finished tea, Mollie tied a neat apron around her waist and started preparing dinner. I cleared away the cups and saucers and washed them up. As I was drying the last plate, and putting it away, Pettifer appeared, bearing in his hand a large key which looked as though it might unlock a dungeon.

"I knew I'd put it somewhere safely, found it in the back of a drawer in the Commander's bureau . . ."

"What's that, Pettifer?" Mollie asked.

"The key to the studio, Madam . . ."

"Heavens, who wants that?"

"I do," I said. "Grenville said I could go down and choose a picture to take back to London."

"My dear child, what a task you'll have. The place must be in the most terrible mess, it hasn't seen the light of day for ten years."

"I don't mind." I took the key which weighed heavy as lead in my hand.

"Are you going now? It's getting dark."

"Aren't there any lights?"

"Oh, yes, of course, but it's very cheerless. Wait till tomorrow morning."

But I wanted to go now. "I'll be all right. I'll put on a coat."

"There's a torch on the hall table, you'd better take that as well, the path down the garden is quite steep and slippery."

And so, buttoned into my leather coat, and armed with the torch and the key, I set off, letting myself out of the house by the garden door. The wind from the sea was still violent, carrying with it squalls of thin, cold rain, and I had to struggle to get the door closed behind me. The dismal afternoon was turning early to darkness, but still there was enough light to pick my way cautiously down the sloping garden, and I did not turn on the torch until I reached the studio when I needed its beam to find the keyhole.

I fitted the key and it turned reluctantly, needing oil; the door swung inwards, creakingly. There was a damp and musty smell, a suggestion of cobwebs and mould, and I quickly put my hand inside and felt for the light switch. At once a single naked bulb, high in the roof, sprang to a chill and insubstantial life, and I was surrounded by leaping shadows, for the draught caused the long flex to swing to and fro like the pendulum of a clock.

I went in and shut the door behind me and the shadows, slowly, were stilled. Around me, dust-covered shapes loomed in the half-light, but across the room was a standard lamp, with a crooked, broken shade. I picked my way over to this, found the switch and turned that on, and at once everything looked a little less forlorn.

I saw that the studio had been designed on two levels with a sleeping gallery at the south end, reached by a stair like a ship's ladder.

I went halfway up the ladder and saw the divan and the striped blanket. Over the bed was a window tightly shuttered, and a pillow had shed feathers, perhaps the work of some marauding mouse. The remains of a small dead bird lay, twig-like and dehydrated, in the corner of the floor. I shuddered slightly at the desolation, and descended again to the studio.

The wind banged and rattled at the huge north window. A complicated contraption of strings and pulleys worked the long curtains, and I struggled with these for a moment, but was finally defeated by their mechanics and left the curtains closed.

In the middle of the floor was a model's throne, with a sheeted shape in the middle which proved to be an ornate gilt chair. The mice had been at the seat of this, too – scraps of red velvet and horsehair were scattered about, along with mouse-droppings and a great deal of dust.

Under another sheet I found Grenville's workbench; his brushes, his trays of paint-tubes, palettes, knives, bottles of linseed oil, piles of unused canvases, grimy with age. There was also a little collection of *objets trouvés*, small things which, perhaps, had taken his fancy. A sea-polished stone, half a dozen shells, a bunch of gulls' feathers, probably collected for the practical purpose of cleaning his pipe. There were curling, faded snapshots, of nobody I recognised, a blue and white Chinese ginger jar filled with pencils, some bottles of fossilised Indian ink, a scrap of sealing wax.

It was like prying, as though I were reading another person's diary. I put back the sheet and went on to the true purpose of my visit, which was the stack of unframed canvases standing around the wall, each with its face turned inwards. These had been dust-covered too, but the sheets had slipped, draping themselves about the floor, and as I dislodged the first pile my fingers touched cobwebs, and a huge, disgusting spider went scuttling across the floor and lost itself in the shadows.

It was a slow business. Five or six at a time, I lifted out the pictures, dusted them off, leaned them in rows against the model's throne, shifting the rickety standard lamp so that the light should shine on them. Some were dated, but they were stacked away in no sort of chronological order, and for the most part I could tell neither when nor where they had been painted. I only knew that they encompassed the whole of Grenville's professional life and all his interests.

There were landscapes, seascapes – the ocean in all its moods, charming interiors, some sketches of Paris, some that looked like Italy. There were boats and fishermen, street scenes of Porthkerris, a number of rough charcoal sketches of two children, whom I knew were Roger and Lisa. There were no portraits.

I began to make my selection, setting aside the pictures which I found particularly engaging. By the time I had reached the final pile, there were half a dozen of them propped against the seat of a sagging couch, and I was dirty and cold, with grimy hands and cobwebs clinging to my clothes. With the good feeling of a task nearly completed I went to sort out the last pile of canvases. There were three pen and ink drawings, and a view of a harbour with yachts at anchor. And then . . .

It was the last canvas and the biggest of all. It needed two hands and all my efforts to lift it out of its dark corner and turn it around to face the light. I held it upright with one hand and stood back, and the face of the girl leapt out to meet me, the dark, tip-tilted eyes smiling with a vitality undimmed by the dust of the years that passed. I saw the dark hair and the bumpy cheek-bones and the sensuous mouth, not smiling, but seeming to tremble on the brink of laughter. And she wore the same fragile white dress, the dress that she had worn for the portrait that hung over the fireplace in the drawing-room at Boscarva.

Sophia.

Ever since my mother had mentioned her name I had been fascinated by her. The frustrations of never knowing what she looked like had only increased my obsession. But now that I had found her and we were face to face at last, I felt like Pandora. I had opened the box and the secrets were out, and there was no way in the world·of packing them back and locking the lid once more.

I knew that face. I had talked to it, argued with it; seen it scowl and smile; seen the dark eyes narrowed in anger and glint with amusement.

It was Joss Gardner.

11

All at once I was bitterly cold. It was dark now and the studio was icy, but as well I could feel the blood drain from my face like water out of a basin; I could hear the laboured thumping of my own heart, and I started, violently, to shiver. My first instinct was to put the portrait back where I had found it, pile some other canvases on top of it and hide it, like a criminal trying to conceal a body, or something worse.

But in the end I reached for a chair and arranged it carefully, so that it supported Sophia's portrait like an easel, and then I backed away on shaking legs and carefully lowered myself on to the sagging seat of the aged sofa.

Sophia and Joss.

Sophia the enchanting, and the baffling Joss, who I had finally learned was not to be trusted.

She went to London, she got married, she had a baby, I think, Pettifer had told me. Then in 1942 she was killed in the Blitz.

But he had not mentioned Joss. And yet Joss and Sophia were so obviously, inextricably linked.

And I thought of my desk, my mother's desk that she meant me to have, hidden away at the back of Joss's workshop.

And I heard Mollie's voice. *I don't know why Grenville's so taken with Joss. It's frightening. It's as though Joss were able to exert some hold over him.*

Sophia and Joss.

It was dark now. I had no watch and I had lost all track of time. The wind drowned all other sound, so that I did not hear Eliot coming down the garden from the house, picking his way through the darkness because I had taken the torch. I did not hear anything until the door burst open, as though on a gust of wind, causing the light to start up its demented swinging, and frightening me nearly out of my wits. The next instant Rufus bounded in and flung himself up on the sofa beside me, and I realised that I had company.

My cousin Eliot stood in the open doorway framed in darkness. He wore a suede jacket and a pale blue polo-necked sweater and he had slung a raincoat around his shoulders like a cloak. The cruel light drained all the colour from his thin face, and turned his deep-set eyes into two black holes.

"My mother told me you were down here. I came to . . ."

He stopped, and I knew that he had seen the portrait. I couldn't move, I was too petrified with cold, and anyway, now it was too late to do anything about it.

He came into the studio and closed the door. The leaping shadows, once more, were slowly stilled.

We neither of us said anything. I held Rufus's head, instinctively seeking comfort in his soft, warm fur, and watched while Eliot shrugged off his raincoat, dropped it across a chair, and came slowly to sit beside me. His eyes never left the portrait.

At last he spoke. "Good God," he said.

I said nothing.

"Where did you find that?"

"In a corner . . ." My voice came out as a croak. I cleared

my throat and tried again. "In a corner, behind a lot of other canvases."

"It's Sophia."

"Yes."

"It's Joss Gardner."

There was no denying it. "Yes."

"Sophia's grandson, do you suppose?"

"Yes. I think he must be."

"Well, I'll be damned." He leaned back, and crossed his long, elegant legs, suddenly relaxed, like a knowledgeable art critic at a private view.

His obvious satisfaction puzzled me, and I did not want him to think that I shared it.

I said, "I wasn't looking for it. I've been wanting to know what Sophia looked like, but I had no idea there was a portrait of her down here. I just came to look for a picture because Grenville said I could have one to take back to London."

"I know. My mother told me."

"Eliot, we mustn't say anything."

He ignored this. "You know, there was always something funny about Joss, something unexplained. The way he turned up in Porthkerris, out of the blue. And the way Grenville knew that he was there; the way he gave him a job, and the run of Boscarva. I never trusted Joss farther than I could see him. And the desk disappearing – the desk that should have come to you. It was all fishy beyond words."

I knew that I should tell Eliot then that I had found the desk. I opened my mouth with the intention of doing just this thing, and closed it again because somehow the words would not be spoken. Besides, Eliot was still talking and had not noticed my incipient interruption.

"My mother swore he had some sort of a hold over Grenville."

179

"You make it sound like blackmail."

"Perhaps, in a modified form, it was. You know, 'Here I am, Sophia's grandson, what are you going to do for me?' And Pettifer must have known as well. Pettifer and Grenville have no secrets from each other."

"Eliot, we mustn't say that we found the picture."

He turned his head to look at me.

"You sound anxious, Rebecca. On Joss Gardner's behalf?"

"No. On Grenville's."

"But you like Joss."

"No."

He pretended to be amazed. "But everybody likes Joss! Everybody, it seems, has fallen under his spell of boyish charm. Grenville and Pettifer; Andrea is besotted by him, she never leaves him alone, but I think there may be something just a little physical in that attraction. I thought that you were bound to have joined the club." He frowned. "You *did* like Joss."

"Not now, Eliot."

He began to be intrigued. He shifted his position slightly, so that we half-faced each other on the sofa, his arm along its carved back, behind my shoulder.

"What happened?" he asked.

What had happened? Nothing. But I had never felt quite easy about Joss, and all the coincidences that seemed to tie our lives together. And he had stolen my mother's desk. And he was now, at this moment carrying on his clandestine affair with the unsavoury Andrea. At the very idea of this, my imagination was apt to turn and run.

Eliot was waiting for my reply. But I only shrugged and shook my head hopelessly and said, "I changed my mind."

"Could yesterday have had anything to do with it?"

"Yesterday?" I thought of sitting with Eliot on the sunbaked terrace of the little pub; of the two boys sailing their dinghy down the blue waters of the creek; and finally Eliot's arms, encircling and holding me, the feel of his kisses, and the sensation of losing control, of sliding over a cliff.

I shivered again. My hands, cold and grimy, lay in my lap. Eliot put his own over them and said, in some surprise, "You're freezing."

"I know, I've been here for hours."

"My mother told me you want to go back to London." We seemed to have dropped the subject of Joss and I was thankful for this.

"Yes, I have to go."

"When?"

"Tomorrow night."

"You never told me."

"I didn't decide until this morning."

"You seem to have changed your mind and made a lot of decisions all in one day."

"I hadn't realised how the time had flown. I've been away from work for nearly two weeks."

"Yesterday I asked you to stay."

"I have to go."

"What would make you stay?"

"Nothing. I mean . . . I can't . . ." I was stammering like a fool, but I was too cold, too dirty and too tired for such a conversation. Later, perhaps, I would be able to cope . . .

"Would you stay if I asked you to marry me?"

My head shot up. Something like horror must have shown on my face, for he put back his head and laughed.

"Don't look so shocked. There's nothing shocking about getting married."

"But we're cousins."

"That doesn't matter."

"But we don't . . . I mean . . . You don't love me."

It was an appalling thing to say, but Eliot took it in his stride.

"Rebecca, you are stammering and stuttering like a shy schoolgirl. Perhaps I do love you. Perhaps I would have loved you for a long time before asking you to marry me, but you've precipitated this situation by suddenly announcing out of the blue that you're going to go back to London. So if I'm going to say it at all, I'd better say it now. I want you to marry me. I think it would work very well."

Despite myself, I was touched. No one had ever asked me to marry them before, and I found it flattering. But even as I listened to Eliot with one part of my mind, the other part ran round in circles like a squirrel in a cage.

Because there was still Boscarva, and the land that Eliot needed to sell to Ernest Padlow.

You are not my only grandchild.

". . . it seems ridiculous to say goodbye and walk out of each other's lives when we've only just met each other, and there are so many good things going for us."

I said quietly, "Like Boscarva."

His smile froze slightly around the edges. He raised an eyebrow. "Boscarva?"

"Let's be honest and truthful, Eliot. For some reason you need Boscarva. And you think that Grenville might leave it to me."

He took a deep breath as though to deny this, hesitated, and then let it all out in a long sigh. His smile was rueful. He ran a hand over the top of his head.

"How cool you are. The Ice Princess all of a sudden."

"You need Boscarva so that you can sell the farm to Ernest Padlow to build his houses."

He said, carefully, "Yes." I waited. "I needed money to build the garage. Grenville wasn't interested so I approached

Padlow. He agreed and the security was the Boscarva farm. Gentleman's agreement.''

"But it wasn't yours."

"I was sure it would be. There was no reason why it shouldn't be. And Grenville was old and ill. The end could have come any day." He spread his hands. "Who would have imagined that three years later he'd still be with us?"

"You sound as though you want him dead."

"Old age is a terrible thing. Lonely and sad. He's had a good life. What is there for him to cling on for?"

I knew that I could not agree with Eliot. Old age, in Grenville's case, meant dignity and purpose. I had only just got to know him, but already I loved him and he was part of me; I could not bear to think of him dying.

I said, trying to stay practical, "Isn't there some other way you could pay off Mr Padlow?"

"I could sell the garage. The way things are going I might have to do that anyway."

"I thought you were doing so well."

"That's what everybody's meant to think."

"But if you sold the garage, what would you do then?"

"What do you suggest I should do?" He sounded amused as though I were a child with whims to be indulged. I said, "How about Mr Kemback, and the car museum in Birmingham?"

"What an uncomfortably good memory you've got."

"Would working for Mr Kemback be such a bad thing?"

"And leave Cornwall?"

"I think that's what you should do. Make a new start. Get away from Boscarva and . . ." I stopped, and then thought, *in for a penny, in for a pound*, ". . . and your mother." I finished in a rush.

"My mother?" Still that amusement, as though I were a beguiling fool.

"You know what I mean, Eliot."

There was a long pause. Then, "I think," said Eliot, "you have been talking to Grenville."

"I'm sorry."

"One thing's for certain, either Joss or I will have to go. As they say in Westerns, 'This town ain't big enough for the two of us.' But I'd rather Joss went."

"Joss is unimportant. He's not worth taking a stand over."

"If I sold the garage and went to work in Birmingham, would you come with me?"

"Oh, Eliot . . ."

I turned away from him and came face to face once more with Sophia's portrait. Her eyes met mine and it was as though Joss sat there, listening to every word we were saying, laughing at us. Then Eliot put his hand beneath my chin and jerked my head around so that once more I was forced to meet his eye.

"Listen to what I'm saying!"

"I am listening."

"We don't have to be in love with each other. You know that, don't you?"

"I always imagined it was important."

"It doesn't happen to everyone. Perhaps it won't ever happen to you."

It was a chill prospect. "Perhaps not."

"In that case," his voice was very gentle and reasonable, "would a compromise be such a bad thing? Wouldn't a compromise be better than a nine to five job for the rest of your life and an empty flat in London?"

He had touched me on the raw. I had been alone for too long, and the prospect of staying alone for the rest of my life was frightening. Grenville had said, *You were made for a man and a home and children*. And now they were all there, waiting for me. I had only to reach out my hand, to accept what Eliot was offering me.

I said his name, and he put his arms around me, and drew me very close, kissing my eyes, my cheeks, my mouth. Sophia watched us and I did not care. I told myself that she was dead, and Joss I had already put out of my life. Why should I care what either of them thought of me?

Eliot said at last, "We must go." He held me away from him. "You must have a bath and wash all those dirty marks off your face, and I must get the ice out of the fridge, and be all ready and dutiful to pour drinks for Grenville and my mother."

"Yes." I drew away from his arms, and pushed a lock of hair out of my face. I felt deathly tired. "What time is it?"

He looked at his watch, the strap that I had given him still shining and new. "Nearly half past seven. We could stay here all night, but unfortunately life has to go on."

I got wearily to my feet. Without looking at the portrait I took it up and put it back in its hidden, dusty corner, along with the cobwebs and the spiders, its face to the wall. Then I picked up other pictures, at random, and piled them around and against it. Everything, I told myself, was just as it had been before. We tidied up in a cursory fashion and covered the canvases with the fallen dust-sheet. Eliot switched off the standard lamp, and I picked up the torch. We went out of the studio, turning off the light and closing and locking the door. Eliot took the torch from me, and together, following the bobbing circle of light, we went up the garden, stumbling a little over hidden verges and tussocks of grass, mounting the shining wet steps of the terrace. Above us the house loomed, lighted rooms glowing behind drawn curtains, and all around us was the wind and the silhouettes of leafless, tormented trees.

"I've never known a storm to last so long," said Eliot, as he

opened the side door and we went inside. The hall felt warm
and safe, and there was the good smell of the chicken casserole
that we were to have for dinner.

We parted, Eliot heading for the kitchen, and I upstairs to
shed my filthy clothes, draw a bath and wallow in warm, scented
steam. Relaxed at last I thought about nothing. I was too tired
to think. I would fall asleep, I decided, and probably drown.
For some reason the idea of this did not alarm me.

But I did not fall asleep, because as I lay there, I heard,
above the noise of the wind, the sound of an approaching car.
The bathroom faced over the back of the house, the drive and
the front door. I had not bothered to draw the curtains and the
headlights of the car flashed for a second against the dark glass.
A door banged, there were voices. Thus disturbed, I climbed out
of the bath, dried myself and started across the passage to my
room, but stopped dead when I heard the raised voices carrying
up the stairwell from the hall.

". . . found her halfway up the hill . . ." a man's voice,
unrecognised.

And then Mollie, ". . . but my dear child . . ." This was
interrupted by a wild cacophony of sobbing. I heard Eliot say,
"For heaven's sake, girl . . ." And then Mollie again. "Come
in by the fire . . . come along now, you're all right. You're safe
now . . ."

I went into my room, pulled on my clothes, buttoned the
neck of the brown caftan, brushed and plaited my hair, all in
the space of moments. I painted on a layer of lipstick – there
was no time for more – thrust my bare feet into sandals and ran
downstairs, screwing on my ear-rings as I did so.

As I reached the bottom of the stairs Pettifer appeared through
the kitchen door with a face like a thundercloud and bearing in
his hand a glass of brandy. It was indicative of the gravity of
the situation that he had omitted to put it on a silver salver.

"Pettifer, what's happened?"

"I don't know what's happened, exactly, but it sounds as though that girl's having hysterics."

"I heard a car coming. Who brought her home?"

"Morris Tatcombe. Says he was driving home from Porth-kerris when he found her on the road."

I was horrified. "You mean *lying* on the road? Had she been hit by a car, or something?"

"I don't know. Probably just had a tumble."

At the far end of the hall the drawing-room door burst open and Mollie came towards us, half running.

"Oh, Pettifer, don't stand talking, hurry with the brandy." She saw me standing, quite at a loss. "Oh, my dear Rebecca, what a terrible thing, quite terrible. I'm going to ring the doctor." She was at the telephone, thumbing through the book, unable to see because she had somewhere mislaid her glasses. "Look it up for me, there's a dear. It's Doctor Trevaskis . . . we ought to have it written down somewhere, but I can't find . . ."

Pettifer had gone. I took the telephone book and started to look for the number. "What's happened to Andrea?" I asked.

"It's the most ghastly story. I can hardly believe it's true. What a mercy Morris found her. She could have been there all night. She could have died . . ."

"Here it is. Lionel Trevaskis. Porthkerris 873."

She put a hand to her cheek. "Oh, of course, I should know it off by heart." She lifted the receiver and dialled. While she waited she spoke to me, swiftly. "Go and sit by her, the men are so useless, they never know what to do."

Mystified and oddly reluctant to know the details of Andrea's unhappy experience, I nevertheless did as she asked me. I found the drawing-room in something approaching a shambles. Grenville, apparently nonplussed, stood in front of the fireplace with his hands behind his back and said nothing. The rest of them

187

were grouped around the sofa; Eliot had given Morris a drink, and they watched while Pettifer, with commendable patience, was trying to trickle some brandy down Andrea's throat.

And Andrea . . . despite myself I was shocked and frightened by her appearance. The neat sweater and the pressed jeans in which she had set out so gaily were soaking wet and smeared with mud. Through the tear in the jeans I could see her knee, cut and bleeding, vulnerably childlike. She had lost, it seemed, a shoe. Her hair clung, like seaweed, to her skull, her face was blotched with crying, and when I said her name she turned her head to look at me from pathetic, streaming eyes; I saw with horror the great bruise on her temple, as though she had been savagely struck. The Celtic cross on its leather thong was also lost; torn off, perhaps, in some unthinkable struggle.

"Andrea!"

She gave a great wail and heaved herself over to press her face into the back of the sofa, spilling the brandy as she did so, and knocking the tumbler clean out of Pettifer's hand.

"I don't want to talk about it. I don't want to talk about it . . .!"

"But you must!"

Pettifer, exasperated, collected the glass and went from the room. I told myself that he had never liked the girl. I took his place beside her, sitting on the edge of the sofa, trying to turn her shoulders towards me.

"Did somebody do this to you?"

Andrea flung herself back at me, her body convulsed. "Yes!" She screamed at my face as though I were deaf. "Joss!" And with that she dissolved once more in a welter of sobs.

I looked up at Grenville and was subjected to a stony, unblinking glare. His features might have been carved from wood. I decided there was no help to be expected from that quarter. I turned to Morris Tatcombe.

"Where did you find her?"

He shifted, one foot to another. I saw that he was dressed as though for a night on the town. A leather jacket, decorated with a rash of embroidered emblems, and spotted with rain, skin-tight jeans and boots with high heels. Even with high heels the top of his head scarcely reached to Eliot's shoulder, and his long hair hung damp and lank.

He tossed this back, a gesture both aggressive and self-conscious.

"Half-way up Porthkerris Hill. You know, where the road narrows and there isn't a pavement. She was half-way up the bank, half in the ditch. Lucky I saw her, really. Thought she'd been hit by a car, but it wasn't that. Seems she had this row with Joss Gardner."

I said, "He asked her to go to the cinema with him."

"I don't know how it all started," said Morris.

"But this, it seems . . ." said Eliot gravely ". . . is how it ends."

"But . . ." There had to be some other explanation. I was about to tell them this when Andrea let out another wail, like some aged sibyl keening at a wake, and I lost my temper.

"Oh, for goodness sake, girl, shut up!" I took her by her shoulders and gave her a little shake so that her head bobbed on the silk cushion like a badly stuffed rag-doll. "Stop making that dementing noise and tell us what happened."

Words began to spill out of her mouth, made ugly with weeping. (I thought briskly, *at least she isn't missing any teeth*, and hated myself for my own hard heart.)

"I . . . we . . . went to the cinema . . . and wh . . . when we came out, we went to a pub, and . . ."

"Which pub?"

"I don't know . . ."

"You must know which pub . . ."

My voice rose in impatience. Behind me, Mollie, whom I

189

had not heard come into the room, said, "Oh, don't shout at her. Don't be unkind."

I made an effort and tried again, more gently.

"Can't you remember where you went?"

"No. It was d . . . dark . . . and I . . . couldn't see. And then . . . and then . . ."

I held her firmly, trying to calm her. "Yes. And then?"

"And Joss had a lot of whisky to drink. And he wouldn't bring me home. He wanted me to g . . . go back to his flat with him . . . and . . ."

Her mouth went square, her features dissolved into uncontrollable weeping. I let her go and stood up, backing away from her. At once Mollie took my place.

"There," she said. "There, there." She was more gentle than I, her voice as soothing as a mother's. "Now there's nothing more to worry about. The doctor's on his way, and Pettifer's putting a nice hot bottle in your bed. You don't need to tell us any more. You don't need to talk about it any more."

But, perhaps calmed by Mollie's manner, Andrea seemed anxious to make a clean breast of it, and, through interminable sobs and gasps, we were to hear the rest of the story.

"And I didn't want to go. I . . . I wanted to come home. And I . . . left him. And he came after me. And . . . I tried to run, and I tripped on the p . . . pavement, and my shoe . . . c . . . came off. And then he c . . . caught me, and he be . . . began shouting at me . . . and I screamed and he *hit* me . . ."

I looked at the faces around me, and the same horror and consternation, in varying degrees, was mirrored upon them. Only Grenville appeared coldly, deeply angry, but still he did not move, he did not say a word.

"It's all right," Mollie said again, her voice shaking only a little. "Now, everything's all right. Come along, upstairs."

Somehow Andrea, wilted and bedraggled, was eased off the sofa, but her legs would not hold her weight, and she started to collapse. It was Morris who, standing nearest to her, stepped forward and caught her before she fell, swinging her up, with surprising strength, into his puny arms.

"There," said Mollie, "Morris will carry you upstairs. You'll be all right . . ." She moved towards the door. "If you'll come this way, Morris."

"OK," said Morris, who did not appear to have much option in the matter.

I watched Andrea's face. As Morris moved, her eyes opened and looked straight into mine, and our glances clashed and held. And I knew that she was lying. And she knew that I knew she was lying.

Leaning her head against Morris's chest, she began to cry again. Swiftly, she was borne from the room.

We listened as Morris's burdened footsteps went down the hall, started up the staircase. Then Eliot said, with masterly understatement, "An unsavoury business." He glanced at Grenville. "Shall I ring the police now or later?"

Grenville spoke at last. "Who said anything about ringing the police?"

"You surely don't intend to let him get away with it?"

I said. "She was lying."

Both men looked at me in some surprise. Grenville's eyes narrowed and he was at his most formidable. Eliot frowned. "What did you say?"

"Some of her story may be true. Most of it probably is. But still, she was lying."

"How was she lying?"

"Because as you said yourself, she was besotted with Joss. She wouldn't leave him alone. She told me that she'd been often to his flat, and she must have been, because she described it to me and every detail was right. I don't know what happened this evening. But I do know that if Joss wanted her to go back with him, she'd have gone like a shot. No arguments.''

''Then how,'' asked Eliot smoothly, ''do you account for the bruise on her face?''

''I don't know. I said I don't know about the rest of her story. But that bit, for sure, she made up.''

Grenville moved. He had been standing for a long time. Slowly, he went to his chair and lowered himself carefully into it.

''We can find out what really happened,'' he said at last.

''How?'' Eliot's question came out like the shot of a gun.

Grenville swung his head around and fixed his gaze on Eliot. ''We can ask Joss.''

Eliot let out a sound, which in old-fashioned novels would have been written as ''Pshaw''.

''We shall ask him. And we will be given the truth.''

''He doesn't know what the truth means.''

''You have no justification for making such a statement.''

Eliot lost his temper. ''Oh, for God's sake, does the truth have to be thrown in your face before you recognise it?''

''Don't raise your voice to me.''

Eliot was silent, staring in disbelief and disgust at the old man. When at last he spoke, it was in scarcely more than a whisper. ''I've had enough of Joss Gardner. I've never trusted him nor liked him. I believe he's a phoney, a thief and a liar, and I know that I'm right. And one day you too will know that I'm right. This is your house. I accept that. But what I will not accept is his right to take it over, and us with it, just because he happens to be . . .''

I had to stop him. ''Eliot!'' He turned to look at me. It was as though he had forgotten I was there. ''Eliot, please. Don't say any more.''

He looked down at his glass, finished the drink in a single

mouthful. "All right," he said at last. "For the moment, I won't say any more."

And he went to pour himself another whisky. As he did this, with Grenville and I watching him in silence, Morris Tatcombe came back into the room.

"I'll be off then," he said to the back of Eliot's head.

Eliot turned and saw him. "Is she all right?"

"Well, she's upstairs. Your mother's with her."

"Have another drink before you go."

"No, I'd better be off."

"We really can't thank you enough. What would have happened if you hadn't seen her . . ." He stopped, the unfinished sentence conjuring up visions of Andrea dying of exposure, exhaustion, loss of blood.

"Just lucky I did." He backed away, obviously anxious to be off, but not quite sure how to get there. Eliot put the stopper into the decanter, left his freshly filled glass on the table and came to his rescue.

"I'll see you to the door."

Morris ducked his head in the general direction of Grenville and myself.

"Night, all."

But Grenville had hauled himself to his feet with massive dignity. "You've handled things very sensibly, Mr Tatcombe. We're grateful to you. And we would be grateful, too, if you would keep the girl's version of what happened to yourself. At least until it has been authenticated."

Morris looked sceptical. "These things get around."

"But not, I am sure, through you."

Morris shrugged. "It's your affair."

"Exactly. Our affair. Good night, Mr Tatcombe."

Eliot led him away.

Grenville laboriously settled himself once more in his chair.

He passed a hand over his eyes, and it occurred to me that such scenes could not be good for him.

"Are you all right?"

"Yes. I'm all right."

I wished that I could confide in him, tell him that I knew about Sophia, and Joss being her grandson. But I knew that if there were any telling to be done, it had to come from him.

"Would you like a drink?"

"No."

So I left him alone, busying myself in tidying the cushions on the flattened sofa.

It was some time before Eliot reappeared, but when he did he seemed quite cheerful again, the sudden row which had flared between him and Grenville now quite forgotten. He went to pick up his drink. "Good health," he said, raising his glass to his grandfather.

"I suppose we're in debt to that young man," said Grenville. "I hope one day we'll be able to settle it."

"I shouldn't worry too much about Morris," Eliot replied lightly. "I should think he's quite capable of settling it for himself. And Pettifer has asked me to tell you both that dinner is ready."

We ate alone, the three of us. Mollie stayed with Andrea, and in the middle of dinner the doctor arrived and was taken upstairs by Pettifer. Later, we heard him talking to Mollie in the hall, then she showed him out and came into the dining-room to tell us what he had said.

"Shock, of course. He's given her a sedative, and she has to stay in bed for a day or two."

Eliot had gone to pull out a chair for her, and she sank into this looking exhausted and shaken. "Imagine such a thing happening. How I'm going to tell her mother, I can't think."

"Don't think about it," said Eliot, "till tomorrow."

"But it was such an appalling story. She's only a child. She's only seventeen. What could Joss have been thinking of? He must have gone out of his mind."

"He was probably drunk," said Eliot.

"Yes, perhaps he was. Drunk and violent."

Neither Grenville nor I said anything. It was as though we had entered into some sort of an unspoken conspiracy, but this did not mean that I had forgiven Joss, nor condoned anything that he had done. Later, probably, when he had been interrogated by Grenville, the whole truth would come out. By then I would probably be back in London.

And if I was still here . . . Slowly, I ate a little bunch of grapes. This could be my last dinner at Boscarva, but I truly did not know whether I wanted it to be or not. I had reached a crossroads, and had no idea which was the way I should take. But soon I was going to have to make up my mind.

A compromise, Eliot had said, and it had sounded tepid. But after the histrionics of this evening, the very words had a solid ring to them, sensible and matter-of-fact, with their feet planted squarely on the ground.

You were made for a man and a home and children.

I reached for my wineglass and, glancing up, saw that Eliot watched me across the polished table. He smiled, as though we were conspirators. The expression on his face was both confident and triumphant. Perhaps, while I was thinking that I would probably end up by marrying him, he already knew that I would.

We were back in the drawing-room, sitting around the fire and finishing our coffee, when the telephone started to ring. I thought that Eliot would go to answer it, but he was deep in a chair with the paper and a drink, and managed to linger so long that it was Pettifer who finally took the call. We heard the kitchen door open and his old feet go so slowly across the hall.

The ringing stopped. For some reason I glanced up at the clock on the mantelpiece. It was nearly a quarter to ten.

We waited. Presently the door opened and Pettifer's head came around the edge of it, his spectacles glinting in the lamplight.

"Who is it, Pettifer?" asked Mollie.

"It's for Rebecca," said Pettifer.

I was surprised. "For me?"

Eliot said, "Who's ringing you at this hour of the day?"

"I've no idea."

I got up and went out of the room. Perhaps it was Maggie, wanting to tell me something about the flat. Perhaps it was Stephen Forbes, wondering when I was going to return to work. I felt guilty, because I should have been in touch with him, letting him know what I was doing and when I planned to go back to London.

I sat on the hall chest and picked up the receiver.

"Hello?"

A small, mouse-like voice began speaking, sounding very far away.

"Oh, Miss Bayliss, we were passing, and he was lying there . . . my husband said . . . so we got him up the stairs and into the flat . . . don't know what happened. Covered in blood and he could hardly talk. Wanted to call the doctor . . . but he wouldn't let us . . . frightened leaving him there on his own . . . there ought to be somebody there . . . said he'd be all right . . ."

I must have been exceptionally slow and stupid, but it took me a little time to realise that this was Mrs Kernow, calling me from the phone box at the end of Fish Lane, to tell me that something had happened to Joss.

12

I was amazed and gratified to find myself in a state of almost total calm. It was as though I had already been prepared for this crisis, been given my orders and told what to do. There were no doubts and so no indecision. I must go to Joss. It was as simple as that.

I went up to my bedroom and got my coat, put it on, did up the buttons, came downstairs again. The key of Mollie's car lay where I had left it, on the brass tray in the middle of the table in the hall.

I picked it up, and as I did so the drawing-room door opened and Eliot came up the passage towards me. It never occurred to me that he would try to stop me going. It never occurred to me that anyone or anything could stop me going.

He saw me, bundled into my old leather coat. "Where are you off to?"

"Out."

"Who was that on the telephone?"

"Mrs Kernow."

"What does she want?"

"Joss has been hurt. She and Mr Kernow were walking home along the harbour road, they'd been visiting her sister. They found him."

"So?" His voice was cold and very quiet. I expected to be intimidated, but I was not.

"I'm going to borrow your mother's car. I'm going to him."

His thin face hardened, the skin drawn tight over the jutting bones.

"Have you gone out of your mind?"

"I don't think so."

He said nothing. I slipped the key into my pocket and made for the door, but Eliot was faster than I, and in two strides was in front of me, standing with his back to the door and with his hand on the latch.

"You're not going," he said pleasantly. "You don't really think I'd let you go?"

"He's been hurt, Eliot."

"So what? You saw what he did to Andrea. He's rotten, Rebecca. You know he's rotten. His grandmother was an Irish whore, God knows who his father was, and he's a womanising bastard."

The ugly words, which were meant to shock me, slid off my back like water from a duck. Eliot saw this and my unconcern infuriated him.

"Why do you want to go to him? What good could you do? He won't thank you for interfering, if it's thanks you're looking for. Leave him alone, he has no part of your life, he's none of your concern."

I stood watching him, hearing him, without making sense of anything he said. But I knew, all at once, that it was over, the uncertainty and the indecision, and I felt light with relief, as though a great weight had been lifted from my shoulders. I still stood at the crossroads. My life was still a confusion. But one thing had made itself abundantly clear. I could never marry Eliot.

A compromise, he had said. But, for me, it would have been a poor bargain. All right, he was weak, and probably not the most successful of businessmen. I had recognised these flaws in his character and had been prepared to accept them. But the welcome he had shown me, the hospitality, and the charm which he could turn on and off like a tap, had blinded me to his vindictiveness and the frightening strength of his jealousy.

I said, "Let me go, Eliot."

"Supposing I say that I won't let you go? Supposing I keep you here?" He put his hands on either side of my head, pressing so tightly that it felt as though my skull would crack open, like a nut. "Supposing, now, that I said I loved you?"

I was sickened by him. "You don't love anyone. Only Eliot Bayliss. There's no room for anyone else in your life."

"I thought we decided that it was you who didn't know how to love."

His grip tightened. My head began to pound and I closed my eyes, enduring the pain.

"When I do . . ." I told him through clenched teeth ". . . it won't be you."

"All right then, go . . ." He let me loose so suddenly that I nearly lost my balance. Savagely he turned the handle and flung the door open, and instantly the wind poured in, like some monstrous creature that had been waiting all evening to invade the house. Outside was the dark and the rain. Without another word, not stopping to look at Eliot, I ran past him and out into it, as though to some sanctuary.

I had still to get to the garage, to struggle with doors in the darkness, to find Mollie's little car. I was convinced that Eliot was just behind me, as frightening as an imagined bogey man, waiting to jump, to catch me, to stop me from getting away. I slammed the car door shut, and my hand shook so much I could scarcely get the ignition key fitted. The first time I turned it, the engine did not start. I heard myself whimpering as I pulled out the choke and tried again. This time the engine caught. I put the car into gear and shot forward, through the darkness

199

and the rain, up the puddled driveway with a great spattering of gravel, and so at last out and on to the road.

Driving, I regained some of my previous calm. I had eluded Eliot, I was going to Joss. I must drive with care and good sense, not allow myself to panic, not risk a skid or a possible collision. I slowed down to a cautious thirty miles per hour. I deliberately loosened my death-like clutch on the driving wheel. The road ran downhill, black and wet with rain. The lights of Porthkerris came up towards me. I was going to Joss.

Now, the tide was at full ebb. As I came out on to the harbour road, I saw the lights reflected in wet sand, the boats drawn up out of the reach of the storm. Overhead tattered scraps of cloud still poured across the sky. There were people about, but not very many.

The shop was in darkness. Only a single light glowed from the top window. I parked the car by the pavement and got out and went to the door and it opened. I smelt the new wood, my feet brushed through the shavings which still lay about the place. From the light of the street lamp outside I could see the staircase. I went up it, cautiously, to the first floor.

I called up, "Joss!"

There was no reply. I went on, up into the soft light. There was no fire and it was very cold. A squall of rain swept the roof above me.

"Joss."

He was lying on his bed, roughly covered by a blanket. His forearm lay across his eyes, as though to shut out some unbearable light. When I spoke he lowered this, and raised his head slightly to see who it was. Then he dropped back on to the pillow.

"Good God," I heard him say. "Rebecca."

I went to his side. "Yes, it's me."

"I thought I heard your voice. I thought I was dreaming."

"I called up, but you didn't reply."

His face was in a terrible mess, the left side bruised and swollen, the eye half-closed. Blood had trickled and dried from a cut in his lip, and there did not seem to be any skin on the knuckles of his right hand.

"What are you doing here?" He spoke muzzily, perhaps because of the lip.

"Mrs Kernow rang me."

"I told her not to say anything."

"She was worried about you. Joss, what happened?"

"I fell amongst thieves."

"Are you hurt anywhere else?"

"Yes, everywhere else."

"Let me see . . ."

"The Kernows bandaged me up."

But I stooped over him, gently drawing back the blanket. As far as his rib-cage he was naked and below this tenderly swathed in what looked like strips torn from an old sheet. But the ugly bruising had spread up and on to his chest, and on his right side the red stain of blood had started to seep through the white cotton.

"Joss, who did this?"

But Joss did not answer me. Instead, with a strength surprising in one so hurt, he put up an arm and pulled me down so that I was sitting on the edge of his bed. My long, blonde plait of hair hung forward over my shoulder, and while he held me with his right arm, his left hand was occupied in slipping off the rubber band which held the ends together, and then, using his fingers like a comb, he loosened the strands, unravelling them, so that my hair hung like a silken tassel, brushing on to his naked chest.

He said, "I always wanted to do that. Ever since I first saw you looking like the head girl of . . . what was it I said?"

201

"The head girl of a nicely run orphanage."

"That's it. Fancy you remembering."

"What can I do? There must be something I can do?"

"Just stay. Just stay, my darling girl."

The tenderness in his voice . . . Joss, who had always been so tough . . . dissolved me. Tears sprang into my eyes and he saw these and pulled me down, so that I lay against him, and I felt his hand slip up beneath my hair and close around the back of my neck.

"Joss, I'll hurt you . . ."

"Don't talk," he said, as his seeking mouth found mine. And then, "I've always wanted to do this, too."

It was evident that none of his infirmities, his bruises, his bleeding, his cut lip, were to deter him in any way from getting exactly what he wanted.

And I, who had always imagined that loving was something to do with fireworks and explosions of emotion, discovered that it was not like that at all. It was warm, like sudden sunshine. It had nothing to do with my mother and the endless procession of men who had invaded her life. It was cynicism and preconceived ideas flying out of an open window. It was the last of my defences gone. It was Joss.

He said my name and he made it sound beautiful.

Much later, I lit a fire, piling on the driftwood so that the room was bright with flickering firelight. I would not let Joss move, so that he lay with his dark head propped on his arms, and I felt his eyes following every move I made.

I stood up, away from the fire. My hair fell loose on either side of my face, and my cheeks were warm from the fire. I felt soft with content.

Joss said, "We have to talk, don't we?"

"Yes."

"Get me a drink."

"What do you want?"

"Some whisky. It's in the galley, in the cupboard over the sink."

I went to find it, and two glasses. "Soda or water?"

"Soda. There's a bottle-opener hanging on a hook."

I found the opener and took the cap off the bottle. I did this clumsily and it fell to the floor, rolling in the maddening manner of such things into a dark corner. I went to retrieve it and my eye was caught by another small and shining object, lying half under the kickboard beneath the sink. I picked it up and it was Andrea's Celtic cross, the one that she had worn on a leather thong around her neck.

I kept it in my hand. I poured the drinks and took them back to Joss. I handed him one, and knelt on the floor beside him.

I said, "This was under the sink," and showed him the cross.

His swollen eye made it difficult for him to focus. He squinted at it painfully.

"What the hell's that?"

"It's Andrea's."

He said, "Oh, to hell." And then, "Get me some more pillows, there's a good girl. I could never drink whisky lying down."

I gathered up a couple of cushions off the floor, and propped him against them. The action of sitting up was agony for him and he let out an involuntary groan.

"Are you all right?"

"Yes, of course I'm all right. Where did you find that thing?"

"I told you. On the floor."

"She came here this evening. She said she'd been to the cinema. I was working downstairs, trying to get the shelving finished. I told her I was busy, but she just came up here, as though I'd never said a word. I followed her up and told her

203

to go home. But she wouldn't go. She said she wanted a drink, she wanted to talk . . . you know the sort of drivel.''

''She's been here before.''

''Yes, once. One morning. I was sorry for her and I gave her a cup of coffee. But this evening I was busy; I had no time for her and I wasn't sorry for her. I said I didn't want a drink. I told her to go home. And then she said that she didn't want to go home, everybody hated her, nobody would talk to her, I was the only person she could talk to, I was the only person who understood.''

''Perhaps you were.''

''OK, so I was sorry for her. I used to let her come and get in my way when I was working at Boscarva, because there wasn't much else I could do about it, short of bodily throwing her out of the room.''

''Did you do that this evening? Throw her out?''

''Not in so many words. But finally I'd had enough of her batty conversation and her totally unfounded belief that I was ready, willing and eager to jump into bed with her, and I lost my temper and told her so.''

''What happened then?''

''What didn't happen? Screams, tears, accusations, routine hysteria. I was subjected to every sort of vilification. Face slapping, the lot. That was when I finally resorted to force, and I bundled her down the stairs and threw her raincoat and her beastly handbag after her.''

''You didn't hurt her?''

''No, I didn't hurt her. But I think I frightened her, because she went then, like the hammers of hell. I heard her clattering down the stairs on those ghastly clogs she wears, and then I think she must have slipped because there was the most frightful thumping and bumping as she went down the last few stairs. I shouted down to make sure she was all right, but then I heard her running out of the shop and slamming the door behind her, so that I imagined she was.''

"Could she have hit herself on anything? Bruised her face when she fell?''

"Yes, I suppose she could. There was a packing case full of china standing at the bottom of the stairs. She could have collided with that . . . Why do you ask anyway?''

I told him. When I had finished he let out a long, incredulous whistle. But he was angry too.

"The little bitch. I think she's a nymphomaniac, do you know that?''

"I've always thought so.''

"She was always talking about some guy called Danus, going into the most gruesome of intimate details. And the bloody cheek of telling everyone that I had asked her to go to the cinema with me. I wouldn't ask her to empty a dustbin with me . . . What's happened to her now?''

"She's been put to bed. Mollie got the doctor.''

"If he's worth his salt he'll have diagnosed self-induced hysteria. And he'll prescribe a good walloping and send her back to London. And that'll get her out of everybody's way.''

"Poor Andrea. She's very unhappy.''

As though he could not keep his hands off it, he reached out to touch my hair. I turned my head and kissed the back of his hand, the lacerated knuckles.

He said, "You didn't believe her, did you?''

"Not really.''

"Did anyone else?''

"Mollie and Eliot did. Eliot wanted to call the police but Grenville wouldn't let him.''

"That's interesting.''

"Why?''

"Who was it who brought Andrea home?''

205

"I thought I'd told you. Morris Tatcombe . . . you know, the boy who works for Eliot . . ."

"Morris? Well I'll be . . ." He stopped in mid-sentence, and then said again, "Morris Tatcombe."

"What about him?"

"Oh, Rebecca, come along. Pull yourself together. Use your wits. Who do you think gave me this beating?"

"Not Morris." I did not want to believe it.

"Morris and three others. I went along to The Anchor for a glass of beer and a pie for my supper, and when I was walking home, they jumped me."

"You knew it was Morris?"

"Who else would it be? He's always had this grudge going for me ever since we last crossed swords and he ended up on his backside in the gutter. I thought his putting the boot in this time was just a continuation of our running feud. But it seems that it wasn't."

Without thinking I began to say, "Eliot . . ." and then stopped, but it was too late. Joss said quietly, "What about Eliot?"

"I don't want to talk about Eliot."

"Did he tell Morris to come after me?"

"I don't know."

"He could, you know. He hates my guts. It fits,"

"I . . . I think he's jealous of you. He doesn't like your being so close to Grenville. He doesn't like Grenville being so fond of you. And . . ." I looked down at my drink, turning the glass in my hand, feeling suddenly nervous. "There's something else."

"From your expression one would think you'd murdered somebody. What is it?"

"It's . . . the desk. The desk downstairs in your workroom. I saw it this morning, when you were telephoning."

"I wondered why you'd suddenly gone cantering out into the rain. What about it?"

"The desk and the Chippendale chair. They came from Boscarva."

"Yes, I know."

His calmness shocked me. "You didn't *take* them, Joss?"

"*Take them?* No, I didn't take them. I bought them."

"Who from?"

"A man who runs an antique shop up beyond Fourbourne. I'd been to a sale about a month ago, and I dropped in to see him on the way back, and I saw the chair and the desk in his shop. By then I knew all Grenville's furniture and I knew they'd come from Boscarva."

"But who took them?"

"I regret to have to shatter your innocence, but it was your cousin Eliot."

"But Eliot knew nothing about them."

"Eliot most certainly did. They were in one of the attics, as far as I remember, and he probably imagined they'd never be missed."

"But why . . .?"

"This is like playing the truth game. Because Eliot, my love, my darling child, is head over heels in debt. That garage was financed by Ernest Padlow in the first place, it cost a bomb and it's been losing money steadily for the past twelve months. God knows what use fifty pounds would have been to Eliot, a mere drop in the ocean one would have thought, but perhaps he needed a little ready cash to pay a bill or put on a horse or something . . . I don't know. Between you and me, I don't think he should be running his own business. He'd be better working for some other guy, being paid a regular salary. Perhaps, one evening, when you're sitting over drinks at Boscarva, you could try and persuade him."

"Sarcasm doesn't suit you."

"I know, but Eliot makes me edgy. Always has done."

I felt, obscurely, that I must stand up for Eliot, make excuses for him.

"In a way, he thinks that Boscarva and everything in it already belong to him. Perhaps he didn't feel it was . . . stealing . . .?"

"When did they realise the things were missing?"

"A couple of days ago. You see, the desk belonged to my mother. Now it belongs to me. That's why we started to look for it."

"Unfortunate for Eliot."

"Yes."

"I suppose Eliot said I'd taken them."

"Yes," I admitted miserably.

"What did Grenville say?"

"He said that you'd never do a thing like that."

"And so there was another monumental row."

"Yes."

Joss sighed deeply. We fell silent. The room was growing cold again, the fire beginning to die down. I got up and went to put another log on it, but Joss stopped me.

"Leave it," he said.

I looked at him, surprised. He finished his drink and put the empty glass down on the floor beside him, and then pushed back the blanket and began, carefully, to get out of bed.

"Joss, you mustn't . . ."

I flew to his side, but he pushed me away, and slowly, with infinite caution, got to his feet. Once there, he grinned triumphantly down at me, a bizarre sight, bruised and battered, and dressed in bandages and a crumpled pair of jeans.

"Into battle," he said.

"Joss, what are you going to do?"

"If you'll find me a shirt and a pair of shoes, I'll get dressed. And then we're going to go downstairs, and get into the truck and drive back to Boscarva."

"But you can't drive like that."

"I can do anything I want," he told me, and I believed him. "Now find my clothes and stop arguing."

He would not even let me take Mollie's car. "We'll leave it there, it'll be all right. Someone can fetch it in the morning." His own little truck was parked around the corner, up a narrow alley. We got in, and he started the engine and backed out on to the road, with me giving directions because he was too stiff to turn around in the seat. We headed up through the town, along streets that had become familiar to me, over the crossroads and up the hill.

I sat, staring ahead, with my hands clasped tightly in my lap. I knew that there was still something else we had to talk about. And it had to be now, before we reached Boscarva.

For some reason, as though he were immensely pleased with life in general, Joss had started to sing.

> The first time ever I saw your face
> I thought the sun rose in your eyes
> And the moon and stars . . .

"Joss."

"What is it now?"

"There's something else."

He sounded shocked. "Not another skeleton in the cupboard?"

"Don't joke."

"I'm sorry. What is it?"

I swallowed a strange obstruction in the back of my throat. "It's Sophia."

"What about Sophia?"

"Grenville gave me the key of the studio so that I could go and choose a picture to take back to London. I found a portrait of Sophia. A proper one, with a face. And Eliot came to find me, and he saw it too."

There was a long silence. I looked at Joss but his profile was stony, intent on the road ahead. "I see," he said at last.

"She looks just like you; or you look just like her."

"Naturally enough. She was my grandmother."

"Yes, I thought that was probably it."

"So the portrait was in the studio?"

"Is . . . is that why you came to live in Porthkerris?"

"Yes. Grenville and my father fixed it between them. Grenville put up half the capital for my shop."

"Your father . . .?"

"You've met him. Tristram Nolan Gardner. He runs an antique shop, in the New Kings Road. You bought a pair of balloon-back chairs from him. Do you remember?"

"And he found from my cheque that I was called Rebecca Bayliss."

"Right. And he found out, by cunning question and answer, that you were Grenville Bayliss's granddaughter. Right. And he found out that you were catching the train to Cornwall last Monday. Right."

"So he rang you up and told you to meet the train."

"Right."

"But why?"

"Because he felt involved. Because he thought you seemed lost and vulnerable. Because he wanted me to keep an eye on you."

"I still don't understand."

"You know something?" said Joss. "I love you very much."

"Because I'm being stupid?"

"No, because you're being marvellously innocent. Sophia wasn't only Grenville's model, she was his mistress as well. My father was born at the beginning of their relationship, long before your mother arrived. Sophia married, eventually, an old friend she'd known from childhood days, but she never had any more children.''

"So Tristram . . .?''

"Tristram is Grenville's son. And Grenville is my grand-father. And I am going to marry my half-cousin.''

"Pettifer told me that Sophia meant nothing to Grenville. That she was just a girl who'd worked for him.''

"If it meant protecting Grenville, Pettifer would swear that black is white.''

"Yes, I suppose he would.'' But Grenville, in anger, had been less discreet. " 'You are not my only grandchild!' ''

"Did Grenville say that?''

"Yes, to Eliot. And Eliot thought he meant me.''

We had reached the top of the hill. The lights of the town were far behind us. Ahead, beyond the huddled shapes of Ernest Padlow's housing estate, lay the dark coastline, pricked with the tiny lights of random farms, and beyond it the black immensity of the sea.

I said, "I don't seem to remember you asking me to marry you.''

The little van bumped and lurched down the lane towards Boscarva. "I'm not very good at asking things,'' said Joss. He took his hand off the wheel and put it over mine. "I usually just tell people.''

As once before, it was Pettifer who came out to meet us. As soon as Joss switched off the engine of the van, the light in the hall went on, and Pettifer opened the door, as though he had known instinctively we were on our way.

He saw Joss open the car door and ease himself out, in obvious discomfort and pain. He saw Joss's face . . .

"For heaven's sake, what happened to you?''

"I had a difference of opinion with our old friend Morris

Tatcombe. I probably wouldn't look like this except that he had three of his chums with him.''

''Are you all right?''

''Yes, I'm fine. No bones broken. Come on, let's go in.''

We went indoors and Pettifer closed the door.

''I'm glad to see you, Joss, and that's the truth. We've had a proper how-do-you-do here and no mistake.''

''Is Grenville all right?''

''Yes, he's all right. He's still up, in the drawing-room, waiting for Rebecca to come home.''

''And Eliot?''

Pettifer looked from Joss's face to mine.

''He's gone.''

Joss said, ''You'd better tell us about it.''

We ended up in the kitchen, around the table.

''After Rebecca had gone, Eliot went down to the studio and came back with that portrait of Sophia. The one we looked for, Joss. The one we never found.''

I said, ''I don't understand.''

Joss explained. ''Pettifer knew Sophia was my grandmother, but no one else did. No one else remembered her. It was all too long ago. Grenville wanted it to stay that way.''

''But why was there only one picture of Sophia with a face? There must have been dozens Grenville painted of her. What happened to all of them?''

There was a pause while Joss and Pettifer looked at each other. Then it was Pettifer's turn to explain, which he did with much tact.

''It was old Mrs Bayliss. She was jealous of Sophia . . . not because she had any notion of the truth . . . but because Sophia was part of the Commander's other life, the life Mrs Bayliss didn't have no time for.''

"You mean his painting."

"She would never have anything to do with Sophia, more than a frosty 'good morning' if she happened to meet her in the town. And the Commander knew this, and he didn't want to upset her, so he let all the pictures of Sophia go . . . all except for the one you found. We knew it was somewhere around. Joss and I spent a day looking for it, but we never turned it up."

"What were you going to do with it if you found it?"

"Nothing. We just didn't want anyone else to find it."

"I don't see why it was so important."

Joss said, "Grenville didn't want anyone to know about what happened between him and Sophia. It wasn't that he was ashamed of it, because he'd loved her very much. And after he's dead, it won't matter any longer, he doesn't give a damn who knows then. But he's proud, and he's lived his life according to a certain set of standards. We probably think they're old-fashioned, but they're still his own. Does that make sense to you?"

"I suppose so."

"Young people now," said Pettifer heavily, "talk about a permissive society as though it were something they'd invented. But it's not new. It's been going on since the beginning of time, only in the Commander's day it was handled with a little more discretion."

We accepted this meekly. Then Joss said, "We seem to have gone off at a tangent. Pettifer was telling us about Eliot."

Pettifer collected himself. "Yes, well. So down to the drawing-room Eliot went, and stormed in, with me behind him, went straight to the mantelpiece, and dumped it up there, alongside the other picture. The Commander never said a word, just watched him. And Eliot said, 'What's that got to do with Joss Gardner?' Then the Commander told him. Told him everything. Very quiet and very dignified. And Mrs Roger was there too, and she just about threw a fit. She said all these years the Commander had deceived them, letting Eliot believe that he was his only grandson, and he'd get Boscarva when the Commander died. The Commander said he'd never said anything of the sort, that it was all surmise, that they'd simply been counting their chickens before they were hatched. Then Eliot said, very cold, 'Perhaps now we can know what your plans are?' but the Commander said that his plans were his own business, and *quite right* he was too.''

This little bit of championship was accompanied by Pettifer's fist coming down with a thump on the kitchen table.

''So what did Eliot do?''

''Eliot said in that case he was going to wash his hands of the whole lot of us . . . meaning the family, of course . . . and that he had plans of his own and he was thankful to be shed of us. And with that he collected a few papers and a briefcase and put on his coat and whistled up his dog and walked out of the house. Heard his car go up the lane and that was the end of him.''

''Where's he gone?''

''To High Cross, I suppose.''

''And Mollie?''

''She was in tears . . . trying to stop him doing anything stupid, she said. Begging him to stay. Turning on the Commander, saying it was all his fault. But of course, there wasn't anything she could do to stop Eliot. There's nothing you can do to stop a grown man walking out of the house, not even if you do happen to be his mother.''

I was torn with sorrow and sympathy for Mollie.

''Where is she now?''

''Up in her room.'' He added gruffly, ''I made her a little tea-tray, took it up to her, found her sitting at her dressing-table like something carved out of stone.''

I was glad I had not been here. It all sounded very dramatic. I stood up. Poor Mollie. ''I'll go up and talk to her.''

"And I . . ." said Joss ". . . will go and see Grenville."

"Tell him I'll be there in a moment or two."

Joss smiled. "We'll wait," he promised.

I found Mollie, white-faced and tear-stained, still sitting in front of her frilled dressing-table. (This was in character. Even the deepest excesses of grief would not cause Mollie to fling herself across any bed. It might crease the covers.) As I came into the room, she looked up, and her reflection was caught three times over in her triple mirror; for the first time ever, I thought that she looked her age.

I said, "Are you all right?"

She looked down, balling a sodden handkerchief in her fingers. I went to her side. "Pettifer told me. I'm so very sorry."

"It's all so desperately unfair. Grenville's always disliked Eliot, resented him in some extraordinary way. And of course, now we know why. He was always trying to run Eliot's life, come between Eliot and me. Whatever I did for Eliot was always wrong."

I knelt beside her, and put my arm around her, "I really believe he meant it for the best. Can't you try to believe that too?"

"I don't even know where he's gone. He wouldn't tell me. He never said goodbye."

I realised that she was a great deal more worried about Eliot's abrupt departure than she was about the evening's revelations concerning Joss. This was just as well. I could comfort her about Eliot. There was not a mortal thing I could do about Joss.

"I think," I said, "that Eliot may have gone to Birmingham."

She looked at me in horror. "*Birmingham?*"

"There was a man there who wanted to give him a job. Eliot told me. It was to do with second-hand cars. He seemed to think that it might be quite interesting."

"But I can't go and live in *Birmingham*."

"Oh, Mollie, you don't have to. Eliot can live on his own. Let him go. Give him the chance of making something of his life."

"But we've always been together."

"Then perhaps it's time to start living apart. You've got your house at High Cross, your garden up there, your friends . . ."

"I can't leave Boscarva. I can't leave Andrea. I can't leave Grenville."

"Yes, you can. And I think Andrea should go back to London, to her own parents. You've done all you can for her, and she's miserable here. That's why all this happened, because she was unhappy and lonely. And as for Grenville, I'll stay with him."

I came downstairs at last carrying the tea-tray. I took it into the kitchen and put it on the table. Pettifer, sitting there, looked up at me over the edge of his evening paper.

"How is she?" he asked.

"All right now. She's agreed that Andrea should go home, back to London. And then she's going back to High Cross."

"That's what she's always wanted. And you?"

"I'm staying here. If that's all right with you."

A chill gleam of satisfaction crossed Pettifer's face, the nearest he could get to a look of delight. There was no need for me to say more. We understood each other.

Pettifer turned his paper. "They're in the drawing-room . . ." he told me ". . . waiting for you," and he settled down to the racing page.

I went and found them, backed by the two portraits of Sophia in her white dress, Joss standing by the fire, and Grenville deep in his chair. They both looked up as I came in, the long-legged young man with his villainous black eye, and the old one, too tired to pull himself to his feet. I went towards them, the two people I loved most.